BLOOD AD INFINITUM

LMBPN Publishing
PMB 196, 2540 South Maryland Pkwy
Las Vegas, NV 89109

Version 1.00, May 2021
eBook ISBN: 978-1-64971-805-1
Print ISBN: 978-1-64971-806-8

BLOOD AD INFINITUM

BLOOD & ANCIENT SCROLLS™ BOOK THREE

RAVEN BELASCO

DISRUPTIVE IMAGINATION

DEDICATION

To Cairngorm McWomble the Terrible: you are my essential co-author. Thank you for napping by my desk as I write, taking me for walkies when the plotting gets tricky, and always making sure I never forget that the main character in my life is your own stubborn little self.

And to Christine Stewart: Many days of this pandemic, you've sat by me as I worked and quietly read your book or done your own work. For a writer to let any human do that, never mind an eleven-year-old, is exceptionally rare because most people insist on interrupting the poor writer. But the one thing I'll miss when we all find our "new normal" is you quietly keeping me company as I write. You're basically already as kick-ass a hero as I could ever write—and don't you ever forget it!

THE BLOOD AD INFINITUM TEAM

Thanks to my JIT Readers:

Jeff Goode
Dorothy Lloyd
Micky Cocker
Jackey Hankard-Brodie
Zacc Pelter

Editor
SkyHunter Editing Team

CONTENTS

PREFACE

Hey there, Reader!

This book has a bunch of words and phrases that are not in English. Some are in the am'r language, and some are in the languages from around the world, since the am'r get around and often speak the language of the country they grew up in, or the country they are in now.

The am'r words are given definition when they are first used, but if you forget any of them, there is a glossary of the am'r language in the back of the book.

Likewise, there is an index of all the non-English words and phrases you will encounter along the way. If the meaning of those words is vital to the understanding of the story, I've made sure they get explained in the text. However, sometimes our protagonist Noosh doesn't understand what she is hearing. So you have a choice: you can experience the moment as she is experiencing it, or you can go to the index and look up the words if you don't like not knowing.

Whatever you choose, I hope you enjoy the book!
Raven

PROLOGUE

There was no direct flight from Buenos Aires to Bucharest, so we went on vacation.

Well, it was a vacation for *me*. The vampires I was with saw it as a continuation of the mission we'd been on. As "missions" went, it had been a complete and utter clusterfuck. I really wanted to draw a line between it and the rest of my future.

And I deserved a break. A holiday. A nice period of time when I was not being chased by bad guys or locked up in underground prisons or having to decapitate and burn endless villain after villain, just to ensure they did not start up all the drama again. *Ever* again.

You might imagine that doing things like decapitating and burning people (after said people had imprisoned you and done other horrible things to you and those you loved) might cause a person to need more than just a vacay. Something more like long-term talk therapy and some nice calming medications.

I used to feel that way myself. I spent my first months

with the *am'r*—that being what the vampires call them-selves—being quite sure I was a woman most desperately requiring therapy, more than anyone had ever needed it before.

This last adventure (although that was far too positive a term for it; "debacle" was more apt) had changed some-thing in me. Now, I found myself just wanting some fun. I wanted to live, not just go from horror to horror and fear to fear, but be able to enjoy this bizarre existence I found myself inhabiting. I didn't feel the need for emotional help anymore. I felt oddly stable.

It might have been all the am'r blood I'd drunk when I nearly died. Of course, I no longer meant "died" the way I used to. What had nearly happened to me was the "vis-tarascha," which was the am'r term for dying as a mortal human (a "kee") and then, over a period of time—an inde-terminate period of time: days, weeks, months, who knows?—resting and transforming into a full am'r and rising again from the grave.

I was an "am'r-nafsh," you see, not kee anymore, not am'r yet. I was the platypus of supernatural beings: not one thing or another, an oddity who was neither fish nor fowl. I'd hated it, hated the way I was trapped in the am'r world but still had to do embarrassing kee things like eat, and to complete that cycle, use a toilet.

I'd hated that I was a super yummy snack for the am'r and that none of them could help but sniff around—liter-ally—and tell me how delicious my blood smelled. I could never tell who liked me for me and who was just huffing me like glue.

Then all of that nearly ended, although I was too

messed up to appreciate it until the danger was over. When I could and did get it, the realization that I'd nearly lost my last tie to my kee life made me appreciate my situation more. That probably was helping with this weird sensation of emotional stability.

I'd lost people. That part still hurt, and I had plenty of mourning left to do, but that was nothing unnatural. I could have experienced those emotions even if I'd never let Dracula exchange blood with me for the third time in a hot tub back in Nowheresville, USA. Those were honest human emotions and meant I was not turning into anything, well, *inhuman*.

Not that the am'r I'd met were inhuman. So far, "am'r" meant "all the human flaws taken to the next level." Extra centuries meant extra time to hold grudges and grow chips on your shoulder. Really dig into those flaws in your character, and/or just go stark raving mad.

I'd been a big reader of vampire fiction back when I'd been a kee librarian, and the only excitement in my life had been found between the pages of whatever book I was reading at the moment. One question I'd asked with those books back then was, "If vampires are real, why haven't they taken over—if they are so all-powerful and immortal and stuff?"

I'd discovered the answer the minute I joined the am'r world: the am'r couldn't organize their way out of a paper bag, never mind rule the world. The clashing personalities, the in-fighting, and the sheer irrationality all combined to ensure that the am'r kept fighting the same stupid battles they'd fought all their human lives. They killed each other with the same casualness as stepping on an ant. Immortality proved to be all too fragile, and while their powers increased with time, that didn't seem to help with anything beyond killing each other more expeditiously.

The one exception was Bagamil, my lover and—in the bizarre world of am'r relationships—my grandfather. He had seemed pretty god-like when I'd first met him, above the petty bickering of the rest of the am'r, who themselves treated him a bit like a deity. But in the recent fiasco I was so happy to put behind me in terms of both spatial and temporal distance, Bagamil had proved to be far too fallible. He'd been captured with shocking ease and held captive for months, requiring rescue. Then, during the Benny Hill Show of a rescue, he had not been particularly more skilled at escaping the booby-trapped caves and multitudinous minions than the rest of us.

The rest of the am'r still treated him like a god. For myself, I knew I loved him, and I knew I needed to find out more about this man with whom I'd shared the most intimate of living and loving. He was not a god, but he was a mystery, and I needed to start getting to know him.

But first, *vacation*.

PART I

Am'r Of London

"Man is a rope, tied between animal and superman—a rope over an abyss. A dangerous crossing, a dangerous journeying, a dangerous looking back, a dangerous shuddering and ceasing." — *Friedrich Wilhelm Nietzsche*, Thus Spoke Zarathustra

CHAPTER ONE

"I want to do the Tower of London. I want to see the bit of the oldest remaining Roman wall, and I have a list of museums somewhere. I did it on the flight. Here it is! I won't read the whole thing, but it includes the Museum of London, the V&A, the Natural History Museum, the Horniman Museum, the Sherlock Holmes Museum... Oh, and the libraries! Obviously, the British Library and the London Library—and there are evening tours!—but as an archivist, I really can't miss the Guildhall and the St. Bride Libraries. Oh, there're too many things, and I want to do them all *now*—!"

Lilani, she of the blue-black skin and mohawk of many microbraids, and Vivian with his russet-brown skin and short dreads both looked at me and then at my patar Sandu and then at their patar Nthanda. They didn't know what to do with my kee-like enthusiasm for kee things.

I was fascinated to see that Viv, whom I'd last seen with his whole right arm off at the shoulder, had a functioning right arm that matched the left. It filled me with a million questions about how much "vhoon-vaa"—am'r-style healing with blood—he'd must've had to regrow an arm so fast. Daciana, one of Sandu's Romanian crew, had said regrowing limbs would take a "long and painful" time, so how had he pulled it off so fast? Or did it just *feel* like a long time because it was so painful? And what would the process look like? Did it grow inch by inch down to the fingertips, or did the bones come in, then the muscle, then the skin?

I'd done my own speed-healing, boosted by vhoon-am'r—that was the fancy way to say "vampire blood"— but it had just been deep puncture wounds, not limb regeneration. And those wounds had been bound under dressings—albeit a dirty plaid shirt ripped into strips, but you do what you can with what you have—so I'd not been able to watch the process. All I knew was how incredibly *painful* it had been, which was not a precise measurement.

Nthanda gave them that utterly infectious smile of his and then turned it on me. I could see why they had each fallen for him. He was tall but not skinny; instead, his muscle made fascinating shapes under his fitted light-weight sweater and black jeans. All in black, of course, because with the am'r diet being what it was, that best hid potential spills from your meals.

Nthanda had rich, dark, reddish-brown skin. His heart-shaped face, topped by little twists of coily black hair fading down to shaved, was a background for his huge round eyes under dramatically arching brows, a broad triangle of a nose, and entirely distracting lips. That smile of his popped out his high cheekbones and squinted his eyes into sparkling dark depths. It made one want to ensure that he smiled often.

Happily, I seemed to be able make him smile. I had met him the very first time I'd met any amount of am'r, at a conference which was supposed to be for Sandu and Bagamil's "allies"—but which I'd still be abducted from, anyways. That first time I met him his smile had impressed me, but it hadn't lasted very long, because a gathering of am'r is necessarily a stressful occasion. Am'r don't play well together.

Tonight was different. It was an intimate group of allies as true as you could get in the am'r world. Firstly, Sandu, my "patar." That is, the man who made me into an am'r-nafsh and his "frithaputhra," which translates out to something between "beloved lover" and "beloved child." The am'r world obviously had no issues with weirdly incest-y-sounding titles because incest literally wasn't possible, am'r not being able to have children in the kee biological sense.

That made it slightly easier to explain that my other lover Bagamil was the patar of my patar—Sandu's lover and his father, thus my grandfather, or "gharpatar" in the am'r language. They all acted like this was totally normal, and I'd been out of the kee world long enough that it only weirded me out when I spent too long thinking about it.

That was my immediate family, plus the allies to whom we'd become closer during the farcical "rescue" of Bagamil: Nthanda and his two frithaputhraish, Lilani and Viv. (Don't *talk* to me about how plurals work in the weird am'r language.) They had collected us from Heathrow airport and brought us to see the flat (that's Brit-speak for "apartment") in London where we would be staying. It was spacious and very comfortably decorated. It was also underground; you had to go down steps from street level to open the front door. I could imagine it getting bad reviews from any kee who might stay there—"Great space, but no natural light! I got Seasonal Affective Disorder after staying there only two days!"—but an underground flat was pretty perfect for creatures who could not abide the cruel rays of the sun. Not that we burnt up into a dramatic pile of dust or anything; we just *wished* we would while a migraine of superhuman proportions threatened to make our brains explode. Sadly, while being an am'r-nafsh didn't confer the complete powers of being am'r, one experienced the downsides.

Nthanda had brought his immediate family as an honorary escort for my strange little am'r family, a very formal mark of respect for Bagamil, as the Aojysht-of-aojyshtaish, that is, the most ancient of the am'r, for whom age meant increased power, not being fed oatmeal in an old folks' home.

There was no red carpet, no uniformed guards, no marching band, just a few Londoners collecting their Yank friends from the airport and taking them 'round to their rental flat. It looked like nothing to the mass of kee that flowed like a river around us. A river of smells: food, beauty products, sweat, the leather in shoes and jackets, plastics, and other chemical odors, but most of all, the underlying perfume of kee blood that kept the am'r from relaxing in the company of kee—even this am'r-nafsh.

Nthanda and his fam hand-delivered us and ensured that the flat met with Bagamil's approval, then they very politely fucked off. After flying from Buenos Aires to

Munich (no direct flights, argh) and then back to London, surrounded by people—kee people—the entire way, the last thing we wanted was to be social, even with fellow am'r. Even with fellow am'r we *liked*.

Oh, there was one thing they did before they fucked off. Viv was carrying a big, awkward bag, and I knew what came in those. We had an am'r holiday party, and he was Father Christmas, letting us choose what we liked from a selection of bladed and projectile weapons. Sandu and Bagamil chose a longer sword and a serious knife each and took some guns to tuck around the flat. Still deeply feeling the loss of my beloved Terry Smatchett, I took a long knife that had decent balance, clearly military. It was decent, but I felt no connection; it was just to tide me over until the promised replacement smatchett was in my hands, I assured myself. Anyway, we were just here for some meet-ings—and for my vacation. Nthanda had the south of England under control, we were assured, so there were no Bad Guys with a Plan for us to have to deal with.

The first thing we did on our vacation was stay in bed for three days. No regrets. Those were three days of sleep-ing, loving each other for hours, napping, and then resuming our very detail-oriented, hands-on proving to each other that, "I'm so glad you're still alive, and I'm still alive, because for a while there, it seemed a not very likely outcome."

Normally I ask a lot of questions. Not only is it very much who I am, but ever since I discovered how easily my ignorance could get me (or someone I love) killed, my desperation to level up to "not being a liability" was high.

Not this time. I was either asleep, or my mouth was full.

Full of blood. Or other parts of Sandu and Bagamil.

The am'r insist that sex be a part of healing. More than once, I've mocked their horndog nature. This time, I understood it entirely. I could have handled another few days of it before engaging with anything else in the world, but there was important am'r business to attend to. And also, I was still technically alive and needed to be fed, well, actual *food*.

Happily, Sandu and I didn't have to go far in the city twilight. There was a mini grocery store with a sign that said M&S Simply Food right around the corner from our underground love nest. Sandu, who had accompanied me out, called it "Marks and Sparks," and when I exclaimed over the excellent fresh produce and amazing meat and cheese selection, he laughed at me.

"I do not know why you Americans persist in asserting that British food is terrible. It *was* terrible. After the Germans had blitzed this city into rubble, the whole country was on rations for decades. Did you know, *dragă* Noosh, after that war was over, your birth country made a lot of money from the British debt? In the end, the UK paid twice what it had borrowed from the US. They paid right up until the early 2000s."

"Um. No. I had no idea."

"And I may not eat...food, but I can certainly *smell*. In the 1950s and the 1960s, what people in your country did to meat and vegetables was a *crime*."

"Ah, yes. I've seen the cookbooks in the library. Jello salads and stuff."

Sandu shuddered. When he'd brought me home to his birth country—Romania, obviously, although when he was

Dracula there, it was called Wallachia—he'd eagerly shared with me the traditional foods of his people, sniffing the aromas with appreciation even though he could no longer eat. The food was hearty and delicious. I could see how someone who had spent his mortal life eating such honest and well-seasoned cuisine would be offended by the smell of boiling canned vegetables down to gray mush.

We bought enough food to keep me going for a while, plus a fun selection of wines for me to try. I couldn't get drunk anymore, but I could enjoy the taste, dammit! Sandu had a sizeable wad of British currency, and I wondered at what point our host had slipped him the generous spondulix. The am'r seemed to be free of financial woes, and I was going to have to figure out at some point who their cash earners and their bankers were and *how* they slipped so freely through the complicated kee world.

But those were all questions for another time. (*Would I ever stop making lists of questions about my new people and feeling like I'll never get them answered?*) We required more formal apparel than our travel clothes. Nthanda had issued an invitation for tonight, and it was *his* city we were in, so declining and staying home for more hours of nonstop fucking wasn't an option.

Since nonstop sex, blood-drinking, and sleep were all we had done, no one had a decent outfit for this outing, and the am'r were vain creatures. Bagamil joined us, and out we went again.

I'd been promised a *real* shopping trip since our recent misadventure had left me wearing nothing but cargo pants cut into uneven (and blood-drenched) shorts. I was *owed*, I felt.

We didn't have all night, so we ended up with outfits for tonight and for a couple of days, and promises to me of a future spree in one of the great shopping capitals of the world. The simple kee pleasure of being in a clean, well-lighted store and the glitter of Western consumerism catching my crow-like eyes was yet another span of much-needed distance between me and my recent stressful past.

I ended up with a black silk midi-dress, high-necked—always good forward-thinking around a group of am'r—with drapey sheer sleeves and a narrow-pleated skirt. I felt deeply elegant. After a hot shower and the application of the freshly bought makeup and hair products—my neglected curls got a much-needed deep-conditioning—I felt very far from the gal who had been drenched in blood, hacking off heads.

Not that that couldn't happen at any time tonight. I knew the am'r well enough by now not to take a peaceful evening for granted. But I could *hope*.

Off we went, out into the nighttime streets of London. It was the wrong supernatural creature, but of course I had *Werewolves of London* playing in my head. Bagamil looked at me inquisitively as I quietly howled, "Arrrooo!" I smiled and shook my head. Some things you couldn't explain to the old fogeys.

He didn't *look* like an old man, though. He wore a slick black suit with a black shirt under it. His one concession to individuality was a sunny yellow tie almost the same shade as the sunflower-yellow robes he'd been wearing when I met him and named him "Mister Sunshine" in my head. His socks matched, which delighted me. I would find out about his perverse-seeming desire to wear that bright color, dammit, and all his other secrets, too. Eventually. For now, I just enjoyed seeing his golden-olive skin set off by the black fabric, the hint of yellow from the tie bringing out the wicked spark in his dark, dark eyes, and his Freddie-mustache trimmed perfectly. His long, thick black hair was pulled into a braid this evening and was draped over his shoulder.

Sandu looked different from his patar. He was also in black, but more casual, an expensive modal shirt under a sports coat, and the type of well-draped fitted trousers he tended to wear; the obvious price tag made them not-so-dress-down. He was smooth-shaven, which Bagamil always said he preferred, despite his own mustaches— maybe having a mustache *and* kissing one was awkward?— and his shoulder-length black hair was slicked back in glossy waves. When his hair was pulled back, it emphasized his strong beak of a nose and high cheekbones. He felt me objectifying him and glanced over with those sexy gold-flecked green eyes. I felt a rush of love and lust for him, the two emotions intrinsic and inseparable. I tried to put all I was feeling into my return smile, and from the smolder in his eyes and the twitch of a smile back, I knew he'd gotten it.

But we were walking through the streets of a nighttime city, where threats could be kee or am'r in nature, so his lips went back to unsmiling and his nostrils flared as he used them, as well as his superior am'r eyesight, to search for danger.

Nthanda kept tight discipline in his metropolitan area, however. No am'r threats bothered us as we moved through the cool bustle of London-at-night.

It was better than the kee world by day, at least as my nose perceived it. The rancid scents of sewer and unwashed kee bodies were still all-too-pungent, but between them, I could enjoy the rich smells from kebab shops and the greasy temptation of fish-n-chips. The pubs and nightclubs didn't smell very nice because alcohol processing through kee bodies was not a lovely scent, but then there would be the unexpected nostalgia of a laundromat pumping out the scents of detergent and hot air, or passing a kee walking their dog, and smelling that canine must.

I had briefly been in the kee world over this past year, but it had mostly been rushing through the cities—and countryside—to get to an am'r stronghold well away from the ant-like activity of the kee masses. Staying in a kee city was oddly thrilling.

It was also strange to think that less than two years ago, I'd had no idea the am'r even existed. I would have been excited to be in London as my old kee self but in a very different way. I'd let myself be transformed so very easily and had Stockholm-Syndromed into a life of using living sentient people as food and killing anyone who looked at me wrong without a qualm.

OK, so I usually have help with the killing part, but it's the thought that counts.

We moved out of the bustle of wide urban thoroughfares to skinnier backstreets and fast-food places named after random US states, Michigan Fried Chicken being even more jarring to my mind than Alaska Fried Chicken, and then into a warehouse section in what I'd been waiting my whole life to call "the Smoke." There was no yellow Victorian fog, however. Although I'd known that intellectually, it was still disappointing.

There was a small bustle of life—the usual selection of nighttime workers and street people. And rats. Plenty of rats. I could smell all that, unfortunately.

The huge boarded-up warehouse we entered had once been a junkie squat and smelled like it. I had to stop breathing as we moved through filth and detritus, the ammoniac scents fighting with the fecal and putrescine. Sandu took my arm, Bagamil led the way. If he could scent another am'r through *this*, I could gauge how much my sense of smell would improve when I eventually became full am'r. On the other hand, the last thing I wanted to do in this environment was breathe through my nose. I hoped Bagamil had good verbal instructions from Nthanda or knew the way from previous visits.

It was just like getting to Dracula's underground castle from Bucharest. Enter via a place most kee would avoid like the plague, then go through a hidden door—in this case, a piece of the floor only someone with the strength of an am'r could lift, pull to the side to expose steps down to a freight elevator, which was not evidenced in any way in the dilapidation above.

There were three buttons. We were going to the first one. They let me push it. It paid to be with people who loved you and would indulge your childish whims.

I did wonder what the *lower* levels of a vampire den could possibly house.

All freight elevator experiences were pretty similar. You stood in a big, banged-up utilitarian box and listened to both the regular thrum of the machinery and the occasional surprising and concerning crashes and clunks, slowly inching down into the vampire den. Well, perhaps that last part was not common to the *kee* freight elevator experience, but being trepidatious as I headed into a group of am'r, even supposed allies, was starting to feel all too normal to me.

Neither of my lovers said anything, so I piped up. "Hey, guys, anything I need to know? *Beforehand* would be nice."

Sandu chuckled, and I had a flash of annoyance because he had been the worst perpetrator of keeping me in dangerous ignorance. Bagamil spoke in a calming tone that reminded me he could read my emotions.

"You have been in groups of our kind before, cinyaa—" It was a good time to call me "my lover," and remind me that there were times when I didn't want to slap them both. "You have always had good instincts for when to stay quiet. While you have been through some intense events," that was *one* way to put it, "with Nthanda and his people, do not forget that he is an aojysht in his own right, and this is his territory. I am afraid that my being so casual with you may have perhaps led you to believe that we are always that way. It is not so. This may not technically be a formal gathering, but act as if it is and treat Nthanda as the respected elder he is. Decorum around the am'r is never regretted. Insouciance may be regretted for an all-too-short period of time."

"Sandu once told me to keep my mouth shut and just look pretty."

"I never said…"

"I am certain my frithaputhra did not use those words. They have a very American flavor to them, so I assume you are rephrasing a warning he gave you before meeting me for the very first time. It is not utterly incorrect advice, cinyaa." Here he looked at me wryly. "Try to be a good girl for your poor old gharpatar."

Sandu pulled up the freight elevator door while I was coughing on clumsily stifled laughter.

Nthanda was beautiful at the best of times, never mind how his muscular body filled out his clothing, but tonight he'd gone all out. Once I saw him lounging with deliberate insouciance on a battered Victorian fainting couch, my coughing turned to an awkward choke.

He was in a classic tuxedo, wearing it as comfortably as James Bond did. The geometric shapes of the tux made the curves and planes of his face even more starkly beautiful. Well, if I stayed silent because he'd taken my breath away, at least I wouldn't say anything humiliating.

The room was filled with furniture and other décor stolen from BBC period-piece sets. Actually, since I was in the country where those historical dramas were actually *history*, possibly they'd been re-appropriated from real castles and country estates and shit like that. It was anachronistically lit, however, with neon signs advertising XXX, Peep Show, Adult Video, Private Booth, and GIRLS GIRLS GIRLS. Some blinked, some didn't. It was maddening; how was I supposed to keep my eyes on potentially unfriendly am'r in this flickering, uncertain light? With my am'r-blood-assisted eyes, full dark might have been preferable.

I'd only met a couple of Nthanda's people. There were more tonight, and they were as diverse as London was. Every shade of humanity was present from the blue-black skin of Lilani to a heavily freckled ginger—*seriously, a vampire with freckles?*—who set off his pallor by wearing a pristine white tracksuit and what we in the US called "sneakers" and he would call "trainers." It was strange, but somehow the tracksuit looked as formal as the tux.

Bagamil led our threesome forward, and he gave a nod and a smile while Sandu bowed and glanced at me to make sure I was doing so, too. It was weird. I'd never bowed to Nthanda before, but we were all standing on ceremony tonight.

"Aojasc' am'ratv! Thank you, Nthanda, frithaputhra-of-Chausiku, for receiving us. I have not spent time in the company of the am'r of London in far too long."

"Strength and immortality to you, Aojysht-of-aojysh-taish, and your frithaputhraish. You are all known and welcome to me, and may those of us who have not personally met you yet be gracious." He swept a look around his own am'r, and he looked even fiercer at that moment than when I'd seen him fighting another am'r to their inevitable doom. It was a good reminder to me that even the am'r who are technically on your side could be just as dangerous as foes. Indeed, with a known enemy, you never let down your guard...so maybe allies were in their own way *more* of a threat.

"Now I will leave you to introductions," Nthanda

continued. "However, attendance is not mandatory for the rest of the evening. If anyone thirsts, there is a city vhoon-plump at your disposal."

I shuddered as I heard his words. Maybe when I was fully am'r I'd get over my residual kee squeamishness, but until then, thinking of human beings as walking, fuckable juice boxes upset me whenever I was forced to confront it. I should probably take that discomfort back to first principles and become vegan for what years of eating kee food were left to me, but I never seemed to have the time to work through my philosophical issues before I found myself killing someone before they killed me.

It meant I spent a lot of time feeling uncomfortable, psychologically speaking. It also meant I was a teensy bit terrified that if I ever became comfortable, it would mean I'd become a monster.

It was, thank everything, not as terrible as the vampire receiving line had been back in what I liked to think of as the "Rave Cave" in Castle Dracula. Meeting new am'r by standing around and chit-chatting was still pretty bad, though. I'd never been good at this sort of thing, even when it was just normal people I was talking to. Now, I knew that each person who met me was sniffing my tempting am'r-nafsh scent and considering how they might get me alone for, oh, just a wee tipple of the most delicious blood imaginable—and those were the ones who weren't actively restraining themselves from grabbing me and rushing off to drain me dry.

Lilani and Viv waved at us from other parts of the room, but as much as I longed to rush over and greet the few am'r I knew—and maybe spend the whole evening talking to them to put off awkward introductions to strange am'r—they didn't enable my social anxiety. I felt disappointed and even more stressed.

Nthanda started things off by coming over with an am'r who, as he moved through the neon reds and pinks and greens, looked manscaped within an inch of his life. Then I wondered, is she a lady-am'r after all? They were presented to me as "Nadim," and they looked perfectly androgynous in a gorgeously fitted shiny satin-y suit with a rainbow-sequined shirt under it. Their makeup made me feel shame at my single shade of eyeshadow, mascara, and lipstick. I should have at least taken the time to do my eyebrows. Theirs were…perfection, shaped perfectly and drawn in as I could never achieve.

They rocked designer stubble with the length fading to zero wherever it didn't sculpt their face, using it as another form of makeup. Their eyelashes were so long it made me hope they were wearing falsies. Behind the lashes, every color in their sequined shirt made an appearance around their brown eyes. They smelled amazing, too, a spiced musk scent. Most am'r didn't wear perfume or cologne, but it didn't surprise me that Nadim did.

I watched their perfectly shaped lips (three metallic shades from peachy-pink to dark plum-brown) move as they said in husky accented English, "A pleasure to meet you, Anushka darling."

I realized I was slightly hypnotized and pulled myself together. Yes, I was a hick from a small town, but the things I'd done over the past year had to have given me enough sophistication not to drool when meeting City Folk.

And then I had it. Anyone who spent that long on their maquillage wouldn't say no to sincere appreciation.

"Oh, it's just Noosh, Nadim!" I let my enthusiasm be the covering reason for my rush of words. "Can I say I am so inspired by your look? I need someone to teach me how to do art like you're wearing!"

Their eyes lit up with even more sparkle than the glitter. "Luv, if your man lets me spend some time with you, it would be my honor to teach you some skills."

"Like I could stop her." Sandu chuckled beside me. "Nadim, O Beautiful One, the woman before you faced down Mehmet at his most insane and more ravening am'r than I can count with less of a pause than she took to admire your bedizened face."

"Oh, it's not just my *face*, Impaler!" Nadim spun, which was when I belatedly noticed they had on killer heels, the kind with the red bottoms, under their perfectly creased suit pants.

I couldn't help myself; I wolf-whistled. Every am'r in the room stopped talking like the record had skipped and turned to look at me. Then they saw who I was whistling at, and the conversation abruptly returned to the normal am'r medium-low volume.

Sandu and Nadim were laughing. Sandu was laughing *at* me, I was pretty sure, but Nadim was laughing with delight. "*You* stop!" they told Sandu, "She's my new best friend, and I'm stealing her from you immediately."

Before I had to worry if I'd gotten myself in too deep,

Sandu turned to Nthanda and said, "I do not see Dubhghall in this gathering. I was hoping to see him here tonight."

"That makes two of us, mate. He left our bit of extra-curricular in Tierra del Fuego with Lope. He may still be there, enjoying his bangin' hospitality."

"Let us hope that he is still there enjoying those delights."

Nthanda called to another am'r to come and join us. He might have looked not dissimilar to Nadim if the latter had not been rainbowed and contoured to the max. Also distractingly handsome, his skin was a slightly darker shade of caramel, and his hair was short and perfectly moussed into tousled warm-walnut-brown waves. His hazel eyes glittered without the need for actual glitter.

Sandu reacted with delight. "My brother in name! How are you? Noosh, this is Sikandar, which in his language is the same as mine: Alexandru. Sikandar. Alexander."

Sikandar laughed. "And we are Great, my name-brother and I!" He dipped his head to me, keeping warm eye contact the whole time. "It is a pleasure to meet one my brother loves. Anushka, yes?"

Damn my name. Introductions are always such hell.

"Just Noosh, please. And it is a pleasure to meet you, Sikandar."

I was going to ask him where he was from originally and how long he'd been in London. I would've loved to know if he'd become am'r in his country of origin or after he'd started living here. I didn't know if this might break some sort of am'r social code, so I stopped short and panicked about what to say next.

I was saved by Nthanda bringing another am'r over to

meet me. Sandhya looked like what I could only categorize as "Bollywood leading lady." She wore a long black tunic with a subtle dark-gray pattern. It went down to her ankles but was split up to her waist. Under the tunic were plain black palazzo pants. Her look was naturally elegant: her long black hair in a perfect blowout, the subtle makeup popping her dark-brown eyes from her golden-brown skin and insisting, "I woke up looking this good" (although as a fellow femme, I knew just how much work went into looking so effortless).

"It is good to meet you, Noosh. I have heard your name; it precedes you! You take after your patar in that way, and you are not even full am'r yet."

I didn't know what to do with that, but Sandu jumped in to save me. "So *my* name proceeds me?"

Sandhya looked impatient. "Of course it does, whether you are going by Sandu or Vlad Ţepeş. You know we have heard all the stories."

Nthanda snorted and elbowed Sandu in the ribs. "Stories about the Impaler, right? Not a rare commodity, eh, mate?"

Sandu smiled darkly, "I do not mind the *truthful* stories. And they who believe the fabricated propaganda, I know they are my enemy. That just makes it easier."

"I did not know you needed help finding enemies."

"It is always helpful to tell false friends from true."

"You have that right, mate. Well, no false friends in this room tonight. Or if there are, I will sort them with my own hands. Not that I wouldn't have willing helpers. Roy, here —" Nthanda looked around, found the ginger in white. "Roy, get your arse over here!"

The pallid am'r made his way over from where he had been lurking against the wall under a red naked woman blinking between two dancing positions. The lurid neon had covered up how intense the orange of his hair was, and being braided in rows made it pop all the more against his fish-belly-white scalp. As he drew closer, his freckles also popped; they were spread thickly over every visible bit of his skin.

"Here's another chap who's good in a bit of argy-bargy. Roy, this is Sandu and his frithaputhra Noosh." I thought Nthanda's tone held a bit of warning, and as Roy's icy blue eyes met mine, I could see he was tense as hell. My hackles, never fully relaxed around a bunch of am'r, abruptly raised as high as they could go.

"Aye, I've heard of bloody Dracula, right enough. But why's he brung his am'r-nafsh nitty here? Is she to share? I'll have a go—"

Sandu had moved with his inhuman speed toward Roy, but Nthanda got there first, actively blocking Sandu and speaking hurriedly back to him without looking around. He had a large dark hand wrapped around Roy's palely speckled neck, a study in contrasts.

Roy met Nthanda's eyes without fear, and I noticed the tension had drained out of his body. He seemed comfortable being almost lifted off the ground by his throat. I tried to remember to breathe and hold my body loose but ready for action.

"My apologies, Sandu. This little sod's not fully housebroken. Yet. He'll either learn or he'll die trying." His voice hardened as he directed it into Roy's face. "We've *discussed* this, you stupid ikkle wanker? You're not in some street gang anymore. If you don't take this seriously, you're *brown bread*, got it? Now be polite to your elders and betters, show 'em the nice manners I taught you. Apologize to Sandu and Noosh. And make it good, yeah?"

Nthanda let go of Roy so suddenly that he should have stumbled backward, but he sort-of flowed down into a comfortable posture. It was the first time he really registered as an am'r to me, and I would have to be careful of that. Nothing good would come of underestimating this obviously unstable creature.

"Sorry for what I said, uh, *Sandu*. And sorry I called you a nitty, eh, Noosh, is it? I just never smelt a real am'r-nafsh before. Got me all worked up, innit? So, sorry…right?"

Nthanda grimaced. "I'm afraid that for now, that's probably the best you're going to get. He was pretty feral when I took him in. He'd been in the hands of this nasty little villain, a roadman named—no joke—Fangs. He'd been a purveyor of rare herbs and prescribed chemicals his whole kee life, and he just kept going once he'd risen from the vistarascha. He lived entirely in the kee world, just made his thugs into am'r so they'd be scarier enforcers. He taught 'em naught and killed 'em as soon as they got too cocky. Me and my lot sorted them a few years back. Had to put 'em all down, but our Roy here, he's a fast talker, and he convinced me to take him in and try to make something of him. I could still change my mind on that, you tosser. You still must prove you're worthy of my time."

This last was to Roy, who looked unfazed by the threat. He also didn't seem to care that Nthanda was casually discussing the details of a life story I personally wouldn't want shared so freely with strangers.

A peal of feminine laughter distracted us all. When I looked over, Bagamil was intimately close to a gorgeous am'r I didn't know. A rush of jealousy moved through me, and I tried to stomp on it. There was no such thing as jealousy among the am'r, so I could not allow that bad kee nonsense to come over into my new life.

"Come and meet Nahid," Sandhya said, and she took my arm, which surprised the hell out of me. Am'r don't normally touch each other so easily.

Nahid was another intimidating beauty, with perfect sable hair parted down the center to emphasize the glorious symmetry of her heart-shaped face. Her nose was straight and strong. Her lips were perfect arches shaded a soft rosy neutral. Her cheekbones were high, and all were background loveliness for her eyes, which were like no eyes I'd ever seen before. They were a rich brown, but that wasn't what caught you. Those perfect almonds were tilted up at the outside, making her look like an illustration, not a living, breathing woman.

Well, she's an am'r, so she's not really living.

Those beguiling eyes were under another pair of perfectly shaped and groomed eyebrows, of course.

I'm really *doing my brows every fucking day from now on...*

She wore all black: a body-con dress that made her every curve a boast. The fact that it was ankle-length was negated by the fact that in the back, it only started its presence on her body at the top of her ass—a perfectly plump and rounded ass.

Bagamil made room as we came over. I arched an eyebrow up at him. *What's all this?*

He smiled comfortably in return. "I was catching up

with an old friend from when I was a younger am'r, traveling across what today we would call Asia. I had an adventure or two along the way." Here he outright smirked, and both women made sounds that were all too knowing. Bagamil continued, "Nahid here, and Sandhya as well, are old enough that they remember me from that time. We are reliving the memories."

I looked at Sandhya and hid my surprise in banter, "Baby Bagamil adventures? I hope the rest of us get to hear it all. My gharpatar has so many stories to tell that I've barely caught up with them." I hated to admit I knew little about someone so vital to me.

Hopefully, it wasn't clear that I just wanted to use these elder, and thus more powerful, am'r for what they knew about my gharpatar. Of course, they had a use for me as well, and that was to spend as much time as they could enjoying being near me for sniffing purposes and possibly to talk their way into getting a sip or two of my blood. Both of them favored me with very warm smiles indeed, with glints in their eyes that were supposed to come across as "excited to meet a new friend" but meant "horny for sex and blood."

Ah, am'r. You're all so dependably...thirsty. We can use each other.

"What I'd really like is to get your own story...Noosh, yes?" Nahid's huge dark eyes met mine unflinchingly. I didn't think she realized she was trying to mesmerize me, not a particularly bright idea in front of Bagamil and Sandu. I think my intoxicating odor was causing her to do it without thinking.

I'm the ultimate am'r excuse for bad behavior. "I'm sorry, I just couldn't help myself!" Blech.

"Yes, it's Noosh. Thanks. But my story is very short so far, so I'm certain it's very boring compared to yours."

"Do not believe her modesty," Bagamil put his arm around me proudly, and all the am'r standing around us got glints of jealousy in their eyes. None of them would have turned down a chance to drink the vhoon-Aojysht, and *I* was practically drowning in the stuff. "Days after becoming am'r-nafsh, our Noosh single-handedly dealt with Fatih Sultan Mehmet, and she survived being his prisoner and gave the tokhmarenc to his second in command."

I started to protest because Dragoş—another frithaputhra of Sandu and my big brother in the am'r sense—had done the lion's share of that work, but Bagamil overran my words. "Not many months went by before Noosh was called to Tierra del Fuego to rescue *my ass*. Her patar was captured, and again she survived captivity through her own initiative and bravery. And we turned out to have *two* sets of enemies to fight in those caves at the bottom of the world. She has experienced more than any am'r-nafsh I've ever heard of in all my existence, which is not a short period of time. And she has lived to tell the story where many a young am'r met an early tokhmarenc. So, please, do share your stories and get to know the frithaputhra-of-my-frithaputhra. I could not ask for a better representative of my vhoon-anghyaa."

Wow. To translate into English, he'd just said that of all his bloodline, which included Vlad Dracula, he couldn't want a better example. I couldn't process that.

I mean, I knew he loved me and was proud of me, but

that statement was pretty...unambiguous. I had done things I was proud of in my kee life—well, graduating with a Master's degree in Library Science was the only one worth mentioning—but I'd never felt such unqualified approval and appreciation in the whole time I'd lived before this moment.

I need to hold onto this for the next time I'm fighting to the death, covered in blood.

Or maybe doing all that "fighting to the death, covered in blood" is something that has been seen and valued. Maybe I deserve this praise.

I would consider that later. I had to get back to the delights of conversational dodgeball with superior beings.

CHAPTER TWO

I ended up with Nahid and Sandhya, sitting, or in Sandhya's case, reclining, on a plush carpet under an ADULT BOOKS sign. There was a huge hookah there with elaborately curved smoky black glass, black-and-gold hoses, and exotic carved-wood mouthpieces, which they taught me how to enjoy. Since I'd never smoked anything more exotic than a little pot back in college, the technicalities of the nargileh gave us a chance to spend some time around each other with a neutral topic to focus on, and the sweet-scented tobacco smoke wafted like incense, which made it easier to slide into storytelling. Knowing that Sandu and Bagamil were in the same room, albeit in other corners, chatting with other groups, made it possible for me to relax as much as I intelligently could around newly-met am'r.

They pressed me, so first I told them about meeting Bagamil by Sandu just throwing me into a public situation, and with no warning, formally and for the first time introducing me to the am'r who'd created him in front of everyone. We all had a good chuckle at how stupid men could be. Then they demanded I tell the whole story of getting abducted by Mehmet, which I could by now narrate in a very condensed recap.

"So, how did you meet Bagamil?" I threw the question out to both of them.

There was a pause while Nahid took a deep lungful of the blue-gray smoke. We watched the process, and I pondered how nice it was to be able to do things like this and not worry about lung cancer.

After she let the smoke dribble between her lush lips, Nahid deigned to tell me her story.

"I was born in Shahr-e Rey in Iran, back when the city was called Rhages by the Greeks. I was a devotee of the goddess Anahita, although at this time, the priests had made her but an aspect of Ahura Mazda, not his daughter and a goddess in her own right. Still, it was remembered that there was a time when she alone had been the Goddess of the Strong, Undefiled Waters, Source of All Water and the Cosmic Ocean, and no matter where the priests told us she ranked, we venerated her accordingly."

I was caught up in Nahid's story, imagining a busy temple of sunbaked brick and priestesses in light linen robes attending to sacred pools and accepting offerings from women trying to conceive. I could almost smell a dry wind from the desert mixing with the cool air of the oasis, rattling the palm leaves and cypress branches.

I tentatively reached out with the mediocre skill of my nose to reconsider Nahid's vhoon-scent. She was vastly older than I could have imagined—*Must stop assuming am'r aren't old just because they look young, dammit!*—and I had not had the slightest hint of it until I focused on it. To survive as an am'r, I knew I was going to need to be instantly aware of the strengths of every am'r around me, and "how long have they survived?" was the most reliable indicator of their power, followed by figuring out their vhoon-anghyaa, followed by observing them do shit.

Nahid was still talking, so I closed my eyes and tried to both listen to her tale and also process what I was ever-so-subtly scenting.

"Bagamil was in that age called Mazdak and he was a reformer, trying to bring the priesthood back to the true spirit of Zoroaster's words, which were many generations in the past even then.

"He traveled up and down the Silk Road as you call it now, spreading his words to Zoroastrian temples, and in between, to the people he stopped overnight with, to merchants he traveled with, to anyone who would listen.

"I met him at night as I sat by the temple pool, dreaming of the splendor and magnificence of my goddess. He was freshly arrived, the dirt of the road still upon him, but I was struck by his beauty, by the power that emanated from him. I offered to bathe him, and I undressed him by hand, slipped off my robes, and led him into the pool to wash and refresh him.

"By the time the rising sun was softening the sky, we had talked for hours, and he had refreshed himself with more than Anahita's cool waters. He rested that day, and the next night again, we delighted in discourse both verbal and sexual. But sadly, I have never been blessed with the vhoon of the Aojysht-of-aojyshtaish, only the pleasure of his company and wisdom now and then over the centuries.

"After he moved on, I used the insight he bestowed upon me to move up the ranks to head priestess. I was able to influence the other temples around me for many miles, and for a while, Mazdak's message of social justice, equal rights for rich and poor, and freedom to love spread like ripples in the Cosmic Ocean."

We sat for a while, digesting her words and giving her the best applause that can be given to a storyteller: a moment of silence.

Finally, I asked, "Did Bagamil not make you an am'r, then?" She didn't *smell* like he had, but I was so new and ignorant that it was best not to make assumptions.

Nahid laughed at me gently. "Are you asking if we are sisters? No, most regretfully Bagamil is neither my patar nor a bakheb-vhoonho—a giver of blood. Thus, we are sisters only in the wider sense. Although, I would be a much closer sister if you would like and your patar and gharpatar approve..."

Fucking A. Am'r and their damned blood-horniness. They probably have some stupid unpronounceable term for that, too. I just haven't learned it yet. I can't go one step around the am'r without getting propositioned. Even for someone who spent too many years in a long-ass dry spell, it's amazing how quickly that gets old.

I made myself stop my internal complaints and listen as Nahid started speaking again. "No, to my eternal regret, it was not Bagamil who became my patar. He only drank from me and shared exquisite passion. It was years later, at the height of my career as the head priestess, that I met she who became my patar. Shazia has met her tokhmarenc now, alas. I mourn her ceaselessly. She was, besides being a patar whom I loved most passionately, an amazing companion for many centuries of adventure. I could tell you so many stories!"

Sandhya had sat up from her lounge to puff upon the hookah. She spoke up now, smoke wafting from her mouth was as if she were a lazy dragon. "I am from a later time than Aojysht Nahid, frithaputhra-of-Shazia, but the same part of the world to the Western mind. I grew up in a city called Sanjan in Gujarat, in what we then called Hindustan, the earliest settlement of Parsis in that country.

"Bagamil then went by the name Baghodat, which in our language meant 'Created by God.' He was the head of the *dastūr*, our high priests, and the wise leaders of our Parsi community in exile. It was said that he had personally brought us safely away from the Muslim conquest of Persia, but no one believed it because it was over a hundred years later, and how could even the holiest of men have lived so long? But no one alive could remember a time when Baghodat was not leading us, looking as he always did: young yet radiant with wisdom. And so we venerated him and held ourselves blessed to have such a one among us.

"When did this take place? Ah, that is so hard to explain. I still think in the Zoroastrian calendars—of which there are three—when I think in kee dating at all. In your 'Common Era'...bah, I hate maths! Well, the Sassanid Empire fell in the middle of your 600s, and then my people traveled from place to place, looking for their new home, for twenty-five years or so. This would have been about thirteen hundred years ago, I guess. It feels much longer sometimes, and sometimes it feels like it was only a moment ago."

Over a thousand years old. She is another aojysht, and I never noticed. Now that it had been pointed out to me, of course, I was able to work through their complex blood scents and catch in each a depth that slowly intensified in am'r blood over time. It was the opposite of aging. It was the smell of might.

Missing that all-important base note of mightiness could well be the thing that brings you to an early tokhmarenc. Do better.

"There is a written narrative of all of these troubles. It is not entirely wrong, and more importantly, it is beautiful. I enjoy hearing it recited; it makes me forget the modern world for a while.

"My people lived in Sanjan for about five centuries after we fled our original home in Persia. As I said, I was born about one hundred years into that peaceful and prosperous time, when the *Atash-Warharan*, our temple of the Sacred Fire, had been safely alight for years and Parsis came from where they had been scattered to the winds to celebrate festivals with their own people at the one place where the Ancient Fire still blazed with the pure divinity of Yazdan, as our people had come to call our One God.

"Women had no role in the temple anymore, but I was always drawn more to worship than I was to play with girls my age—or to planning my eventual marriage with my aunties and grandmothers. I would slip out of helping my mother around the house and go be solitary in the woodlands around Sanjan, gathering twigs for the priest's sacred bundles as an excuse to loiter around the temple. I would fantasize that I'd been born a male so that I could have become a priest myself someday. Baghodat noticed me, and one evening when I was gathering twigs alone, I found his august presence somehow beside me, and we spoke for hours about the worship of Yazdan, about the saintly Zartosht...and about how unfair it was that women could not be priests. Baghodat told me that once women were priestesses in their own right, which seemed unbelievable in my world, but of course whatever he said must be truth. I hung on his every word.

"The next day, late in the afternoon, I was back skulking around the temple, as far in as a laywoman could go. I was ostensibly praying for a sick auntie for my mother, who could not take the time away from her household duties, but mostly I was hiding from all the other aunties because I was now of marriageable age, and there was much pressure for me to stop disappearing in the woods and start preparing. We followed the traditions of the Hind in this regard; we wore the sari and performed our elaborate marriage ceremonies at night. There was much preparation required; that was what I wanted least in the world, of course. But Baghodat called me to him that day and offered that if I would come and live with him and keep his house, I could get out of a marriage, and he would teach me more than any other living woman about Yazdan and Zartosht and our sacred rites. I was filled with joy! My mother didn't believe me when I told her, but then Baghodat came to our home and verified all I had said. They had to accept it and the honor done to our family.

"Baghodat always had a housekeeper, never a wife. It wasn't that rules did not apply to him, but that he had been around for so long that traditions existed that applied solely to him. He had a wizened old lady caring for him now, and I remember I that to my youthful eyes she looked so old, like she would die any minute. He obviously cared deeply for her to the point of doting on her, I was amazed to discover when I joined his household. She taught me all of the ways he liked his house run, and it was little enough work for I did not need to cook for him; he was so holy he did not need to eat, and I did not have to clean out a chamber pot from his room, either.

"After a few weeks of getting accustomed to my new situation, however, I did learn what was expected of me that was unlike any other task I had ever envisioned. I was not surprised when he wished to take me to his bed. I was only surprised he did not do that the first night I was there, for I understood well about men, even if I did not wish to be a wife. But the vhoon-drinking was most unexpected. However, as I am sure you understand, he made it very pleasurable, and I was more than ready for the next night of my unusual household duties.

"Baghodat's old housemaid died shortly thereafter, and I took her place in running his household. We passed some years in that way. I can see you are wondering if we are sisters. No, not in that way, Noosh of the Sweet Vhoon. In those days, he resisted making frithaputhraish, although of course, I knew nothing of that at the time. I only did not suffer the fate of his old housekeeper because Baghodat decided in that time to travel to see if other communities of Parsis could be built up as successfully as Sanjan had been. I begged to be brought with him as I was now as educated a scholar as any priest. I could read and debate theology with Baghodat all through the night when we were not otherwise engaged. He agreed, for it was easier for him to fill his vhoon-need from me during travel than to seduce strangers along the way.

"While we traveled, however, we met one of his old fritha-puthraish, Vijaya. At first I assumed this old friend who greeted Baghodat so very warmly was male, but then I realized she was born a woman but traveled the world as a man for safety and ease. By the time we stopped traveling together, she and I were deeply in love, and she begged Baghodat to let me remain with her. He smiled and told us he never stood in the way of love and left us happily when our road went one way and his another. In short order, Vijaya and I had exchanged blood the requisite number of times, and I experienced more passion than I ever thought possible. So, Noosh, we are cousins, yes, but not sisters. But I am very pleased to meet you and to see my old mentor again." With that, she sat back, was handed the mouth tip of the hookah by Nahid, and took a deep lungful of the scented smoke, then handed it back.

"Had you seen him before this over the years?" I dared to ask.

"Oh, of course. It is a small world when you live a long while. Not all of those reunions are nice memories, however." Sandhya took another long draw, and I pondered how I could possibly ask for more details about that without being inexcusably rude. Or would it not be offensive? It was the unexpected things that always tripped me up, dealing with the am'r.

"Excuse me," came a new female voice behind me, and I jumped. Letting am'r sneak up on you is a very bad habit that will fast be cured by a surprise death.

This am'r was another intimidating beauty. She wore a pleated black tank top that mostly existed to cup her distractingly braless small breasts. The lack of fabric exposed a lot of parchment-colored skin. Her hair was the darkest auburn, almost burgundy, cut short and tousled artistically, framing her chiseled face. Huge warm-brown eyes examined me from under dramatically arching thick brows. She was all cheekbones and eyes and lips, soft pink lips.

"Vérène! I didn't think you would make it!" Sandhya rose gracefully and threw her arms around the newcomer. After a very sensual kiss, which I watched with interest because it was rare to see am'r kiss each other in greeting, they settled down on the rug Sandhya had been lounging on by herself, arms entwining about each other. It made a very distracting picture.

"I am very sorry I am late." Vérène spoke earnestly and in a charming accent. I almost didn't realize it was a French accent, it was so strangely fluid. "The flight was late, and then..." She finished her sentence by waving her hands dismissively, a *very* French gesture.

"Kee transportation can be so tedious," Sandhya said caressingly to the am'r in her arms, then added, "My love, Noosh here was just asking about the time in my life when you became my frithaputhra."

I was?

Vérène focused her warm brown eyes on me. "I have heard about you." She faltered, "Noosh...*mouais?*"

"Yes, yes, it's Noosh," I assured her, trying not to sigh.

"I have heard about you," she explained to me in her

flowing accent, "and you seem a very accomplished lady. So, you wish to know about me?"

I mean, sure, I did. I hadn't been expecting a third tale-around-the-hookah, but all of this was amazing, and I didn't want it to stop. "I would love that, please, Vérène."

"It is not a glad story," she warned me. Her face was serious. Sandhya snuggled closer to her, also looking solemn. What the hell were they about to lay on me?

"It was the year 1244 in this new Gregorian Calendar, but we still used the Julian when we bothered with dates at all. We were more interested in other things: the growth of our crops and our cattle and our children. And the growth of our souls. We were Cathars, you see, and they also called us Albigensians. We followed the teachings of the Bogomils, the true Friends of God, those who had rejected the corrupted church. We rejected the cross, the gaudy houses of worship, for our bodies were our temples.

"I saw you start at the name. Yes, he who still calls himself Bagamil was our leader then. He was Ignace the Bogomil when my beloved Sandhya, then going by the most-lovely name Sandrine, introduced me to him in person. The name 'Bagamil' has evolved from that over the years since, I suppose. You must ask him. As I smell it in your vhoon-anghyaa, you are lovers with him, so it will not be hard for you to ask questions of the Aojysht-of-aojysh-taish. *Je dois dire*, I would much rather hear *your* stories than bore you with my own."

"Because you were late, you missed her stories." Sandhya/Sandrine gave Vérène a squeeze that made her wriggle distractingly. "Maybe you can get her to repeat them all to you later. But now, you tell her that part of our tale."

"*Oui, madame!*" Vérène pretended to be submissive and kissed her patar's cheek. From the look Sandhya shot her, I could tell this was far from the truth.

Vérène sobered. "As I say, this is not an amusing tale to recount. We good Christians knew that the Pope so far away in Rome hated us, that his corrupted worship of the Evil God and not the Good God was threatened by our telling the truth. But we were no threat to him! He could call himself Christian and run the rest of the sinful world just as he wanted. We just wanted to live well and support our *bonhommes*, our *Parfaits*, who supported us *Croyants*—Believers—in throwing off the sin of the material world. It was a hard life, but full of love in our community.

"Sandrine was a Parfaite, for women could equally be adepts in our faith. She seemed to us all very holy because she did not eat the food of the earth, and she did not commit fornication with men. When she took me on as her particular student, she showed me that she could be sustained on the holy blood from my body and that her feasting was graced by the Good God by the joy and repletion it brought to us both.

"I can see you are wondering, did she tell me about the am'r? Not at that time. It would have confused me, and indeed, she was very committed to the ideals of Bogomolism."

"As indeed I still am," added Sandhya softly. "The fact of the am'r being who they are does not change my beliefs, as it never changed our Aojysht's. They have not changed since I called him Baghodat. The Good God is the Wise Lord. Christ spreads the message of eternal life and love, as did Zartosht. It is only the kee languages that speak of our faith that are mutable."

"*Oui, mon amour*. But at the time of which I am telling, I did not understand this. And I did not understand the threat to our tough but cherished life, not until Pope Innocent III began his hateful prosecution of us. There was no doubt for any one of us as his soldiers chased us from our villages, killing any and every one of us they could catch. Eventually, what had been thriving communities throughout the Languedoc, thousands and thousands of people, were killed, hundreds at a time hanged or burnt at the stake, or just hunted down like animals, dispatched, spat upon.

"We fled to Monségur, a small fortress on a high hill which had become the seat and head of our church. Cowering within its fortified walls were about two hundred bonhommes and other refugees. A hundred fighters defended us against ten thousand troops sent by the seneschal of Carcassonne and the archbishop of Narbonne, paid off by the His Vileness the Pope. We were besieged there from May through a summer and a winter that was more bitter than you can imagine. We were starving, freezing, filthy, yet our faith brought us endurance. We made it until March when the food ran out entirely. Our Parfaits were am'r, I now understand; it was how they could survive without eating. But they needed blood, as any am'r does, and there were too many am'r in that small space and too few kee. As it was, it was too many kee for the small amount of food we'd carefully hoarded through the winter.

"Our Parfaits told the kee laypeople to give themselves

up. They would be allowed to survive, albeit with yellow crosses sewn onto their clothing, shunned from community life. Our bonhommes were not given such generous terms, and they were burned, two hundred of them, on a massive pyre. As you know, this is the way to keep an am'r from rising again. The Church knew that our powerful Parfaits could survive almost anything on the strength of their faith…but not the fire.

"It was at Monségur where I met Ignace the Bogomil. He was rumored to have been descended from the first Bogomil himself, the very first to preach our beliefs, back in the 900s in Bulgaria. I now understand, of course, they were one and the same man, but even having the family connection meant impossibly much to us who could not know of am'r lifespans. Ignace kept us together those nine terrible months. He gave his own vhoon to am'r who were becoming weak, and he gave the wisest counsel to all. He of course was gratified to have Sandrine, the woman he remembered so fondly as his little Sandhya, at his side, helping him in every way.

"And where Sandrine was, there also was I. She had made me her am'r-nafsh, and my vhoon strengthened her in those impossible nights. Before long, Ignace and she were asking me if I would let others partake of my vhoon to help them survive. We could not have made it all those months without the am'r-nafsh who were made in the desperation of those nights. Who let themselves be drained near-dry over and over to feed the starving bonhommes. There were only izchhaish, no am'r giving back in the blood-giving role of bakheb-vhoonho. I…do not wish to describe anything more than that. It was *horrific*. I often felt that I would not ever feel warm again, nor ever be able to eat or drink enough to fill my hunger and thirst.

"At the end, it was decided that Ignace and a few others should escape the night before the rest of the Parfaits made their big sacrifice. Sandrine and I joined him and a couple other am'r. We dared not risk any more because if it were known that any Parfait had escaped, they would never have ceased tormenting our people to hunt them down.

"There was a well; its water had kept us alive these nine months. But it was also an unexpected means of escape. If you swam down, down, past where you thought your lungs would burst, there was a ledge you could climb out upon, gasping in gratitude for that first sweet, burning breath. There were some caves and a series of tunnels that led down the bottom of the *pog*, the peak upon which the fortress rested and away from the enemy encampments all around it.

"We ran for our lives. We hid in the woods during the day, in caves if we could find them. Once we got out past Nice, we felt brave enough to hide in people's homes. Along the way, we found scattered fugitives of our faith. They were meeting surreptitiously in forests and mountainous wilds. We told them they must escape past anywhere within Papal reach. We kept pushing through Italy and did not feel safe again until we reached the Balkans. Bulgaria was where Bogomil had begun his reformation, so it called to us fugitives as the only home we could imagine. Sandhya and I—now living under the names Sashka and Zornitsa—remained there for some years until we both felt the call to go our own ways in the world. Ignace, now going by Ignác, left us to go to Romania, the results of which have shaken the am'r world ever since."

Oh! She's talking about Sandu. I'm never *going to get used to having Vlad the Impaler as my lover.*

Vérène ended her horrifying tale by grinning at me. It was not in any way un-am'r. They had all survived horrors, as kee or an am'r or *both.* Apparently you got used to it and learned to look on the bright side, which for the am'r was the next sexy dinnertime.

Nahid passed the hookah back to Sandhya, who still sat resting her arm over her frithaputhra's shoulders. Vérène took the mouthpiece next, and she and I sat and listened as the two formidable ancient am'r compared how their countries had changed over time. This normally would have fascinated the historian in me, but I was so over-whelmed I could barely process all my thoughts. I *was* keeping watch since Roy had drifted very casually toward us, working very hard at looking like he didn't care about anything. The back of my brain assessed his threat level and classified it as "pay attention but don't let him notice you are doing so." If I tried to put it into words, I would have said that he was too attracted to the scents of power and my am'r-nafsh essence and also that we were four attractive women, and he hadn't flowed our way out of any conscious decision, just generalized lust.

But that was all in the back of my mind. The conscious part was caught in the swirls and eddies of Nahid's and Sandhya's and Vérène's stories. So many centuries of continued existence; I could not imagine what it was like to be so full of experience. I tried to imagine Bagamil so very long ago as the Mazdak Nahid had known, or the

Baghodat Sandhya had experienced in India. I could visualize him as the Ignace Vérène had met because it was the same man Sandu had told me about when he told me about his own experience of becoming am'r.

Bagamil ties all these stories together. He's not just the most ancient of the still-extant am'r; there's something more than that. Who is my beloved?

CHAPTER THREE

The party went on all night, but of course, that was am'r life. At some point before it was too close to sunrise, I found myself alone, just observing everyone else being social, which, knowing how anti-social am'r are, was an amusing game. I tried to imagine telling my two-years-ago-self that I would be living a life that involved partying with the most powerful people in London and staying up all night every night. And, uh, having endless amounts of great sex...and drinking blood while doing it.

I was quietly laughing at the imaginary shocked face of my former self when Nthanda spoke from beside me, having successfully snuck up on me. I'd thought I was getting better at catching swift and subtle am'r movements, but I'd let myself down again.

I made myself let go of that and calmly turned my head and smiled at Nthanda. He was always worth smiling at. He returned my greeting with a radiant grin and leaned against the same probably priceless antique accent table I was resting my ass against.

We watched the room in companionable silence for a while. Sandu and Bagamil had split up, the better to spread out their ongoing pitch for the am'r intranet and increased community. My patar had a group around him in spirited discussion. My gharpatar held forth with his own group, which was larger and listening in respectful quiet, I wryly noted.

"They've not got much selling to do here." Nthanda spoke from beside me. "They already convinced my fritha-puthraish back in those bonkers caves. And the Aojysht-of-aojyshtaish has not taken such an active role in the lives of the am'r in all my days; he'll find an eager audience for his ideas."

"Hm. Not many were so eager when we had that pan-am'r conference in the Rave Cave."

"The Rave Cave? Oh!" Nthanda laughed, a deep, rich sound that delighted the ears. "You mean in Vlad's strong-hold. Heh!" He paused to chuckle a little more. "But it was different then. Mehmet and his followers were dribbling venom into the ears of any who'd listen. He had many of the most powerful of us on his side, although now that he's dead, most are pretending they never made time for him."

"Most?"

"We are am'r. Some are too proud to change their stance. Some will stand up to the Aojysht for the sake of flicking the Vs to authority. And there are still voices drip-ping venom into ears, just different voices. Your fam has enemies, treasure."

Although I might have bristled at being called that by most anyone, Nthanda calling me "treasure" didn't get under my skin. I considered what he'd just relayed to me as we sank back into a comfortable silence. He wasn't over here for "a bit of natter." He wanted to communicate something serious to me.

I knew we had enemies, but I guess I knew it only in an intellectual way. Sandu and Bagamil knew who our enemies were—I assumed—after lifetimes of *making* those enemies, but they had never shared the master list with me.

I should probably add to my Am'r Things I Really Need To Learn list, "Who are our known enemies, and in what priority must they be triaged?" Are a thousand years long enough to catch up with everything I needed to know yesterday?

I realized I needed to respond to Nthanda, and preferably, not sound like an ignorant simpleton in the process.

"I hope if you hear such poisonous words, you'll let us know who is speaking them, sir." I didn't know how old Nthanda was, but he was the leader of the London am'r, so he was either pretty old or strangely powerful for a youngish am'r. Either way, dropping an honorific in there wouldn't hurt. My beloveds had emphasized that strongly enough on the way in.

"Do not doubt I am your friend."

I looked over to see him smiling at me again. I felt some of the tension I'd held all night drain out of me and gave him my most real, most relaxed smile of the night. "It's lucky for us that you are!"

"It is." He chuckled. Compliments never went amiss. I was surprised, however, when he changed the subject.

"I hear you want to go and do tourist nonsense."

"Um. Yeah. I do. I never got to come to London when I was a kee. I don't want to miss that part of it."

51

"My lot would be happy to escort you 'round. Just give us a list of places you fancy a dekko."

"Oh! That would be really kind! I know I'm being silly. Thank you for indulging me."

"Some of us do far dafter things. If we can't enjoy being am'r, what's the point?"

"That's a good point. Thanks for putting it that way. I'll say it like that to my patar." I grinned.

"Heh. Your patar has gotten up to some rum doings in his time. Ask him about what he was doing here in the late 1800s if he gives you any barney."

"I've been intending to do. Just. That." The words might have come out with a direr intent than I'd intended because every time I'd asked that, Sandu had managed to wiggle out of answering.

Nthanda looked as mischievous as a little kee boy. "Right, then."

I wasn't really tired at sunrise; I had too much on my mind. Poor Bagamil and Sandu had to deal with me pestering them with questions. This was not the first time the two powerful aojyshtaish were overwhelmed by the demanding curiosity of one little am'r-nafsh.

We were back in our bed in our little underground flat. It was a king-size bed, which was nice for us all stretching out in comfort, and for the more inventive sexual positions. The room wasn't very large, so there wasn't space for much more than the bed. We didn't *need* much more than a bed, though, so there were no complaints.

Well, no complaints about the furniture.

"*Draga mea*, now is not the time to be discussing these matters. It has been a long night. I can feel the sun outside these walls. Can we not talk in the evening?"

"If I wanted vhoon-vayon, you wouldn't be sleepy."

"Indeed because vhoon-vayon is healing, revitalizing. It is a good thing to do before the day's rest. Talking is *not*." The man once feared across many lands as Vlad the Impaler had diminished to being a whiny *grump*. A morning person, he was *not*.

"I'm only trying to start learning the things I need to know before we all find out the hard way what you should have taught me ages ago."

Bagamil gamely put himself into harm's way. "Cinyaa, my frithaputhra has owned his mistake in not educating you thoroughly from the start, but now is not the time to throw it in his face. Nor continue correcting it, as you must admit he has been doing. As *we* have been doing."

I would not be gentled. "I am always surprised to find out who the next enemy to kidnap me—or you!—will be. I need to know who to be looking out for, who has sworn vengeance, who has made a blood vow to bring you down at all costs, who thinks that there would be nothing finer than getting Dracula's am'r-nafsh all to his or herself, and draining me as a special 'fuck you.'"

"We will be up all day if you want *that* list," Sandu muttered and rolled over, trying to pretend he was already asleep.

I bristled, ready to fight. Bagamil sighed and gently tugged me into his arms, pretending not to notice my initial cranky resistance. It said a great deal about my trust

—or my level of annoyance—that I would even try to resist a being who would find it easier to break my bones than hold on to me with the amount of calculated firmness so as not to leave a bruise.

"Cinyaa, shhh." He wrapped himself around the now-compliant me. "Listen, you are overtired. The kind of evening we had this night—not fighting with the body but fighting with the mind, being smart, witty, and effectively discrete—is as exhausting as any battle and less *fun*.

"Let us rest. Let us greet the next night with the vhoon-vayon you mentioned, and then let education and discussion begin. I have not lived these many kee lifetimes not to have learned to sleep when it is time to sleep. Nothing good comes of staying awake unless it is for love or war."

I sighed deeply to let them both know I was not satisfied with this outcome, but I relaxed into Bagamil's arms and closed my eyes.

I had planned to lie there and make a bullet-pointed list for the next night's discussion—a list that would be inexorable and undodgeable. But I fell immediately asleep.

The next night did indeed start with vhoon-vayon. I wasn't really awake when I was prodded in a butt cheek by something blunt but very firm. Then I realized I was likewise being poked in the front of my left thigh by something similar.

It was hard to retain a bad mood when you woke up to two insistent lengths of morning wood, so I didn't try.

Sandu was the one behind me, and Bagamil was

partially under me as I semi-sprawled across him. Sandu was teasing his fingers up and down my back from neck to farther cheek, drawing little swirls with a fingertip, then more teasing spirals lightly along my ribcage, not touching my breasts. My skin came alive under his touch, which was more awake than my brain. My body responded on its own, my ass arcing toward his cock invitingly while at the same time twisting my upper body toward him to facilitate his access to my breasts.

It was Sandu who had helped my breasts first come alive, the very first time we shared what I did not yet know to call "vhoon-vayon." I just called it the best sex of my life.

The memory of sitting on Sandu's lap that first time flashed through me: the fire crackling behind us and bringing out the gold flecks in his green eyes, feeling his cock against me but having not yet had it inside me. The recalled responsiveness of my nipples shocked by the intensity of sensation, not just at the point of touch but hardwired directly to my pussy. My breasts had never responded like that before then. I'd never figured out if it were because I was mesmerized by Sandu or if in the long dry spell before him, my body had changed and improved with age.

Whatever it was, the reminiscence mingled with the fingers now obligingly playing across my proffered breasts, and the sensations hit me with double the intensity. I moaned, and that brought Bagamil fully awake and into the action.

He took over the breasts from Sandu and added kissing my neck, always an action that with an am'r, was a promise as well as bringing immediate pleasure. His cock brushed eagerly against my body, seemingly of its own accord.

Meanwhile, Sandu's hand had moved down between my legs and was doing more directed teasing, making sure my clit was fully aroused and ready to enjoy all the tactile sensations to come. His fingers dipped lower and tantalized between my labia, as if I needed *extra* help being hungry to have him inside me.

Between the two of them, they worked me into a mindless mass of craving. I squirmed and cried out under their hands, begging for more. No specific directions, just *don't stop!*

Happily, they had no intention of stopping. When that delightful period had gone on long enough, Bagamil rolled back onto his back, and Sandu lifted me bodily onto him. If I had been going at my own speed, I would have rushed to have him all inside me, but Sandu held me back and made me take him only a few millimeters at a time, so by the time Bagamil's cock was half inside me, I was begging shamelessly for them to hurry the fuck up.

They didn't. Time slowed as my aching hunger was ever-so-slowly filled. It didn't matter how much I wriggled and pleaded; both were in complete synchronicity and absolutely no hurry.

Finally—finally!—my thighs, my ass, and my labia were pressed with my full body weight against Bagamil, and he was buried within me as deep as he could go. I was given back full control of my body, so for a while, I moved very vigorously indeed on top of my cinyaa, using his cock to get myself off over and over.

Finally, I slowed to get my breath and because the

orgasms had made my thighs too quivery to keep going like that. Also, there was an element missing from the picture, although that element was patiently waiting and enjoying the show.

I leaned forward to kiss Bagamil; without even having to think, I ducked before my top lip hit his so I could slide in perfectly under his Freddie-stache—the sweet little habits of a long-term love.

He slid his arms around my back to kiss me, and my breasts pressed hard into his chest. After a minute, certain he was still well settled within me, I wiggled my ass invitingly, which gratifyingly made Bagamil gasp in our kiss. It also immediately had the desired result: Sandu's cock pressing against the offered opening.

I'd never had time to build up any issues about anal sex. It had never, ahem, come up in my extremely limited sex life before Sandu. Well, my former girlfriend's finger surely didn't count. Before I had time to think about it in terms of a threesome with two men (in a position very similar to this one, our first time), it was just sort of *happening*, and since I was in the hands of experienced and caring lovers (and hopped up pretty high on Bagamil's powerful blood) everything had felt comfortable, and if not perfectly easy, well, the challenge was one I was very much up for. As, haha, were they.

Sandu went almost as slowly as he had in lowering me onto Bagamil, who'd taken his arms from around me and was reaching behind me to, as far as I could tell, flick across them Sandu's nipples to heighten his pleasure at first penetration. All I knew for certain was that Sandu's cock impossibly got even harder inside me.

There was a particular angle in this position where if they both held still, I could move and fuck both of them without anyone falling out, each having as much pleasure as the other. My thighs having recovered, this we did for a good long while, and I didn't bother to try to count the orgasms.

When it was time for something new, we decoupled—detripled?—and Bagamil moved over to the doorframe and smiled invitingly. We both laughed at him with shared delight. Since arriving at this tiny flat, we'd had to work around the lack of space, and Bagamil had become very fond of us all standing in the doorway from the bedroom to the bath, with them taking turns: one holding me up, and the other stabilizing us all by holding onto the doorframe. (Us all squished in sideways was also an enjoyable variation.) Sandu stepped out of bed, and I climbed up and into his arms, and he managed to get himself inside me as he took the two steps to the doorway. I held onto his neck as Bagamil took his place inside me.

This was a fun position, and one only am'r could maintain for a very satisfying period of time. But the part we all liked best about it was how easy it was for them both to drink from me while inside me.

The downside was that neither could drink for as long as they liked, seeing as how I was being doubly drained, but intensity made up for the brevity. They would time it so that each put their lips on me at the same moment, each pair of lips opened as one, each set of long, sharp canines pricked my skin simultaneously, and then all I could do was breathe and hold on as four teeth penetrated my skin in concert. The sensations blew my mind out of my head, into a million pieces, to maybe coalesce eventually.

After they finished drinking this time, they kept on fucking me for a good long while. I was a little woozy from how much they had taken, but my limits had been extended after the healing I'd done from our last big fight. In all the loving we had done since we got to London, I wondered if they had been testing me, putting me through controlled trials to get a feel for my new strength and limits.

I also had the vhoon-anghyaa of Astryiah inside me, and no one was sure how that would affect me. I now mingled the blood of just not my patar and gharpatar and my fellow frithaputhra Dragoș, a direct bloodline, but the also the divergent blood of Neplach, my uncle-in-blood who'd fought with me against Iblis the Insane Genie, and from just a week or so ago (although it felt like a century already) the equally powerful blood of Astryiah. Apparently, no one had ever tried this with an am'r-nafsh before, so I was a walking science experiment. *Fun.*

So our never-dull sex life had gotten even more inventive. Neither of them had bothered to tell me why, but I wasn't stupid. I could also see why it might seem like a good idea *not* to say something like, "Hey! We are going to run you through some tests to see what the result of your drinking different people's blood is. And we'll do it during sexy times." If I was worrying about the test results, it might not only impact the results but also possibly ruin the simple joy of sex. Insert a scientific-sounding comment about the disturbance of an observed system by the act of observation here.

Since I had figured it out, I could have mentioned it to them, but I didn't want *them* worrying about *me* worrying.

Here I am, transforming into a super-vampire, while two of the world's most powerful vampires watch over me, and we still have to play stupid human games. It's no wonder the am'r have never taken over the damn world.

I didn't have time to think about non-sex stuff for very long, though. After the fun and games in the doorway, Sandu bent me over the sink and kept fucking me while Bagamil drew a bath. Am'r love water, the only thing they do not have in common with cats.

I cycled through some more waves of orgasm while the tub filled, then we all squeezed in. My little knife, Sa'mah—which had for many, *many* years previous been Bagamil's own and which he'd given me as a lover's gift—had been brought in and set on the tub edge. Bagamil was inside me as I sat on his lap in the warm water. Sandu stood in front of me, feet to either side of Bagamil's legs, and the sight of his cock in front of my face was very pleasing. He took Sa'mah, raised one foot to rest it on the tub edge, and nicked a vein on his inner thigh.

I moved so fast to get to the carmine fluid that rushed out that I nearly dislodged myself from Bagamil, who laughed and held on tighter to my hips. As I drank from Sandu, those hips moved on Bagamil automatically, but whether my orgasms came from that penetration or from the blood rushing down my throat, I couldn't have said.

Sandu's was the first blood I'd ever tasted. It was a combination of tasting like home but also intense, like the most robust red wine ever. I could guzzle it like a seasoned lush by now, though.

I was still filled with thirst when the cut in Sandu's skin closed on its own. I knew better than to try to keep it open with tongue and teeth, so I turned my attention to the pretty thing sticking out at quivering attention. There was another way to get blood out of a male am'r.

I had first discovered this to my profound dismay after waking up in a dried-blood "wet spot" after my first night with Sandu. He'd had to do some serious Noosh-whispering to calm me down and not have me running away screaming. (Although mostly in humiliation, not disgust if I was brutally self-honest about it.)

Any reticence or uncertainty was long gone, now. I slid Sandu deep into my throat, a skill I had been able to work on perfecting only recently and liked showing off. He dropped his leg to get stable on both feet and groaned in appreciation. Smugness swept through me. It was *good* to feel so confident in my sexuality; it made my enjoyment of all of it so much greater.

Mixing blowjob techniques while keeping Sandu's preferences in mind—not that there had been a formal education, just what I'd figured out over time and regular repetition—it did not take long to get the extra blood I craved.

After he moaned again and again (at that moment, he was like any kee man) and I drank the lesser quantity of am'r ejaculate, I leaned back against Bagamil, who was still pressing erectly up inside me. He idly played with my nipples as I smiled up at Sandu.

"Now what?" I asked playfully. I knew I would still get blood and a final orgasm from my gharpatar—he was skilled in what the kee world would have called "Tantric sex practices," so he orgasmed as many times as he liked along the way, saving ejaculation for the grand finale. Sandu could do it as well, but not as easily as his patar. Maybe thousands of extra years of practice had something to do with that?

"She is too impatient, my frithaputhra," Bagamil said to Sandu, pretending to ignore me even as he was gently moving up and down inside me. "What have you been teaching her? She must learn patience if she is to exist for endless centuries."

"*Hei, pur și simplu nu e cinstit!* I thought you had a *special* connection with her! *You* teach her patience. It's too big a job for me!"

"You should not make a frithaputhra if you cannot handle them," my gharpatar said primly, his mustache twitching slightly with laughter. "Let me teach both of you since evidently *you* have never learned, either."

Bagamil then sat back and directed us to wash ourselves and him with body wash and the loofah. I tried to get things back on the sexual track, knowing I would fail but enjoying playing the game. Each time, I was mock-sternly rebuffed. The tension of knowing more sex would eventually be happening made my body tingle with still-unfulfilled lust.

Finally, Bagamil declared us all clean—"at least your bodies, if never your minds"—and we returned to the bed. There, more brutal lessons followed as Bagamil told Sandu to go down on me but not let me come. I was not used to this since normally, both men enjoyed giving me as many orgasms as my body could handle. I twisted and writhed under Sandu's ministrations, finally shamelessly begging to be given a damn orgasm, already. Sandu stopped and Bagamil took over on my nipples, licking one and flicking the other with his finger, just the way I liked best. I almost snuck in an orgasm from that, but he caught me—we were all able to read each other's bodies intimately by this time —and backed off on that, too.

"What have I done to either of you to deserve this?" I complained as I lay back, mock-glaring at them. I was playing up my discomfort, but only a bit.

"You've gotten quite brash for a mere am'r-nafsh." Sandu was enjoying it all way too much. "My patar is correct. I have not taught you respect for your elders."

"You wouldn't know respect for your elders if it bit you on the ass," I informed him.

"This is correct," Bagamil said, still pretending to be the dignified elder, although he was often the most childlike of us, especially in matters of love and joy. "I have been very remiss with both your educations. That changes starting now."

His idea of "education" was right up my alley, literally and figuratively. Sandu was more than ready to go again, and Bagamil directed how we fucked in a series of positions, making us both hold off on orgasms and joining in where he liked, when he liked, for a timeless period of passionate play.

Finally, Sandu was inside me when Bagamil nicked a vein in his thigh's vellum-smooth, toughly resilient olive-gold skin. It was an echo of when I drank from Sandu, except that both men were kneeling on the bed, Sandu taking me doggie-style and Bagamil letting me cover his cock in hungry kisses. Once his blood began to flow, I dropped to my elbows so I could angle my head up and suctioned my mouth upon the cut. As I always did, I marveled at the difference in taste between them. Bagamil's blood was similar in taste—of course, that was the most specific meaning of what they called the vhoon-anghyaa—but it was so much...*more*. It was so intense that I'd come to think of it as trying to drink fire, the way drinking neat whisky felt as it exploded in the back of your palate.

The intensity did not slow me down, not anymore, and they could not have stopped me from orgasming if they had tried. But nobody tried. As the powerful old blood hit my brain, I lost the ability to see us on the macro-level. We were all just energy, flickering between particle and wave in my perception, the blood and pleasure moving through us as though only they were real, and our bodies mere conduits.

There was orgasm—mine in endless waves, theirs in sudden tsunamis—but I had left orgasm behind, and this alternate plane of being was the true reward for the building hours of withheld gratification. This was truer than a physical spasm; it was like dreaming when your brain pulled together your experiences and sorted them for storing, except this time I was learning new things about the universe at a level I couldn't describe in words. This was not in any human language: it was pure learning through experience.

And then it was over, and I was back in my body. I could feel their bodies wrapped around me, legs and arms real and solid, and all of us holding each other tight. That was just as wonderful because it was something I had words for, something I could carry forward with me as a memory because I could *understand* it.

Our sexy times had taken up half the night, I discovered when they sent me to the kitchen to feed my remaining kee appetite.

Half a night of not having any difficult conversations.

I didn't think they had planned to try to wriggle out of talking by distracting me with amazing, prolonged sex. I just didn't think, once things started going in that direction, that they were at all bothered about how it would cut into the time we'd have for answering hard questions before the sun rose again.

Goddam. Am'r.

While I microwaved one of the pre-made dinners I'd fallen in love with, a Keralan fish curry—we had no prepared foods like this back in the States—I decided I would carry my food back to the bed. Q-and-A time would start *now*.

CHAPTER FOUR

"So, tell me about our enemies." I shoveled fragrant fish curry into my mouth.

"It is not...that easy," Sandu said, the area between his eyebrows developing a W of crankitude.

"Why can't it be? Just start listing the bad guys for me. Who should I be watching out for? Who's moved up to the arch-enemy slot? Who has sworn vengeance on you that you haven't killed yet?"

Sandu sighed deeply, expressing how put-upon he was. He might well be regretting having given up his penchant for extreme violence against anyone who even mildly annoyed him.

Bagamil was in the bathroom, ostensibly braiding his hair in the mirror. I'd seen him do a neater job than I ever could with no mirror. He simply wanted no part of this, wise elder that he was.

"Look," I said, trying to get Sandu past whatever emotional block he was having. "What about some of the am'r I met back at the convention at your place? Some of those really raised my hackles with just a few words. There was a French am'r...umm, his name was something like... Gérard? Gaston? Germain?"

Sandu was drawn in despite himself. "You mean Gilles." He snorted and spoke toward the bathroom. "She thinks *Gilles* is an enemy worthy of note."

"De Rais? Well, she's right that he's not a friend." Bagamil came out of the bathroom wearing only a long braid and leaned against the doorframe upon which we'd just been fucking. He was a beautiful sight, but I didn't let it distract me.

Sandu turned back to me. "This is what I mean. There are too many am'r who are simply 'not friends.' De Rais was a serial murderer of children in his life as a kee. However, since he was made am'r, he has not committed any crimes that would require us to give him the tokhmarenc. He has kept to himself, as most am'r do. He has never crossed me, nor given me any reason to assume he would try to give me my tokhmarenc, at least not more reason than any other am'r."

Unable to stop myself from being tempted off-track, I asked, "What crimes get, uh, *capital punishment* among the am'r? How is it decided? You don't have, like, a tribunal or something?"

"No, no gathering to discuss law, although a couple am'r might share the news of the crimes and then decide to hunt down the miscreant together to make certain of the results. A cornered am'r will fight with unexpected ferocity.

"Capital crimes, as you call them, are few. You have heard of one: the pat'rkosh, one who kills their patar. From

earliest times among our people, that has been an unforgivable transgression. You do not have to love your patar."
He paused, then added, "I am very lucky in mine." He gave
Bagamil a smoldering look. Bagamil blew a kiss in return. I
smiled because I loved their love and it made me feel safe
and warm, knowing they loved each other *and* me. Sandu
got back to his train of thought. "But it is always wise to
offer respect to elder am'r. In particular, since your patar
has given you the gift of his vhoon-anghyaa, to repay him
with death is just not…" His voice trailed off and he waved
his hands, helpless to explain. "Just not *acceptable*."

"Also *not acceptable*," Bagamil added, "is killing or otherwise disturbing so many kee that they might actually
notice, despite how oblivious they normally are, that am'r
exist and share the world with them. I think you have
heard that word, *adharmhem*, for one who endangers the
am'r as a whole. There are not enough am'r in the world so
that if all the kee agreed to obliterate our people, we could
be certain of survival. We could," he said pensively, "go into
the ahstha and stay in it for several kee generations,
reawakening when we were forgotten, merely a myth. But
it would be a nuisance." He grinned at me. "We am'r are too
lazy to wish to deal with such an inconvenience."

"That's it?" I asked. "Only two crimes?"

"We do not need much excuse to kill another am'r."
Bagamil laughed. "I only need be irked by an am'r of lesser
or equal powers, and then I might kill them. So you could
say that we use capital punishment frequently and almost
exclusively for any severity of 'crime.' The only difference
between those two situations and the more idle death

sentences is that no other am'r will try to avenge the killing of a pat'rkosh or adharmhem. If you kill an am'r out of spite, or even honest self-defense, they may have a frithaputhra or a friend who takes it upon themselves to avenge them."

This was fascinating, but it had gotten way off-track. "Thank you for teaching me that, my gharpatar." I ducked my head formally to him, and he looked amused. "But what about that list of our enemies?"

Bagamil smiled mildly at me, knowing I'd trapped him in the very conversation he'd been trying to avoid. But he knew how to play games far better than I did.

"You said you could sense our enemies at Sandu's stronghold. Who else did you sense meant us harm?"

I wanted to protest that that was not what I'd said, but I let it go, hoping Bagamil might be willing to answer my questions as opposed to stubborn Sandu.

"Well, the Russian one. Maxym. He was, ugh, *oily*. Smarmy. He would backstab you as soon as look at you."

"Ah, yes, I know him. He is young and a nasty little piece of work. You were right not to trust him. He fought on Mehmet's side; I remember well. But does he walk among us still?" He turned to Sandu, who was still lounging on the bed, hoping I'd get distracted from a conversation which, for some reason, he did not want to have.

He was happy enough to answer his patar, though. "I do not know. It was, *ei bine*, a busy day. I know which am'r I took the time to make sure would never trouble me again. He was not among their number."

"So he is a potential enemy?" I demanded.

Sandu sighed and shook his head. "If he is alive to bother us, it would be at a gadfly level."

"Like Monserrate? And Apolinar? And Julio? You did not see them as serious threats, and they stole Bagamil right out from under your nose."

Sandu looked more like the pictures of Vlad at that moment, and Bagamil hurried to step in. "I left with them of my own choice. I was not 'stolen,' and it was not Sandu's mistake."

"But they were gadfly-level, right? And no matter how it started, you ended up in a terrible situation. We *all* ended up in that terrible situation."

"Cinyaa, you are not used to life as an am'r. I have been in equally dangerous situations in my long existence. I have fought in wars with your patar. Life is *dangerous* when you are am'r. Indeed, it is hazardous when you are kee; you are just less aware of it most of the time. We cannot make lists of every am'r whom we suspect of being bad actors; they would be too long to be useful."

"The list is Everyone We Know," Sandu growled.

"But you have called Lope an ally. Nthanda is an ally, right? Or why did we just go have a get-together with him?"

"Among the am'r, alliances may be shifting things. Or at least, not entirely to be counted upon. When you need assistance, your allies may be busy doing something else. Or not busy, but simply not willing to be bothered," Bagamil offered.

"Although if you're offering a good fight, you can usually get decent attendance," Sandu admitted. "But that is not about true respect for you and your agreements, but simply the love of vhoon and violence."

I tried not to snicker at Vlad Dracula dismissing blood and brutality as lesser than negotiated agreements. However, this was the first time he'd contributed anything but snide unwillingness to the conversation, and I wanted to keep him participating.

"How can you live like that, not knowing when another Mehmet or Julio will abduct you with maadak?" I asked, meaning, "How the hell can I live with that?"

There was a pause. Sandu looked at Bagamil. Bagamil looked at Sandu. I didn't like that.

"*Sufleţel*, this is am'r life. There is someone waiting around every corner to steal your am'r-nafsh or give you your tokhmarenc. That is why we train with our weapons and drink plenty of vhoon—to keep us growing stronger and faster as the years go by."

Bagamil, probably disliking the look on my face, jumped in. "Cinyaa, this is how it *has* been. This is what we are trying to change. This is *why* we have allies like Lope and Nthanda when in the past, our kind never bothered with such things. We are trying to build a new am'r world. It will take a while, however. You yourself will be a full am'r for many years before the changes we are fighting for now will take effect. You must be patient with the am'r. They will fight change. And true change it is; in all these long years, we have never tried another way."

"I...just don't want you to keep being in such terrible danger. And be worrying about me, too." That was the least cowardly way I could put it.

"There is a way to minimize the danger to you. We

could go to one of our more hidden strongholds. We could hide from the world. You could have a normal am'r-nafsh existence away from all other am'r. For many decades, we would see no other am'r. Or if we did, they would not walk away to tell their friends where we had taken shelter. That is the old way. For long years, we have tried to pretend that air travel and satellites and other kee technology have *not* been making that life less and less practical. Now, with you as our guide and inspiration, we are trying to change that. But if you like, we could put off the experiment for some time. I would not mind a few decades of being with just my Sandu and you."

They were offering to let me be a craven weakling, no blame or shame. I felt a rush of anger at them both, then realized it was a heated mix of humiliation and resentment. Why weren't they calling me out and telling me what a loser I was? That I had tasted not even two years of am'r life and it had me running for the hills, screaming, a quitter before the game really got started?

Fuck.

"If we run off and *hide,*" I said slowly, careful with my words, "it will just put off the changes you're hoping to see. I definitely *don't* want that. But *how* are we going to make am'r society change? I don't see how my archiving the records of am'r history will change how the am'r behave now."

Bagamil took that on. "One thing you dislike—and we *all* dislike—is how vulnerable maadak makes us. It is impossible to sense a maadakyo. Even I am powerless against it. The first order of business for us is to pool the knowledge that might have been built up over the

72

centuries about maadak and to set up new scientific studies to add to it. The sooner we have an antiserum, say, something we could give to any kee to ensure it is safe to drink from them, or something we could drink like an antivenin once we feel the results of maadak in our systems, the less chance of you, your patar, or me ever being in any real danger again."

"We are here to discuss that on this very trip," Sandu added, glad to be able to say something to which I would respond well. "We have been putting out the call for anyone who has special knowledge of maadak. Or anyone who received scientific training in their kee life."

Bagamil turned to me. "Now, what about this sight-seeing you want to do?"

It felt like a girl's night out. Lilani met me at the door of the flat and promised my patar and gharpatar she'd have me home before sunrise. That made me blush with frustration at being a pathetic "mere" am'r-nafsh, but I soon forgot as we made our way to a pub. "Drinks to start the evening," she announced.

Lilani didn't have myriad microbraids this time. Her mohawk was now in two thick braids that hung down to her ass. I guessed even am'r could get extensions, although I carefully did not let myself giggle aloud at the thought.

The pub was as purely British as anything I'd ever imagined. Wood paneling up the lower half of the walls, the top painted dark red and covered with old British beer and cigarette advertisements. There were random wood and metal things that had obviously had purposes in times past but were now bulky curios suitable only for pub walls. It was dimly and unevenly lit, and it was *loud*. The volume of the music was too high, and all the kee in the place were shouting over it—or singing drunkenly along. The only theme the music seemed to have was that there was a Queen selection about every six songs.

The smell was louder than the noise. There were about thirty kee, and the booze they were chugging seemed to be oozing directly out of their pores. The overheatedness of the rooms was not mitigated by all the windows being thrust open. They let the sound and smell pour out into the street without any relatively refreshing air coming back in.

I came to a dead stop as we walked up when I hit the first wall of throbbing music, chaotic babble, and pore-recycled beer and cider.

"Oh, don't I know!" Lilani laughed at me and shoved me forward. "You have to practice, girl, or you can't handle it at all, like some fussy old aojysht. And the drinks are on tap!" She laughed at her own joke and I grinned at her, panicking on the inside because I wasn't planning to drink from any kee tonight. I hoped she didn't expect me to do so.

But when we got in, she said, "Whatcha havin'? First round's on me!" When I tentatively said I'd have a cider, she came back with two slopping-over pints.

The cider was amazing. I'd never had it except out of a bottle, and this was fresh and foaming, crisp and tartly sweet. I could no longer get a buzz from alcohol, but my palate had doubled in discernment. I took big gulps in pleasure while Lilani's stayed untouched at her elbow. She was scanning the crowd for a different beverage.

"You're lucky you wanted to go to the V&A," she shouted to me over the noise. "I never even knew this one would come in so handy!" I smiled at her, trying not to look puzzled.

After I'd just about worked through my pint and was considering asking Lilani if she wanted to swap cups, her face lit up in delight. She waved her hand and shouted, "Oi! Nads! *Nadia*! Babe, here!"

A woman managed to get a crowd of drunken fuckboys to move apart for her, and she was followed over to us by their crude and unimaginative catcalls. She was plumply rounded, all curves under a nicely fitted suit dress—professional but sexy. I felt my archivist-radar come online and start pinging. Something about the glasses, the tidy updo, and the way she carried herself outed her to me immediately: this was a woman in a profession similar to mine, whose big, beautiful mind craved order and to be getting her hands dirty reducing the entropy in the universe. I liked her immediately.

I had a little more time to admire her since she turned back and yelled something quashing at the boisterous lads. Her suit dress was a perfect shade of hot magenta for her light brown skin. A few dark-brown tendrils had escaped from her chignon, and the humidity was making them curl in a way I knew all too well. She turned back to us, laughing. Whatever lucky genetic combinations had formed her sparkling beauty, they'd resulted in huge warm-brown eyes and a few adorable freckles scattered decoratively across her high cheekbones. Her full lips flaunted their perfect arcs in a hot magenta gloss that perfectly matched her dress.

She made it to us and shamelessly stole Lilani's cider, taking a huge chug in perfect comfort and strange grace. She put it down and announced, "Getting through that mess was thirsty work, right?"

"No doubt!" Lilani agreed, and they hugged. I was taken aback because am'r do not hug kee. At least, I'd never seen it before. In my experience, am'r didn't have casual friendships with kee either, but then, my experience was painfully limited.

Nadia turned from Lilani's arms to reach out to me, smiling broadly. "Any friend of Lilani's…" she gushed as she gathered me into her soft and deliciously fragrant embrace.

This is why we're not friends with kee. Oh, shit!

I was ready to act like one of those crazed vampires in the horror flicks, ripping Nadia's carotid open and devouring every spraying droplet in a blood frenzy.

Focus. Just give the same amount of pressure in returning her squeeze. Do not turn your head to her neck to get a better whiff of that hot kee blood thrumming just under the surface of all that lovely brown skin.

I tried not to seem stiff and distant, but that was a secondary goal after not attacking her.

Finally, many of her heartbeats later—and trust me, I was listening and counting as her strong heart pumped the blood through her veins and arteries—she pulled back from the embrace. I was finally able to hear the ambient noise of the pub again and process information that wasn't directly involved with Nadia's blood *and me not drinking any of it.*

"I missed your name in all this noise," she said, British politeness coming to the fore since I hadn't told her my name.

Aw, shit. I hate this part.

"My name is *Noosh,*" I said as firmly and clearly as I could above the fourth Queen song to play since we'd arrived. The other patrons of the bar were singing along in a varied selection of keys.

"Noosh?" She wasn't sure she'd heard right. Even if everyone in the bar was not a champion at this moment, she'd have asked that anyway.

"Yeah, Noosh. It's a nickname." I shrugged and laughed as if I hadn't gone through this a million times.

"So how do you know Lil, Noosh?"

Good, we don't have to discuss my name. But dammit, how am I supposed to know Lilani, that isn't, "We've had a grand time shooting and hacking up our enemies together"?

Thankfully, Lilani jumped in. "Noosh is a friend of a friend, visiting the UK for her first time! And you're going to love her. She's an archivist, too!"

"What? For reals?" Nadia lit up with enthusiasm. "Where do you work? And is this, like, truly your first time here?"

I had to think on my feet. "Um, I worked as head librarian for about a decade at a library in the States. Now I'm working on a private collection, but it's a bit hush-hush. And yeah, it's totally my first time in the UK, but I've wanted to come here for so long. Just never had the money until now."

"Oh, a private collection! Keep drinking with me, and I'll get all the info out of you, girl. Is it my round?" she asked, eying my glass and her empty one, which had once been Lilani's untouched cider.

"Not yet!" Lilani told her. "Last one was Noosh. I'll get this one."

As Lilani went to get three more ciders, Nadia leaned closer so that she didn't have to shout quite so loudly to be heard. I focused on breathing through my mouth, so her blood-perfume didn't overwhelm the less attractive scents of boozy sweat and old spilled booze.

"So, me? I'm a Records and Archives Assistant at the V&A. That's the Victoria and Albert Museum, yeah? National museum of art and design?"

"Oh, I've heard of it," I told her, my head now swimming not from smells but from information. No wonder Lilani was connecting with Nadia tonight: this was the very night she was supposed to take me to enjoy the V&A after hours, alone in the empty museum, free from bustling, distracting kee and the always irksome daylight. "It must be a great job," I said weakly. Most of my brain was devoted to wondering how Lilani was going to play this.

"It's brill!" Nadia told me, oozing contentedness. "I mostly work in the Archive and Registry, the Word and Image Department. I help manage the museum's institutional records and archives, both paper and electronic information. Not just documentation, but appraisal and disposal of records, too. I also get to help to provide information and records retrieval services to the staff and the public too. I love it all!"

Lilani returned with overflowing pints and joined the discussion as she handed them around. "Yeah, all Noosh can talk about is getting to visit your V&A. It's, like, the highlight of her whole trip, like, a bucket-list thing." She grinned widely at me behind Nadia's head.

"Oh, you must come see us! I'll get you a free visitor pass any day you like! If you come on my lunch break, I'll take you behind the scenes for a, you know, special archivist tour!"

"Nads, c'mon girl, you can do better than that. Let's go tonight. You know I've always wanted to have a look 'round, too."

"Oh, it's after hours now," Nadia said, obviously torn between wanting to jump right up and go and the realities of how complicated it would be if we did. "Getting in right now is a proper pain in the arse. Let's plan a day this week—"

"Nads." Lilani was looking at her very intently. "Let's all go have a girl's loo run, yeah?"

"Oh...yeah, gotta have a slash!" Nadia giggled like she was drunk, but she'd barely touched the second cider, and I had a feeling she was a lady with a well-seasoned tolerance.

"C'mon, Noosh!" Lilani instructed me. "Gotta piss as a group. Just not safe to go to the khazi on your own these days."

I followed them, bemused and excited. Nadia was holding hands with Lilani, her generous curves jiggling with each step. I was far enough behind to watch all eyes follow their impressive promenade to the bathroom. Something for everyone, from Nadia's eye-catching bounce to Lilani's tautly muscular stretch of height, black leather mini-dress like a second skin, and those two long braids swinging like pendulums behind.

The loo was a nasty place; any charming old-timey-ness stopped at the door. It didn't quite reach "The Worst Toilet in Scotland" level, but for someone with am'r senses, not dulled and drunken kee ones, it was bad. The walls had been gouged and chipped throughout the years, with so many coats of paint sloshed over it all that there was no indication of what they were made of. They were currently a dark green color that upped the claustrophobia and nausea factors. They had been liberally graffitied with phone numbers and insults and drawings of genitalia. There were three stalls, also painted "oppressive green," and a sink I would not have washed my hands in if you'd paid me. *The smell.* I won't talk about the smell. I stopped using my nose and mouth-breathed like my life depended on it.

Lilani didn't seem to care, however, and Nadia was too mesmerized to notice.

There was an empty area between the final stall and the wall that perhaps had once held a trash receptacle. That level of orderliness had obviously long been given up, so now it was just a space, one into which three bodies could fit if they didn't mind getting intimate. That was obviously what Lilani intended since she pushed Nadia against the wall, holding both arms up with one hand and running the other over the kee's generous curves.

I would have given them more space, but I found myself drawn to Nadia. Her blood was calling to me from under her skin, which was clean and lightly perfumed with something that had gardenia in it, a perfect complement to the underlying saline richness. As long as I stayed close to her, I could pretend the repulsiveness around us did not exist.

Lilani was murmuring into Nadia's ear, telling her how beautiful she was, how perfect and delicious and luscious. I had noticed long before that am'r compliments tended toward descriptions you could also use for food—no surprise!—but now I really got it. Nadia was lovely, but it was her blood that was the loveliest part of her.

Of course, when an am'r whispers in one's ear, it puts them close to a certain other part of one's anatomy where a big fat vein throbs invitingly under delicate skin. Lilani was kissing there between flatteries, and Nadia was squirming with lust. The necklines of both her suit jacket and the minimal black shirt underneath were in no way obstacles to blood-drinking.

I watched, almost as hypnotized as Nadia, as Lilani's hand—the dark skin set off aesthetically against the magenta fabric tight around plush curves—fondled breasts, teased the lighter brown décolletage, and slid slowly down to start pushing up the hem of the not-particularly-long skirt, exposing more lush brown skin to my view.

I was salivating. The time I had been with Astryiah a breathtaking memory I often replayed in my head. But she was am'r, not kee. This was entirely different, and I was not prepared for the intensity of my lust.

Lilani's fingers moved out of view under the bottom of the skirt, which fig-leafed Nadia by a bare few millimeters. What I could not see in pornographic detail, I could see the results of. Nadia moaned and writhed against the fingers sliding up inside her.

It was a classic am'r move. At the same time, Lilani's

teeth dug into Nadia's neck so the pain of the bite got confused with the pleasure of the other penetration. I knew exactly what sensations Nadia was experiencing, and that made the whole thing even more arousing for me as I imagined the thrills now tingling up and down Nadia's nerve endings.

Watching Sandu and Bagamil together had always been arousing, but a big part of it was that I was happy two people I loved were sharing joy and passion. Here, there was not the same deep love, and for some reason, Nadia being kee changed the whole dynamic. It was a type of visceral voyeurism I'd never expected to find in myself— getting off on *watching*.

Nadia rolled through several orgasms, and a distantly rational part of my brain was glad for the ambient noise level of the pub. The rest of me didn't give a fuck because each time Nadia came, I felt a warm throb of pleasure go through my body as well.

Lilani pulled her head back from Nadia's neck and smiled at me. Her teeth were coated in blood. "Come, have a sip," she invited me.

With a shock, all my pleasure drained out of me. "Oh! No, I couldn't!"

My mind threw me back to a terrible memory, all-too-recent in my past, of me holding a dying kee in my arms and draining the last drops of blood out of his unsavory neck in a dark cave under miserable circumstances.

He had a name. Brodie. I killed him.

I felt almost sick with repugnance now. "I don't drink from kee," I lied to Lilani.

She made a face, and I wondered if someone had told

her about Brodie. But only Bagamil and Sandu knew. Why would they tell *her*?

"Vhoon-kee will not harm an am'r-nafsh," she told me, and I sighed in relief that she did not know. "It is perfectly fine as nourishment. But if you are squeamish…"

Lilani leaned back into Nadia, who was lolling languidly in her arms, a smile plastered on her face. She put her lips back on the bite mark, which had been oozing blood. I relaxed back into voyeur mode.

After a moment, Lilani's near arm shot out, grabbed my upper arm with a python's grip, and pulled me in, then she turned her head and planted her blood-smeared lips against mine. They opened, and mine opened in mindless instinct, then hot kee blood, tasting just as I expected Nadia's blood to taste, spilled into my mouth. I swallowed it as if I'd never had any ethical quandaries, and all guilt was lost in the savor of it.

When Lilani finally pulled back from the kiss, she licked her lips and grinned at me, teeth still blood-tinged. "Now you've had a snack. No worries!"

I smiled unsteadily at her. I supposed since Nadia was obviously fine and was currently cuddling up to Lilani, I had nothing to feel bad about. I could feel the kee blood moving through me, better than the first sip of morning coffee.

Lilani, who'd had a good deal more of Nadia's excellent blood, was practically glowing. Her blue-black skin took on a sheen of pure youthful health, and her eyes sparkled with vitality. She was beautiful at the worst of times; now, she was almost too stunning to look at.

Nadia was gazing up at her, and she obviously felt the

way I did, except more so. Lilani pulled away from the wall and guided the dazed kee out of the nasty loo. "It's time to go have a visit to your workplace. Show it all off to us, right, Nads?"

"Yeah! You gotta come see it! I'll give you both the best tour ever!" Apparently, being mesmerized by an am'r removed Nadia's inhibitions, and she was now free to do whatever her enthusiastic heart desired.

Which, happily, was giving me my own personal after-hours tour of one of the finest museums in the UK.

Nadia took us to a back entrance to the museum and entered a code on a keypad. We were in, but what we were in looked like an office with particularly long hallways. And that was the first part of the tour: the archival collections offices. This must have been overwhelmingly tedious to Lilani, but seeing other archivists' workspaces was so fascinating for me that I forgot Nadia was kee and I part-am'r. We geeked out entirely on that shared level.

"It's utter *pants*, Noosh, that I can't show off the manuscripts, but they are stored at the National Art Library. We have five of da Vinci's notebooks!"

"It's...pants?" I knew that for the Brits, "pants" meant underwear, but I was stymied as to how undergarments related to the situation.

Lilani snorted. "You forgot she's a Yank, Nads."

Nadia giggled. "You know, I did! 'Pants' means, like, 'rubbish.' Something very..."

"Suboptimal?"

"Yes, you got it!" Nadia was encouraging in that way all people treat foreigners—like they are a bit slow, but if you talk deliberately and loudly, possibly they can be taught.

We moved along to the museum part of things. This involved Nadia calling out hellos to a kee security guard. Lilani stepped in and had a low discussion with him, after which he told us to have a brilliant time and wandered dazedly away.

An empty museum is the finest thing in the world. No noisy kids running around, no inconsiderate tourists standing too long in front of what you want to look at next, no having to pay to see the current special exhibits. Nadia accompanied me for a while, pointing out favorite items in the permanent collection. Then she said she needed "a wee and a tea." It was nice being around kee in this regard because they didn't judge me for needing to use the facilities now and again.

Nadia giggled about it in the loo. "Lil never needs a slash. I think she's superhuman or something. I mean, look at her! She's too *perfect* to be a mere mortal, right?"

Then I realized, *She doesn't know Lilani is a vampire. She thinks they are just having hot lesbian sex. Holy shit.*

I weakly agreed with her and passed on the tea part of things. Lilani offered to go with her for a cuppa, which of course she wouldn't drink. I had a feeling that as soon as Nadia had rehydrated, Lilani would be right back up her skirt. I was happy for them, but the randomly amazing pieces of history and art scattered around the museum were far more of a lure to me.

They returned a perfect, timeless time later. I was just

thinking that it was good I was am'r-nafsh because my feet would have been very sore by now if I'd been kee.

"It's almost sunrise," Lilani told me.

"That's around when the cleaners come in," Nadia explained. It hit me again that Nadia had no idea what Lilani was.

Sandu had always said he didn't mesmerize me, but I'd never really believed him. Now, seeing Lilani interacting with a kee for so long, I began to understand just how much a kee could be convinced to believe. I'd seen the am'r around me using the power when we took kee air travel or stayed in a hotel, but those interactions had been brief, and I'd always been more focused on not breathing in over-much the clashing pungent scents in kee public spaces.

We exited via the same door we'd used to enter and walked the pre-dawn streets of Kensington, looking for a black cab. Nadia looked, well, *drained*, and I hoped she'd go get one of those full English breakfasts to make up for all the blood she'd lost tonight. Thinking about it, I wanted one of those myself.

We found a greasy breakfast-all-day place before we found the cab, so Nads and I got to fill ourselves up with eggs, bacon rashers, sausage, beans, mushrooms, fried bread, and milky tea while Lilani looked impatiently at the lightening windows.

I was glad we pushed it because Nadia looked much healthier after a good meal. We finally piled into a cab and she was dropped off first, then I was, and I waved goodbye to a decidedly grumpy Lilani, hiding behind huge sunglasses as the cab took off into the early morning city. I did not stay longer than I had to on the street but rushed down the stairs to our basement-level flat, eager to get out of the already too-bright sunshine and also to tell my beloveds about everything I'd seen at the museum.

The next night was the Tower of London with Viv. I wondered if "Noosh tourist duties" were being passed around to all of Nthanda's people, and if so, if they were enjoying doing something other than the usual am'r shit.

Viv was evidently enjoying it. Normally, he was a quiet, somber man. Even his smiles were solemn. This evening, it was like I was meeting a different Vivian, and that took the thrill of the evening up a notch. I had thought it couldn't be much better; who doesn't love the idea of sneaking into the Tower of London to check out the Crown jewels?

The black cab had come around to collect me with Viv already in it, and we didn't say much on the way to the Tower, although he did point out the White Chapel area as we were going through and winked at me. The cabbie heard him and started on a long ramble about Jack the Ripper, which I listened to with a tourist's delight.

Our cabbie had more to say on the subject (he'd barely managed to cover the first three victims and had touched only briefly on his belief that Jack the Ripper was probably an obstetrician to Queen Victoria's daughter), but Viv had him drop us off by the Thames, the Tower behind us.

"You know that lot's all closed up for the night, right, mate?" the cabbie asked, gesturing at the medieval-looking wall with turrets behind it.

"Cheers, mate," Viv replied blandly, waving him off.

As the cab rattled off over the cobblestones, it felt very lonely where we were. The towers inside the walls were decoratively lit, and there were streetlights along the river, but in every direction, the street was utterly deserted, unlike every other nighttime London street I'd seen. I shivered, not because I was cold—I was never *really* cold anymore, now that am'r blood flowed through my veins—but because it was a lonely night in the city of Jack the Ripper, Bill Sykes, Professor James Moriarty, the Kray Twins, and modern terrorists. Being half-a-vampire didn't seem quite so formidable a thing with the city stretching around me like a huge beast that uncaringly subsisted on puny creatures like me.

Then Viv touched my arm and I looked up into his face, the streetlight picking out his eyes and casting highlights across his nose with its low curves like a Porsche and high cheekbones and full lips. Some of his short dreads caught the light, others stuck up in fascinating shadows. I realized I was no longer cold. This was a big, bad city, but Viv was a big, bad am'r—I'd seen him fighting very capably back under that mountain in Tierra del Fuego—and I felt better with him at my side.

Don't get too comfortable with am'r who aren't Sandu or Bagamil, silly girl. Stop being so damn trusting, or you will not enjoy your inevitable disillusionment.

Viv had broken into a smile which was much less *solemn* than his usual ones, though, and it was hard not to let his obvious excitement be contagious.

"Shall we go have a peep at the Crown jewels, eh?"

I grinned back at him. "Well, since we're in the area, it seems impolite not to."

I figured security would be pretty tight, all those price-less relics and pieces of history considered, but Viv used the same method Lilani had. When we loitered for a second too long at the gated entrance, a night-watchman showed up. Not one of the gaudily dressed Beefeaters, but a man with military bearing wearing a dark blue uniform made to impress not tourists but those who were up to no good.

We *were* up to no good, but we were not impressed. Or at least Viv was not. He played at being lost at first, holding out a piece of notepaper and saying, "Sorry! Do you mind? We musta got turned 'round. Can you help? These directions don't make sense."

The guard came closer, reached for the paper. Viv murmured something I couldn't make out, and the guard made the mistake of looking up from the paper and meeting Viv's eyes.

"No worries," Viv told him soothingly. "Everything's right tonight, and you feel easy in our company. What's your name, lad?"

"Alfie…" The guard's voice was slow and a bit tentative.

"Alfie, is it? Named for Alfred the Great, yeah?"

"Nah, for my uncle Alfie." His eyes were unfocused, his voice slurred like he'd had too much to drink. Viv had really laid it on him.

The am'r laughed warmly. "Of course, good ol' Uncle Alfie, what a chap. Now, you let us right in—yes, good—and you're going to give us the private tour, like. Old friends, we are."

Yeomen Warder Alfie no longer had the tense body language he'd had when we showed up. He got out the key to the gate with unhurried ease, welcomed us in warmly, and locked up after us.

"We'll start with the Crown jewels, won't we?" Viv told him, and the guard smiled affably.

"Every'un does," he told us.

When we left right before sunrise, gold and jewels still flashed in my vision like I'd been staring at the sun. My head spun with dark and violent histories. Viv had held my arm as we strolled along a parapet because his night vision was still better than mine, and because I was walking like I was drunk, peering at all the archaic graffiti carved into the Tower's stone walls.

If you get a chance, visit the Tower of London. You won't get a personal nighttime tour from Alfie, but I promise it's worth it anyway.

I was supposed to take in a few other touristy destinations with my am'r-guided late-night tour service, but our actual reason for being in the UK got in the way.

Nthanda arrived at our flat when I was expecting another high-octane ladies' night with Lilani. I was smart enough not to assume this meant he himself was going to escort my ass around the Museum of London. However, the next person down the stairs was Roy, and I had an uncomfortable moment of worrying that maybe Nthanda was going to force me to accept the dubious am'r as my attendant for the evening.

One room of the flat was an open-plan mini-kitchen/dining/living room. It made sense for a couple tourists who were just going to crash here at night after full days of sightseeing, but not much sense for anything else.

Nthanda and Roy sat on the two-seater sofa. Bagamil and I sat at the table in the kitchen. Sandu leaned on the wall between the two areas.

"Right," Nthanda started. "My Roy has some interesting news."

Roy looked pleased but did not volunteer to tell us his interesting news.

"You lot remember Roy's ikkle origin story? Patar named 'Fangs' and all? Well, this wasn't down here in the Great Wen, but up in Brummagem. Eh, that's Birmingham."

At this point, Sandu and Bagamil assured him they knew that. Since I hadn't, I smiled and tried to look generally world-wise.

Nthanda continued, "Roy still has his northern connections, and he just heard that Croglin would like to invite you up for a weekend in the country." He gave us a look I could not understand and waited for a response.

I glanced at Sandu. I could tell from his still face that he was wracking his brain. I looked at Bagamil, and he had much the same expression.

Nthanda looked smug. "Do we not know of the Vampire of Croglin Grange, gentlemen?"

I would have protested being left out, but it was obvious that I knew nothing, having never even been to the UK before. Bagamil and Sandu had been many times (although getting details from Sandu about a particular period around the year 1893 had long frustrated me) so if there was an eminent vampire in the British Isles, they ought to know.

"Croglin..." Bagamil mused.

"I feel like I have *heard* the name," Sandu added.

"No shame to you if you've not," Nthanda told them, but the smile on his face made it clear to me that he liked having knowledge that both the Aojysht and Dracula did not have. "He's our resident am'r of mystery.

"He lives far Up North, out where there's only sheep and the fractious descendants of Reivers. Many rumors have circulated about him over the years: that he is an aojysht in hiding, or that he was the *real* Dracula of the story...with apologies." He turned to Sandu, and I saw mischief sparkle in his eyes.

"*Nu, nu.* That would explain much. I was not in England at that time, but *something* inspired Stoker." Sandu looked at me as he said this and spoke with sullen insistence.

"Hmm..." Nthanda said, his smile now more private. "Well, our 'Vampire of Croglin Grange' was certainly here because a story of that name was published in the penny dreadfuls in 1875. And *that* might be considered a case of adharmhem, a matter about which something should have been *done.*"

"I was of course here in that year. As you may recall, I arrived in London in the year of the Slavery Abolition Act —1834, if that date is not as deeply burned into your memories as it is into mine. I remember meeting you both in the early years of my leadership of the am'r of southern England."

I was hanging on his every word. I had no idea how you convinced an am'r to tell their whole life's story since getting them drunk wasn't an option, so I had to hear Nthanda's tale now while he was in the mood to tell it.

Bagamil responded, "I am a little vague about Victorian times. I traveled so much in that era—such a time for it, and in comfort like never before! I do know I was here for the Great Exhibition—that was 1851—but shortly after that I was in the Americas and then a return trip to South Asia for many decades.

"I do remember you during the Great Exhibition! What a figure you cut in those days. You wear a suit like none other, my friend."

Nthanda laughed heartily. "I was a young fool trying to impress the Aojysht, but thank you. We all looked more impressive in those suits."

I glanced at Nthanda, who was wearing black skinny-cut slacks in a black-on-black check print and a silky black tee under a matching check sports coat. His shoes were some crazy mixture of sneaker and Oxford, and he wore no socks under them. The black clothing made his dark-reddish-brown skin look even warmer. Highlights from one small side lamp, the only light anyone had bothered to turn on, caught in the planes of his face and the divot between his collar bones, a rich glow. I wondered how he could look more impressive than he did right now.

"But these events happened after the Exhibition. In 1875 the story was published, although a certain Augustus

Hare, Esquire, had been down to London, telling the story at every supper he could get himself invited to long before he got it in print.

"It was a proper bother to go up and check on it, back then. The easiest thing to do would have been to take the London and North Western Railway, which had expanded its service as far as Edinburgh at that time, but I had a specially-made carriage with light-blocking shutters so I could sleep in it during daylight hours. Instead of relying on the rail and then finding shelter in the day, I felt it safer to travel in my own carriage with a driver accustomed to my wants.

"But what a nuisance that was. One couldn't get there in less than a day, and the horses needed a proper rest, so one had to stop at a coaching inn to take care of one's needs and get a meal for the driver and supper for oneself as well.

"Eventually, I was in the Border country. I understand those am'r who want to live far away from the kee world, but me, I like living in their delicious swirl of chaos. A little danger just adds spice, and they kill each other with such regularity. With a little moderation, a city like London can sustain a good number of am'r with no adharmhem.

"But out in the desolation of the fells, an am'r can have as much privacy as they like. There was no Croglin *Grange* at this time, but a house called Croglin Low Hall, which was twenty or so miles from the nearest city, Carlisle." He paused, then spat, "*City*, hah! Carlisle is more a collection of buildings than it in any way resembles my city."

The way Nthanda spoke of London made me realize that despite the city teeming with kee, in Nthanda's mind, it was an am'r city. As he said, *his city*. All the other am'r I'd met shunned kee...until it was time for dinner. Nthanda and his people spent all their time surrounded by kee. I had already experienced that many parts of London were as bustling after dark as during kee working hours.

I'd not been in the am'r world for long, but already the city-am'r life felt...almost *unnatural*. The chance for things to go wrong, for what they called "adharmhem," seemed all too obvious.

It's better than keeping a cattle ranch of kee in your underground lair, though. That thought shook me up. Maybe being around the kee world every single night was better? Maybe am'r were more able to remember where they had come from and view kee as more than ambulatory juice boxes? My respect for Nthanda, which had never been low, rose even higher as I considered that he kept a group of fiercely independent, actively unsociable, and mostly-immortal beings from making such bad choices that the am'r world was exposed to the light of kee attention. And he'd been doing that since the mid-1800s. Maybe that didn't make him an aojysht in the eyes of the am'r world, but it was fucking impressive.

Nthanda had paused to consider the inferiority of places that were *not London* for long enough. He continued, "Asking directions of suspicious villagers after nightfall is never fun, right? Thank God for pubs, because showing up after dark at a pub is never dodgy, even if you're a flash Southerner *and* your skin's a funny color to boot. I was the first Black man most of those rustics had ever seen, and I had questions asked of me, like 'Does that black wash off?' in such a thick Cumbrian dialect that I could barely understand them, even if I wanted to. After the first pub, I sent my driver in to ask for directions. He could barely make out the local vernacular either, but at least he was white and thus had less nonsense to sort through.

"After a night of such *delights*, I ended up at Croglin Low Hall about an hour before sunrise. There was candle-light in one of the rooms, but no one in evidence when I arrived. This was a time when most large houses had a number of servants to keep them running, so some amount of activity could be expected. I was at highest alert, for I was in the territory of another am'r uninvited. I did not have much time to get things sorted before I would also be dealing with daylight, and I wanted nothing more than to finish this chore and get back down to civilization.

"Since no one had come out at the sound of our arrival, I went and knocked on the door myself, leaving my driver to water and attend to the horses." Nthanda paused, and I realized he was enjoying making as much of this story as possible. That was fine with me because I was enjoying it.

"Before my third knock, the door opened from under my raised hand. I got the scent of him first: the strongest vhoon-anghyaa I'd ever encountered until I met you, Aojysht. He was dressed in only a battered damask dressing coat and trousers. He had long black hair, dark olive skin. He did not look like any of the locals, and he didn't talk like them, either.

"'Ah, leader of London,' he said to me. I knew not to show surprise around an aojysht, but I was dismayed that he knew me by sight or smell—because I was certain I'd never met *him*.

"'Certainly, you must come in after such lengthy travels,' he said to me, and I entered Croglin Low Hall, bemused and wary.

"Moving through the hallway and into a drawing-room, I saw that both were a bit faded and out-of-fashion but not dilapidated. I mostly had eyes for my host. He had brought me into a room where a fire was laid and offered me a chair.

"'Would that I could offer you refreshment, Nthanda, frithaputhra-of-Chausiku, but I keep a modest home here and have no izchhaish on the grounds. But I have no doubt that you did partake of one of our many public houses along the way.'

"'Have you been following me?'" I demanded.

"'Have you sensed me?' he replied teasingly. Before I could work through my hot anger, he was saying soothingly, 'No, my good man, I have not been following you 'cross fell and dale, but I do know my land and most of what happens therein. I can stretch my senses out for many miles in each direction, up toward the highlands and down to the lakes. Not much happens near me that I do not feel and know.'"

I was rapt, but Sandu had made a coughing noise, and Nthanda flicked his eyes to him, then looked self-consciously away from all of us. "Oi! Hush, *Impaler!* No, I don't remember what he said word for word, but he spoke like we were in a story; I remember that. And I retain, all these years later, the gist of what he said. It made a bit of an impression, like."

I realized that as Nthanda had been telling the story, his current slang had dropped away from him, and he been speaking as he had in the past. Lots of am'r I'd met still talked like they were in those more formal days; Nthanda had been an exception. It was funny hearing him slip between the two times, linguistically speaking.

"Let him tell his tale as he likes, frithaputhra," Bagamil gently admonished Sandu. "It's not like you've never spun out a yarn to newly-made am'r wanting tales of Vlad Drăculea."

Sandu looked away. I did enjoy it when Bagamil took him down a peg.

"Well..." Nthanda said, obviously flustered from having been caught getting too into his storytelling, "Well, then I asked him about the stories being told by a certain Mister Augustus Hare—and published, as well!

"'Indeed, I know of the boldly mustachioed raconteur. He makes his way from one country house to another, singing for his supper with stories he has lifted from penny dreadfuls, indiscrete society gossip, and tedious tales of his own adventures abroad. However, he has never been to this house, nor have I had the dubious honor of making his acquaintance. His story of a bloodthirsty ghoul haunting this address is just an unfortunate coincidence with my own predilections.'

"'Sir,' I told him, 'I do not believe in coincidences. Has there been no activity related to this property that could not have engendered gossip? Perhaps a problem with a frithaputhra being a bit too voracious?'

"'Sir,' he replied, 'I have no frithaputhraish at this moment, and no guests of our kind...except for your good self this very evening.'

"I questioned him again, trying to trick a different answer out of him, but he insisted the association of

Croglin Low Hall with Mister Hare's little ghost stories was but extraordinary chance.

"'Come! Sense it for yourself!' he cried, and led me on a tour of the whole house. Indeed, I could smell that he had kee servants who came in by day to clean the place, and he insisted they were his main vhoon-sources as well. 'I have not even an am'r-nafsh!' he declared, and it was true; I could not smell that any of that most precious of vhoon."

Nthanda suddenly remembered that he'd gotten pretty used to sniffing *my* precious vhoon for he threw a quirk of a smile my way. I was embarrassed to find myself blushing in response. I'd just *never* get used to being the extra-yummy vampire snack. I wished the low-light conditions would have hidden my blush from am'r eyes as well as it would have from kee eyes, but that was a wasted wish.

Nthanda continued, "As we moved through the house, my questions became more far-ranging. I'd long known of an aojysht in the north of the country who personally kept what order needed keeping in the local am'r population. I hadn't until then given it much thought, except to be grateful that I didn't need to do anything about it myself."

"Um?" I found myself asking. "I *know* I don't know anything about how am'r do business, but why hadn't you bothered to meet him before to, you know, coordinate your efforts and stuff? How were you comfortable with a complete stranger right next door?"

How were you comfortable with a powerful stranger who was apparently going around killing other am'r right and left? Why did you think he wouldn't come down and take your spot? That was what I *didn't* ask, having evolved a self-preservation instinct.

Nthanda just grinned at me, though. "Innocent lit'l Yank! You have no idea how much this island—which may seem small to someone from the States—is almost two different countries. And I'm not even talking about Scotland and Wales. The inhabitants of northern England look down on us "soft Southerners" as almost as bad as *Europeans*, and in return, we see those 'Up Norf' as uneducated peasants who are pretty much only good for producing the star of the Sunday lamb roast. Now, we am'r no longer get to enjoy a good lamb roast, but the attitudes don't otherwise change much after death.

"You may note that I'd only been in London for about forty years when this all happened, but I'm a Londoner right through, and I'm afraid I'd already soaked up all the attitudes, proper indelible. I saw the north as nothing but sheep and rough-and-tumble farmer-kee and mud, and I was just chuffed I didn't have to waste any time on it. It seemed to be taking care of itself, like. It didn't really feel like my problem, right? The nameless aojysht who had dug in up there wanted his privacy; I saw fit to give it to him. He obviously didn't have his sights on London-town, or else I'd have had to kill him back in '34 when I got here."

Ah, am'r logic: if I haven't had to kill them already, they aren't something I need to stop drinking from this nice kee long enough to go do something about. I liked Nthanda a lot, probably more than I should like any am'r I wasn't related to by blood, but he was perfectly typical of his species.

Of course, this is the species I'm fast-tracked to join and spend the rest of a possibly very long "life" among. In a couple of centuries, will I sound like that too?

There was one more question I felt compelled to ask.

"Wait! Everyone keeps telling me that sexism is gone among the am'r, and so far, it seems like that's true. Unless you tell me otherwise, I'm going to assume what I've been told—that racism is a silly kee thing and am'r get over it—is true too. So, are you telling me that am'r can just let go of something human society in centuries of evolution has failed to fix, but that the am'r from the northern and southern parts of the United Kingdom can't see each other as equals as long as they exist in this world?"

Nthanda guffawed and slapped his knee. He looked at Sandu and Bagamil. "I see why you keep this one so close. She has a refreshing way of looking at things, and she's not afraid to call shit out!" He chuckled for a few moments more, then turned his smile on me again. "Treasure, I'm glad you've seen that women can be truly equal in the am'r world. And racist am'r tend not to last very long. I've done my own part to help with that..." As he said this, his look became less a smile and more a baring of teeth, "but there are some things in life that are just *right*. The sun rises in the west, and all's fair in love and war...and Northerners are uncultured sheep-fuckers. It's not prejudice, it's just...*truth!*"

Nthanda had the biggest grin I'd ever seen on a face that was not averse to smiles, so I decided he was doing the British "taking the mickey" thing they love to do to Americans. I tried to get us back on topic...and off mocking me.

"So, you didn't think this guy...what was his name? That he really had anything to do with the odd fluke that people were saying there was a vampire in his house... when there really *was* a vampire in his house?"

I suddenly had four scowls in my direction. Call me

immature, but it was one of the few ways I could get my own back. I haven't yet met an am'r who is OK with being called a "vampire."

Nthanda answered slowly, "Well, that's the funny thing. I think it *was* just a coincidence. The story was all about a ghoul who drained a tenant renting the house; there was no evidence of the house being let during that time. There was this whole thing about the creature scratching the window and then attacking her without finesse. Like a zombie movie. On the second attack, her brother was able to shoot her assailant, who they found the next day mummified in a vault in a nearby church-yard. It seemed to have nothing to do with anything am'r, just overactive kee imaginations. This was the time of Varney the Vampire"—he said the "v" word like he had something nasty in his mouth—"and table-tapping mediums and all the sexually repressed hysteria of that age.

"You ask his name, though. It wasn't until I went to take my leave I realized that in all the touring of the house, of the questions asked and the answers given, I'd not gotten that from him. It was only after we came to a rough agree-ment to keep all as it had been—he'd continue to cull the northern am'r as he liked, preventing adharmhem and keeping his privacy, and I'd continue to rule the am'r from Manchester southward—that I asked.

"'It was very well to come to this understanding with you, Nthanda of London,' he said as he escorted me to the door, the considerate host.

"'It is well indeed that I made this journey. But wait, sir! I find I still do not know your name.' It shocked me to realize that in all my interrogation, I hadn't managed to learn that.

"'Kurgan is the name. I know, a funny old surname. You must know all about how the British expect one to pronounce Cholmondeley but can't handle even two sylla-bles of *furrin'* appellations. Anyway, the locals have long since mixed it up to 'Croglin,' and I'll answer to either by now. Kee may be short-lived, but they are so *dogged*. But *tempus fugit!* I see your carriage is equipped for handling the excruciating aggravation of the daylight hours, but no doubt you'd rather be on your way back to your dim city of smoke.'

"As there was nothing I wanted more than that, and as I felt I'd wasted more than enough of my valuable time in pursuing this ridiculous kee ghost story, I took my leave of Kurgan/Croglin, and we have never crossed paths in all the years since. He has lived up to his end of our bargain, and I've been hunky-dory with that.

"But now he's gotten word to our Roy here that he wants a word with *you*, Aojysht. I'm a fair bit curious about *that*, I must admit."

While Nthanda had been telling his story, we'd all forgotten about Roy. Now that he'd been reintroduced to our awareness, all eyes were on him. He flushed an unat-tractive shade of red that didn't go well with his freckles and defensively started to explain.

"Like 'e said, I do the rounds, stay on top of shit. I was up with me Brummie mates when an am'r I never met came up to us—too bold as far as I'm concerned. 'E said that 'e was Croglin's frithaputhra 'n all, 'n that 'is patar wanted a meet with the Aojysht whilst 'e was 'ere. So I come back down and reported it, didn't I, and that's all I know."

"Roy," Bagamil said gently, "a smart lad like you must know a bit more than that. Did you recognize his *vhoon-anghyaa*? Are you sure you've never seen Croglin or his *frithaputhraish* around before?"

"Eh? No, guv. Only thing ever 'eard about Croglin was to stay away from 'is territory. All us northern am'r know that. Stick in the cities; no going out to the farms 'n such. But I never smelt this bloke's like before. It was proper strong, kinda like the Aojysht's if you wanna know. Old 'n powerful."

Everyone looked pensive except Roy, who still looked warily self-justifying.

"Well," Bagamil said, "I guess I have a date with the *Vampire of Croglin Grange*." He turned to Sandu with a teasing grin. "*Dracul meu*, you shall be eclipsed as the most famous *vampire* I know!"

"Patar, I've been waiting for this day my whole life," Sandu replied. He seemed quite serious about it.

Of course, we didn't leave right away. There was planning to do. The trip "Up Norf" was not quite as onerous as when Nthanda had made it in 1875, and we had been *invited* this time. Or at least Bagamil had been, but there was no way Sandu and I were not going along. It was still a weird situation, and as such, it needed decent consideration.

The first was a disappointment. Nthanda was not coming with us. Roy was.

"Croglin chose Roy to get in touch with you, so he'll expect him to escort you to him. It's only manners."

"But—" I was feeling desperate because I couldn't imagine Roy being a delightful travel companion. "But didn't you say you were curious what the Croglin guy wants?" Neither Bagamil nor Sandu shushed me, so I had a feeling they were doing the thing where they let the brash and ignorant American say things aloud for them.

"Oh, do not doubt I am curious as all fuck, treasure." While I realized "treasure" was a common term of endearment you might get called by a shopkeeper or a cab driver, it still made me quietly happy when he said it. "But remember, we've all just gotten back from that little jaunt to the bottom of the world. I do not often leave London, but have done so three times recently at your patar's call—"

"For which I am...in your debt, Nthanda. You are a valued friend," Sandu put in. The way he struggled over the phrase "in your debt" gave me the feeling he didn't say it very often.

Nthanda smiled ominously in return. "Oh, don't you think I do not appreciate your debts to me, Țepeș. I'll call them in in due time, no worries."

Sandu did his emotionless face, which meant he was worried.

Nthanda turned back to me. "Any road, I have left my city for too long too often, and now I'm that back, I've heard about some young 'uns who think they might be able to step to me. Your visit has been lovely, but it has been a distraction for my people. I won't mind seeing you lot off to the countryside whilst I put these matters right."

"Would we not fight by your side?" Sandu asked, stung.

"Eh, mate, I don't doubt you at my back if there's ever a right dust-up. But you know better than any that I have to sort this myself. Calling in *bloody Dracula* as backup would only prove I've gotten soft to those who want to see it that way. So, thank you, *no*. Take yourselves off and hobnob with the sheep-fuckers for a bit, won't you?"

So Nthanda left and left Roy with us, unwanted by all.

"I still don't see why *he* has to come with us," I hissed to Sandu as we packed our bags.

"Because it's am'r etiquette, *prostie*. And if there are any messages to send back down to Nthanda, Roy can be dispatched with them. Also, you may wish to remember that Roy, being am'r, can hear everything we are saying from the other room."

I groaned in frustration. "Don't any of you believe in *phones?*"

"Of course we do. You have seen me use phones. I have planned our trips with phones. But they are not always the correct method of communication."

Am'r could be the most frustrating creatures.

We did go on a train since, apparently, it was less annoying than traveling by airplane and less tedious a car journey. The train left Euston Station at 10:30 p.m. and arrived at five a.m. in Carlisle, the city which had impressed Nthanda not at all back in 1875.

I can report that trains are much nicer transport for am'r than air travel. The station was huge, so the kee scents of blood and food and cleaning products and toilets were much better ventilated. And inside the train, we weren't bunched together as you are in a plane, even when flying first class. The smell of kee past and present was a distraction, but not so intense that you couldn't even think.

Bagamil and Sandu and I sat at a table that had two seats facing each other. Roy sat alone at another table and growled at a kee when they made the mistake of trying to sit there as well.

We ignored him after that. I ate a variety of sandwiches because I'd forgotten to eat for too long: cheddar and pickle, egg and cress, ham and mustard, and a delicious one called "Coronation chicken." I ate two of all of them and went for a third egg and cress. I found they also sold cans of cider, so I drank some of those. And tea, of course.

I'd never been on a train, so it felt like some kind of adventure.

I've been to fucking Turkmenistan and run around killing vampires. I've been to Tierra del Fuego and killed vampires there, too. I've been to the real Dracula's castle and have been nearly killed by actual historical figures of both greater and lesser importance, and I'm excited about being on a fucking train.

But there it was, and Sandu and Bagamil indulged me and smiled at me, taking joy in my simple pleasure. But they had other dining options in mind.

"*Sufleţel*, we do not know what this Kurgan/Croglin wants from us or how powerful he may be."

"How powerful can he be? More powerful than you and Bagamil?"

"Cinyaa," my gharpatar put in, "it might not be just him and the one frithaputhra we know of. You asked the other day about enemies. We do not know that this am'r is not one. Therefore, it is sensible that we make ourselves as strong as possible prior to the encounter."

I know what that *means. Fucking am'r.*

"So, you need to go get some dinner too, huh?"

"Yes, precisely, cinyaa." A kee lover would have reached out to caress my hand or some other comforting gesture. At least neither of my lovers condescended like that. They cared about bringing me as gently as possible into the am'r world, but it was not a gentle world, and we never seemed to have much time for discussions of boundaries or the processing of feelings.

"Well, I ate. I guess you need to get your strength, too."

I tried to keep my residual discomfort out of my voice. My am'r-nafsh blood was the best thing for both of them, but they had been hitting it pretty hard for a while, and they did need to get more than they could take from me alone. We had been through this all before, but it still wasn't perfectly easy for me to experience.

I told myself the am'r language should help me with my jealous discomfort. Exchanging blood with an am'r-nafsh or a fellow am'r could be called vhoon-vaa (healing) or vhoon-vayon (sex), but taking sustenance from a kee—even if sex were involved, which let's face it, knowing the am'r, it generally was—was called "frangkhilaat," feeding. If I couldn't get jealous of former kee partners for having a burger, I shouldn't feel this pang now.

On the other hand, my previous lovers had never fucked their burgers. At least, I hoped not.

Bagamil went off for about an hour and returned looking bright-eyed and bushy-tailed and smelling strongly of the kee he'd snacked on. There were sleeper cars on this train. I wondered if he'd just invited himself into one for ultimate privacy and comfort. I didn't ask.

Sandu smiled at me and his patar, then went off to attend to his own needs. I focused on looking out the window.

After I'd exhausted the thrills of the dining options, I gazed around and discovered the free entertainment of watching the British countryside roll past for hours and hours. Thank goodness for am'r night vision because I was hypnotized by what to kee eyes would have been a very dull view. I was grateful for the distraction even after Sandu came back, flushed with good health and smelling also of kee blood—and someone else's perfume.

The sky was getting worryingly light as we pulled into Carlisle Station. Roy hustled us up a few cobblestone streets to a hotel, and we found a single surly employee at the desk who was extremely dubious about the very foreign-looking group of us. If Bagamil had not been so powerful in his mesmerism, I think his profound distrust of Europeans, Yanks, and "Southern fairies" would have led to us being told there was no room in the inn.

Finally, we were in a room alone together, Roy having been installed in another room, by everyone's preference. Despite the sun being well over the horizon by now, my beloveds were full of energy. They would have been very happy to spend a long part of the day preparing for tonight's meeting by cycling blood through our bodies in what one could only call "preventative vhoon-vayon." The thing was, these two had been back-to-back against the world since the 1400s. They hardly needed to discuss plans because they knew each other's minds far better than any kee married couple ever could. But me, I hadn't lived even two years of this life, and even less of it with Bagamil also actively sharing blood and love with me. I needed to be told what the plans were, which I guess for am'r was *tedious*.

They could suck on that tedium dick, though. They had chosen me, all fresh and young—well, young compared to an am'r, at any rate—and trained in modern technology skills, so they also had to deal with all the ignorance and curiosity of my comparative youth. They also had to deal with me not being willing to head into danger again without at least getting an overview of the proposed agenda. It wasn't that I was less eager than they for hot sex; I just put a greater emphasis on having a fucking clue what I was doing. Maybe when I was hundreds of years old, I would be more carefree about skipping heedlessly into unknown dangers. Until then, I would prioritize planning was over sex every time.

We showered together to get the smells of train travel off us. Before either of them could move things in a sexy direction, I lobbed the question at them. "So, what is our plan for tomorrow?"

"We visit Croglin," Sandu said, unconcerned. He continued lathering my back.

"Well, duh. That's why we are here. But do we show up unannounced on his doorstep, or do we send a messenger? What is am'r etiquette, since fucking up that etiquette clearly leads to a message-sending tokhmarenc? What do we actually *know* about Croglin, and what can we expect in dealing with him? And *why* do you act like I'm unreasonable for asking this shit?" I asked the question because Sandu had sighed hugely. I was feeling like we were over our honeymoon period and were now in the first blush of finding all the ways our personalities clashed.

Bagamil jumped on the potential grenade. "It's not *unreasonable*, cinyaa. It is just that your patar and I have few worries that we will come up against anything we cannot handle, so we don't worry, we just *do*."

I nearly growled. "But recent events show that you do kinda hafta worry, though. Sandu got drugged by maadak and abducted. So did you. So did I, right out from under your noses. Can you see why this is worrying me?"

Sandu went all cold and distant in his body language and left the shower to dry off. He used the towel in short sharp tugs to demonstrate that I'd offended him deeply—by speaking the truth. Happily, Bagamil was much harder to piss off.

"Cinyaa, you are not wrong, but we have spoken of this already. It is a known problem, and one of the goals of this trip is to start gathering information so that we can create a solution. Until then, what is the good of worrying about it? Your patar freed himself from his capture. We freed you. Later, you both freed me. I think this is proof that we do not have to worry. That as long as we work together, there are no circumstances in which we cannot prevail."

Sandu strutted nakedly out of the bathroom, vindicated by his patar's words. I was less impressed. "I'm afraid I see it more as a worrying trend of things getting *worse*. We keep scraping by, barely getting everyone out in a condition where they can still heal, where they haven't met their tokhmarenc. So for me, it feels like it would be irresponsible not to worry because this time, one of us really *could* die. And I'm the only one who would raise up from death. I don't want to wake up all alone in a grave, starving and feral, and find you both are gone forever!" My last words were shriller than I'd intended. I hadn't fully explored my fears, so they burst out of me in a rush of unexpected emotion.

Bagamil pulled me into his arms. Sandu rushed back in from the bedroom, and Bagamil opened his arms again. I found myself being practically crushed by the strength of their concern for me.

"O, săracuțul! Îmi pare rău!" Sandu said, muffled by my

damp curls. Bagamil was crooning words in a language I did not recognize, and normally he spoke perfect English. I realized what he was speaking had that slushy sound of the am'r language, and I wondered how much more of it there was. Was it just keywords or a fully functional tongue? So much I did not know about my new world.

Mostly, though, I just luxuriated in their love and attention. I finally felt like they had *heard* my concern, so the near-constant stress that had been plaguing me for so long —probably since I'd started having nightmares that Bagamil had been captured—finally started to melt away. I hadn't even realized *that* was what was driving me crazy— and taking Sandu with me.

They sat me down on the bed, each staying in physical contact with me. Sandu pulled me between his legs and wrapped his arms around me. Bagamil sat in front of us and stroked my legs and arms as he talked.

"I had not realized, cinyaa—"

"Neither did I!"

"—that this was such a pressing fear for you. But of course, it is. Not so long ago, you were a very mortal kee who could slip and fall in the shower and be dead at any time. Who lost friends and family in car accidents, with cancers and viruses and heart attacks.

"I have been am'r for a *long* time, long removed from the ever-present fear of death. But that is no excuse, for I am not absent entirely from the kee world. I have brought over enough kee to our life. I should have remembered that these fears are still all too real for you. I am so sorry, Anushka."

My eyes were tearing up, mostly with relief at being

understood at last. But I wasn't entirely comforted. "But...
Neplach was an *aojysht*. He met the tokhmarenc
protecting me. And Araceli had barely begun am'r life; she
only had about sixty years of it before she was killed
protecting me. That's a lot of *me getting immortal people
killed*."

Sandu now hugged me so hard that I squeaked in pain,
worried that a couple of ribs would be broken and I'd have
to go through the equal-if-not-worse pain of vhoon-vaa
speed-healing. He let up, but only a little.

Bagamil met my eyes, and I could feel him using
mesmerism to relax me and open me up to his words. He
spoke slowly and carefully. "It was a terrible loss when
Mehmet and his benighted followers ended the long life of
Neplach, our dear friend. He was indeed strong, and we
were indeed devastated. And I remember the dynamic
young Araceli; you are right to mourn her death when
there was so much potential in her to become a truly
powerful am'r.

"However, you must remember, I am not the Aojysht-
of-aojyshtaish for nothing. And Sandu is my frithaputhra
and has the strongest vhoon-anghyaa an am'r can have.
You saw Mehmet throw his full might against us and fail.
In Tierra del Fuego, you saw us prevail over two enemies
at once. We might not always stamp out our enemies right
away like little bugs, but we are *survivors*. I have avoided
the tokhmarenc for more centuries than I care to count;
you will not *jinx me*, little one. And your patar, even before
he was am'r, survived decades of plots and myriad enemies
until he was made safe from kee death. Do you think your
bad luck so strong that you will bring the tokhmarenc to

Vlad Drăculea? That would be surprisingly egotistical of you.

"Do not fear that you will slow us down or otherwise bring us harm. We are experts at getting out of tight places with our skins intact. This is why we seem so careless to you. We know each other's strengths, and we have faith in that."

"And backing up our faith," Sandu put in more practically, "we have *power*. We have not just strength of body, but strength of mind, strength of powers you still do not fully comprehend as they cannot yet flower in your am'r-nafsh body."

"We have been in worse situations than we overcame in dealing with Mehmet, with Julio Popper, and...what nickname did you come up with for the other? 'Orélie the Self-Anointed?'"

I remembered Sandu and Bagamil in the medieval torture chamber, helpless in the hands of Julio, and shuddered. It seemed an awfully close call to me. I couldn't imagine a *worse* situation.

"There is perhaps a lack of experience, due to your fewer years, and those lived in this modern world. You cannot imagine how hard life was for most of human existence. You come from a time and a place where life is made soft with modern amenities, with modern medicine, with a decrease in the near-constant war and strife that made up so much of the span of humanity.

"For your patar and me, these infrequent skirmishes are nothing new. To you, they are shocking, deeply troubling, a whole new type of life to learn how to survive. To us, all that you experienced in the last year was...business as usual. A little more *vigorous*, perhaps, but nothing that dismayed us."

"But we should have remembered how it would seem to you, *draga mea*." Sandu squeezed my ribs alarmingly again. "You have fit so well into our world that it is too easy to forget you are so new to it. *E adevarat*, I often forget what to kee eyes might seem an issue."

"Neither of you finds recent events to be problematic? You don't have any worries you're just not troubling me with?"

"Cinyaa, tomorrow we confront the unknown. That is always of concern, but I am not worried. Just prepared for anything."

"How do you prepare for anything?"

"My preferred way is to have a restorative session of vhoon-vayon, followed by rest until sundown."

"*Argh!* That's not an answer!"

"It is for an am'r. Our skills are adaptable to circumstances. We just need to be well-fed and rested to use them most optimally."

"What if this Croglin guy has an army of enemy am'r waiting to cut us down?"

Sandu snorted. Bagamil smiled. "That seems highly unlikely, cinyaa. Nthanda would notice if legions of am'r came flooding into his country. Yes, even if they arrived in the north. Just because he left Croglin to deal with local problems does not mean he doesn't have any sources of intelligence. And while we have not heard from Dubhghall, I doubt he has left Scotland unwatched. If an army of unfriendly am'r tried to come in through Edinburgh or Glasgow, warning would have gone out...or, more likely, those am'r would have been unceremoniously given their tokhmarenc, and Nthanda would have gotten notice of *that*."

Bagamil paused and then looked directly at me. "What would you propose we do, Noosh, to go into this situation most optimally prepared?"

Well. Shit. I wasn't expecting that. I was prepared to shoot down *their* lack of obvious preparation, but coming up with ideas of my own? Dammit, they were the Aojysht-of-aojyshtaish and the famous Wallachian Voivode. *They* were the ones with experience in this shit. This little am'r-nafsh librarian shouldn't be required to come up with any sort of plan.

But I did my best. "Well, possibly we should have more backup? I mean, not Roy, but some real allies? Strength in numbers?"

"Again I tell you, cinyaa, that you are not taking into account that I am the Aojysht-of-aojyshtaish and your patar is Dracula. For us to bring 'backup' would look like an act of war or that we are uncertain in our strength and fear Croglin. Neither of those is as optimal as what we are already doing."

I wasn't certain of that, but I had to bow to his greater experience.

"OK, then. How about, um, gathering intelligence on him?"

Sandu responded to this one. "We already know from Nthanda all there is to know about him from a distance. One of the things we do know is that he keeps close tabs on all am'r activity in his area. It is more than likely any spies we sent out would find out nothing he did not want us to know...if they returned to us. But we do not have time to peek into his windows since he expects us to arrive at his front door imminently. And again, it would make us look like we are afraid of him."

"I *am* afraid of him!"

"Why, *micuțo*? What about him scares you more than our previous enemies?"

"If I'd known about our previous enemies in advance, I'd have been scared of them too!" I let my own words sink in for a moment. "All right, maybe a little knowledge *is* a dangerous thing. All this time, I've been running around, not really knowing what was happening before it actually happened. At this moment, I have time to think about everything that could go wrong. To get the willies. I'm telling you, I have a bad feeling about Croglin. About all of this."

"Instinct is not something to be ignored, cinyaa. Just because you are new to this world doesn't mean you cannot have worthy insights. We will add your 'willies' to our considerations, but you must not let your fears impact how you respond. Keep your eyes and your mind open. Observe closely, but do not let fear cloud your judgment. You are already one I value at my back in a fight. Just keep being the strong woman you are, and between us, we can handle anything."

I won't lie. It was very nice when Bagamil called me a strong woman. Part of me preened like a peacock, but there was another part screaming, "This is still a bad plan!"

Then Sandu made me perk up happily. "We are sending Roy along first, you know."

"Oh! I didn't know. That's good!"

If Croglin had, in the past days since sending his message down with Roy, changed his mind about us or gotten into a cranky mood, well, at least he'd kill Roy first. That was something.

Sandu brought Roy into our room. He was sulky and didn't see why he couldn't just take us over to Croglin, drop us off, and go back about his life. Most am'r were hero worship-y around Bagamil and at least a bit respectful to Sandu. I'd thought I hated being attached to celebrity am'r (particularly when it stuck me in the rôle of "the rockstar's girlfriend"), but Roy's resentful indifference made me miss it at a moment when I thought we needed it most.

So Roy went out on his despised errand, and despite my recent shower, I went and took a long soak bath. By myself.

CHAPTER SIX

"The *Marstar* of Croglin Grange invites you to Croglin-fuckin'-Grange and is *delighted* that you took up his invitation so *promptly*. Can I fuck off now?" Roy slouched inside a doorframe and picked his nails.

"You can fuck off soon, Roy." Sandu and I both sighed in hopeful anticipation at this. Roy gave no indication he either noticed or cared. Bagamil continued, "Just give me some information. How many am'r were at Croglin Grange?"

"I only noticed the Big Man."

"What about his frithaputhra, who you met before?"

"I didn't see 'im. Or smell 'im."

"Did you smell other am'r having recently been on the property?"

"I weren't tryin' to be your fuckin' spy. I dunno."

"Roy. You want to be away from us. We want you away from us. Be helpful, or I will report back to Nthanda that I was very displeased with your lack of cooperation. You may have no concern for what Vlad Dracula or *I* could do to you..." Bagamil's voice trailed off to let the threat sink in. "But I know you respect and rightly fear Nthanda of London. So. What am'r did you sense around Croglin?"

Roy scowled, not a pretty look on his pallid, freckled face. "Right. Well, I *could* have sniffed the frithaputhra, but 'is patar's scent got in the way, like. I didn't get *that* super-power, right? I think I could smell some other am'r, but none of it was fresh. So, I already *told* you all I knew, but you 'ad to be a tosser."

Bagamil ignored his whine. "Were there any kee or am'r-nafsh in the house?"

"There definitely 'ad been kee. Regular scents of 'em, like 'e 'as staff or such. No surprise, right? Lord Fauntleroy an' all."

"Did anything make you uncomfortable?" Roy's scowl deepened at this, so Bagamil added, "Not that you are a coward, but did anything seem odd?"

"The 'ole ting is messed up if you ask me. Geezer lives by 'imself out in the middle of nowhere, acts like 'e runs the place. But 'e's got no gang, 'as 'e? No backup. Nobody ever sees 'im. But word's gone round, and I mean, never knew a time when it 'adn't, don't try to go up further than Gunchester, right? Am'r what do, don't get 'eard from again. And we ain't allowed to go 'n get some vengeance. Nthanda just says that's what 'appens. Don't go Up Norf, don't bother Croglin.

"I were proper gobsmacked when 'is frithaputhra came up to me, right? But I brung the message down like I was told, and I done all Nthanda said to do. So my job's done, right?"

After he finished, Roy glowered at all of us. Bagamil

sighed. "Yes, Roy, you're done. You may go." He turned away as if Roy had ceased to exist for him. Sandu and I followed his example. Roy paused as if he were surprised not to have more drama and was considering making it himself. Then he stalked out of the room, and I sincerely hoped we wouldn't have to spend any more time in his eternally adolescent company.

"That was not overly useful," Bagamil noted dryly. "We have no more information than before."

"Did you get any feeling he was lying to us?" Sandu questioned.

I jumped in. "Oh! Can you tell if another am'r is lying? Is that a special am'r skill?"

"What?" Bagamil looked surprised, then smiled wryly. "I'm afraid not, cinyaa. But the longer you live, the more lies you are told. You learn how to tell if someone is not telling you the truth. It is especially easy with kee, who might perspire more under the stress of their prevarication. One could say in that case that one can smell a lie. But with am'r, it's about reading small cues in body language. And asking the right questions."

"That's basically the same with kee."

"Ah, yes. But our reflexes are faster, and our minds also work faster. If we work on it over the years, we can train ourselves not to have any 'tells.' Or so we think; an older am'r might find some other factor we had not considered to be very telling. We will teach you how to read these things, cinyaa. And how to lie with your whole body."

"So, was darling Roy telling us the truth?"

"He was...not entirely honest. However, he is so deceitful by nature that he would give off those same cues just saying, 'Hello, how are you?' I have never interacted with him where he has not been equally..."

"Shifty?"

"Yes, that is the word. In his way, he is as hard to read as a talented aojysht since it's not a matter of *if* he is lying, but if anything he says is true. Obviously, this does not help us much. We knew already that none of us found him trustworthy, but I have not known him long enough to know if there is more here than his baseline deceitfulness. I would advise that we assume none of his information can be counted upon."

"Obviously," Sandu agreed. "And I would further say that I am assuming we are going into a situation where this Croglin has unknown numbers of subordinates on or near his property."

"So, uh, that doesn't bother you?"

"*Dragă* Noosh, we have taken on overwhelming numbers before and prevailed. No, I am not worried in the slightest."

Sandu said this to me with a loving smile, but there was something dark in his eyes, and I wondered if perhaps fighting with just one am'r would be boring to him by now. Maybe if he didn't have to fight "overwhelming numbers," he wouldn't think it was worth getting out of bed for. It probably shouldn't have cheered me up, but it did.

That concluded our discussions on the matter. We had all dressed as practically as possible without having discussed it with each other. Sandu and Bagamil were of a size where they could trade clothing, although Sandu was built more solidly and Bagamil was about two inches taller. Neither was as tall as I would've said I preferred in a man, but they both came from earlier time periods where people didn't grow as tall as they do nowadays. Which is a crazy thing to be able to say about your partner. Or partners. Since I had two, however, that seemed a fair trade for one tall guy. Sometimes I just had to shake my head and wonder yet again how I got here.

They shared a pile of black cargo pants in a nice mole-skin fabric. When we'd been shopping, Sandu had word-lessly pointed them out to Bagamil, and they had bought all that were available in their size. Sandu wore a black knit button-down shirt that fitted him with pleasing snugness. Bagamil wore a more traditional black button-down. It was all very am'r chic in that bloodstains wouldn't show much, except that I knew Mister Sunshine had on bright yellow briefs and matching socks. Right before we left, Sandu donned his faded black duster, and I sighed with pleasure. Nothing beats a handsome man in a sexy coat.

I was wearing a black silk shirt that draped elegantly. Silk is not the delicate fabric I'd always assumed it was; it can stand up to hard use, which is convenient around am'r. The black bottoms in a heavy knit flattered my curves while being more pant-like than leggings. The nice ankle boots Sandu had just bought me looked elegantly hip. In my head, I called them my "London boots."

When we had selected our weapons from Nthanda's stockpile, I'd also grabbed an ankle sheath for Sa'mah. It was hidden in my boots, holding her obsidian sharpness safely until I needed her. I had seldom felt as sexy in any piece of clothing as I did with that little strap hugging me under my boot. My patar and gharpatar carried similar concealed blades but did not bother to bring any of the larger knives or swords with them. I remembered being strapped into a flamethrower what seemed like a thousand years ago and felt a pang of regret that that was not an acceptable fashion accessory for a weekend in the country. I would have felt much better going into this wearing a flamethrower statement piece.

Attired thusly, we left our rooms and exited the empty hotel lobby into the northern English night. Once we got outside into the brisk late-October air, I realized I had no idea *how* we were going to get ourselves there to engage with this whole Bad Idea or *where* we were going. I mentioned that to my beloveds.

"We are going to acquire a car and drive," Bagamil told me. "Your patar loves to drive." This I knew from the first time I went home with him. "And I have directions from Roy, the way he went last night. Those, at least, I believe we can trust."

"But won't all the car rental places be closed now?" I asked.

"Car...*rental*?" Sandu was overcome by a fit of something between coughing and laughing. I hoped he choked. Bagamil, the wise elder, chose that moment to become supremely interested in an historical plaque on an old brick wall near us.

"*Draga mea*, I have never rented a car. Never in all my life!" Sandu was gasping as he tried to control his laughter.

I thought back to all the travel we had done. A driver had always been arranged for us—after our first fateful long weekend, that is. "You own the, um, the car you drove us in back," I found I could not call it "home" anymore, "back in the States?"

"Ah, the Zagato." His voice sounded wistful. "Yes, I own that. I told the oily little kee at the dealership that he had indeed sold it to me, so it is mine."

He smiled widely at me. "And when we find a suitable vehicle, it shall become mine for as long as we require it."

Thus we wandered the nocturnal streets of Carlisle, looking for a vehicle that would suit Vlad the Impaler and apparently also the Car Thief.

After a long time breaking in my boots on cobbled streets, we came back to a car we'd passed a couple times, a boxy, shiny thing I could only describe as a "fancy jeep." DEFENDER was emblazoned across the back, an oval reading Land Rover underneath.

"This will work," Sandu announced, and I sighed in relief. Bagamil gave me a raised eyebrow, which made me have my own coughing fit. Sandu nobly ignored us as he stood by the driver's side door and scented the air. Really, he *huffed* the car, leaning toward the edge of the door where it met the side of the car. He inhaled in fast little sniffs, pausing occasionally, then snuffling more.

Then he straightened. We were on a narrow side street, poorly lit for kee eyes but as clear as day for us. I watched in fascination as his nostrils flared, then Bagamil and I followed him as he went off after the scent-spoor.

He led us unerringly, with me trying not to giggle as I pondered what breed of scent-hound he'd be, to a restaurant that was still open in what you couldn't call a bustling metropolis but was too big to be called a town. It was a pretentious Italian eatery, promising small plates and over-priced cocktails. I was suddenly hungry for kee food as the smells wafted out to my nose, but I shoved that aside. Now was not the time.

Sandu went into the restaurant. Bagamil and I moved into a shadowed area on the other side of the street. We didn't have to wait long. Sandu was soon preceded out of the restaurant by a large, angry-looking man, who was gesticulating and speaking fast in that thick accent I had barely been able to understand in the hotel's desk clerk. Knowing it was technically English somehow made it harder for me to understand him, and I felt like I'd had a more intuitive understanding of Turkish and Arabic than I did of this.

"Yon jalopy's a spanker, and thoos darn weel dunshed it! Thoo cud a gitten a bus throot gap!"

Sandu was speaking calmly, explaining that he wasn't used to these tight streets, and he had just misjudged. He'd pay for any damages of course, but he wanted the man to check the car and make sure it was just scratches before they exchanged information.

The man wasn't having it. "Thoo lot frey owert watter reckon thoo can hannle laal lonnins bloody white liners! Thoo shud mon lait a taxi!"

Sandu played up his attempts to calm the man as they moved to the Land Rover, Bagamil and I coming up quietly behind. The guy was so busy venting his wrath at Sandu that he never noticed.

The man stopped short when we got to his car and looked around, puzzled. "Eh, where's thy car? Ah can see nowt!"

Sandu slid into his personal space, forcing the man to meet his eyes as he told him, "The car was totaled. There was no one there to explain it. There was nothing you could do. You will catch a cab home tonight. You will not call the police. You will just buy another car. Do you understand?" The last was said with great intensity as if the words were being bored into the man's mind.

"Ahreet, mate."

"Repeat it back to me. The car was totaled..." As Sandu worked the man through the mesmerism, I watched in fascination. I'd never seen Sandu do his thing, not like this. Most times when he spoke with kee, they just gave him what he wanted. I couldn't usually tell if he was using low-level entrancement or that was just the privilege that came with being a handsome European man who, as actual royalty, was used to getting his will without hesitation.

But this was different, not low-level, not at all. I could feel a throbbing at the edge of my brain, and if I could feel it, I couldn't imagine what that guy was experiencing. It must be a bit like drowning. He repeated it back, his voice dull and slow but certain.

Dammit. This means Sandu didn't *lie about not mesmerizing me.* I'd almost counted on Sandu having made me make those rash decisions in that that long-ago weekend that had changed my life. In all the times I'd been abducted and stuck waiting around to be rescued ever since, I'd always come to a moment when I'd asked myself how I'd gotten here (or gotten here *again*) and replaying the past, I'd concluded that Sandu *must* have enthralled me and made me do things contrary to my core self.

Nope. It was all me. Fuck. Well, maybe he was low-level persuasive, but it was *mostly* me. I had been so recklessly horny and idiotically thrilled to discover vampires were real that I'd gone and joined the Dark Side without a second thought.

It can't be the Dark Side. We are the good guys, dammit. Well, that was a fun internal debate for another day. For now, Mister Former Land Rover Owner was done being bound to Sandu's will, and he toddled off toward the high street and his interrupted dinner without a backward look.

Sandu stood smiling at us, dangling the key fob. "I have acquired a suitable vehicle. Shall we go?" The fob chirped, and the doors unlocked. *Damn. He can be smooth when he likes. Bastard. There was no way I could ever have turned him down. Bastard.*

And then we were rolling through the English countryside again, and I had the window down to smell the cool night air, full of autumnal decay, the occasional harsh sweetness of manure, and the smell of peaty water as we crossed bridges. Bagamil had the map open on his phone as we drove toward Croglin Grange—thirty miles until the Bad Idea became a Bad Reality.

After Carlisle, the houses and buildings were spaced farther apart until we came to a huge supermarket with a big lit sign saying Tesco—We're open 24 hours. My tummy growled at the thought of getting more sustenance, and I told it to shut up. Recently I had been close to forgetting about kee food, only remembering to eat when it was pressed upon me. What was going on with me now? Before I had time to work up a greater anxiety, we went through a roundabout. Sandu was driving our fancypants jeep as though he were totally comfortable with driving on the wrong side of the road.

Once we got to that roundabout, however, even with

the few cars that were in it at this time of night, the experience was almost worse than the remembered terror of thinking Sandu and I would be painfully drained of blood by Julio's minions while Bagamil was used as the am'r version of a chocolate fountain for the rest of his pitiful existence. Those fears were only a few weeks in my past, yet the experience of going the wrong way in a chaotic circle of cars merging to and from any and all directions was almost as terrifying. I white-knuckled it until we finally exited on the A69—and it was a measure of how shaken-up I was that I didn't have a moment of giggling very maturely to myself about "sixty-nine"—in the direction of something called Aglionby.

A bit later, we crossed Warwick bridge and proceeded through a town delightfully called Little Corby. Another waft of that peaty-water perfume showed we were near something called Cairn Beck. Then we passed a sign for Heyton Hall Castle, although I couldn't see a castle. Soon after that, signs promised Castle Carrock, and eventually we did pass, in the distance, a true castle lit up in the night. As an American, this was a pure shivery delight for me, and I wished that instead of driving toward the Bad Plan, we could go in a different direction both figuratively and literally and throw ourselves into doing the tourist thing.

I hadn't collected myself from that before we passed Tottergill Farm, then a place called Cumrew—and then I did giggle. This far out from the city, it was all farms on hillsides and little villages tucked into valleys. I'd never been any place like it in the world. It felt like every story I'd ever read about England was true—even *Lord of the Rings*, potentially—and we'd unquestionably come across hedgehogs dancing in a circle in the moonlight around the next bend.

And there were a lot of bends. The road kept getting narrower, sinking down into the landscape. I realized with a start that carriages had been cutting into the dirt on this path since before Alfred the Conqueror. Before the ancient Romans built a wall somewhere around here! In some sheltered places, trees grew over the road in an arch so that the moonlight filtered down between the branches. I wanted to ask Sandu to slow down, not only so I could enjoy the view better, but because the few times we passed other cars, I felt certain there was not enough room for us both, and one of us would end up crashing into the hedge.

Because there were hedges. Actual *hedgerows!* They looked satisfyingly like you'd expect a hedge to look, except you probably hadn't expected to be nearly driving into them at regular intervals. It was not what I had envisioned while reading cozy murder mysteries in my American bed in the evenings, back in my old life where adventure was comfortably in the pages of a book and not most of my waking moments.

I wished fervently that this upcoming encounter would be with a deeply introverted recluse who just wanted to donate some books to my library and talk to us about am'r history. That this time we could interact with a fellow am'r without knives or guns or flamethrowers coming into it. That no one would try to end Sandu's and Bagamil's long existences, or my potential one. Just a social call, and then we could rest for a while up here in this amazing part of the world and go for long night walks in these hills, breathing the remarkably refreshing air and visiting castles and stately houses. And pubs! The thought of a warm pub with a fire in the fireplace and a glass of single malt whisky and a big plate of food that would include "chips" made my tummy growl again. What was going on with me? It couldn't be stress. I'd had plenty of that in the recent past without being famished. For kee food, that is. Better not to contemplate my increasing need for blood as sustenance, as well. I'd never been so hungry in my life—any life.

After we passed a place improbably named Newbiggin, Sandu slowed, so I was able to hear the burbling sound as well as smell the water as we crossed a small river that was signposted as Croglin Water. Holy shit, we must be getting close now. I leaned in, looked at the map app, and saw the destination only a short line away above a stream called Briggle Beck in an area of green labeled Bank Wood. We took a sharp right onto a very bumpy, potholed driveway and drove down a long drive lined with trees that made me very glad I had almost-am'r vision because I wanted to see what we were coming up on: the infamous Croglin Grange.

There was a stone wall of the kind I'd become familiar with in my short time in the north to either side of the drive. We had to stop at a long wooden gate, and Bagamil popped out of the passenger side to open, hold, and then close the gate behind us after we'd pulled through. I looked askance at him as he climbed in the car, and he shrugged. "I've lived around agriculture my whole life, cinyaa. It doesn't matter what time you live in; you leave gates as you found them."

The main buildings of the house were enclosed like they were a castle inside defensive walls. Everything was built from warm sandstone, although some places had big blocks of it and the others used what seemed like the rubble. In the outer wall, there was an ancient arched gate, but weeds had grown up around it, and it obviously wasn't used often. We drove to the right and into a roughly paved courtyard filled with a battered 4x4, old planter pots and other farm detritus, and more thriving weeds.

The wings of the building were of many heights and obviously from different time periods, with differently shaped windows and doors. One roof was greenish slate, the other darker gray-black slate. It seemed like it had grown organically, extending both upward and outward over time, with a single-storied wing going off to the extreme left and a two-story wing at s right angle to the main building. It had clearly been expanded at some point to create a passage to an adjoining barn. I was not used to houses like this. In the first place, nothing in the States was as old as parts of these buildings were, but this was not a fancy manor house like on TV. These were buildings that had been housing people since, like, the fifteenth century or something, which had been cobbled together with various equivalents to duct tape over the centuries. There was a feeling of imposing age, but also the prosaic utilitarianism of a farm. I had seen caves that the am'r had inhabited for many centuries and I'd been living in Dracula's underground castle, but *this* left an impression on me, perhaps in part because it wasn't a vampire-gnawed warren but a place where kee generations had been born, lived their too-short lives, and died, and their descendants had kept the cycle moving in very human ways—shortcuts and half-assed repairs included.

The main building had a plank door, black paint chipped from age, inside an arch painted a somber dark-gray. When we got out of the car and approached it, the door opened with a full-on tortured *creeeeeaaaaak* of unoiled rusted metal. All my body-hairs stood on end, despite how ridiculous it all was.

The figure inside the arched doorway was silhouetted. It was a masculine shape, and I almost expected a Nosferatu kind of thing or...I don't know, something *monstrous*. The backlighting revealed a moderately tall, well-muscled but not bulky form. His long dark hair made a penumbral halo in the light around his head and shoulders.

"I invite you in, my guests. You are welcome to enter! You come to a house storied in vampire legend and myth, so shall we not observe the formalities?"

As he spoke, he stepped back and to the side to encourage our entry. The movement facilitated scent particles in the air to move toward us, right after the speed of sound brought his voice to our ears. I felt Bagamil turn to stone and I stopped dead too, my whole self now more alert than I thought possible, staring at my gharpatar. Sandu, on my left, did the same, but with less comedic effect.

Am'r don't sweat. At this moment, Bagamil would have broken out in a sweat if he could. He would have been shaking if am'r did that. Being Bagamil, he wasn't hyper-ventilating, although he may have forgotten to breathe for a while there. He stopped looking anything like a human being, although I could not have told you what that meant, only that it happened.

Sandu and I stood there, looking at Bagamil. Bagamil stared at the shape in the doorway.

"Will you not come in...Vohuni-sura?" When our enemy spoke that unknown word, Bagamil looked like a person again, but now he looked like an old man. I did not know his age, but he looked as old as anyone I'd ever seen. It was like we were in a fairytale, and some sort of name magic had been invoked, but with far more terrible implications than Rumpelstiltskin had ever had to deal with.

"My...*son?*" The words were pulled out of Bagamil's mouth like information he'd been tortured for hours to get. We had only been interacting with this creature for minutes. This was bad.

The man inside the doorway laughed, a bitter sound. "The Earth will plummet into the sun before you hear me call you 'patar,' Vohuni-sura." He stepped back into the hallway to make it less complicated for us to enter without coming too close to him. "But do come in, and let us catch up. It's been simply *ages*."

After walking down a depressing hallway painted an unattractive brown on the bottom half and an age-yellowed cream above, we were ushered into the "warming room" and found ourselves in a small space which had a choice of an uncomfortable loveseat, probably Victorian, a set of padded chairs with intricately carved legs and backs that looked to have been lifted from Versailles right after shit went down, and a dubious rocking chair. Having been instructed to "Sit, get comfortable!" by our host, Sandu and

I parked our butts on that loveseat in unison since it was the safest-seeming furniture in the room. Bagamil perched gingerly on one of the fancy Louis chairs. Our enemy poured himself into the rocking chair, looking bonelessly comfortable. Sandu and Bagamil usually rocked that look; now they looked like teenage boys meeting their love interest's parents for the first time. I wished I could be amused by it, but I had recently seen Bagamil look more comfortable while hogtied with all his limbs broken. Sandu looked confused and dismayed, and he had not looked that way even when he'd been nailed into a medieval torture device.

All Sandu's and Bagamil's brash confidence, born of ages of physical and mental superiority over a world full of am'r, had been broken in one sniff and a few words. I was fucking terrified.

And a little voice screamed internally, *I fucking told you we needed to worry about this!*

Another part of me was screaming for another reason. Kurgan/Croglin/Whoever was *hot*. Stunning. Painfully gorgeous.

I had been attracted to Sandu upon first meeting, his high-cheekboned face sculpted by an intense life, his strong nose framed by wide green eyes, his full lips. I loved looking into that face as our bodies joined. Even with all the times he'd lied by omission, even with all the ways he'd been frustrating me recently, I always felt a rush of love and attraction when I looked at him.

Bagamil was attractive in a very Freddie Mercury way: beautiful, wide-set, warm-brown almond eyes under long, straight brows, a perfect strong nose balancing the face over his neatly shaped mustache, and a pouty lower lip that begged me to kiss it endlessly. High cheekbones under that golden-olive skin. His long, thick hair made him look like young Freddie with the mustache of the older Freddie. By now, to look at him was to love him.

But Kurgan…love was not needed to be blown away by him. He had the same thick, gorgeous long hair as Bagamil. He had the same nose. The same amazing cheekbones, although his skin was a cooler olive. He had equally full and impressive eyebrows, and beyond a mustache, he had an impeccably trimmed boxed beard, showcasing full, oh-so-perfectly-shaped lips. But all that was beside the point. The point was his eyes, and once you met them, you had trouble looking away. They were almond like Bagamil's but not set quite as deep, and they were just…*stunning*. They were darker than Bagamil's, an almost-black which made the whites pop even more—pure drama in ocular form. They returned my glance with a sultry, regal look that affected me far more than it should have.

I forced myself to look away, around the room. A few paintings hung on the walls, and nobody needed to tell me they were priceless. They also weren't in great condition, with the wooden frames damaged in a variety of ways and the paint cracked or faded in places. A daguerreotype sat on a delicate side table beside the door we'd come in. It was of our host in an old-fashioned suit, probably from the time of the invention of photography, which was, what, the 1830s? The man in the photograph had the same disgustingly handsome, smug visage he wore now. If I'd just been looking at the photo, I would have said I wanted to knock the smirk off his face, but in his presence, my recently acquired predilection for violence was smothered by fear.

A small fire burned in a tile fireplace, and for long minutes, the only sound was the crackling of the flames. When a burning log gave a sudden CRACK, I was the only one who jumped, but the tension level of the room shot even higher, which shouldn't have been possible.

"Well, gentlemen," he finally drawled. He didn't bother to add, "and lady," which either was better than having said it or *worse*; I couldn't tell which. "How kind of you to accept my invitation. You spend so much time in the States or on the Continent, and I was never sure I'd get a chance to welcome you to my home. But now here we all are, and not past time, either, at least on my end. *Aojasc' am'ratv*, as you would say. You, however, seem a bit unsettled." His thick accent—Russian?—made his every word fascinating to the ear. He also seemed to be having trouble not laughing with every word, and that countered the fascination by setting my teeth on edge.

Glancing at Sandu, I saw that he was looking at Bagamil with an almost pleading on his face, but his patar only had eyes for our enemy. Finally, Sandu sighed, turned to Lord Ego, and spat at him, "Who the fuck are you, anyway?"

That caused the laughter to boil over our enemy's lips. *Those full lips.* He finally regained control and replied, "*Cine dracu sunt eu?* Why, Wladislaus, is your sense of smell so weak?"

"I have never smelled you before, nor any of your vhoon-anghyaa. *Cum ar trebui să te cunosc, nenorocitule?*" Sandu asked coldly.

"Ah," Lord Ego replied, mockery dripping from every

syllable. "But you should recognize me as a most familiar note in any am'r perfume. You have met countless of my frithaputhraish over the centuries, *micuțule*."

I was only starting my education in the fine art of Romanian swearing, and I'd never heard *micuțule* before, but it made Sandu nearly fling himself out of his seat. I had heard its component parts; "*micuțo*" was "little one," a nickname Sandu used for me, and the "-ule" was a masculine ending, so it must be like, "little man." Oh, dear. Sandu would not handle that well.

Lord Ego continued, "And speaking of Bagamil. *He* knows who I am. Once he counted me dearer than vhoon itself. Has he never spoken of me? No? Oh, my. A sin of omission so great...that *must* count as a lie, an unforgivable lie."

He turned to me. "And has his frithaputhra not lied to *you*, little cousin? There is so much dishonesty in this dysfunctional family, you must regret ever joining your blood to ours. But I will bring everything out into the cleansing light of truth, do not worry."

Why are the Bad Guys always telling me that? Is it some special tier of mansplaining? More importantly, how the everloving fuck does he know about that? And "our family?" How is Lord Ego part of our family?

I did not have time to ponder imponderables, however, for onward Lord Ego flowed. "You frithaputhraish of Bagamil now see your hero come to the end of his journey. Look at the Aojysht-of-aojyshtaish. There he sits, unable to speak, unable to fight. The very sight of me has quite unmanned him."

Lord Ego had slouched sideways as he spoke to demonstrate how relaxed he was, how little he saw any of us as a threat. By now, he was sitting sideways in the rocker, one leg up over the curving arm, swinging gently. His elbow perched on the other arm, and he rested his head in his hand. It was like he was posing for a portrait titled "Study of an Unbothered Handsome Young Man." How I hated him, but I couldn't take my eyes off him as he monologued, delighting in the sound of his own voice.

"The am'r have seen this pathetic creature as their leader, even as their *god*. Has he told you that none can match him in age, in strength, in wisdom? *Lies*. Although, no, I must be fair. Not *active* deception, but merely profound ignorance. I have been working to counter him down these long ages, preparing for this moment through a span of millennia your infantile minds cannot comprehend.

"I am sorry for you, my cousins. You must be in shock. Perhaps not a shock as great as your Bagamil is feeling, but still, I have pulled the rug out from under your feet. Your whole universe is upside-down! In the end, what I am doing will make your world a better place, but you cannot know that now.

"For now, all I can do is tell you your prophet is false! But why should you believe me? After all, you came here believing me to be a mysterious malefactor, and why not? That was what your patar, your gharpatar, told you to believe. Why would you doubt his wisdom? Why would you doubt the words of the Aojysht-of-aojyshtaish?"

And why would I believe one word Lord Ego has to say to me? Sandu and I exuded that from our whole beings as we listened. Bagamil, worryingly, still sat in silent shock.

"*Khorosho*. I do not have your trust. Yet. So, I will let your beloved leader explain to you who I am and why he is no longer the Aojysht-of-aojyshtaish. I will let him admit to you who he *really* is. When you want confirmation or further details, you will find me out on the hillside behind the house, admiring the stars."

Lord Ego swung languidly out of his pose, and I felt Sandu hold his muscles ready for attack. My gharpatar sat as he had been sitting, looking as crushed as our enemy had implied. *Why?* Sandu could have saved himself the extra energy he'd just burned through in preparing for anything because Lord Ego sauntered out of the room, and we heard the far door creak as he went out for his promised evening constitutional.

Sandu and I turned our heads in unison to look at Bagamil. "Patar, *what is this?*" Sandu's voice conveyed the anxiety I was feeling, and his words spoke for me. "Why did you call this creature 'son?' Why have you let him say all these vile things? Are you just letting him believe he has cowed you to take advantage of his ego? I suggest we conclude this nonsense *now*. I have heard enough to know he is delusional, as mad as Mehmet was. Is he an am'r whose vhoon-anghyaa is unstable? *Who is he?*"

Sandu moved through a cascade of emotions as he spoke. He ended with his voice more high-pitched than I'd ever heard it. Lord Ego's words had profoundly shaken him.

I realized the emotion that I was feeling—finally!—was anger. I was angry, not at the Bad Guy, but at my beloved idiots, who just hours before had assured me that I need not worry about a thing; they could handle anything the world threw at them. Maybe my ongoing concerns about this had just been fear of the unknown, but that unknown had just reared up and bitten us all on the ass, and these fuckers both looked even more shell-shocked than I. They were so egotistical, they had assumed they wouldn't ever meet a problem big enough to, well, really be a problem.

We were still waiting for Bagamil's response. Finally, he shook himself, the most kee-like physical reaction I'd ever seen from him, then made a point of meeting our eyes. His skin was still a nasty gray over his usual golden olive. "Who is he? He did not lie; there was a time when I called him 'son.' And he did not lie when he said that I believed until just a short while ago that I had killed him."

Sandu sat motionless in a way I knew all too well by now; it meant he was furious. "Why am I hearing about all this *only now* and from an enemy? I believed I knew about any potential threats. You know about all my enemies, those who still exist. You know all the secrets of my life, my patar. *Sufletul meu*, we have known each other over five centuries, more than plenty of time to tell all our tales to each other. Why are secrets of your past rising up to threaten us now? Why do you have secrets from *me*?"

Bagamil met Sandu's anger with steady acceptance; his own eyes were brimming with sorrow. "Frithaputhra-mine, I truly thought this was an old grief, long past troubling anything except my memories. How could someone who was millennia-dead be a threat to anyone living? I have lived so much longer than you; there are stories I have not told you simply because I have forgotten them. And this tragedy I was happy never to tell you, for it shames me to remember it, and I was glad that no one existing today should ever know my worst mistakes, my deepest regrets."

"Since your 'worst mistake' is now here, laughing at us, perhaps you should have been more willing to share that part of your past with me."

"*Dracul meu*, there was no way to imagine this would ever happen. I have no idea how he has existed in this world for so long without my knowing of it."

"Well, patar-mine, I had never thought to accuse you of a lack of imagination or understanding, but here we are." With that, Sandu pushed up out of the uncomfortable loveseat, and we heard him slam the screechy door as he left the house. Was he going to talk to Kurgan or go stand in another part of the property and glower at the night sky alone? I didn't think it likely he'd just take the car and go; for all his flaws, Sandu didn't abandon people. He might have impaled hundreds of people in his time or worked them to death building his castles (I'd never dared ask about the rumored execution that involved flaying the victim alive, followed by salt and then *goats*), but he had always stood by his people and had never been afraid to risk his life right along with them.

I tried to get comfortable on the loveseat. It was impossible, even after spreading out to take over Sandu's space. It must be psychological, since after becoming am'r-nafsh, I'd been able to nap comfortably on stone blocks. Bagamil was not looking bothered by his ridiculous chair, or rather, he was already so miserable that physical discomfort couldn't worsen things.

"What the fuck is going on?" I asked him.

He sighed. "Cinyaa, you were right. We had become too

brash in our conviction that there were no threats we could not handle in this world. I truly did not see this coming, and I have dragged you both out here when it should be me alone meeting the consequences of my sins."

"Before I say, 'Oh, fuck that,' say the first bit again."

"Which? Oh. *You were right.*"

We sat for a moment while I savored that. But Bagamil was feeling shitty enough, so I finally let go of my glorious moment and continued, "Why the hell should you be facing this alone, though? Would you leave *me* to face my 'sins' alone, or would you demand to fight beside me, giving me a lecture about how that's what love is?"

Bagamil sighed again. Even the Aojysht-of-aojyshtaish could have a really terrible day, and that was sad news for the rest of us because it meant *no one* ever outgrew bad days.

"Is this Kurgan a true threat, though? I mean, why can't we just chop off his head and set him on fire?"

"Obviously that is our goal, cinyaa, and nothing has changed there. But he is more of a threat to me than any other am'r I know to exist today," he said this with more bitterness than I'd ever heard in his voice before, "because he is almost as old as I, and as such is the most real threat I have faced...since the last time I faced him."

"But who the fuck is he?"

My gharpatar sighed even more deeply, and I wondered if he'd ever look like Mister Sunshine again, or if a shock like this could age an am'r the way it could put gray hairs on a kee head. He tried to sit back on his chair, but it made an ominous creaking noise, so he got up, moving like an old man, and sat down on Sandu's side of the loveseat. I was glad he was closer to me, and I took his hand, hoping it might be a comfort. He squeezed it and shot me such a grateful look that I felt a pang I couldn't do more for him.

"I will tell you who the fuck he is, but it will take a while."

PART II

Bagamil's Tale

"Who are they that will make peace with the bloodthirsty Liars? To whom will the Lore of Good Thought come?" — Yasna 48.11

CHAPTER ONE

It was so long ago that we must use the language of myth to give it feeling: "in the time of the ancestors," "a thousand thousand years ago," "once upon a time."

That was when this story began. That was when *I* began. That was when the am'r began. The story of the am'r and my own tale are too interwoven to be able to tell separately.

I was born in a time the kee now call the "Neolithic." The dating system the kee use puts that at roughly 9,500 to 4,500 BCE. I know it is not something one born in these times can easily imagine. My birth came just as the agricultural growing of crops began spreading through the groups of settlements that had previously been hunter-gatherers. It was a time of profound change and disarray. Civilization had barely been born, yet already we were experiencing civil unrest.

The human species was changing in countless ways. None of us alive then could have predicted that such a drastic change was in progress, as great as the change from

Homo erectus to *Homo sapiens* had been, but in radically less time.

I was born in a proto-city. If you are visualizing huts or roundhouses, wipe that picture from your mind. We had rectangular buildings, timber-posted, made with mud-bricks and lime plaster, that huddled against each other as the settlement expanded outward. Inside it was dark and often smoky, for ventilation was far from perfect. No one yet had invented streets, so we spent a certain amount of time on our rooftops, as city-dwellers do to this day, and our thoroughfares were across the tops of the buildings. One thing about humanity has never changed: this led to a certain amount of required gossiping as you crossed a neighbor's roof and they sat outside weaving or sewing in the brighter light, or just resting in the evening and drinking beer.

You ask if we had beer back then? Oh, of course we did, cinyaa. Fermented grain and fruit beverages had long been invented and refined to suit fussier palates. People had their *priorities*, after all, and the craving for intoxication is older than *Homo sapiens*. Life was as raucous and disorderly as any collection of human beings living in close contact can make it, but it was interconnected and warmly familial, which many kee places have lost in these times. I remember it with the full sentimentality of reminiscence.

My family was the priest-caste of our settlement. From father and mother down to son and daughter, nieces, nephews, cousins, all had roles in the rituals of our religion. And there were many rituals, intricate and lengthy. Some would go on all through the night; others required regular ceremonies at set times of the day for days or even weeks leading up to a holy day.

We worshipped gods that looked much like the ones kee still adulate: great gods of sky and weather, local gods of spring and grove, domestic gods of childbirth and hearth. Our ancestors became spirits who guided our lives, in their own way more powerful than the gods because they were still so close to us, their influence and goodwill still so vital to our day-to-day lives. My people were rather literal and also deeply pragmatic; for many generations, we had kept our ancestors close by removing their heads after death, and after we carefully defleshed the bone, we painted the skulls and kept them in places of honor in our homes to facilitate the receiving of our ancestors' wisdom.

The seismic changes to our society had profoundly affected my family's fortunes. My father argued passionately for Asera-Masdheh, our Wise Lord, a sky god who was worshipped with fire and blood. Our main rivals were the old gods of our hunter-gatherer predecessors, who were worshipped with regular blood sports and dramatic retellings of mythic hunts and battles, reenacted by priests wearing costumes including outsized animal heads, skins, and body paint, which, when the feast or fast had been supplemented with enough strongly fermented drink, became terrifyingly real to those who did not know the priestly secrets of performance and manipulation.

All faiths need to ensure they do not lose their followers, but my family's needs were greater than most, for we drank the vhoon—this was the word for blood in our language, and so the am'r still call it—of our followers, as well as accepting offerings of food and the labor of their hands.

If you have heard the term "*haoma*" or "*soma*," it was the birth of these. Those have come down in the kee form of the religion, which is still worshipped by sadly diminished numbers even to this day. But the hallucinogenic plant aspect was for others; when the priests were my family, we continued the ways of our past, which was to take offerings directly from our followers, and under the influence and power of the vhoon, we made predictions and translated the will of Asera-Masdheh, made judgments for the community, and of course, kept up the rituals and rites that propitiated Him.

No, cinyaa, I do not know how vhoon-drinking began as a sacrament in our worship. This was a settled tradition by the time of my birth. The story told by my family was that Asera-Masdheh enlightened one of my great-great-grandfathers—this is not a precise measurement of lineage—that he had been gifted with a special connection to the Wise Lord, one that must be supported by the community. That all who worshipped must make regular sacrifices of their vhoon to keep the connection with Asera-Masdheh strong and running through his priests to our whole society.

Was that true? I do not know. Perhaps a genetic mutation left an ancestor of mine with a need for vhoon like an anemic kee who requires blood transfusions to survive, and the ability to derive more nutrition from it than the average kee. Even if that is true, could that not have been a subtle but powerful commandment from Asera-Masdheh, deep-writ in our very genes? And how they figured out the need to ingest vhoon if not commanded by the Wise Lord is another question. But this was a time when it was understood that vhoon was a vital thing. The phrase from the Christian Bible, in the book Deuteronomy, "the blood is the life," expresses the concept well, and the writers of the Judeo-Christian sacred texts were undoubtedly deeply influenced by the sacred works that many generations later, my people would commit to parchment and the earliest paper made of flax and hemp. Other religions involved drinking the blood of animals in their ceremonies, so it is not hard to imagine how the step to human vhoon was made.

Still, centuries later in Zoroastrianism, the concept of haoma sounds just like am'r vhoon-drinking. The sacred writings claim haoma promotes healing, enhances sexual arousal, is intoxicating, is physically strengthening and nourishing, stimulates alertness and awareness, and is "most nutritious for the soul." All these are true with vhoon for am'r, and for yourself now as well, cinyaa.

My family had already begun to show alterations from the rest of humanity. We had eyes that preferred the dark of night, and more and more, our rituals took place after sunset. We aged more slowly and had longer lifespans than the other members of the community. Some of us were physically stronger or showed amazing powers of healing.

That was *not* me, not at first. I was a sickly child. After weaning, I could barely manage to eat solid food, and most often after a meal, you would find me at the latrine pits or outside the walls of our settlement, in the back of the communal gardens, trying to hide that I had vomited up my dinner *again*. My photosensitivity was the truest handicap, and I could not help with any tasks that took place during daylight hours. It was widely assumed by my family that I was a runt who would die soon enough.

There was not yet a prohibition against what would later be seen as the negative, "sinful" practice of incest. In my world, there was no word for it, and it was common sense for my family members to intermarry to keep the priesthood well within our control. You could see my childhood infirmity as a product of inbreeding, but with that came the side-effect that this difference in our genes was being passed through cousin marrying cousin, uncles marrying nieces, and even brothers marrying sisters, just as the Egyptian royalty practiced, many centuries later. Generation after generation, our unique vhoon was reinforced and strengthened. What I was—what I had the potential to become, that is—had been created brick by brick like a building, baby by baby down our bloodline, our vhoon-anghyaa.

My name even hints at that understanding, although it was more in a poetic sense than a scientific one. Vohuni-sura I was named, "He of Mighty Blood." While I was a sickly child, that name was used mockingly by the other children around me and also some adults when speaking of me to my parents.

No, my name was *not* Zarathustra. He was my younger kin, and later I was his advisor and mentor. In a way, I was the prototype for him, and parts of his story are *my* story, woven together over the centuries to make the myth of the prophet. I was at his side his whole life, and after his death, I spent many decades holding the Zoroastrian communities together, traveling up and down the ancient highway that later became Darius the Great King's Royal Road, looking for cities and settlements where the way of the Wise Lord was being lost, corrupted by priests who wanted to gain power over adversaries, or other scheming. I have been the loyal defender of my people, stepping forward from the shadows to better their lives or save them from exploitation over and over as the years flowed by. I went with them in the Zoroastrian Diaspora, and I helped them set down roots and consecrate the Fire Temples after each persecution. I helped them escape from the rise of the Muslim world. Later, I helped the teaching of Zoroaster move up into Europe, where it grew under many other names, and I watered those faiths with my knowledge and strength.

It was after the disastrous genocide of the Cathars by the Catholics that I realized I could and should no longer try to manage kee lives. I had grown too far from their experiences and realities to be a good counselor to them, and the kee world was now too teeming, too disparate, to hold any attraction for me.

Ah, but that is all another tale for another time. I have gotten ahead of myself and skipped past the most vital part of my story.

As I said, I was a frail child, but I survived day after day, despite the doubts of my elders and the taunts of my peers. At age fifteen, I became a man and was allowed to do more than chores—what chores I was strong enough to manage —around our temple-home complex. I could finally take part in the priest's sacrament.

I will never forget the first time I tasted vhoon. Being required to fast since the night before had not been a problem for me. I barely managed to consume solid food as it was and had survived mostly on milk for years, although even that led to terrible stomach pains.

I enjoyed the ritual bathing and meditation, and as any child raised in a priestly family, I knew how to pray for hours—or at least *look* as if I was doing so.

Finally, there I was in my stiff new ceremonial robe, and an izchha, the person selected to offer up their vhoon, knelt before me. The izchha was my age, and while that might have made another nervous first-timer more comfortable, to me, it merely seemed to emphasize the difference between his healthy, sun-kissed, well-muscled body and my scrawny limbs and sickly pale skin. I was more excited than nervous, yet this was a great discomfort to me, and I had to fight to keep from trembling as I knelt before him, took his outstretched arm, and held my ceremonial knife to his wrist. The knife was a short but beautifully worked obsidian blade, which I had named Sa'mah— "dark," as her smooth black curves are—and was a gift from my mother just moments before I stepped into the area you would call the 'sanctuary,' or perhaps 'chancel,' where only the participants in the ritual could go.

Then I noticed that *he* trembled, too, and I realized it was his first time to be izchha since my people did not allow anyone under the age of adulthood to offer their vhoon. With a rush of confidence, I took Sa'mah, nicked his wrist precisely, and brought it to my mouth without wasting even a drop of the sacrament.

And everything changed.

For the first time in my life, I swallowed something that seemed to be welcomed by my tastebuds, my throat, all the way down into my stomach. With each mouthful, I felt new wellness and vitality spreading through my body. I could almost feel it enter my bloodstream, move up to my heart, and then be sent out, heartbeat by heartbeat, into every part of me.

As it reached my brain, it was as if I experienced pleasure, true pleasure, for the first time in my short life. It was a combination of mitigation of pain and a wash of well-being, of *bliss*, that relaxed a tension I never knew I'd been holding and yet energized every part of me.

Thank goodness I had experienced vhoon-drinking vicariously and had the proper practices discussed with me, or I would have drained that boy, my equal in age, until there was not a drop left in his body. But my new strength brought me new clarity as well.

From that moment on, my life changed. I *thrived*. My body filled out with muscle. My skin glowed with health. I easily dominated conversations and physical activities. My miraculous improvement was seen as a sign from Asera-Masdheh, and as the favored new acolyte, I was given regular priestly duties. Indeed, our followers asked to be izchha to me in particular. Since that meant other priests would have more time for themselves, there was no jealousy from my family, and of course, I was more than happy to take the extra services because every drop of vhoon made me stronger.

In a year's time, I was the obvious choice to take over from my father, who was then the head priest. My older brothers might have been resentful except that my presumed blessedness had brought so much prestige to our family that we all were richer, and our temple no longer struggled with the other sects for offerings and influence.

That is my story. That was how the first am'r—for so I believe I am and have never found evidence to prove me wrong—came to be. It is, I know, too mundane to be thrilling and too imprecise to be scientific, but perhaps that makes it all the more *real*.

But that does not explain our enemy, and his story is very much entwined with mine. What, cinyaa? You wish to hear about Zarathustra first? As you wish.

Zarathustra was the son of my eldest brother's youngest son's eldest son. His name, which means "Golden Cattle," demonstrates how much our community had come to focus on the agrarian lifestyle that had rapidly changed the quality and shape of our lives. There was little that happened in the world in those days that was not tied in one way or another to the gods. In this case, the early teachings of Asera-Masdheh, whom Zoroastrians would later name Ahura Mazda, became entwined with the ways of the tilling of the land, of irrigation, and of the new science of animal husbandry that did not involve migrating with your herds.

He was a bright child with an irresistible smile and a powerful personality. The blood that had so twisted me worked differently in him, and he was vibrant with kee life and power.

The stories of his life you read in the Gathas and the Younger Avesta are a hodge-podge, many truths from many centuries that have been commingled, first by the metamorphosis in oral tradition over centuries, then altered further over the years of written history as parts of the story were added or removed to fit the changing needs of the audience.

I have worked as well to remove myself from his story. While I was a mentor to the first Zarathustra in his life and to the many other prophets that came after, I have always pushed Zoroastrianism to be a kee religion for the best good of its kee adherents. Now, only the poetry of some of the oldest Avesta texts holds a hint of what culture my cousin was shaped by and what my earliest world was like.

That is enough about Zarathustra. You wanted to know about me, and you wanted to know about our enemy. My first frithaputhra. The world's first frithaputhra and second am'r.

He was another cousin, my mother's younger sister's eldest daughter's youngest daughter's eldest son. By the time he was born, I had been head of our family for many years, the highest priest of Asera-Masdheh, blessed by Him to be unaging, ever stronger and more learned, increasing in the Glory and Understanding of the Wise Lord, His Voice on Earth. After I took over from my father, I was the high priest for so long that the kee of our settlement, which was grown even more populous and city-like now, became used to me as their ageless leader, watching over generation after generation of kee lives.

As the generations rolled by, I looked with increasing anxiety for another who was like me. As my family continued their unintentional genetic experiment, I found many who had some difficulties with photosensitivity, and there were more than a few the vhoon obviously had a salutatory effect upon, giving them euphoria, strengthening their limbs, and gilding their beauty. But none had mutated as fully as I, and after a couple of generations, I began to wonder if I would always be alone in my god-gifted glory.

Then my little first-cousin-twice-removed was born. His parents named him Vohun-ukhra, which was, I believe, an attempt to tie him to his powerful cousin the high priest. As my name meant "He of Mighty Blood," his meant "He of Powerful Blood," but at the beginning, he seemed as unworthy of his name as I had.

With excitement and fascination, I watched the sickly, undersized nursling barely make it through childhood. I started spending unprecedented time at his family's home, ostensibly exchanging news with the adults, but in actuality watching little Vohun-ukhra out of the corner of my eye. He was a bright child who made up for his physical handicaps with creative solutions and prevented his relatives from seeing him as a burden by putting on a cheery demeanor and being quick of wit and eager to offer help where his weakened condition would allow.

I thought I was being subtle, but his mother noticed my interest. Soon, young V'ukh was being seated beside me during meals, called over to show his crafty ways with painting or carving, or instructed to recite his lessons to me to show off his ability to memorize and declaim our ritual prayers.

I did not fight it. I took him as my apprentice early and went so far as to move him into my home, where I lived alone with only a girl, Frehnai, to cook and clean for me and see that I was not lonely at night. Priests in my time took no vows of chastity, and indeed my family encouraged and rewarded productive unions as the worship of our Wise Lord spread to other settlements and new temples needed to be built and maintained.

V'ukh and Frehnai and I made a nice little family. He followed me around like a puppy, and I understood his drive to feel special, to feel valuable, since I was not so far from my own grueling childhood. He was always to be found at my side as we went around the temple tending to the sacred duties, and he was not denied entrance to our most holy places. Although my living quarters were spacious enough to give him a small room with its own straw pallet, still, in the evenings when I woke up, I would often find him curled against my back, his bony little body pressed to mine for warmth.

Once he came to me, he no longer needed to pretend to eat as I had done at his age. I instructed Frehnai to always have fresh milk for him but not to try to force solid food despite her admirable desire to mother him. Once he realized I understood, his love for me grew even more fervent. He followed me with shining eyes and eagerly learned all the teachings I had for him.

I finally knew what it was like to have a son. Once I had become strong with regular frangkhilaat, the blood-gift of the izchhaish, I was no longer shy about exploring intimacy with anyone who caught my eye. And once I became robust and vital, there was much pressure from my family to provide children who would carry on my connection with Asera-Masdheh. I worked my way through many of the unmarried young women of my family and even a few married women of known fertility who wanted the honor of carrying my children, but I got no child upon any of them. In time, I had to invent a vision from the Wise Lord, explaining that as His holiest high priest, I should have no children, for all our people (and my family most of all—so shut up, aunties!) needed my undivided attention. That worked, as I knew it would. As a sickly child and now as a man apart, I had studied people: their words, actions, and intentions. It was one reason I was so popular as a priest and such a good mentor, later, to Zarathustra.

V'ukh, of course, had developed that same ability, and I deepened his understanding. We talked for hours through the part of the night where only lovers and temple devotees were awake, and his mind matured until I could soon forget I was discoursing with a child.

He was ready for his first rite of izchha well before the age of adulthood, and I was certain that frangkhilaat would take away all his childish ailments, so at age thirteen, I gave him permission to lead the ritual. I observed from where the worshipers could not see, so they would not think I doubted him, but I knew I had no reason to question his maturity, and I was proven right. I saw him have the same moment I'd experienced after his first mouthful of vhoon; he closed his eyes, and I saw the shock of it move through his whole person. At that moment, I was a boy again, ending my tortured kee life and becoming something new. I experienced my own thrill because I was no longer a man apart; there was another like me.

I had made my first frithaputhra. Not, obviously, using the technique I would come to invent in later years, but with V'ukh, I did not have to put my vhoon-anghyaa into him; it was already there. V'ukh was the only other I found who spontaneously became what later would be called an "am'r." In the beginning, I had no idea what my vhoon would do if drunk by a kee, and I assumed I had to wait for those like me to naturally appear in our family. At that time, I never discovered the formula for the tripartite rite to create the patar-frithaputhra bond, which was very much my loss. But that comes later in my story.

After his first rite of izchha, we were an inseparable team, both united in the common goals of bringing the worship of Asera-Masdheh to the world, prosperity to our family...and for ourselves, regular frangkhilaat. There was no skulking about in the shadows; well, except as with me, the sun became entirely unbearable to him after his first taste of vhoon, so we transacted our lives after it went down. But on days where the izchha ritual did not happen in Asera-Masdheh's temple, it was not hard to get vhoon. I was the head priest, he the hand-picked apprentice, the prodigy, the rising star. Any lover we wanted in our settlements, or over the decades, in the communities that sprang up around us up and down the great Khorasan road, would be ours for just a smile. It was felt we did great honor to whomever we lay with, and if we further honored that lover with the sacrament of izchha in our beds, none would ever think to complain, especially since the sacrament took the loving to greater heights.

At some point, our little family had changed. I do not recall the first time I heard the noises that indicated Frehnai was in V'ukh's bed, but it did not bother me. I was pleased that two whom I cared for so deeply were finding joy together. They were together for many days after that, and I found sustenance elsewhere those days. I was still so young and still so full of hunger that going without vhoon did not appeal.

One evening, Frehnai was attending to my bathing, and out of habit, I admired her graceful form but then realized she looked gaunt where her curves were normally more generous. I looked closer at her lovely face and saw dark circles under her eyes and an unhealthy pallor to her nutmeg skin. As she brought bowls of water and towels, I heard the shortness of breath I would expect from the elderly, and I realized her arms were trembling with the weight of a bowl she used to carry without thought. I immediately rose and took the burden from her and sat her down on my pallet.

I did not have to ask her anything. I knew I was seeing the results of too frequent blood loss. I thought about how many nights I had heard the sounds of their lovemaking and cursed myself for not having spoken to V'ukh about the need to moderate what one took from a regular lover and to rotate between a selection of partners so one never took more than one kee (a word that comes down from the language we spoke then, meaning mortal, an earthborn animal) could recover from with food and rest. At the moment, however, I just held Frehnai and comforted her. I told her she would do no work again until she recovered from her "sickness." I went to our neighbors and got a bowl of meaty broth to feed her, and bread from our communal ovens.

Later that night, I took V'ukh for a walk outside the walls of our growing city to a cypress-dotted hill where at the peak, we could sit and see the stars above us and the lesser glows of dying cooking fires and resinous torches and little stone lamps burning animal fat below us.

"My son," for so I called him, "the kee ones around us

are more fragile than we who are become amar." ("Amar" was a word from our language which meant something like "immortal." It was perhaps a bit presumptuous for me to have taken it on back then, but it has since proven to be true.) "We must honor their vhoon, their gift to us, and never take so much as to cause them harm." I went over the schedule I had worked out, having three izchhaish I visited "in rotation, as our crops go into different fields," and how much vhoon it was safe to take from a kee one time or from a regular izchhaish, who must give lesser amounts.

It was the only time I'd ever had to castigate him despite my having taken him in at such a young age. I might have been a little harsh with him, for I admit I felt a deep disappointment at having to explain these things, which I had worked out so easily on my own. He had seemed like the other half of my own self, the same soul in a separate body, so I felt anger at him for his casual ill-usage of Frehnai, as if I had let my own self down.

I remember his body, now so well-fleshed and vital, sitting stiffly as I chastised and lectured him. When I finished, V'ukh promised he would be more careful, but his voice was distant, and he would not meet my eyes. I told myself he was feeling shamed, as well he ought, and gave him space to come to terms with his mistake and my justifiable disappointment and ire.

He never came to terms with it, although I did not see it at the time. V'ukh never was the boy who adored me ever again, but I did not perceive the loss, at least at first. Our lives were increasingly demanding; the worship of Asera-Masdheh, in part due to my unageing face and body, had drowned out the voices of the other gods for miles in every direction around us, and V'ukh and I were sought-after to do the ceremony of the sacrament at every temple of our Wise Lord. I was too busy to notice the distance that grew between us.

He still lived in my household, although many days we both slept elsewhere, so we did not often see each other even in passing. I was habitually on the road, gone for the long periods that travel by camel or ass imposed. It was after one such journey that I returned home, disgusted by the dirt of the road upon my skin and clothes, and called for Frehnai to bring fresh clothes and a bowl of water for washing. She took a long time to answer my call, and I was beginning to wonder if she was even in my home when she staggered in, barely able to carry a small skin of water, never mind the stone washing bowl.

"Frehnai! What..." But I did not have to ask. The symptoms were the same as before, only more serious. I gathered her up in my arms and carried her to my pallet. She was gasping for air and shivering in my arms. I held her to me, smelling mortality upon her; it was only her devotion to me that had raised her from what was obviously soon to be her deathbed.

I acted without conscious thought. For the first time in my life, I took my ceremonial blade and used it upon *myself*: a quick slit to the wrist, then I pressed my flowing vhoon to her lips. After so many years, so many repetitions of that very action, it feels strange to remember the original occurrence. It was hard to get her to swallow it at first; she seemed to feel that if one not of the priesthood drank the sacred vhoon, it would be a great transgression. But I spoke soothing words to her and told her any action *I* suggested to her could not be wickedness, I who interpreted Asera-Masdheh's laws for the people. And so she drank, and after her first few sips, I felt a vitality come into her. She grabbed my arm and took gulp after gulp until my wound closed, not as fast as they do now, but still faster than a kee's healing.

I gazed down at Frehnai in my arms, and she looked up at me with eyes sparking with their old vivacity, the strength marvelously renewed in her. She brought her lips up to mine for a kiss, and I felt a bond stronger than I had ever felt with anyone in my life. We explored each other's bodies for the rest of the morning, indeed the rest of the day, and I had never experienced such interconnectedness with another. Before this, the only thing remotely comparable had been my connection with V'ukh, my son.

V'ukh. That was the matter I would have to deal with next. Pushing aside my joy at this surprising result of a kee receiving my vhoon, I dealt with my thoughts about my erring son. Was it defiance, or was it uncaring recklessness? I desperately hoped it was the former since I believed I could correct mere youthful rebellion, but if it were not? After these many years of learning at my feet, I did know how to fix whatever flaw in his character had led to such cruel inconsideration not just of love, for Frehnai had loved V'ukh from the moment I'd brought him home, but of life, *her very life.*

I was almost beyond anger that my son was capable of this thing. Frehnai had been afraid of committing sacrilege, but what V'ukh had done was the true desecration.

I did not see him that night or the next few, for he had gone to another community to teach young would-be priests. It was good that I had a few days to compose myself, for my wrath was as a fire that would consume an entire forest. By the time he returned home, I felt ready to talk to him as befitted a high priest, in a calm tone and manner. And I knew what I would say.

"You have let me down, Vohun-ukhra, and what is worse, you have let down the sacred vows you made before Asera-Masdheh. Vhoon is the ultimate gift, the supreme sacrifice. By recklessly taking too much, endangering the health and even the life of the izchha, you dishonor the sacred trust with which it is given.

"And this was *Frehnai*, son, who vhoon-gave to you in perfect love and trust. How could you betray that?

"I have spoken of this to you before. I had assumed that one time would be enough, that you would moderate the enthusiasm of youth with the deeper perception given by your blessed proximity to our Wise Lord. But you are obviously less blessed than I believed. You leave me no choice but to strip you of your role as priest. You must now earn your place, which once was handed to you. You will be a temple acolyte again, and you will serve Asera-Masdheh in more modest roles until I am convinced that you have been taught self-restraint and thoughtful loving-kindness for those who give unto you the sweetest of gifts.

"You will be as a child again, drinking milk for sustenance instead of vhoon. You will learn the lessons of humility and respect that I apparently failed to teach you in your first childhood. Vohun-ukhra, you are my son, and I love you. I know *this* is not who you wish to be, and I know it will not take you long to be teaching the ways of Asera-Masdheh at my side again."

He did not reply, did not try to explain or defend his unjustifiable actions. At the time, I saw it as a hopeful sign for his quick rehabilitation to the man I thought I knew and loved. But he also did not apologize or promise a change in his practices.

The one thing V'ukh asked was that his shame not to be made plain for all who knew him to see, but that he be allowed to go be an acolyte at a temple far from our home. Since that was what I was going to suggest anyway, it cost me nothing to make it seem like I was giving him that mercy.

We traveled many miles to the furthest settlement where the words of Asera-Masdheh had been heard. Happily, I had never brought V'ukh there before, so he was not known as my son and protégé. I simply left him at the temple as an acolyte who came late to dedicating his life to the Wise Lord. As we traveled, I had shared my wisdom with him, and he listened quietly, with neither argument nor debate. I saw this as his submission to my authority and to my superior understanding, and felt assured of a happy resolution after a suitable time of arrogance being unlearned, replaced by modesty and insight.

I left him there and traveled back by a circuitous route, visiting many temples along the way and doing services there. I stopped in smaller villages and spoke of Asera-Masdheh with both his followers and those who had not yet left their old ways, for the words of the Wise Lord were becoming entwined with the new learnings of the land, and those who followed him prospered with abundant crops and plentiful herds of cattle and camels.

CHAPTER TWO

I returned home to a healthy Frehnai, who seemed to have taken no harm from her ordeal. She remembered how I'd saved her with the sacrament of Asera-Masdheh, and now her devotion to me was complete and total. I as well felt a far deeper connection to her, with my vhoon now flowing in her veins. The love between us was profound but also satisfying in the simpler level of domestic comfort we gave each other. While it was obvious that I could not provide her with children, more and more I came to think of her as my wife. In the absence of V'ukh, she became the one I spoke to about temple matters at the end of a long night, and she began to impress upon me her intuitive knowledge of handling community matters and interpersonal conflicts. I turned to her for advice more and more frequently.

After some months, I resolved to pay V'ukh a visit to ascertain his progress. I did not believe he would be *truly* ready to come home again, since he had made too great a transgression, and I wanted at least a year as an acolyte to impress that upon him, but I thought it would be beneficial to praise the efforts he had made thus far, and maybe speak to the local priest about a schedule of reward, what today we would call "fast-tracking." I had no doubts that my son would be thriving in his new community and that, even if he were chafing a little under his lower rank, at least he was dedicated to learning in humility.

I loaded my camel for the long journey; the family had a number which were shared among them, but there was an ornery old beast only I could handle and who was kept alive solely because I was fond of her as a travel compan- ion. Dregvaa was her name, which meant "Containing Wickedness." Ah, I have not thought of her in many years. With Dregvaa as fiendish and entertaining company, I made my slow way to the community where V'ukh now served as acolyte.

Or so I thought. When I got there and asked for him, I was directed to the local head priest, and he looked very grave indeed as he said he had much to impart. He was sorry, but I had been very mistaken about the acolyte I had left there upon my last visit, who had not had *any* vocation after all. When he was with them, he was late to or disre- garded all his duties, and he was disrespectful to anyone who tried to discuss the matter with him. Worse than that, soon it was reported that he lay during the day with women and men. That, in-and-of-itself, was not the prob- lem, for none of our priests were celibate, and being a priest assured that finding willing partners was not diffi- cult. No, the problem was that he demanded that his lovers do the izchha ritual with him in the bedroom. Outside of my home and our very special circumstances therein, the rite of izchha was to be performed *only* in the temple and not as part of lovemaking. As if that were not more than enough, the reports were that V'ukh forced his partners whether they wished to or not and that he drank far more from them than anyone had ever heard of, leaving his unhappy partners weakened and feeling violated both physically and spiritually.

It was good, said the local head priest, that within a week, he had gone. He had just walked off one night, whence to, no one knew, else they would have had to send someone to me to come remove him, for they had already seen that he would listen to none of them.

I was beyond emotion. His abuse of the trust of our community was deeply wounding. Just as hurtful for me, it had never occurred to me that V'ukh would not be eager to return to his rightful place at my side. That he should just disappear, leaving no word? I could not comprehend it. I could not get this extreme response to his penance to make sense. My son had erred profoundly but not irredeemably. I had worked out a very reasonable solution for his rehabilitation, and at the same time, kept his shame from being public knowledge. I could not have been fairer, and there could not have been a more evenhanded resolution.

Yet he had chosen to publicly create an almost incurable rift with his community of worship. This gossip would spread to other settlements faster than feet could walk it there. Further, he had then made the choice to self-exile from his home, from...from his own father. He had so much yet to learn; I had so much yet to teach him! But he had walked away from it all.

I was too shaken to do any services. Instead, I climbed

back onto Dregvaa and let her set the pace back home. I swayed on her back through the nights and listened to Dregvaa grumbling to herself as if she could explain the inexplicable.

I remember seeing the walls of our settlement, and I felt relief that soon I would be in Frehnai's arms. For a little while at least, I could think about something other than my failure as both father and priest to V'ukh. Somehow, I had driven him away from a life he had loved. Somehow, I had driven him away from *me*. I wanted to lose myself in Frehnai's generous curves and enthusiastic welcome. I had deliberately held off on frangkhilaat the whole way home, and my hunger was helpfully threatening to drive other, more painful thoughts from my mind.

I returned Dregvaa to the family's stables, then walked through the streets to my lodging. Life was so normal: children playing when they should have been doing errands for their parents, the people of the community calling greetings to me from their tasks making pottery (the newest innovation in our time of change and a rapidly growing industry), preparing food, or other myriad daily tasks of our newly settled lives. It was a balm to my soul. By the time I got to my door, I was more relaxed than I had been for weeks, and I was ready to share all my hungers with my lovely Frehnai.

When the door opened, the smell of her sweet vhoon reached out to pull me in, but as I stepped inside, I realized that the scent was far too pungent for things to be well. I rushed to her room and found her body lying on the floor as if dropped, her tunic ripped and defensive wounds on her arms. Her throat was ripped open, not as if by a jackal, leopard, or cheetah, but obviously by the smaller jaw and duller teeth of an am'r mouth.

And I could smell him. My son had been here and had left not an hour before my return. I was torn; should I go after him before the trail was lost, or should I forget him and do what I could for Frehnai? There was yet life, weak but still extant, in her body. I gently moved her to her pallet and tried to close the skin back over the oozing wound. There was hardly enough blood left in her body for more to be pumped out with every slowing heartbeat. I ripped my own wrist open with my teeth and tried to get her to drink, but she was not conscious enough. This was the moment when I discovered the healing powers of vhoon, not just when ingested, but acting immediately upon a wound. I watched in wonder as her wound closed under my vhoon-flow until she was no longer in further peril from bleeding out. She was still dangerously close to death from the vhoon that was no longer in her body, but spilled around us on the floor and bed—and most likely energizing the man whom I had once called "son," somewhere out in the world. But I could not focus on that, not yet.

I managed to hold Frehnai's head at an angle where it was easier to keep her mouth open, then reopened the wound on my wrist—not too much, just a light but steady stream of drops—and massaged her throat to make her swallow. It was very complicated, but I eventually got some vhoon into her, and it did not take long to bring her up to a place where she could swallow on her own. Soon after that, she was drinking from my wrist like a baby suckling.

I let her sleep, although my hunger from days of with-holding on the road combined with my current vhoon-loss was intense. But I let her sleep in my arms because I could not bear to let her go. I made many plans for when I found V'ukh, just what I would do to him. At that moment, questions of "Why?" were buried under an anger beyond any I have felt before or since.

When Frehnai woke up, it was to renewed health and vigor. Her skin was glowing, and her wounds were no longer visible even as scars. Her eyes were bright with well-being and also with arousal. I asked her no questions yet, but we made passionate love all through the rest of the day. It was the first true vhoon-vayon, both giving and taking vhoon as we gave and took orgasms from each other. I had no thoughts but for the miracle that was Frehnai and the thing we were creating together.

But as I woke the next evening, my anger resurfaced. Frehnai did not want to speak of it, but I demanded she tell me every detail. Apparently, V'ukh had returned a day before I did. Despite having been his victim before, Frehnai was merely cautious with him, welcoming him home and asking him only how his travels had been. She informed him that I had gone to visit him, she expected my return any day, and that I would be delighted to find him already returned to his home.

He demanded she lie with him and she had to let him, for he was far stronger and faster and would not accept a refusal from her. He drank from her too deeply. She was a smart woman, and after it was over, she went to a neighbor and was fed rich meats and camel's milk with healing herbs to somewhat make up for the loss. But V'ukh was angry with her for going out—he was afraid she was attempting to turn our community against him—and he attacked her, shouting that she belonged to him, not to the pompous and condescending Vohuni-sura, the so-called father who could not love a son as he deserved.

In his frenzy, he had shared with her more of his thoughts than perhaps he meant to. He intended to take from me everything which was mine: from Frehnai, to my position as head priest. But Frehnai, despite her weakened condition and her fear of both his mania and his physical strength, told him that not only would she not change her allegiance from me to him, but that she would no longer have anything to do with him. She kicked him out of the house and told him to leave and never return, nor speak to her again.

That was when he grabbed her, ripped her throat open with his teeth, drank her almost dry, and left her leaking the last of her life's blood out on the floor.

As Frehnai related this all to me, my anger fused into a solid knot of intention. The man once I'd been proud to call my son, him I would now kill. I was responsible for him, for his actions in this world. I had strengthened the weakly child, I had fed his body and mind, I had powered him with the sacred izchha; I had made him. And now, when he had developed into an anti-social brute, it was my duty to protect not just my lover, not just my community, but the *world* from my son's evil.

That turned out to be easier resolved than done. I immediately left Frehnai with the intention of tracking V'ukh, but I was met by some of the priests of Asera-Masdheh, glad I was back from my travels because there was much temple business that had been neglected. I was the head priest, and this was my community, so I could not ignore them. By the time I had sorted through their concerns and relegated everything into the correct hands, I could no longer track him by scent-spoor.

Why could I not? Ah, I was not then as you know me now, cinyaa. I was still a very young am'r, and while I felt much stronger than the kee around me, my abilities were barely more than those of a powerful kee, which I had never been before frangkhilaat had strengthened me. My sense of smell was barely better than kee senses, although at the time it seemed so very enhanced, and the same for my strength, my power of fascination, all those facets which mark the am'r as altered from kee. Looking back on it, the man I was then seems so powerless, so confused. It is not pleasant to remember being that man.

But as it was, all I could do was await his return, for I had no doubt he would return to face me, and prepare myself to end the life of my son.

In the meantime, I prepared others as well. I put it around that Vohun-ukhra had suffered a head injury that had let Evil Thoughts into his mind. This was a pragmatic explanation that worked for both the most- and least-devout thinkers, for back then, everyone *knew* head injuries let demons into your brains. All were warned to give a wide berth to the one they had once cheerfully greeted in the streets and trusted to lead their most sacred ceremonies, and all were told to let me know if they saw or heard tell of him.

After a month had passed with no sight of V'ukh, I began to travel to other settlements in search of him. I no longer left Frehnai alone at home, however. She had grown too dear to me to bear parting from her for long, and I knew that once V'ukh discovered she yet lived, she would be as a red flag to a bull. You will see that was an all-too-apt description.

So, cinyaa, you follow in the footsteps of the earliest of those who were given vhoon-am'r. Never let an am'r tell you an am'r-nafsh must hide away in their patar's stronghold, for the One Who Came First was at my side for the first fight between am'r. Which, yes, as you shrewdly note, began as soon as there were two am'r in the world.

What? Was Frehnai there by my side for me to protect her or to lure V'ukh out from hiding? Ah, cinyaa, you ask that with censure in your voice, but you must understand that Frehnai knew all my mind. She knew I felt it was safer for her to be where I could protect her, but also that, yes, she might be a lure to V'ukh in his frenzied evil. She worried along with me about what he could get up to, left at liberty. He was already proven to have no concern for the sanctity of life or the sacredness of the izchha ceremony. Who knew how many people for whom he had tarnished the rituals of Asera-Masdheh? Who knew how many people he had drained until they perished from vhoon-loss?

And so Frehnai and I, riding Dregvaa and the only other camel whose company Dregvaa would tolerate—no, cinyaa, I do not remember the other camel's name after these many years—became nomads, moving from town to smaller settlement, looking for any trace of V'ukh. When we did not find him, we held a service to honor Asera-Masdheh, for still I sought to spread the word. Now as well, I hoped that by doing so I might counter any evil V'ukh was bringing into the world.

I was not a moment too soon in that goal. As we got farther away from our settlement, we began to notice a strange shift in people's attitudes. I used to be greeted with great excitement, even reverence. Now, at the sight of me, people were wary, their faces closed. And more than just relating to me, I found more and more people outside of settlements embracing the old ways of pastoral nomadism. We were even seeing small bands without any cattle, just their bows and spears and knives.

When I spoke to those people about the words of Asera-Masdheh, about the wisdom and goodness of caring for the land and growing as the grain grew, they threw back at me that the ways of their ancestors seemed better to them—freedom to roam like lions instead of being planted and stuck in one place. When I mentioned the excitement of the new technologies of our time, such as pottery and all of its potential, they countered with the thrill of the hunt and the horizon stretching out, unexplored. Looking back at this through the filter of the years, I see this bifurcation has never left the kee world, but it was my first time encountering this clash of the backward-looking and forward-looking spirits.

I knew when to let go, so I just asked if they had seen a man matching V'ukh's description. Oh, they told me, you mean Kori'kan? He was here, and he taught us many things. He has reconnected us with the teachings of our ancestors. He has reminded us to be bulls among men, to emulate the strength, the determination, the endurance, the potency of the oxen. Their eyes lit as they spoke of him when they should have been saving that reverence for the gods, for Asera-Masdheh.

It was with a terrible weight upon my heart that I heard them out. My beloved son was not just an amoral butcher of kee. He was actually turning people away from the Wise Lord, sending them backward in development away from Good Thoughts, Good Words, and Good Deeds. Back to the time when we slaughtered our fellow humans like animals, when we treated our animals with cruelty and dishonor, when we cared not for the earth beneath our feet and trampled the plants we should be nurturing with tender care.

I do not think you can understand how upsetting this all was to me. I had seen our world on the cusp of a better future. From time beyond measure, human innovation had been thousands of years in evolution, and even then, the advancement was simply a pointier stick or a new idea about how to cure animal skins, not what *you* would understand as innovation today. And those small changes moved as slowly across the world as through time. But in the Neolithic, one could see huge, vital changes being made in the time of one's father's father, or one's father, or even oneself, spreading more rapidly to the increasing number of settlements and making a demonstrable difference in the quality of life. It was like the jump in the computer age, that kind of demarcation between "what came before" and "what comes after."

And these changes were tied inexorably to Asera-Masdheh. To this day, in the holy books of the Zoroastrians is enshrined the idea, "*He who cultivates grain, cultivates righteousness.*" The separation of religious belief from scientific thought was so many millennia away as to be unfathomable. Ideas came from the gods. That was understood and accepted without question or the need for questions. I had lived my life in service to my Wise Lord, who brought us Good Thoughts, and my whole purpose in existing was to spread these innovative Good Thoughts and the better life they guaranteed. To see that being turned backward, retrogressing to a harsher, coarser past? It was not just upsetting in the main, but it also felt like a direct attack on my life's work.

It felt like that because that was what it was. As Frehnai and I traveled, we kept finding ourselves a few steps behind V'ukh, discovering the ripples of damage he was causing to our whole world. My former son's words had a strong influence on the young, who wanted the drama and romance of the old hunter-gatherer times. And some of the elders, those who had resisted change all their lives, were even more easily swayed. Where once there had been communities working together in the new directions our world was taking, now there was dissension. People fought, and they brought the gods into the fight. The voices of the ancestors were twisted and manipulated. Taru, the god of the old bull cult, was rising in power against Asera-Masdheh. At every one of the Wise Lord's temples, attendance was down, and rites were being neglected.

So Frehnai and I traveled behind V'ukh, trying to undo the damage he had wrought and untwist the distortions he'd left in his wake. That became our specialty as priests, for I had made Frehnai a priestess, as was my right as high priest. By now, she knew as much about the teachings of Asera-Masdheh as anyone living. We learned which words best countered the blandishments of the False Prophet

Kori'kan, and we spoke them to all who would sit and listen. We won little battles, but were losing the war. Still, we devoted ourselves to that task, while at the same time, I hoped and prayed to come across my former son in the flesh.

Why did I not track him more diligently? As I said, my abilities were not as you know them today. The journey spanned months, then it spanned years. The speed of life back then was more gradual, more drawn-out. You, hasty child of the twenty-first century, would call it "slow." We moved like the sun and the moon across the heavens, following the paths prearranged by the gods, inexorable, relentless. Sometimes I could scent that he had been in a building, for homes back then did not have windows, only openings in the roof to let out smoke from cooking fires, and scents could easily linger in those enclosed spaces. But mostly, I knew of V'ukh's recent presence by the messes he'd made in the kee minds. He might have been of the same bloodline as me, but his glamor and charisma had always been very strong, whereas mine needed to be developed over many centuries to rival the power with which he'd been born.

And for all that, for all the years of plodding across the landscape on indignant camels who would rather be back in their paddocks, the tension and strain of arguing for your god and your whole society's future with those who have been fired up by one would tear them down on a spiteful whim, for the inability to rest for fear you cannot repair the harm by the time you get to it, we might as well have stayed in our home. For that was where I found

V'ukh, when finally I caught up with him. That was where it all ended.

We were so happy to be back in our home, Frehnai and I, that at first we didn't feel the change in our settlement, the air of uncertainty and discontent. It did not take long, however, as we went about our daily lives—I stepping back in my role of high priest and introducing Frehnai to her new roles in the temple—to discover that V'ukh's influence had spread all the way back to our settlement, and it was ripping our community apart.

The followers of Asera-Masdheh and the new ways were in constant discord with Kori'kan and his preaching the bloody ways of Taru. Arguments flared up around the spring where everyone went to collect their water. Whether one used the new pottery jugs or the older water-skins had become a political statement, as it were, for which side you had chosen. Once work was done for the day, and the serious imbibing of beer and mead had begun for the night, those disagreements became physical fights.

I worked up a series of sermons to address this, to try to encourage the inclusion of beliefs and a focus on a peaceful, harmonious community. But the followers of Taru and Kori'kan were not interested in peace. The hot blood of the bull ran through them, and they were spoiling for a fight, any fight. I could counsel patience all I liked to the followers of Asera-Masdheh, but eventually, enough sharp words would be spoken that only fists could follow.

This all built up like water boiling in a skin over a fire:

the little bubbles rise first, but it seems like nothing will break the surface tension…and then suddenly, the larger bubbles are crashing up to the surface, and all is chaos.

We came to that boil when Kori'kan returned to our home and started preaching in the temple of Asera-Masdheh.

It was just as the sun had dropped below the horizon, the western sky still pale orange, shading into ceramic blue, then into blue-black. One of the under-priests came in a rush to our rooms, calling my name. I was enjoying an early-evening-loving with Frehnai and had to rudely with-draw from her body, throw on my robes, and go running, Frehnai calling out behind me to take care as she hurriedly began to dress.

I was at the temple, the taste of Frehnai's blood still in my mouth and the scent of her body still wrapped around me under my clothing, when another scent knocked every-thing else out of my mind. *That scent.* I knew it like I knew Frehnai's honey-must aroma. Like I knew the pungent odor of Dregvaa from every other camel. The man I had called my son, had loved as none other, my cherished V'ukh. He who had betrayed me and everything we stood for. The scent that for years I had been searching for on every waft of air was right in front of me, waves of it exuding from his pores and pouring from the temple as Kori'kan raged inside, shouting of revolution, anger, and turmoil.

I had felt many types of anger toward him in the intervening years. The smell of him knocked me into stillness, a statue of rage become lucid potential energy, just waiting for his actions to spark my reactions. I felt the utter clarity and calm of knowing the moment was *now*.

What, cinyaa? I seem to you to always have lucidity and calm? Well, do you know, there might be a part of me that is stuck always and forever in that moment. No matter how many millennia I endure, there might be a part of my heart that is eternally held *there*, in the moment I killed my son.

Our settlement had built each building wall against wall, and we did not have streets as you would recognize them now. The temple was no exception. I had left my house by the roof and rushed across the intervening rooftops. I heard his voice rising from inside the temple below me.

He could tell when I arrived on the temple roof since his am'r abilities were almost as strong as mine by then. He climbed the ladder, and I gaped at the sight of him. Our community was justifiably proud of the woven fabrics we produced, of the flax grown around the settlement, and the goat and camel hair from our herds, innovating patterns in the weaving as we had innovated painting patterns onto our pottery. The followers of Taru, just as they refused to carry pottery pitchers to make their anti-innovation point, had also rejected the new textiles in favor of hides as a way to advertise their beliefs on their bodies.

Our ancestors had become quite expert in the preparation of hides. The leather could be made very thin and supple now, stitched with sinew in elaborate patterns. Fashion is no new thing to the human species: with beads of shell and stone worn on cords or sewn to clothing or braided in the hair, it was invented at the same time as the very first tools, so long ago that even my ancestors could not remember.

Obviously, when he'd visited a community who were true masters of leatherworking, Kori'kan had built himself an external persona, a pronouncement of himself and his god. He stepped out of the shadows of the temple into the cool blue of early evening, and the torches already lit on the temple's roof caught a magnificent ochre-red cloak that swirled around him, fluid and dramatic. The tunic he wore underneath had been turned black with iron oxide, and his shoes had been dyed the same shade. With his long black hair and flashing dark eyes, it made a vivid statement, and for an instant, I felt pride in my son.

He did not let that feeling last long. "The Trickster has arrived! The one who lies with the flicker of the Flame! He who would confine you behind walls in the trap of Asera-Masdheh! Do you see now what a liar he is? Are you ready to let the truth of Taru set you free?"

I heard murmurings around me and realized a large portion of our community was audience to this, seated as many were in the evenings on their rooftops to catch the last of the light and catch up with friends and family over a pitcher of beer and the evening meal. Any people who had been inside were climbing the ladders as fast as they could, like ants swarming out of a hill.

Kori'kan continued shouting in much the same vein. He seemed to have an unending stream of words to attack me, that could flow out of him until the end of time. I was the eye of the storm, and I held myself in calm reserve until the perfect moment.

"V'ukh," I said, my voice low and steady but pitched to

carry. "My beloved son, our cherished priest. What has pulled you from the loving arms of your family, from the warm admiration of all here in your home? Once you led us in Good Thoughts, Good Words, and Good Deeds. We need you still to guide us all in the Wise Lord's plan for us to work in harmony in this world, with each other, with the animals we husband, and with the green growing things we tend, yet what you have brought us recently? Violations of the natural order, the order revealed by Asera-Masdheh. It is you, V'ukh, my son, who has been bemused with the tricks and lies of False Thought, of desert spirits showing you mirages of falsehood. But all is not lost! We are here. We all long to enfold you in our arms and have you working side by side with us again. Let go of all this confusion and error. Let the ways of our ancestors recede into the past where they belong. Take my hands, my son, and reach with me toward our joyous and bounteous future!"

Did I think he would, upon hearing those words, renounce the following he had spent years building up? No, cinyaa, no. I was not that stupid, even though I was so very, very young. But I had to give him that chance in the eyes of our community, had to give him that opportunity for redemption and reconnection. They had to see him as the intolerant outsider forcing unwanted change upon a healthy society, and see me as part of them, as "us," a united force standing up to oppressive alteration coming from the outside. Otherwise, I could win a victory against him yet still lose the war against the discontent he had already wrought.

I knew I would win? Yes, of course, I did, cinyaa. I knew

myself, and I knew him. I knew I was the stronger. At that point in time, he was closest to my strength in the whole world, but I still had years of vhoon-drinking on him, with all the strength it brought me. I had been in a stronger body longer. When it is a matter of might-makes-right, I hope I still have that edge to this day, and I would like to think I have added knowledge and understanding to those more external strengths. Yes, I still believe I can beat any am'r. Yes, even our enemy, cinyaa. Do not fear.

What happened next? You are very impatient, cinyaa, but I do take your point. Perhaps I do not really enjoy speaking about what happens next, and I have been taking a very long and winding road to avoid telling it. But I have promised, so...

There we were upon the rooftop of the temple, and I had just pleaded with him to rejoin his community, his religion, and his family. I knew that message would fail to reach his heart.

He laughed and continued mocking me and the Wisdom of Asera-Masdheh. After a while, however, he realized he had lost his audience. Perhaps in the far settlements, his words had converted people easily, but in his hometown, the ways of the Wise Lord had impacted every life, had influenced every mind. He might have sown dissent among the easily dissatisfied, but he had a long way to go to change the hearts of our community.

Failure always made V'ukh angry. Looking back, I see that now. He had a personality that could not accept rebuke or failure. He saw the former as a personal attack and the latter as a general attack. Any and all criticism was intolerable to him; everything was taken personally, and since I *was* personally attacking him at the moment, this was where it had all become true—what his rage had told him was truth—and this was the moment he would finally avenge himself for all of it.

He pitched his rebuttal to be heard by all around us. "If you will not hear the words of Taru, then perhaps you will learn from the *strength* of Taru. Let the gods resolve this as they have always resolved these matters: the winner is the one left standing. All shall bow to him."

In my center of calm, I was more than prepared for this. It was as if my whole life had been in preparation for this moment. It was always coming down to this, my beloved V'ukh rebelling against me, the son knocking down the father. If my son had stood for the new order and I for the unyielding old, perhaps it would have been *right* for him to win. But in a perversion of that truth, the man I'd raised stood for the past we had grown out of, reimposing old ways that would hold back not just the new species of am'r but the whole of the kee as well. I was the future. *I must win.*

He had a long knife, obsidian like most of our best blades, embedded in a wooden haft to give it length. It had been hidden under his cloak, but as he rushed upon me, he swung it out for ease of use. I stepped back from his first thrust easily, so easily that he paused. It was clear he had forgotten, or perhaps never really recognized my agility. His parents had not yet been born when I was learning how to avoid fights my weak muscles and brittle bones could not have handled, using fast wits and fast feet to survive the rough-and-tumble of boyhood. He was not yet implanted in the womb when I experienced the first rush of vhoon-gifted vitality and demanded that all the best fighters of our settlement teach me—and were, eventually, mastered by me.

He was quick of body and of mind as well, however, quick to reassess and react. His next passes made even me have to work to avoid taking damage. I let him make a few more and danced around him, learning his habits. He and I had never sparred. Once he had experienced the vhoon-gift, he'd done as I had and practiced with lads his age, with those who peacocked around the community as its boldest fighters. By then, most in our community saw me only as their ageless head priest and had forgotten the days when I had taken down every man who challenged me.

He had learned my speed, and the minute I saw a perfect opening, he learned my strength as well. I struck and knocked his blade out of his hand, breaking most of the little bones. His standing there in shock gave me a moment to admire the flashing arc of the weapon as it flew across three rooftops, then I had to pay attention to V'ukh again. He had not fully healed—am'r healing has taken many lifetimes in me to become so rapid—but I was certain he could fight through quite a lot of pain, and I knew him to be ambidextrous.

He was in stinging shock, and from that place, he made the decision to grapple me. When he rushed me, I let him make contact. I did not want to keep avoiding him and give him time to think. His pain and anger were making his choices for him. Good.

He had built more muscle on his frame than I and was taller as well, so the fight was a bit more evenly matched than I would have liked. Thrice he managed to lift me bodily, trying to throw me from the roof to the ground. Once he tried to break my spine over his knee. Each time, I used my agility and clear thinking to climb his body in a way that I could get in damaging blows to his organs, his neck, and his head, then jump off him while his arms were weakened from the impact of my blows.

By this time, he had given me some damage: a few broken ribs, various other disfigurements that would still be visible today were I not am'r, and bruising on many parts of my body. He, however, had taken far more from me: his nose was broken, and an impressively bleeding cut on his forehead had left his long hair was matted with blood. He was limping on his left leg. I had smashed his right hand even further, and I could not guess how much internal damage he was fighting through.

The scent of his vhoon was a distraction to my thoughts.

Spectators had moved closer as we fought; rubbernecking is nothing new to the human condition. Many had brought torches since their kee eyes could not see as well in the dark of night. This fight had been going on for at least half an hour by now, and true dark had overtaken us. I had to keep shouting for people to move back, move to another roof. They did not listen, of course, and the temple was large enough to make them feel they had plenty of space to satisfy their curiosity.

V'ukh was frustrated and in more pain than he had been in many years. He had apparently expected an easy victory over me, and that he'd not gotten it was driving him crazy. He had to some extent believed that his chosen god was stronger than mine and would not let him be defeated—but he was not stupid, and he could tell he was losing. He needed to do something.

He snatched a torch from a too-near spectator and lashed out at me with it. The fire roared past me, the pitch coating keeping the flames from going out. I could dodge it easily enough, but I was worried about the people around me. It was harder to protect both myself and them at the same time. I got one group of idiots out of the way at the cost of my robes, which I quickly had to remove. That was fine. They were torn by this point and only getting in my way. I had been trained to fight naked since there was value to clothing back then, but not a nudity taboo or any kind of shame. V'ukh's pretty cloak was long gone. He had removed it after I'd used it to try to choke him.

The time spent tearing off my flaming robes gave V'ukh time to plan. I was standing in front of a group of onlookers who had ignored my many pleas for them to, well, *get out of the fucking way*. This time V'ukh rushed me, grabbed me in his arms, and barreled into them. They were right by the edge of the temple roof, and the buildings around it were not as high, so a number of them fell screaming over the edge. I had to protect myself and block his blows. I could not do anything for them, but it *hurt* to hear their cries. Worse, some had been holding torches, and soon it became clear that where the torches had landed, since those parts of the settlement were catching on fire.

I knocked V'ukh back with a series of blows to the head that should have knocked him out, but he was still standing, grinning bloodily at me. For some time, I had been fighting not to let a vhoon-craving more powerful than any I had ever known distract me from meeting V'ukh's attacks and searching out his weaknesses, but the more he bled, the more the animal part of me began rising, fogging my mind with violence. Not the precise violence of trained muscle-memory, but giving in to the urge to break and crush, tear and rend.

V'ukh had seen and smelled the fires that had started after his last attack on me. He now turned his sanguinary grin from me and rushed another torch-carrying onlooker, ripping the brand from his hands and tossing it onto another roof. It landed on a ladder, the wood of which was old and dry and caught immediately, spreading the flames across the wooden parts of the structure and down to the wooden furniture and straw pallets within.

"Your Wise Lord *loves* fire!" V'ukh mocked as he ran to another torch-holding bystander. "Let's see how well he loves the fire of Taru!" V'ukh punched the man's nose so deep into his brain that he spasmed and died even as his torch flew in a flaming arc of destruction to another home.

With that, the animal part of me took over. I saw V'ukh rush toward a group of onlookers standing along the far wall of the temple, which was part of the external wall of our settlement. It was three stories high, and any who were shoved from there would fall to their deaths. There were also two pitch-bright torches, one in a raised bracket on the floor, and one held aloft. I was thinking, *I must keep V'ukh from them*, but mostly, I wanted to rip out his throat and feel the vhoon spray out as I guzzled it down.

And then I was upon him.

He dodged a blow to the head that would have ended things immediately, leaning back so far he almost fell off the roof. His body came back like a spring, and I moved with a focus that made time stretch dreamily around me to avoid a blow that, with his momentum, would have snapped my neck and left me helpless for him to drain.

I caught him to me, and with my strength and his mass, we were almost a match. We grappled, doing as much damage to each other as we could while blocking the other from either getting in a good blow or getting away.

I saw my moment and grabbed his head, then lunged to lodge my teeth in his neck. I grazed him, but he ducked his chin hard, forcing my head away. Using all his force, he grabbed my waist and pulled my torso down to his meet the knee he brought up like a weapon, trying to crush more ribs and knock the wind out of me. I could not feel pain at this moment, and I pushed myself into his down-ward blow. Grabbing the opportunity he had given me when he lifted his leg, I brought my arm up and knocked him off-balance.

He went sprawling, into a group of people who had not moved far enough away, but I could not attend to them, for I scrambled after him on all fours like the animal I had become and pinned him down. He was bleeding from where my teeth had sliced, and I would let nothing stop me from getting down to the jugular.

I knelt on his legs, held his arms down. At that moment, the strength coursing through me was more ferocious than any I had ever known. My teeth sank into the bleeding wound, and I worried it open. I was probably growling.

I got several deep swigs of blood before his body arced as if shot through by an electric current. He threw me off him and bounded up, and I saw him throw his arms around a person—a flash of feminine curves under a brown and black patterned robe, a sudden catch of familiarity at my mind—and they both flew over the far edge of the temple, which was also the edge of the settlement, down to the bare ground. There was a crunching thud of bodies landing. In his frenzied rush, V'ukh had knocked even more people over the wall, but I did not hear the other plummeting bodies come to their resounding ends.

For once, I did not care about the lives of my people because my brain had finally processed what I had seen. I confirmed it by leaning over the edge and looking down into the dark outside our walls at the ground where V'ukh's body lay sprawled over another's—over the body of Frehnai, my lover, my companion—the woman who had taught me the true depths of love.

The burial customs of my people were evolving at that time. We followers of Asera-Masdheh would come to value sky burial as the holiest way of treating the fleshly remainders of our beloved ones, but at this time, we often did simple burial or even excarnation by hand. We separated the heads and kept them, lovingly decorating the skulls with paint, in our homes so that our ancestors might more easily guide us.

I could not do that. I did not want to use the old ways of dealing with the beloved forms of my son and my lover, but I was not ready to leave them for the birds to pick clean, either. I went a little mad in my pain and my loss.

The rest of that night I stayed by their bodies, keening

with grief. The rest of the community had to deal with the fires that ravaged our settlement without my help, nor did I give them any assistance with attending to the myriad wounded and dead. There were more dead than those who had been victims of our rooftop fight, for the followers of Kori'kan and Taru had rioted upon their leader's death, and few of the homes and public spaces of our community had escaped without significant damage.

But all that I would deal with later. When the sun rose that morning, I threw my tattered robes over my head and dragged the bodies of my beloveds to a cave near the settlement's walls that had been home to a pack of hyenas before a hunting party from our camp had dispatched them. In that shaded place, I sat with the loves of my life and I spoke to them, sang to them, prayed despairingly to the Wise Lord to return them to me.

Three nights and three days, I sat with Frehnai and V'ukh, mourning them. Time has never moved so painfully slow as it did in that cave. But the world would not wait for me; my family came, which meant the leadership of the temple came as well. They pleaded with me to give Frehnai and Vohun-ukhra—both beloved by more than just myself —proper burials. They implored me to come out and help the settlement rebuild from the destruction caused by the fires. I knew I was letting my people down, but the bodies of those I loved were on either side of me, and I could not, would not, leave them.

Part of my mind was still reasoning logically, a seabed buried leagues under an ocean of pure emotion. I knew I must attend to their bodies before decay started to set in.

Again and again I ran through options, rejecting them, and reconsidering, and rejecting again.

Finally, something as mundane and menial as appetite threw me out of my fugue-state. I had lost a great deal of vhoon fighting the final battle with my son. Now that he was dead, I could call him that again with only love for him in my heart. While the vhoon of his that I had tasted had been unexpectedly vitalizing, it was not enough for much-needed healing. At first, the slowness in the rebuilding of internal organs, bones, and muscle tissue felt like an outer manifestation of my tremendous pain and loss. I welcomed the pain, cherished it as a connection to my beloveds' deaths.

But the am'r appetite is not something that can be ignored. Kee can disregard their body's requests and starve themselves for a multiplicity of reasons, both good and bad, and apparently forget to do such basic things as drink enough water. But we am'r, our bodies will not let us ignore or neglect. If one does not take frangkhilaat consciously, one will be so overtaken that one will find oneself feeding *unconsciously*. That lesson is learned in the first frangkhilaat after the vistarascha. When one rises that first time, one is comprised entirely of ravenousness, and one's first meal, the fraheshteshnesh, rarely survives the encounter. But that is what I have experienced vicariously over the millennia with am'r made in what is now considered the usual, the *only* way for an am'r to be born into this world. But that is beside the point. At that moment in time, I had no concept of those things. I knew only that I must find an izchha. That it was time to heal, at least in body.

But I could not leave my beloveds just lying in a cave—a

rather less effective form of sky burial. My new incisiveness led me to the decision to keep them whole, not bring back the skulls to my home in the old way, but to let their bodies rest and return to the earth.

I left V'ukh in the cave and took Frehnai to a beautiful place, a high hill of cypress and cedar that looked down upon a natural spring, the very one that fed our community. Under the light of moon and stars, I buried her deep enough to keep scavengers from her body, that it might gently become one with the earth again. I wanted a being as wholly beautiful as she to be part of the beauty of the world forever and ever.

When I got back to the cave, I realized it was the perfect final resting place for V'ukh, a quiet place for his unquiet self to finally find respite and surcease. As he lay in peace at last, I filled the space with dirt and rocks to keep his body from being consumed by larger animals. I found a weighty stone, a boulder really, and with all my strength—at that weakened point, almost not enough—I moved it in front of the opening to protect him from disturbation for all time.

Those vital tasks complete, I could turn to first taking frangkhilaat, as I was now in a dangerous state of hunger, then returning to my community and helping them rebuild and move forward. With the threat of Taru and his followers now behind us, all were united and ready to embrace Asera-Masdheh and the new ways that would bring us prosperity and comfort in the changing world.

What, cinyaa? You seem unhappy with my story. What is it?

Oh. Why did Frehnai not have her vistarascha? That is

the deepest tragedy of all, one from which my heart shall never recover. As I told you, I had not figured out how to make an am'r-nafsh, had not realized that after a *third* exchange of blood, she would be safe from kee death. Although I had drunk her delectable vhoon many times, I had only given her my vhoon twice. She lacked that final intermingling of my am'r essence with her own to give her that gift.

Years later, when I learned the formula of the tripartite ritual, it sent me into such a fugue that I left the world, blocked myself into a tomb such as I had made for my son, and ripped my wrists open again and again until I lost so much vhoon that I sank into the *ahstha*, the coma-state. I did not die, but I rested there through many years until I was awoken the same way you helped wake me from another ahstha less than a year ago. But that is another story.

Yes, cinyaa, what *now* is wrong?

Ah. Yes, yes, it is now clear that my son Vohun-ukhra did *not* rest in his tomb for all time. I knew it the minute that I smelled his vhoon this night. I do not know his story. He has obviously managed to exist for all these millennia without my having the slightest knowledge of his existence, which prior to this, I would have told you with utter certainty was impossible. But now my certainty is shaken, for my son is alive, here in this house, and thus my world is turned upside-down. I feel I understand nothing anymore.

But this I do understand, at least. Kori'kan, which could easily contract to "Kurgan" over the stretch of so many years, is indeed our enemy. He is my enemy most of all, but also enemy to any whom I love, as he has always been. Why he hid all this time and why he reveals himself now? Well, it cannot be for good reasons. Be careful around him, cinyaa. Indeed, stay as far away from him as possible. For all that I felt much older than him back in our first life, by now, it is the same as twin brothers born minutes apart. Although the technically "older" brother could claim his status, they are the same age to those around them. The passage of time makes this just as true with us, which means he is as powerful as I. Indeed, I cannot guess how his powers have grown. I must assume they are as great as mine, with only minor variations.

No, cinyaa. No, I do not know what to do next, not precisely. I do want to hear from him what he wants from me; it has been a long time coming, after all. After that? Well, I guess I shall have to kill him *better* this time.

PART III

Ad Infinitum

"May we be those who renew this existence." — *Yasna 30.9*

CHAPTER ONE

About halfway through Bagamil's tale, Sandu returned. He lingered in the hallway for a while, although Bagamil and I sensed him there, and he knew it. Eventually, he slid through the partially open door and leaned against the wall. He didn't fully forgive his patar, but the story was too compelling not to empathize as it wound ever downward to its heartbreaking conclusion. As Bagamil spoke, his pain was as raw as when he'd first lived it, even after all these...millennia.

Millennia. I knew he'd lived a very long time, but it had never occurred to me that he'd been around on this planet since, like, humans were barely past being *cavepeople.* Before the Iron Age. Before the pretty much everything. He'd seen it all invented and then seen all those inventions become old news. He'd been around longer than most of the world's religions. How was he so stable, so *not insane*? How was he not bitter? How was he still excited about new things? Well, *normally* he was joyful and full of passion. Right now, his strangely youthful enthusiasm was lost under old wounds savaged open, and the weight of all those millennia weighed him down.

When my gharpatar stopped speaking, there was a long silence as Sandu and I tried to digest all we had heard. It was a *lot*. Bagamil just sat there, and I guessed he was processing having told others this story for the first time since 4,000-something BCE.

Sandu finally spoke. "I still wish you had wanted to share *everything* with me, patar. I also understand why you did not. You are right; I cannot understand that stretch of time. Five hundred years ago feels so long in the past now, and there is plenty I do not wish to remember or speak of from that time. From so much farther back...*da*, I understand why you wished to leave it buried when you thought it *was* buried.

"But what do we do now when your former son has had a whole new type of rising from the grave? Has anything truly changed in our plan? He is but one, and we are three."

Bagamil gave this thought. So did I. Sandu was right. No matter how powerful this Kurgan was, it was three-to-one. Even if his frithaputhra showed up, and we'd only heard about the one, it was still three-to-two. We'd taken on far worse odds.

"I must speak with him, of course." Bagamil knocked both of us out of our thoughts.

"*Da bineînțeles.*" Sandu was not bothered by this. "And after you have had your therapeutic chat, we kill him."

This was a rare moment, when remembering that Sandu was Dracula was *not* a bad thing. You could count on the man to be there for you when it was time for action.

It was nearing sunrise, and we could all feel it. Also, we

were all keeping our ears and noses open for Lord Ego. He had not told us how amazing and powerful he was for some hours, and that can't have been easy for him.

"Did you speak with him?" Bagamil asked Sandu.

"*Da*. He was waiting for me up on the hill behind the house. He tried to bend me to his way of thinking with words and mental influence, calling me cousin and implying he would value me as an ally against you. I left him thinking I was swayed by my own anger if not by his cajoling. He hates me too much to be effective at persuasion and he knows it, but he trusts the negative emotions well enough and feels we had a meeting of the minds in a shared revulsion for you. I could stand no more of him, so I told him I must consider further."

As if speaking of him had invoked him, we heard the front door creak in that ridiculous way but did not hear his light tread down the hallway. However, even my am'r-nafsh nose got a whiff of him as he pushed the warming room door open and the cooler air of the hallway rushed in.

Yes, now that I was looking for it, there was a commonality in scent with Bagamil's vhoon-anghyaa. Before this moment, I would have characterized it as "basic am'r vhoon." Then I thought, *Wait, is every am'r in existence a descendant of Bagamil?* That shook me up, but it had to be true. No wonder all the am'r were so damn worshipful of him. He was everybody's *daddy*, whether it was one generation back or hundreds of generations. Bagamil was the commonality in the scent of the am'r. He was our shared ancestor, no matter where in the world you came from, no matter who your kee parents had been.

Fuck. And I've been naively fucking him. Exchanging blood with him. Fuckity fuck.

I had gone into loving him without the slightest idea who or what he was. He'd just been Sandu's patar, just "Mister Sunshine" to me. I hadn't had have the least idea what Aojysht-of-aojyshtaish meant, and I hadn't bothered my pretty little head about it. I just jumped on his dick, opened my veins to his mouth, and opened my mouth to his blood.

All along, I'd been bothered by Sandu being this rock-star am'r. Dracula was *nothing*, not compared to Bagamil. I'd been fucking the am'r equivalent of humankind's oldest discovered ancestor. Casually cuddling the first am'r in existence. Probably farted in my sleep beside him. *Fuck.*

There was a torrent of panic threatening to shut down my brain by asking, "Why me? Why does he say he loves *me*?" I was going to have to swim in that ocean of self-doubt later since we still had Lord Ego to deal with.

Lord Ego. Who, since he hadn't stayed buried in his cave, was the *other* progenitor of the am'r species, the other oldest living—well, for some value of "living"—creature in the world.

And there he was in the doorway, directing a supercilious smirk at all of us: Bagamil and me on the loveseat and Sandu holding up the wall. "I see there has been much necessary communication in this little family. I would say I was sorry to bring discord, but I am proud to have brought the light of truth to the long-built-up shadows of lies. And now another light comes that cannot be ignored. I have rooms where you may rest for the day, whether you prefer to rest together or separately." He arced an eyebrow at this, and I wanted to cold-cock his arrogant, too-handsome face because he was certain he had come between us, destroyed our loving connection, and he was deeply pleased with himself about it.

"Yes, we must rest and continue to discuss matters," Bagamil replied. Only because I was trying to watch both their faces at the same time did I see the briefest of flickers through his eyes, exchanged with his frithaputhra.

"I, for one, would prefer some time to think about all of this *alone*," Sandu whined, hurt dripping from his words. If I hadn't just seen the look Bagamil had given him, I'd have freaked out, but now I just thought, *Don't overegg the pudding, you big drama queen*. Kurgan did not know Sandu well enough to understand that of all the emotions he never let people see, pain was the most carefully hidden.

"Come then, my cousin," Lord Ego urged Sandu with all the warm concern of the most gracious of hosts. "Let me take you up to your room first." Sandu stomped off behind him like a sullen teenager, making me want to giggle.

Bagamil leaned close to my ear and subvocalized, "We must let him believe he is successful at creating wedges between us." I nodded; I'd gotten that on my own. "Please act as if you are wounded and uncertain." That was not going to be difficult since I *was* uncertain. I would also have been as wounded as Sandu was except I'd barely known Bagamil two years, and I didn't expect to have learned all his dirtiest laundry in that time. He continued *sotto voce*, "But I do not want you alone. Ensure that you are with me or your patar at all times. I do not know what Kurgan might try to do with you, but considering his repeated mistreatment and abuse of my beloved Frehnai, I do not want to find out."

I shuddered. Me neither. Bagamil was going to speak again, but Lord Ego materialized in the doorway, and after having observed us sitting stiffly for a moment, put on his effusive host act again and led us up to a room on the upper floor. The rooms in this old house were tiny. Our room featured a huge old empty dresser and a bed that took up most of the room, but it would not have fit all three of us, even if we hadn't been playing that Sandu was too mad at Bagamil to want to be around him. There was a thick tapestry on one wall. Having been poorly cared for, the colors were muddy, and the edges were fraying. It had a squarish lump raised in the center. When I investigated, a small window was behind it, which would have let in barely enough light to bother us anyway. Still, I appreciated the am'r-ish decorating priorities.

When we climbed into it, we discovered the bed was made for very short people. My patar was not overly tall, but he had to lie on the diagonal to be able to straighten his legs, leaving me to curl up in the remaining triangle of bed.

Thank everything he was am'r and I am'r-nafsh. To a kee, this bed would have been too lumpy and miserable to allow any sleep. As it was, I wondered for a few minutes if I wouldn't be happier lying on the floor before I was pulled down into blessed unconsciousness.

Something in am'r blood knows when the sun sets. It's not a matter of light changing, because hopefully one is in a room where all light is blocked. It's not a big thing in vampire myths—I mean, being able to change into a fog or a bunch of bats is way more impressive—but it's one of the things the kee myths about vampires got right. The sun sets, and in the coffin, the vampire's eyes pop open, ready to do nefarious vampire-y things.

In our stupidly short, lumpy bed, my eyes opened, even though I was a half-vampire at best. As I turned my head, I saw Bagamil's beautiful almond eyes already open, watching me. They were a very dark brown, and from a distance, you couldn't see where his pupils left off and the irises began. If you were close, you could see how warm that dark brown was. If you were painting them, you'd use burnt umber, but that wouldn't capture them perfectly because they changed with all his moods. Now they were very warm and affectionate as he looked at me. I snuggled closer. This would probably be the last safe, relatively comfortable moment we had together before a deeply stressful period of unknown length.

We listened to the evening sounds of birdsong and the semi-regular baaing of sheep. I'd never been around sheep very much. They all seemed to think they were in immediate danger of slaughter. It was not the peaceful, bucolic background noise I'd imagined.

Speaking in the subvocal voice he used when trying not to be overheard by acute am'r ears, he said, "I love you, cinyaa. There are some things we must discuss before meeting the night."

"I love you, too. Do you think *he's* outside the door?"

"There is no way of knowing, short of going over and opening it. However, I strongly believe his resting place is not in one of the rooms of this house. He is under it, or more likely, under one of the outlying buildings. I think we have a few moments to speak before he will have roused himself, dressed for the day, and made his way over to listen at our door."

"OK. So, what's the plan?"

"Insofar as there is a plan, it is for you to let me have some alone time with *him* today. Stay with your patar. Do not let yourself be separated from him. And stay alert. At any point in this evening, we could go from the long-overdue father-son chat to finishing what I thought I'd completed millennia ago. And he is a powerful creature, even more so now. I will not underestimate him again. I may require Sandu's assistance and yours."

I knew he did not *need* the assistance of the youngest am'r-nafsh, barely trained in either weapons or hand-to-hand fighting, but I really appreciated him pretending I was a vital part of the death-and-destruction squad, so I kissed him. He kissed me back with passionate enthusiasm. I had to force my stupid brain not to take this moment to marvel about the ages of humankind that he had witnessed or consider how many others he had kissed or wonder if I rated in the top thousand. I simply enjoyed the feeling of his lips on mine, his skin against my skin, and knew he wanted to be nowhere else in this instant.

Actually, the skin-on-skin and his enjoyment of the moment became clear when his erection poked my hip. Am'r really *could* get horny anywhere, any time. I let myself giggle into his kiss, and he pulled his head back to smile ruefully at me. "This would be a most optimal moment for me to strengthen myself on your potent vhoon, cinyaa, and to take comfort in your exquisite body, but as I said, while we have some time, it is probably not very long. I do not doubt that if he found us *in flagrante delicto*, he would just walk in and pretend he had not heard for the purpose of ruining it for us. Possibly, he'd ask me to hand you over when I was done."

"I haven't known him long, but I feel like I've known him too long already. That sounds just like him."

"I don't believe I ever truly *knew* him, but from what he has shown me of his character, you can trust him to be scheming, vindictive, revengeful, and violent."

"Um. That's kind of every am'r I've met, more or less. Except you."

Bagamil snorted and squeezed me tighter. "That is a fair point, cinyaa, although your patar has mellowed out over the centuries. Most am'r do, or they end up rushing to meet their tokhmarenc. What sets Kurgan aside is how discreet he has been for all this time. That speaks to a depth of cunning that concerns me. If existing this long has taught me anything, it is that this is a very small world, and am'r have very big footprints. It should not have been possible for him to have hidden himself from me all this time. He has been calculating and cautious. This is not headlong violence, but something quietly Machiavellian. I cannot guess it, so it discomfits me. I must find out what his plans are and put an end to them by putting an end to him."

He paused, and I had a moment to consider how he in whose arms I snuggled was the *least* violent of the am'r but was with no doubt a stone-cold killer who would be considered a serial murderer in the kee world. One day I would come to terms with the fact that I had jumped into this world without a second look and that I would do the same thing again. There was still a tiny part of me that was dismayed by that—and, honestly, I associated that dismay with the "still kee" part of me and was holding onto it tight.

"I'm still confused that you never found any hint of him. Like, he must have made frithaputhraish—we know he has at least one, at present—and you obviously never noticed them. You have this amazing knowledge of vhoon-anghyaa and the most discerning of all am'r, um, noses. How did you never bump into any of his offspring? And since you must have, why did you not recognize them?"

"I am as bemused as you. All I can think is, not expecting him to still be in this world, and our vhoon being of such close connection, I must have met descendants of his over the millennia and simply thought they were descendants of *mine*. I do not take time with every am'r I meet to trace their ancestry back to me. I did that for some centuries. But after many thousands of years? Too many am'r have had their vistarascha, made any number of frithaputhraish, and then met their tokhmarenc, and I have never met them or heard their names. If I were to meet an am'r descended many times down from Kurgan, I cannot say that they would clearly *not* be of my vhoon-anghyaa, to my senses. But most especially, it was because I simply wasn't looking for it."

"Oh. That makes sense. I mean, as much as any of this makes sense."

"It does not make me feel very…masterful. I have gotten used to being the Aojysht-of-aojyshtaish. I have…hmm, there is a phrase I have heard: 'believed my own hype.' That describes it perfectly. Finding that V'ukh..." His voice ground roughly to a halt, and he took a few deep breaths before continuing. "Finding that I have mourned killing him for thousands upon thousands of years but that he is *not* dead. Finding that I made such a huge mistake, left it all unknowing, and wandered around this world thinking myself the eldest of the ancient, the most powerful of all? I feel disgust for myself, cinyaa. I feel more uncertain than I have since I became am'r. It is not a...*good* feeling."

A worse feeling was hearing him say *that*. I had come to depend on my gharpatar to be, well, the Platonic ideal of a grandfather: a warm, safe harbor in the storm, a fount of all the answers, someone who was strong when I was weak. Seeing the one I counted on for all that now crumbling with all-too-human self-doubt was threatening to move me into full-blown panic. "Gharpatar? Um, if this were me saying this to you, what would you tell me?"

Bagamil paused, then started to laugh. It started as a low chuckle and progressed through to a deep belly laugh. I didn't know why we were laughing, but seeing his face wrinkled up in mirth, hearing him gasp for breath before spasming with laughter again, well, I couldn't help but join in.

It was really effective stress relief.

Finally, Bagamil could speak again, although he wheezed a little at first. "Cinyaa! The student becomes the master! No, I do not joke, not at your expense. You were just right to appeal to my Socratic side. You know how to handle me, and that is good! No, do not pull away. I needed to be properly handled right then, and that was more effective than a slap to the face.

"*I* would have advised *you* to not let something like this shake your faith in yourself. It is, after all, the first such mistake I have made in, oh, about 6,500 years and I suppose I am allowed a great big mistake, say, every 5,000 years or so?" He paused for a few more spasms of hilarity. I wondered if a being so old could get *giddy*.

Since we were naked, I felt the small series of muscular contractions as he pulled himself together. Then he added soberly, "Thank you, Anushka, darling Noosh. I could have let Sandu see this, or you, but no one else in the world. I am lucky to have frithaputhraish I am so close to. As an am'r continues to exist, often they pull away from others. There will be times when one has suffered too much loss, too much betrayal, when too many memories are still too raw in one's heart, and one shuts down emotions altogether. I have seen it in many others. I have gone through it myself, centuries of it, where it's not even worthwhile to make a frithaputhra and you just get enough frangkhilaat to continue existing, as free from *feeling* as possible."

"I, uh, I don't know what to say. Honestly, I haven't even begun to handle how someone with your life experience could want, could love...*me*. I'm not even going to try to start processing what you just said there."

Bagamil abruptly deflated. "Oh, cinyaa. Your patar and I have obviously failed in our efforts to reconstruct your shockingly low self-esteem. I promise you *that* will be our first priority once this is over. We shall praise you and worship you as a goddess and give you so many orgasms that you forget you ever existed in a place of no praise and no joy.

"But we have taken long enough. If our enemy is

standing and listening outside the door, he is undoubtedly very confused, and I remember a time when 'Confusion to the enemy!' was a popular saying. So, let us take our accidental lead and run with it, yes?"

"I like 'Confusion to the enemy!' very much," I told him and kissed him on the way out of his arms and into my unwashed clothing and a very uncertain night to come.

Breakfast was not what I expected, not that I had any useful expectations. No one was lurking outside our door, of course. We wandered over to Sandu's room, which still had a nice strong scent trail to it. He had already left, so we followed our noses down to the ground floor, where other scents joined in, distracting ones that included a kee. *Not good.*

We made our way into the biggest room we'd so far found, a gorgeous old farm kitchen with an antique Aga-style stove taking up one wall and a substantial wooden table, a sturdy old plank affair that would have been a gorgeous antique if it had been properly cared for at any time in the previous century, centered in the space. Sitting on one side of that table was an unknown am'r who was immediately recognizable by vhoon-anghyaa as Kurgan's frithaputhra. Sitting on the other side of the table, drinking a cup of tea, was a kee woman. Well, girl. She was way too young to be sitting in this den of evil vampires wearing a short skirt and a clingy shirt, with caked-on makeup including shocking blue eyeliner and the thickest mascara application I'd ever seen. She looked defiantly at me and crossed a befishneted leg over the other to make sure that all the male attention came back her way. She couldn't place what kind of threat I was to her: either competition, or the kind of woman who would lecture her not to make bad decisions. Apparently, my librarian side was more obvious than I'd realized. Either way, she wanted me to leave her alone to make her bad decisions in peace.

Her blood smelled *delicious*. Fresh and rich with kee health. It would be refreshing and satisfying, a perfect way to energize myself for what was to come. I could almost taste it...

The memory of Brodie, now a decaying corpse in a cave at the bottom of the world, who would *maybe* be found by spelunkers someday, flashed across my mind and slammed into my heart. It made me feel sick.

Your first kee victim. Never forget his name, and maybe you won't end up being a crazy am'r Bad Guy who needs to be removed from the world for the betterment of all. Also, do everything in your fucking power to keep this girl from becoming a victim tonight.

"Make her some tea," Lord Ego's toady snapped at the Wee Strumpet.

"Ahl nut dyeu it!" she snapped back. But she got up and turned the electric kettle on.

Have I just seen the Ultimate British Thing? That even in a house maintained by undead beings who don't eat or drink, there's still a functioning setup for making tea?

Lord Ego's toady smiled a wide false smile at Bagamil and me. "Hullo! I'm Norvyn. Welcome to Croglin Grange. I have a Full English here for both of you."

I looked at the table. There was no spread of bacon,

sausage, eggs, beans, tomato, fried bread, etc., a breakfast I'd become addicted to from my first day in the UK. Norvyn was making jokes. Haha. Tea and a strumpet were what was on offer.

Wee Strumpet chose this moment to slam a mug of hot water with a teabag floating in it in front of me. "There's ney milk, so there's nowt else," she snarled.

I picked up the mug and cupped my hands around its heat, an automatic response. In the past as a kee, it would have given me something to do with my hands during an uncomfortable social situation. Now, in the am'r world, I had a sort-of-weapon in my hands, at least as long as the water was nice and hot.

"Thank you, Norvyn, but we are not hungry just now." My gharpatar was well-practiced with both social niceties and am'r sub-context. "Where is my frithaputhra, do you know?"

"Oh, him. He and the Lord of the Manor went for a walk. I expect they'll be a while. They have a lot to talk about." The toady gave us a perfect example of a sneer that implied we were fucked. "I'd have some breakfast to help pass the time."

"Again, my thanks, Norvyn, but no. We shall explore the house and its fine antiques. I believe there are some examples of fifteenth-century architecture? We'll leave you and your guest," he bowed to the Wee Strumpet, and she smiled delightedly at him, making her look even younger under the garish face paint, "to enjoy your evening."

I put down my mug. Bagamil took my elbow and escorted me from the kitchen.

We went down the hall as far as it led, and the final

door opened into a library. "Oh…" I moaned softly, taking in walls full of books, many as vintage as the furniture, some even more antique. "*Oh, look!*"

Bagamil shook me. "We do not have time for this, cinyaa!" That did not achieve the effect he desired, so he moved to stand in front of me, blocking my view with his sternest face. "I promise that once we deal with Kurgan and Norvyn, you can come back here and gather up all the books you want. We will take them with us, and you can cherish all of them. *But not now.*"

"OK," I muttered unhappily, trying to restrain myself from peeking around his imposing head.

"Norvyn will not leave us alone for long. When he arrives, I will dispatch him. Then we will look for Sandu. I would ask for some time alone with Kurgan, but do not go out of voice range, for I may need your help when the time comes to complete things." I knew yet again that *my* help was not what he really meant, but I didn't interrupt. "Then this will all be over, and we can get back to your *vacation.*" He smiled at me, and I loved him very much.

So, of course, the toady ruined the moment by slamming the door open. "You checking out the old books, eh? Not my thing, really. But young madam here had something she wanted to tell you." He shoved Wee Strumpet forward so that she fell into Bagamil's arms, which he automatically opened to catch her.

Out of the corner of my eye, I saw Norvyn, still moving forward with his entry momentum, stretch his arm out to my gharpatar. Bagamil responded almost as fast by shoving Wee Strumpet out of his arms and to the floor. She cried out in angry surprise.

It had been perfectly timed. Bagamil slammed Norvyn against a wall of books with a heavy *thump* and smashed a blow to the side of his head while his other forearm pressed into the toady's throat, lifting him off the ground by the neck. Since Norvyn was slightly taller than Bagamil, I thought this was pretty impressive...except that valuable books were getting damaged by the pressure. Norvyn wasn't fighting, just trying to pull away from the tautly-muscled forearm that was crushing his trachea and larynx.

Things were moving fast, but the moment froze when I noticed the syringe sticking out of my gharpatar's neck, right where it met the shoulder. A syringe with the plunger all the way depressed. A translucent layer of blood was left along the path of the plunger. *Fuckity fuck fuck fuck! What fresh hell is this?*

"Bagamil!" I started to warn him, but then a change came over him that I knew far too well. His eyes began to glaze over. "No!" I screamed as he sank down, fighting the drug rushing through his system. Maadak, the one thing that could take down the oldest and strongest am'r. A proven kryptonite, since that was how my gharpatar had been abducted and held captive before. *Goddammit, not a-fucking-gain.*

We all watched him slide bonelessly down onto the threadbare antique Persian rug. Then the Toady-boy turned to me, grinning. "M'Lord would like to speak with you now."

Of-fucking-course.

The Wee Strumpet chose this moment to communicate her confusion and disappointment. The evening had not gone to her plans, which had probably involved intimate intercourse with one or more partners, a decent meal, and maybe some financial incentives since she was a busy young lady whose time was valuable. She'd gotten none of those things. She'd had only an inferior cuppa, nobody was paying attention to her, she was most decidedly *not* having any fun, and it was *not* OK. This she explained to us in strident Cumbrian dialect, and while Toady-boy might have understood her words, I only got the gist. I was fine with that.

She had lurched up from the floor as she increased in volume and verbal momentum. I have to say that in full flow, she was damn impressive. Norvyn and I watched her for some moments in sheer appreciation. Then he backhanded her across the room. As she slumped to the floor again, I was dismayed by how much I also appreciated the sudden silence. On the other hand, if she was unconscious for a while, it meant I didn't have to worry about trying to save her insolent kee ass while also figuring out how to survive my current crisis.

Toady-boy turned to me. "Right. Shall we go?" I nodded. What else was I supposed to do? We left two bodies slumped on the library floor like an ambitious game of Clue.

This was really not how I wanted this evening to turn out. I liked Plan A so much better. And this makes no sense! Why did they knock Bagamil out? What is their plan? What other five thousand things don't I know that I need to know?

I followed him down the depressing hallway and through the arched doorways. We went past the farm buildings and up the hill to where I guessed Lord Ego had spent the previous evening admiring the stars and having a short, unsatisfactory discussion with my patar. Well, he was continuing that dialogue with Sandu now, and I was, not of my own free will, going to join this terribly important conversation as well, so he was getting his heart's desire for attention.

Maybe I'll find out what the hell this has all been about, which is definitely a bucket list item. Although since dying isn't off the table tonight, maybe I shouldn't be joking about that, even in my own head.

I could smell that Sandu had come this way, and Kurgan, and his Toady-boy. At least it was only the three scents, not some army of Kurgan toadies, waiting to overwhelm us.

There were trees on the way up the hill that blocked the moon and starlight, but at the top, it was open to the sky. The stars were very pretty and bright so far from any light pollution, but my eyes were all for the solitary Byronesque figure who waited for me.

Solitary. As in, Kurgan waited for me alone, no Sandu in sight.

I'm in so much trouble.

CHAPTER TWO

"Please, little cousin, sit down and talk with me."

I let myself drop to the grass of the hilltop, but I was not relaxing. "Where's Sandu?"

"Wladislaus? He is...resting."

"He rested all day. *Where is he?*"

"He has been taken back into the house. He is *sleeping*, as is your gharpatar."

"What? *Why?* Why have you gone through all of this... this fucking kabuki?"

"To get you alone, sweet cousin."

"Huh. You've shoved the oldest am'r and Vlad Dracula out of the way to get to *me*? I'm sorry, but I'm not buying that. I'm not even fully am'r yet. I'm *nobody*."

"Cinyaa, do not say that! You carry—"

"*Do not call me 'cinyaa!'*" My voice was shrill with sudden anger. How *dare* he call me by Bagamil's love name for me?

"It is but a term of endearment from back in my earliest

days. However, if you do not care for it, I shall call you...*myshka*, then."

"My name is Anushka." I didn't even like my name, but I liked him calling me by a nickname far less.

"Myshka will be my pet name for you. It means "mouseling" in Russian, my adopted tongue. As I was saying, you carry the vhoon-anghyaa of one of the eldest am'r—do not forget I am the same age!—and the blood of Wladislaus Drăculea, which is *not* very significant in itself but deepens that immediate bloodline. And from other am'r of your patar's vhoon-anghyaa, as well. You also have the vhoon-anghyaa of the Abbot Neplach, and very precious indeed, the aojysht Astryiah. You have more disparate vhoon shaping your development as an am'r than any I have heard of in my long years of life. You have the possibility to be something new, something uniquely powerful. I want you at my side, learning from my experience, being shaped by my teaching, being made even more powerful by my vhoon. I know I have more to offer you than the insipid, played-out *proigravshiy* who claims he is the Aojysht-of-aojyshtaish when he has never fathomed that for all these years, I have existed alongside him, the greatest threat to his existence. He is *pathetic*."

I did have a lot of questions for Kurgan...or Croglin, whatever he wanted to call himself, and in my experience among the am'r, the bad guys often ended up giving me more useful information than my patar or gharpatar ever did. I wasn't buying what he was selling, but I couldn't help but be curious about what he was up to. So far, every baddie I'd ever met had loved talking about his evil plans, monologuing being a trope from books and films that I had validated by my personal experience. Since Sandu and Bagamil would be out for hours with that maadak in their systems, there was no reason not to let Lord Ego work through his smarmy sales pitch for changing allegiances. It wasn't like I hadn't heard it before, although at least the last bad guy who'd captured me had paid me the compliment of assuming I'd stay loyal to my beloveds.

Never thought I'd have anything nice to say about Julio Popper, AKA "Señor Super-Colonizer." If you live long enough to learn, you hit some real surprises along the way.

"Kurgan? Is that what I should call you?"

"It is my name by now as well as any."

"Well, I do have many questions for you—"

"I am delighted, little cousin. I will answer them all."

Well, then don't interrupt me while I'm trying to ask, Lord Ego, I thought, but I kept my face wide-eyed and curious. "I hardly know where to start! Um, how do you know so much about me?"

"It is not hard to get any information at all from your patar's stronghold. Not all his frithaputhraish are as loyal to him as he assumes, and your gharpatar has no security. He presumed he did not need any, the fool.

"I have been aware of you since before you arrived in Romania. I have followed you, seen how poorly they have cared for you. I was on the periphery the whole time. You were always safe; you always had a safety net. If they had not been able to catch you, nor you rescue yourself—as you have done all along, my brave little cousin—then I would have stepped in to save you."

I saw red. "I-I nearly *died* in Julio's caves. And Mehmet...his Bat Bitch nearly killed me herself, and then if Sandu hadn't—if Dragoş hadn't—*flamethrower!*"

I was tripping over my words. He had taken me from "not delighted with the situation" to "ready to rip out his eyeballs" faster than Sandu's cherished little supercar could go from zero to sixty.

"Peace, myshka. Firstly, you cannot die; only the little mortal encumbrances will fall away. But it was I who convinced Mehmet he was jinn—this was not difficult; he was quite mad—and sent him on his path. Once he had completed his goals, I would have removed him and reeducated his followers.

"And the dreadful little Popper and the ludicrous Orélie-Antoine de Tounens were even easier puppets to control. None of them would ever have truly harmed you. And I would not have let you go through the vistarascha without my vhoon-anghyaa improving you first."

I tried to process that, but I couldn't. I was frozen in thought and deed. Lord Ego had taken me to a place of such wrath that I was like a crashed computer. But as I sat there with my own personal blue-screen-of-death happening in my brain, I realized it was more than that. It was his *vhoon*.

Normally, with am'r and their vhoon-anghyaa, it was like back when I'd been a normal living person. If someone I was around had body odor or were wearing perfume, I'd really notice it at first, but after a while, I didn't think about it anymore. Now, when I caught a whiff of a kee, the intensity of the olfactory input was so strong that it was hard for me to think of anything else, but when I stayed in their company for a while, my focus could go back to my old senses, so that I was vision-dominant again.

But with Kurgan, the similarity to Bagamil kept catching my attention and teasing my brain with the minute differences. It kept distracting me when I needed to be paying one hundred percent attention to the unapologetic killer at my side.

Kurgan seemed to have sensed none of this and was happily rolling along with his infuriating words.

"So you see, you have been in safe hands—my hands—this whole while. But that also means, little cousin, that all you have credited your patar and gharpatar for, now you must acknowledge was *my* loving influence and protection. It might be hard, I understand, to make such a radical shift in your thinking, but it is vital that you recognize and accept the truth. I am your *true* patar. Share vhoon-vayon with me and finalize a process that began back in your library in Centerville and has led you here to this moment."

There were still too many emotions to process, including some I really didn't want to examine, so I stuck with top-level annoyance. "Um. Why weren't you *there*, then?"

"I just said I was. That I have been there at every step."

"No. Why was it Sandu who showed up, then? Why wasn't it you?"

"I was not ready for He Who You Call Bagamil to be aware of me yet. It did not suit my plans."

"So, us kicking Mehmet's ass and us kicking Julio's and Orélie's asses. That was all part of *your* plan?"

"My planning is always fluid. That is a lesson I have learned in the millennia I have existed on this Earth. But they have all been my puppets: Fatih Sultan Mehmet, Popper, de Tounens, Drăculea, and even Vohuni-sura, the man who claims to be my father. I have been behind all their choices, their actions, without their even knowing it.

"And all that you have gone through has made you the singular am'r-nafsh you are today, bursting with unimagined potential. If I had just swept you up from your little library, those experiences, the unique combination of vhoon- anghyaa that rushes through your veins? Well, I could have tried to *force* the same outcome, but often a light hand on the reins yields better results. This, too, I have learned over my long span of years. Just because you did not know it was *me*, however, does not lessen my impact upon your life."

We sat for a moment. I think Lord Ego was assuming I was adjusting to my new reality. I was actually trying to come to terms with the breadth of his arrogance. I was also trying not to breathe from of my nose. His scent was becoming intoxicating to me, the way my am'r-nafsh perfume was supposed to do to full am'r. He didn't seem overwhelmed by me, though. Having his scent overwhelm me, instead, was making me even more confused than his words.

Think about something other than his smell, dammit. Where was I? OK, when am'r went bad, some level of crazy was not optional. Well, that made sense. With longer lifespans and greater strength and influence, the chance of fully realizing one's potential madness was much more feasible.

There was only so insane a kee could get before the law or an enemy took them down, but with care, an am'r could sit back and let those various psychoses grow and flourish for centuries and centuries.

The main risk to ending all that crazy was to commit adharmhem, the one real, punishable crime among the am'r. Risk the mass of kee finding out about the lesser numbers of am'r in their midst, and a bunch of am'r would hunt you down and make sure that fuckery was put to a sudden and very final conclusion. It was one of the vanishingly rare ways you could get any number of am'r to agree on anything and then work together, to boot.

In that way, I had to admit, Kurgan *had* been the mastermind he claimed he was. He had made it all this time without getting himself on that kind of am'r radar. Whatever nefarious shit he'd done down the years, it had never led to other am'r getting out their pitchforks and torches for him.

That scared me. It implied a competent, functional insanity. I had been an all-too-close observer of the batshit-crazy bad guys almost winning twice now in my short span of time with the am'r. If Kurgan was able to keep his shit together and his ego in check, my beloveds and I were real trouble.

Ask more questions. If you keep him talking, you'll find out his weakness. Hold to that. And remember to breathe through your mouth...

"So, you talk about the long life that has filled you with knowledge, but I don't know anything about that. Would you tell me, how have you kept yourself hidden from

Bagamil? What have you been doing since he left you in a cave, thinking you dead?"

Delight transformed his face, his already disturbingly beautiful face. When I'd looked at him up until this moment, I could tell that he was related to Bagamil only in that they were obviously from the same ethnic heritage. Other than that, they did not look as closely related as they were. I could only guess that the long lives of am'r allowed one's personality to be stamped more strongly in one's visage, even if it were not done by the laugh and frown lines of the kee. Perhaps happiness had not been as common an emotion for Kurgan as it was for my gharpatar, who embodied joy every day despite everything the world threw at him. Whatever the reason, when Kurgan felt true pleasure, he looked as close as a brother, as a *son*, to my beloved gharpatar. I had to harden my heart and remind myself that he was the entirely-fucked-up Lord Ego and right now, Sandu and Bagamil were in maadak-comas because of him, experiencing the pain and nightmares of that drug's terrible influence.

"I am so pleased you are wise enough to accept me without a fight. Oh, I know you have not entirely thrown in your lot with me yet. I would be foolish to think you'd abruptly end your former loyalties, and *you* would foolish to think you could trick me with too easy an acquiescence. I observed how you played Mehmet, after all. But I have also seen you stand up to strong am'r when they had you and the ones you love in their power. I am pleased you are being sensible, and I have no doubts that the more I instruct you, the more I will become your obvious choice."

Fuck. His warning came as a nasty shock. He really had

been around, somehow, hiding in the shadows or something, spying on me. I really could not take it for granted that I could fool Lord Ego by catering to his...ego. He knew—and *how* he knew was a very frustrating problem—my playbook for dealing with baddies, so now I not only had the disadvantages of being millennia younger and weaker and merely am'r-nafsh, but also of my enemy knowing me while I did not know him. It was a profoundly bad position.

You can fix one of those factors by letting him talk. That's all you can do right now. Stop worrying and get him to tell you things that might benefit you. The part of me that was always and forever a librarian and archivist added, *And take good mental notes! There is only one other being in the world who can tell a story from this perspective. Hopefully, you'll get to write down Kurgan's story from memory after he is safely given the tokhmarenc. And stop sneaking huffs through your nose, dammit. That isn't helping!*

Lord Ego took a deep breath and started. "You partially know my story from Vohuni-sura's point of view. It is very wrong on many details, but I will not waste our time now by correcting them. Later, I will tell it all to you as the winner who finally gets to write my history with clarity and truth.

"But for now... I woke up in darkness. This was, of course, not a problem for one with the eyes of an am'r, even though my night vision was far less acute then than it is now. Now, you cannot even imagine the distances I can see, the vibrancy of color in ranges your hardly-better-than-kee eyes cannot perceive, the fine detail I can distinguish in the darkest of shadows. But at that moment, any sight was good enough. Eventually, my confused memory brought back to me the firelit fight on the rooftops of the community I had once called my home, and I remembered the final betrayal of the man who styled himself my father. Well, I swore it was his *final* betrayal, and I have kept that vow, as you shall see.

"I dug myself out of the packed-in dirt and rocks and rolled away the boulder that blocked me into what *he* thought was my grave, where he would have constrained me to lie in for all eternity and rot as any kee, all maggots and decay.

"I discovered to my dismay that my ability to stand the light of day had decreased during my rest. I had also come to realize in my time of digging to my rebirth that my hunger was greater than it had ever been before. It was, as I know you can understand from your own experience, not an optimal combination.

"My uncontrollable appetite forced me out into the blinding light of the sun, although I was later to realize it was late afternoon, already shading its way into evening. I was confused and disoriented, and instead of making my way to the closest kee habitation and vhoon-source—my own home—I headed the wrong way, out into the wilderness.

"It was, however, the best thing I could have done, for to return home to feed my hunger would have alerted Vohuni-sura to my unexpected vistarascha—I was the first am'r to experience this, after all—and he would have had the chance to give me the tokhmarenc he had so desired me, his disappointing son, to undergo.

"Instead, I got to experience the first-ever fraheshteshnesh when I came across two men bringing trade goods to the settlement. I drained them both fully and was barely satisfied, but they left me their camels and their possessions, and that made it easier for me to travel to another settlement. None were very near each other back in those days, being built around accidents of geography such as natural springs or riverways, defensive hills, or other conveniences. There I could sell the rare pigments they had carried for a good price in trade items. Having done that, I had a place to stay while I found izchhaish to satisfy my needs more sustainably. There, I could plan.

"I knew I must never let my so-called father discover that I still shared the Earth with him. Away from my former home, I built up a trading business with the goods that fortuitously came with my first meal as a true am'r.

"The man you have called gharpatar is not *truly* am'r, you see, not by the definition that began with me. Or which began with his first frithaputhra, if one did not know of my existence, which he, the fool, did not. Vohunisura has never gone through the vistarascha, never awoken to the pangs of the fraheshteshnesh. The frithaputhraish he has populated the world with, they all go through that process to become am'r in truth. But *he* is still technically kee. *I* am the first true am'r, the earliest to experience the vistarascha—as the result of filicide."

I didn't know what to do with that. It was all so long ago, and Bagamil had been making am'r for thousands of years since, so, I mean, what did it matter if the original am'r hadn't had to go through the same process as everyone else? Originals seldom went through the process they innovated, after all. I didn't know why Lord Ego was being insistent about this, but it seemed important to him. I needed to pay attention.

I realized I'd forgotten not to smell him, and that, as I'd been drawn into his tale, I'd begun breathing in slow, deep breaths, savoring the fragrance of his blood as it rushed under his sexy olive skin. It made it easy to see things from his point of view. I panicked and tried changing mid-breath from breathing through my nose to my mouth. I ended up coughing and dying of embarrassment. I finally got control of myself and made a sound that indicated that, really, I was paying attention and I wanted to hear more, and it was true. This was all fascinating. *He* was fascinating. I reminded myself that it would be nice just to be able to listen to it and not have my fate and the fate of my beloveds be hanging on it. Then I could be fascinated with the story and not the man.

"As a trader, I had the perfect lifestyle for moving farther and farther away from my enemy. I needed to ensure that news of me did not make its way back to him, so I let that, and wanderlust, pull me to the settlements to the east and north. I did not hurry, but as the years passed, I made the crossing of the Caucasus mountains and was up in what they now call the Western Steppe.

"I knew immediately I had made the right choice. The first people I met were in the process of becoming what you now call the Hurrians. They were the people of Taru, although they called him Teshub, the very god I had chosen over the megalomanic Asera-Masdheh. Their ways made sense to me, and as I traveled from settlement to settlement, I felt myself growing, my knowledge expanding outward to a wider understanding than I could ever have imagined in my previous confined life. I was free of the stifling shadow of Vohuni-sura and his cult. I was finally a man free to become more than just a subservient priestling, an eternal follower of rules imposed upon me. Now, I could *make* the rules for my life.

"Not that I needed many. I did what I wanted when I wanted. I traded honestly when the mood took me, or if I did not like the deal, I would take the other trader's goods and life. I grew richer and richer, but no lawless men were any threat to me because I was stronger and faster than all of them. I look back upon that time of travel and growth as one of the best and happiest of my long life.

"Once I passed the Caspian Sea, I found myself in the true steppeland. There ceased being settlements as I knew them, places where people lived the whole year round. It was among the hunter-gatherers that I really *knew* belonging. Their gods had foreign names and the people prayed to them in tongues very different from the one I'd grown up speaking, but the gods were just versions of Taru and his pantheon, and those tongues I could learn. And there were none who did not want to trade for rare foreign pigments, so I was welcomed with open arms.

"I spent what you would call the Bronze Age on the steppe. Sometimes I settled with one tribe and worked my way up to ruling them, spending decades caring for them as I would my own family. Indeed, they took the place of family for me. I organized marriages and chose which tribes we allied with and which we slaughtered.

"But I was always an am'r alone amongst the kee, although I did not have that name for myself, or them. I was to first hear those terms, words barely altered from my milk tongue, only many thousands of years later. Time moved more slowly in those days, and the frithaputhraish of Vohuni-sura did not spread so far east for a long time. They stayed in what they thought of as 'civilization' and husbanded the kee as they taught them to husband livestock.

"I did not figure out how to make my own frithaputhraish for quite some time. I was happy to use my tribes to provide me izchhaish, and a few of them I grew connected with and cherished for the short spans of their lives.

"It was the brevity of those relations that finally led me to independently invent the patar-frithaputhraish relationship. It took many decades of experimentation, for how could one guess that the vhoon-bond must be exchanged thrice for the transformation to take hold. I only knew that I had risen from the dead, and I was certain there was some way that I could give that gift to my own favorites. I had the memory, you see, that the last time I drank from Vohuni-sura's *suka*, her vhoon was different somehow. It smelled and tasted of a strange mix of his vhoon *and* hers. That stayed with me, always in the back of my mind.

"Many of my izchhaish died their kee deaths before I figured out the precise ritual, the magic number. And there was one aspect I had not considered, living as I did in such a kee world. Vhoon-anghyaa. It had simply never occurred to me that my bloodline could give away the fact of my existence to my enemy. Once I found the way to create frithaputhraish, I began to do so in all innocence, increasing those who would finally be able to live on, serving me down the long years.

"It was a great shock to me the first time an am'r of Vohuni-sura's make arrived in my world—in the Iron Age, that was. I had by then moved even further along the steppe, through the lands of the Scythians and among the Turkic peoples near the Altai Mountains.

"You would be surprised how much travel the kee did in this time. In years to come, Vikings would visit me in my lands, having traveled unbelievable distances for such fragile creatures. Already I had met people from places you now call China, Mongolia, Siberia. This was in the days when travel was by foot or camel or horse. There was travel by boat as well, the best way to go long distances, yet far more perilous.

"Eventually, one of Vohuni-sura's vhoon-anghyaa explored the world far enough to end up in my lands— indeed, in my tent—brought as an exotic guest by my men. Nekdel was his name, the first time I had heard a name from my childhood in so very long. My people saw him more as a prisoner, and he was going along with it in amusement, as he felt he was the most powerful being for many thousands of kilometers.

"And then he smelled me, and I smelled him, and everything changed. I immediately knew the threat. He did not; he assumed I was just another frithaputhra down from Vohuni-sura. Ha! This maddened me, but I did not let him see that. I plied Nekdel with the strong vhoon of my tribe, for those who breathe the air of the steppe and drink the milk and blood of our horses have the most powerful vhoon of all the kee. While dodging his questions, I had no trouble getting him to answer mine.

"I found out much about the world outside the steppe

then, which I had for so long preferred to forget. And I found out how busy my supposed father had been. He had a been a father indeed, to a whole race of what he called 'amar' or 'immortal,' which has condensed over the centuries down to 'am'r.'

"As Nekdel babbled happily to one he assumed was a friend and brother, I made my plans. I had a few fritha-puthraish by this time, not as many as the shameless Vohuni-sura, but I now realized I had to protect them and protect myself. I sent messages to them—they were with different tribes under my control, khans under me—and they came in a rush to join what Nekdel had been told was to be a grand feast.

"In the end, there *was* a grand feast, but it was Nekdel who was the meal. He was a young am'r, only perhaps one hundred years old. Between my strength and the superior numbers of my frithaputhraish, he was easily enough subdued. I found that breaking his limbs and not letting them set correctly kept him from being any further threat. I wanted his vhoon-anghyaa to be in all of my frithaputhraish, so they drank from him multiple times over the weeks we were able to keep him alive and producing vhoon. After they had taken his vhoon into their bodies, their vhoon-anghyaa did change, the scent less obviously mine. The more they drank, the more Nekdel's influence was apparent. I encouraged them to drain him almost-dry over and over. One day, he sank into a deep coma, and his body stopped producing any vhoon. It was the first time I saw the ahstha, and I did not know Nekdel could be roused from it. I am not sure it would have been worth the effort, in any case. Therefore, we burned his body, and I was well-pleased with the results."

"So, that's how you covered up your frithaputhraish? With vhoon from other am'r?"

"Precisely, myshka. I had invented the concept of the bakheb-vhoonho, although this was less about receiving power from the blood-giver and more about transforming the vhoon-spoor." Lord Ego looked smugly pleased, and I wasn't sure if it was for me for being so quick-witted or him for having been so wise as to choose me as his, well, whatever he wanted me for. Knowing am'r, it would mean I would have to vhoon-share with him, and since am'r don't really like blood without sex, the latter almost certainly wasn't optional.

I realized with a nasty shock that part of my brain was pondering what sex with Kurgan would be like, what he looked like without his clothing, what it would be like to have that delicious aroma all around me as his long hair curtained my face just like Bagamil's. *Oh. Ugh. Who is currently drugged into a nightmarish coma by this monster, remember? Stick to the history lesson.*

Happily, Lord Ego was always pleased to hear the sound of his own voice. "Over the centuries, I built a balance to Vohuni-sura and his am'r with my own loyal frithaputhraish."

This struck me as *just wrong*. Bagamil—was he being called Mazdak by the lovely priestess Nahid at this time?—was not trying to build up an army of loyal subordinates. For the main reason that that really wasn't his style, but secondarily because he had not the slightest idea that an opposing army was being established against him. Bagamil was simply leaving behind a scattering of lovers, who themselves left an increasing stream of am'r created in love and lust. There was no big strategy, just the sort of organic growth you'd expect of a species, if a very strange one. Could you even consider the am'r *organic*? I still wasn't sure how alive the am'r were, but this was not the time to interrupt. I could spend as long as I liked thinking about all the ways Kurgan was wrong later, when he was safely dead. Now I needed to listen. to help me find some way to get him to that nice dead place.

"I built our numbers, carefully choosing the finest women and men to serve me. It took so long for another of Vohuni-sura's am'r to return our way, for the people of the steppe were seen as violent barbarians, and why would anyone want to venture into their lands? Violent, I will accede, for the wildest vhoon flowed through our hearts, kee and am'r alike. But 'barbarians,' I will not allow. But the intricacies of the many cultures of the widespread steppe are more suited to poetry than to dry recital.

"Finally, I had to send a frithaputhra who had the late Nekdel's vhoon-anghyaa in her to lure more of his am'r back to our lands. We needed their vhoon for the camou-flage it lent my frithaputhraish. My own vhoon-anghyaa was not so distinct from Vohuni-sura, and thus this plan worked perfectly from the start and has for all these years. As my frithaputhraish branched out with their own fritha-puthraish, it was no longer even needed, and they were simply assumed to be of Vohuni-sura's line because no one not of my make even knew that there was a second lineage of am'r."

I had to interrupt. "But what about the fact that the

more people who know a secret, the less chance there is of it staying a secret? Are you saying that no one babbled the truth in all these millennia?"

Kurgan had somehow, without any obvious move-ments, had been getting closer and closer to me as he regaled me with his glorious backstory. When I had been in his presence earlier, he hadn't done that highly offensive conspicuous-sniffing thing some am'r do around me, but he was definitely crowding my personal space now. He was holding eye contact with me, and at the same time, he was allowing himself to be seen to visibly breathe through his nose. It was, strangely, one of the less offensive ways an am'r could deliberately indicate they were checking me out. I wasn't expecting any sort of social delicacy from Kurgan, and the surprise of it kept me from moving away fast enough to avoid his touch, although he reached out slowly, letting my eyes track his movements. He was giving me time to pull away, but quite stupidly, I did not. There was a part of my brain screaming, *Get the fuck away, you idiot!* But it seemed far away or muffled by something.

His fingers stretched out the last inches and stroked the back of my hand. I felt that touch between my legs.

I finally managed to snatch back my hand and tried to be subtle about scootching my ass a few inches away, but it was a wasted effort. I had let him touch me, and now I wasn't running screaming. This was all handing over power to him, and I knew it. I didn't know what to do about it, however. And then he was talking again, and, oh, I was supposed to be listening to him to find his weaknesses, right. *Right?*

"Ah, but I realize you are not used to my methods,

myshka. Among the am'r of Vohuni-sura's vhoon-anghyaa, there is no methodology, no plan. His am'r are born much as the kee are, purposeless accidents of lust.

"But my frithaputhraish were all chosen by me for loyalty and obedience. None of my vhoon-anghyaa may make an am'r-nafsh without getting my direct approval, and then they are taught to protect the secret of our hidden line with their lives. There is nothing random, nothing left to chance. And the few who have not handled the transition to am'r well—as you might remember Mehmet and his madness—are swiftly given their tokhmarenc before they can cause my line any adharmhem."

My first feeling on hearing all this was a sense of profound dubiousness. All the am'r I had known were as contrary as cats and just as easy to herd, but maybe if you had a selective, um, breeding program for am'r, you could make them docile and compliant. *Ugh.* A vision of lined-up, blank-eyed am'r soldiers, all programmed to follow Lord Ego's orders, made me shudder in real alarm. *I must find out how much of what he is saying is shit I have to worry about and how much is bad-guy-delusions-of-grandeur.*

"I'm still curious how you kept yourself secret, even if all your am'r had perfect discipline. How did you manage not to bump into Bagamil by accident in all that time?"

"An excellent question, my wise little cousin!" he exclaimed. A rush of anger at his talking down to me freed my mind of lust for a moment. I tried to keep my conflicting emotions off my face. "In part, it was good planning. I tracked him constantly and always had am'r near him. I was at all times prepared to leave my stronghold if he arrived in my city. But here is the sheer comedic luck; he never came my way. I stayed in the country that became Russia—then the Soviet Union, and then Russia again—for most of my years. It was a more than big enough land for me to have all the space I needed; thus my longevity did not arouse kee curiosity. And the systems of rule, which I can modestly say I've had some influence upon, have more than once also created conditions very useful for an am'r. Unlike those of *Bagamil's* get," he said "Bagamil" like it tasted especially bad in his mouth, "I've never needed to go and hide from the kee. I became accustomed to being surrounded by them, and I do best with regular amounts of frangkhilaat. And since I do not make am'r-nafsh for love, the thought of holing up with just one person and being stuck sharing vhoon-vayon with them alone is in no way attractive to me. I can get the benefits of their vhoon as often as I like and still have a city of kee at my disposal. Indeed, I can have as many am'r-nafsh as I can stand around me, educating them while they feed me."

He'd gotten even closer to me without having seemed to move. Part of me was looking for an excuse not to move away, but I was *not* shocked and frozen as I'd been before. Kurgan was entirely consistent in his attitudes toward the world around him. As he worked through his history, it was the same story cycling around and around, just different details.

So why am I not moving away? Lord Ego's complete inability to have emotional connection should have been the ultimate flashing red light. I mean, it all fit with the story Bagamil had told me about V'ukh and how he'd used Frehnai but obviously never loved her. Indeed, he'd killed the woman who had loved him both as a child and as an adult. But once he'd gotten out from under the hated shadow of Bagamil, how had he managed to live thousands and thousands of years and not have a meaningful relationship with even one person?

Do you think he'll have his first real bond with you? You're not that kind of girl! Get up! Move!

I used pacing as an excuse to force my unwilling body up and away from him. Movement helped me think. The grassy hillside had been a soft seat, but I realized belatedly how soggy the ground had been since the fabric of my trousers was now clinging damply to my ass. It was icky and uncomfortable, but I didn't want to be tugging fabric off my butt in front of him. It was moments like these where I wished I were in a book or a film where this sort of thing never happened. Reality was being stuck talking to a terrifying vampire with damp fabric clinging uncomfortably to your ass, and it was *completely unfair.*

"What have I said to perturb you, myshka?" he asked, patting the ground beside him, trying to look inviting. Honestly, dealing with Mad Mehmet had been easier; I'd only had to flatter his vanity, and I could lay it on pretty thick without him noticing. Lord Ego was sane, although it was a cold, calculating "sanity" like none I'd ever experienced in my life. I was stuck between Scylla and Charybdis. I couldn't let him see my complete distrust of him because he might give up on trying to persuade me, and just kill me—or worse. I'd seen Mehmet demonstrate the worse, and I really didn't want to go out like that. On the other hand, not only did I not want to admit my attraction either to myself or him, but he had already warned me that if I seemed to be too easily persuaded to join Team Kurgan, he wouldn't believe it. *How do I get myself into these situations?*

"It's just...a lot of information to process," I told him; I could say that with pure honesty in my voice. "So, my pat... Baga...Vohuni-sura, he never went to...to where? Moscow?"

"That is the main of my cities, *da*."

"How did you get this whole Croglin thing going on, then?" I gestured around and at the hulking black-on-black shadow that was the rambling house below us.

"Ah, another perceptive question. I love your quick mind."

You don't love anything but yourself, I thought, but squashed it and hoped my face stayed empty and attentive.

"The Muscovy Company, a chartered English trading business, traveled to Russia in, ah, the 1550s. Was it 1555? That trading company could bring me connections to Great Britain, which was one of the most powerful kingdoms in the world at that time. In the Muscovy Company was a man with an awkward mouthful of a name, a John Clayton Dacre Croglin.

"He was a man of the world, as those merchant adventurers tended to be, and he immediately understood what I was offering him. Thus, he offered his vhoon to me. The Company stayed in Moscow for some while, guests of the first Tsar of all Rus, Ivan Grozny 'the Terrible,' who was also one of my make. But Croglin was my personal guest, and we strengthened our connection with repeated vhoon-vayon. A pleasant memory, *da*.

"Croglin managed to survive the return trip to England, one of a handful to do so. Having become am'r, with my strong vhoon-anghyaa, the sinking of his ship was less lethal to him than the rest of the crew. After concluding private trade deals for me in London, he returned to his ancestral home and prepared it for my eventual visit."

"Wait! How was he an am'r already? You said he was only there for a while."

"Oh. It was some months, but I could not send an am'r-nafsh out into the world. I gave him the vistarascha and a *very* opulent fraheshteshnesh, sumptuousness as only the Russians could provide. So many naked bodies in the light from the torches, draped on furs, the kee feasting and fucking as we moved through them, drinking from whichever pleased us most in that instant, and then on to the next."

Kurgan paused then, caught up in his version of happy memories. I decided to change my pacing to angle myself in an even wider arc away from him, but with that soft and sudden am'r movement, he was standing in front of me. His eyes glinted in the moonlight, and some part of me that had evolved from a small, scared mammal in the time of antediluvian predators went *Eeeeep!* I had to actively fight my body, which was trying to cower under some form of shelter. I was certain am'r *could* smell fear, and I didn't want that adding to my already-too-alluring blood-perfume.

"I am trying to be patient with you, little cousin," he growled. I didn't think he was actively trying to threaten me; he just couldn't *not* be menacing. "But it is very hard for me not to just take what I want. I know I must give you time to ask me these questions, to let logic sway you to your inevitable choice. But I am not made of endless patience."

I tried to back away, and his hand shot out and grabbed my wrist hard enough to make it feel like those slender bones were being crushed. I was back in that place I particularly hated with am'r bad guys, where I had zero time to figure out the right answer to a riddle that would keep me from being killed, like some particularly obnoxious Greek sphinx.

"Hey!" I protested, working very hard to keep my voice from pitching upward in obvious terror. "You've put me between a rock and a hard place, Kurgan. You've already warned me not to choose your side too quickly or you won't believe me, but now you're saying I'm taking too long to make up my mind. Do you see how I can't win? I can't go with my honest feelings because I'll be afraid that either I'm taking too long, or I haven't taken long enough. That's *not* how you inspire someone to join you."

He froze, then abruptly let go of my wrist. I started to rub it very gently and stared at him. I was pretty sure no one had talked to him like that in…well, maybe since Bagamil chewed him out back in 4,500-something BCE.

I was so tired of all of this. This was the third time since choosing the am'r life that I found myself stuck dealing —*with no help from anyone*—with unstable villains who wanted things from me that I didn't want to give them. This was just too much. Maybe Bagamil and Sandu didn't mind being in some vampirish Groundhog Day where we fought the same fucking battles over and over, but this was not how I planned to accept living for eternity. If I was stuck repeating the same day over and over, it was going to be me having mind-blowing sex with my beloveds, archiving incredible ancient works of am'r lore with inspirational colleagues, and honing my fighting skills. Not because I *needed* them, but because I'd learned that challenging myself on the physical level was as exhilarating as challenging myself on the mental level.

I was not—*not*—going to keep repeating whatever mistake kept landing me in this suck-ass situation. They had laughed at me in London for questioning their *modus operandi*, but I was not going to be laughed at again. I was going to light a fire under the majestic rear-end of the Aojysht-of-aojyshtaish to ensure that I was *never* in this situation again.

That is, if I survived to that point. I should get back to digging for information and distracting Kurgan from his desire for sex and blood of either the willing or unwilling variety.

Speaking of Kurgan, he had been using those seconds to think. He was obviously working through a whole lot of feelings because while his eyes stayed on me, they were not focused on me. He was processing thoughts like a high-speed computer, but if I tried to run, he would have pounced on me without pausing his meditations. I stayed still and waited for his response.

"Ah. Myshka. I hear the truth in your words. You do not try to wound me nor confuse me. I can tell. You are just telling me your own feelings."

What the fuck kind of infantile emotional development am I dealing with here? He has lived how long*, and he still can't tell that things he doesn't like to hear aren't always about being a meanie-pants to him? I thought I was on thin ice before...*

"So, I tell you I have heard your concerns, sweet cousin. You may ask me your questions in peace. I will give you the time you need to understand that I am your only choice."

I nearly let myself sigh audibly at this. Dealing with megalomaniacs was exhausting, but honestly, when dealing with powerful beings who could live ridiculously long stretches of time, only getting more powerful as they went, that was unavoidably going to be the shape of am'r bad guys. Your choice was "vainglorious narcissists."

Get back to finding shit out and distracting him from thinking about raping you.

"So, Bagamil never went to Russia in all that time?"

"It is remarkable, *nyet*? Yet, it is true. Oh, many of his make ended up in my lands. It was only at first that I had to, eh, *import* them. Over the centuries, many were drawn to the promise of riches in Tartary."

"But never Bagamil?"

"I awaited him for many years, never ceasing to watch him from afar. But while he eventually traveled much farther east, he never came closer to me than building his stronghold in Turkmenia. He was entirely uninterested in the northern steppes."

"But you were eating his frithaputhraish for lunch!"

"And dinner and dessert!" Kurgan laughed, and I hated myself for finding his laugh sexy and thrilling at the glint in his eyes as he met mine in the shared joke. "But this he never noticed. In the early days of the am'r, those who explored the still-untamed world could die as kee do, from accidents of underestimating geology or wildlife. Boiling lava is not something an am'r will survive. And I do not know of any am'r who have healed from being eaten by wild animals—or wild *kee*, since there have been plenty of tribes who practiced pragmatic cannibalism across the planet."

"I, uh, I never thought of that."

"It is not a common fate of am'r who live in these times. The kee have brought much science to making world travel survivable, and those creatures who consume kee bodies are hunted to extinction. That is why the am'r have stayed in the shadows all this time. It is easier to 'eat the kee for lunch,' as you put it when no one notices you are doing so."

I shuddered, remembering a pile of naked human bodies in a cave, the remnants of an am'r feast, before my world blew up in fire and was never the same. *He said he was behind that, too.*

"If that's the case, why did you incite crazy-ass Mehmet to try to take over the world? That was the most extreme adharmhem I can imagine. If he hadn't been stopped when he was, the kee would seriously have started noticing."

"Ah, Fatih Sultan. I was working with the tools at hand. He was not…a precise tool, but he almost succeeded. It was a very close thing. If you had not found those *chyortov* flamethrowers, my annoying cousin Wladislaus would have ceased to be a problem, he would not have resurrected Vohuni-sura from the ahstha, and I would have stepped in to put Mehmet down like the mad dog he was. My schedule would not have been delayed."

I took a deep breath. "Excuse me, but would you explain your *schedule* to me, please? I don't understand why you waited so long to kill Baga…Vohuni-sura." This was the first of two questions that had really been troubling me, and both had to be phrased super-carefully because I did not want Lord Ego to decide I was accusing him of cowardice. That would *not* go well.

He paused, and I could not read his face. So far, I'd only been able to read either disdain or lust on his unfriendly physiognomy. He took so long to answer me that my body tensed in preparation for fight-or-flight despite my best attempts to forcibly relax.

"That is a very insightful question, myshka." It did not sound like a compliment. I waited for more, forgetting to breathe. "At first, I just wanted to get as far away as I could from that spiteful man, those wounding memories. I was simply glad he did not know I was inhabiting the same world as he. Then, for many years, I got caught up in my life with my people. I won't say I entirely *forgot* him, but I had far more interesting things on my mind. I prepared to meet him again eventually, but, as I said, he never came my way.

"Once I realized the world was filling with his make, I became determined to fix that balance with those who could stand up to the supercilious hypocrite, those loyal to me and me alone. That was the work of many generations. As soon as my method of making my frithaputhraish unde-tectable to him and his was proven effective, I also ensured that he was surrounded by spies amongst those he trusted best so that tracking his movements and machinations was not too difficult. Obviously, the era of the computer and cell phone has accelerated that considerably."

"Who...who are the spies you have around him now?" I was sure that I both needed to know this, and that I very much did not *want* to know who had betrayed my beloveds and me.

He gave me a list, too long a list. At first, there was no bad news. Many of Kurgan's frithaputhraish had supported and fought for Mehmet, not actually believing his insane ramblings of being jinn but giving them lip service and, more importantly, actively trying to kill as many of Bagamil's and Sandu's allies as possible. A fair number of them had been sliced up, burnt, or blown up in that trifling little fracas in Turkmenistan, so that was all good news from my point of view. More troubling was when he mentioned Llorenç the Catalan, who I knew both Sandu and Bagamil generally trusted, and the frithaputhra of Tryphena, Zopyros. I knew Bagamil had been concerned that neither of them had ever been found in the ruins of his old stronghold or since.

It turned out they were fine, but they were the "make" of Kurgan, as he put it. They had been pulled out in case anyone remembered them fighting on Mehmet's side down in those caves or anyone got around to remembering that all of Bagamil's and Sandu's plans had been known in advance by the enemy and decided to sort out who that enemy agent had been. That was suboptimal, but not too surprising.

The next two "moles" almost made me laugh. Maxym was one, the sleazy Russian who nobody trusted in the slightest. He was not ever going to be a problem for us. The next was Gilles, Gilles de-fucking-Rais. When I remembered the conversation I'd had with my patar and gharpatar about him just a few days ago—although it felt so much longer—I had to be careful simply to nod solemnly.

Of course, both Maxym and Gilles had been deemed untrustworthy, but not for the right reason. They were *not* known to be part of Kurgan's Secret Army. We just thought they were assholes. "Right for the wrong reason" was actually dangerous, in this context.

The next names gave me a true shock, however. "Oh, and Răzvan and Haralamb," Lord Ego tossed out casually. But he also was observing me carefully, and I did not hide it well enough when my body stiffened in disbelief.

"You thought they were loyal followers of Wladislaus, *da?*"

"I...didn't know. Not, like, for sure. I guess I thought they were of Sandu's vhoon-anghyaa, although I'd never asked him about it."

"No. They are *mine*, but they gave the tokhmarenc to two of his make, drained them fully over and over. They are passing as his vhoon-anghyaa several generations descended. You see how perfectly my technique works?"

He mentioned Abilio, an am'r I'd met in Buenos Aires, and I made a private note to get Lope's number from Sandu and let him know about that. Happily, most of the other South American am'r he mentioned had been working as minions to Julio and Orélie, and none of those am'r left the caves in Tierra del Fuego alive. That I was sure of, and I still could not get the stench of all those burning am'r bodies out of my memory.

Then the real blow fell. "And Lilani."

"What, *who?*"

"One of Nthanda's am'r. You spent some time with her in London, did you not?"

You fucking know I did, you asshole. "She...seemed like she was very loyal to Nthanda."

"Well, she does not wish to die. If Nthanda suspected her of disloyalty, he would give her the tokhmarenc without pause. She is not stupid."

Kurgan is really trusting me, I thought. *This is information I could use to his disadvantage.* In the next moment, that little bubble burst when I realized it just didn't occur to him to worry about telling me. I either would choose his side, or he would kill me, so revealing his secrets didn't trouble him. *I swear I will make him regret underestimating me. I swear it.*

I needed to get away from the hurt I was feeling about Lilani. "What about Roy?" I was pretty confident about that one.

"Who?" Kurgan looked blank.

"The redhead who, um, interacted with Toad...Norvyn. One of Nthanda's as well."

"Hmmm. I think Norvyn mentioned him. He is none of mine."

Some dickheads were just dickheads, and not *bona fide* bad guys. Still, the temptation to somehow get Roy accidentally killed in Nthanda's eventual housecleaning was strong.

"I have many more frithaputhraish spread across the world. Those are just a few of the current ones who give me useful information."

That ended that line of questioning. The next one would have to be done even more circumspectly. "So, um, you took care of Vohuni-sura and, uh, Wladislaus, pretty easily just now. I mean, using maadak you always have. Why have you been doing things so, uh, hands-off, until tonight?"

"If I made an appearance, it would be over, *nyet?* As soon as Bagamil knew I existed, our final fight was inevitable. And then I win, and it's over."

He said it like it was so simple. To him, maybe it was. "Yes, but what I mean is, you could have taken down Bagamil with a dose of maadak at any time and then given him his tokhmarenc any way you wanted. Why go at him with Mehmet, and then with Julio and Orélie? That seems like so much trouble."

"Do you think they were the first caltrops I threw under his feet? For years, I was just playing with him, seeing what he would do, learning if his weaknesses were the same after so many years, while I amused myself watching him dance for me. And often I did not have to do a thing, for his own undisciplined get would attack their Aojysht-of-aojyshtaish of their own whimsical accord.

"With the last two traps I laid for him, I thought I was ready to end it, and I thought that that was the way I wanted to do so, still from a distance, leaving him in the ignorance in which he has remained for so long. I thought that was what I wanted. And, indeed, both exercises brought me gains, not the least of which were facilitating *your* growth and strengthening."

My pacing had slowed as he talked since it wasn't from a genuine need for movement but purely an attempt to resist both him and my own treacherous body. The sheer egotism of that statement stopped me cold, and he used that moment to slide up to me in the boneless am'r way again. He reached for the wrist he had grabbed before and I tried to shy away, but he ended up with my hand in both of his, stroking the wrist he'd nearly crushed.

"I did not mean to hurt you, myshka. You…excite me more than anyone has in a long time. I am normally, eh, not *gentle* with my am'r-nafsh. They will heal, and it makes them stronger. But you have not yet experienced my style of training. My am'r have fought with you, and you are not weak, *nyet*, but you are not used to such…rigor…outside of true battle. Even your supposed training has been too easy-going, too undemanding for this harsh world. I cannot wait to teach you, to shape the am'r I know you can become. As well, I cannot wait to taste you, to be within you, to show you the passion of which you are truly capable."

His voice dropped as he spoke, and his fingers stopped stroking my wrist and skimmed up my arm. I could feel them tensing with a desire to grab into my flesh. "When I finally become your bakheb-vhoonho, I cannot wait to feel the moment my blood enters you and begins the change to make you part of me. What satisfaction we will experience! I know this…and I know you feel it too." He matched with his right hand to my left arm what he was doing to my right arm. It was too close to an embrace, but I could not step back and break it. Desperately, I tried to focus on what he had been saying before he'd gotten close enough that his scent surrounded me and turned off my brain.

"What…what were you saying about thinking you were ready to end it?"

"Hmm? Oh, *him*. I just realized after the *polnaya zhopa* in

South America that I was *glad* Popper and de Tounens had both failed. I recognized that I no longer wanted to watch him be given his tokhmarenc from an anonymous distance; I wanted to be looking into his eyes and see the moment when he understood he had lost *at my hands* and that *I* was finally giving him the ending I promised him so very long ago. I thought I had grown out of my desire for revenge and put aside childish things, but this vengeance has been a long time coming, and it is mete that I attend to it personally.

"But I do not want to speak of *him* anymore. He is taken care of for this moment. I do not want to talk at all…" His hands dug into the muscle of my upper arms, then let go and caressed upward to my shoulders. I made the stupid mistake at this point in letting my eyes be caught by his. They were an even darker brown than Bagamil's, almost black, nothing to catch the moonlight. But that mysterious depth made them even more compelling, it seemed to me now. His presence seemed to be surrounding me, and more than that, saturating my whole self with desire for him. It felt *good*; it felt like wanting more.

His fingers brushed the skin at my neckline, and when they moved up my neck, it seemed like I felt his touch in every nerve ending. My body relaxed for the first time in his presence, and I couldn't remember why I hadn't done so before. Being near him felt so *right*. Why had I been fighting this?

His lips were fuller than…than whose? Fuller than lips I was used to, at any rate. When they brushed against mine, they felt lush and perfect for nibbling upon. I would have happily kissed him for hours, but his lips slid across my cheek and down the line of my chin, landing a first soft pressure at the top of my neck, and my brain melted down the last stage to being nothing more than an organ for processing pleasure sensations.

He pressed his kisses down my neck. I lost the ability to stand on my own, and he caught me in his arms, then clasped my body against his and pulled my core forward so my body arced, pressing my groin to his and encouraging my head to fall back, exposing my neck all the more. I could feel his erection against me, but it was a faraway distraction because his lips were exciting me more than I could process. They were parted, breathing across my skin, taking in my scent deeply. My head was pressed into his shoulder, and his long hair was soft under my cheek. I was breathing him in just as eagerly, getting as high from it as a teenager huffing glue.

I was caught intensely in the moment, no thoughts of past or future, only now now *now*. He kissed up and down my neck and pulled me even more tightly to him. I clung to him, not thinking of anything, reveling in the sensations that pulsed through me from the proximity of him.

He pulled his face back and I turned my head to meet his look, hurling myself into the dark depths of his eyes. "I will have you," he told me, his face glowing with lust and triumph. I did the only thing I could do, which was say, "Yes."

With casual strength, he lowered me bodily to the grass and then knelt above me. The moon and starlight streamed down around him, backlighting his long hair, catching on his cheekbones and his strong nose, and making his full lips pop from his neat beard. His eyes were shadowed, but I could catch the shape of their distracting beauty. His black clothing made him a penumbral shape above me and I wanted him to be naked, but my brain seemed to be disconnected from my mouth, so all I could do was lie there and want him.

He leaned over me, and my heart raced faster. His hands went to the front of my shirt and the fingers made fists in the fabric, then he pulled. The silk made a sharp, sad sound and fell in half to either side of my breasts. My bra took less time to remove from his path. He touched me then from face to lower belly, possessive caresses, making my body know it belonged to him. I moaned and writhed shamelessly; any part of my mind that might have had thoughts about my behavior had long been shut down.

Having moved down to my waistband, he tugged, and the button went flying into the night. The zipper below it made the wise decision not to resist and thus survived intact. He tugged the pants off over my hips and left boot. They ended up bunched over my right boot, forgotten entirely in the next second because his hands again possessed me. Each caress and digging-in of fingertips told me that more assuredly than words.

He was undoing the belt and buttons at his own waist. I felt a surge of excitement at seeing him, and at what would follow the seeing. I was disappointed that he didn't remove his clothing; he just lay down alongside me and caressed me, grabbing handfuls of my skin in his appreciative, possessive way. I had never been touched like that before and it was as addictive as everything else, feeling him seize what was his. The thrill of suddenly being his was part of it. One minute I had not been, and then the next minute I was his, in his hands and in his power.

Kurgan was kissing my body now, and as he grew more excited, the kisses became nips that teased but did not draw blood at first. It almost reminded me of something, of another time with another lover, when first I felt the pressure of am'r teeth. But that flash of memory was rolled under the seething urges that were all I had for consciousness anymore.

He was biting me now, really biting, drawing blood. He was doing nothing to give me pleasure to counter the pain of the bites, but why did I even expect that? I couldn't remember. Anyway, it was more than enough to feel his lips pull back and get the rush of anticipation, feeling the first sharp prick of canines against my skin, and only having enough time to start to gasp before they slid through my dermis, creating their own holes to penetrate as they went.

They were not deep bites, just little tastes of blood, like having an *amuse-bouche* before a meal. Some part of me stirred as this went on, almost remembering that there was once a time this wouldn't have been so exciting for me. That it might have been a problem, and not something that was arousing me so much I could feel the wetness spreading down my inner thighs. But that very arousal made me not care about anything that had happened before this moment. There was only now, what was transpiring now, and that it kept on transpiring.

My head was thrown back as I panted through the intense sensations of the bites and the bliss of feeling Kurgan lapping up the little runlets of blood from the punctures. He moved up and down my body as he had with his kisses, from breast to inner thighs, where his lips and tongue discovered my reaction to his...what to call them? Not love-bites. No one was thinking about love. And more than lust-bites. Power-bites, possession-bites, domination-bites—something like that. It was a connection like none I'd ever felt before, and instead of fear for how it over-whelmed me, I dove into it with a strange feeling of relief. I didn't have to worry about attempting to control circum-stances that felt too much for me, anymore. Control was gone; I should have given it away and had no worries long before this. I felt free. I felt like I might float off the ground with this sudden weight lifted off me.

Except there was another weight on me. Kurgan had shifted from lying alongside me to partially atop me. Under the clothing I wished was not there, I could feel his tightly corded muscles. He was not a large man, but those wiry limbs were heavy with his subtle strength.

I could feel something else pressing against me, and it was no longer blocked by clothing. But I did not have time to think about that because Kurgan had moved for the purpose of finally taking a proper drink from me. If asked, I couldn't have told you which penetration I was more excited about, but the choice was not mine. I reveled in the freedom not to bother with thinking or holding onto desires, but just holding on for the ride.

Kurgan raised off me slightly, and I looked down to see my moonlit body covered in bite marks, some still oozing a little, some already closing. I was painted in streaks of blood where his clothed body had brushed up and down the wounds. He made a small sound, and I looked up and met his eyes, circles of living shadow. My head spun even faster, and without needing a command, I let my head fall back and to the right, exposing my neck for him.

There was a second of pause in which I could feel Kurgan taking in my offering myself to him, and I could feel the pleasure radiating off him. Then his weight was fully upon me, and shortly after that, his lips were rough against my neck, but not as rough as his teeth, which tore into me without reserve. The pain was almost enough to knock me out of my floaty place, enough that the thought, *No one has ever bitten me like this!* flashed sharply through my mind, but any concerns that tried to trouble me were removed as a distraction began between my legs. He was pressing himself upward, and with my generous lubrication, it took no time at all for him to be pushing into me and up and up.

The pain from my throat was transformed into a supplement and complement to pleasure, and he had barely begun to move in me when the first orgasm swept across me, then kept building and crashed down on me. My body responded to his in the most primal of rhythms, reaching to him for everything he was giving me, thrusting toward him everything he wanted to take from me.

On the cold hillside, brazen in the blue-white light of moon and stars, we rutted like shadow-animals, nothing as evolved as "am'r," just blood-drinking beasts of the night.

He drank and drank from me, taking blood and pleasure as his due. I gave and gave, and then there was a moment where the light-headedness was not from gasping in ecstasy but because a black curtain was lowering across my sight. Even with am'r sight, it was not a darkness I could see in like, the night's shadows. It was the shade of consciousness slipping away. My body fell back, limp.

In an instant, he pulled me up against him, turning me so I was spooned against him. Once I was settled unresponsively in his grasp, he ripped his wrist open with his teeth and shoved the spurting vein to my lips. For a long minute, the blood was wasted, streaming down either side of my chin, but from a deep place inside me, a more savage ancestry than lizard-brain or mammal-brain awoke me to my need, and my mouth opened. Then his blood was in me, and I was swallowing as if I'd never stop.

And it was *powerful*. Within only a few mouthfuls, I felt it rushing into my bloodstream, up to my heart, and out through deep arteries to superficial ones, down to arterioles, and even farther out to the tiniest capillaries, filling my whole self full of him.

His cock was inside me again, and he held me tight against him as we thrust in perfect rhythm. But that was happening in my body, and my body was far away. I was flying out in all directions at once to the farthest reaches of the universe, encompassing the subzero emptiness of space and the all-consuming heat of stars, stretching until speed and distance had no meaning. Pleasure was too small a thing to notice, and pain was nothing more than the annoyance of a tiny buzzing insect.

I twisted and spun and moved in ways that could not be comprehended by mere human bodies, small and gravity-bound. The world and Kurgan's body moving within mine was so far behind me that I laughed across the universe to remember it.

And then I was laughing within my body, and Kurgan's

arms were clasping me, and he was laughing, too, the harsh rumble of one who didn't laugh very often. He gripped me tighter and became more serious in his movements, and then I was orgasming like a non-universe-sized woman again, and as he came, he growled, "You're mine. You're mine. You're *MINE!*"

And in that moment, that was all I wanted.

CHAPTER THREE

When it was over, I was in a mindless state for an unknown while. Too much had just happened for me to be able to process it. For one of the few times in my life, I could just "be" without having to remember and critique the past or analyze the present or be planning for the future. I just lay there beside Kurgan, feeling the grass soft and coolly damp beneath me. He said nothing, and also for once, I did not feel the compulsion to ask a partner in the quiet post-coital moments, "What are you thinking?"

Without thought, I had no way to track the passage of time. It was not long enough for the moon and stars, which I found myself watching, to visibly progress across the sky. Eventually, that moment changed from present to past, and Kurgan rose and adjusted his clothing.

That led to an awkward moment for me. My trousers were collectible from their damp pile around my ankle and could be put on again no problem, missing only that top button but staying up fine nonetheless. My shirt was beyond fixing, however, and all I could do was let it dangle to either side of my chest. I did have to take it off to remove the demolished bra and then shrug back into the clammy ripped silk, but I didn't feel cold. I felt more vibrant and vigorous than ever before.

He moved unhurriedly down to the house. I followed him, watching his shadowy shape with unceasing fascination. Then I stepped into a hole dug by some small animal and yelped in surprise. He paused and turned back to me.

"Are you alright, myshka?"

I pulled my leg out and tentatively rested my weight on it. There was a slight ache, but I knew that even if I had sprained it, it would heal within minutes. "I'm fine. I'll just walk carefully for a moment."

"Catch me up in the house. It is time for your new life to commence."

The portentousness of that didn't faze me. "I'll be right behind you," I promised him. I didn't want to leave his side because he was the only thing of real interest to me in the world.

I reached down to massage the damn ankle, wanting to increase the blood flow to the area so that Kurgan's strong vhoon could work its fastest. He moved down the hill and out of sight into the courtyard. As I rested there, bent over and rubbing my leg, I started to feel...funny. Really funny. *Really...* I sat down abruptly, since it seemed like I'd black out in the next instant.

I took a few breaths to steady myself, and the wooziness passed. Something else passed with it. It was fortunate that I was already sitting because I was rocked with emotions so rough that I might have fallen over.

My fascination with Kurgan was fading. In its place was

pure seething anger, although at whom I could not say. Knowledge flooded into me and memories of the past hours played in my mind, a whole new perspective coloring them.

"Oh!" I gasped, then, "Oh!" again. I didn't sob. It hurt too much to cry. I just sat there, more shaken than ever I had been in a life that for the past couple of years had been full of shock and devastation.

What have I done? I mean, beyond cheating as comprehensively on Sandu and Bagamil as I could possibly do, and with their arch-fucking-enemy of all people! I had not paused to think of them; I had actually forgotten them. I had not paused to consider anything.

You were mesmerized, I told myself. *You thought it couldn't happen to you, but you were wrong. You can't hold yourself at fault. You literally couldn't think, you could only do as you were told. Remember how all-encompassing it was? When you can't realize something is happening to you, how can you overcome it?*

That was true, accurate, right. I was, however, also certain there was still a whole world of guilt to go along with it that, which I'd eventually have to work my way through. Not right now, though. I had no idea how much time had passed, save that sunrise wasn't imminent. But Kurgan was headed to my helpless beloveds, and he had said some nonsense about my "new life" commencing, and I was damn sure that meant *sans* Bagamil and Sandu. I got up and tested my leg. The time spent in profound moral turmoil had given my ankle time to be perfectly happy again. *That's one part of me, at least.* I ran down the hill carefully to make sure I didn't misstep again.

I pushed the antique door open and moved down the hall to the library. I could hear Kurgan and Toady-boy talking —*Is my hearing already that much improved?*—but more distressing, the closer I got to Kurgan, the more I felt our connection.

I did *not* want this connection. More than that, I was terrified of what would happen when I got within mind-melting range of Kurgan. It was the worst of quandaries; I needed to get near them and find out what was being planned for my beloveds, but I also needed not to go back to being a mindless sex zombie. I had no knowledge upon which to base my decisions, so planning my next move was essentially impossible. I had a feeling that Kurgan could feel me through our connection, so sneaking up to the library door and listening seemed unlikely to work as a plan. As I rested my hand on the doorknob, I froze. Out here, I was still *compos mentis*, dammit, but I had a feeling that if I walked right up to his side, my mind would again liquify into nothing more than the lubrication of arousal.

I couldn't just stand here, and I couldn't run away, so I forced the muscles in my arm and hand to respond to me. The doorknob turned, so I forced the muscles of my legs and feet to respond as well, and I bearded the dragon in his den.

I was right. Once I entered the room, I could feel Kurgan's influence washing over me. The last time I had not been able to fight it, but having gone under and come back up again, I understood the process better. I slowed my breathing and kept a certain percentage of my brain focused on it. It didn't help that I needed my whole brain, and more, to keep up with one of the most ancient and powerful of aojyshtaish, but the most vital thing right now was simply to be contesting his mesmerism.

"Ah, myshka. Your ankle is well?" He wasn't interested in my answer, which was fine because I wasn't yet ready to try to talk. "You bring your vhoon and your familiarity with those involved at the perfect moment. Norvyn and I were discussing which we should wake first, Wladislaus or Vohuni-sura."

Shit. I *had* to speak now. My voice cracked a bit on the first syllable, but I got it steady. "Um. Why are we waking them? What's the plan?"

"I will kill each in single combat. I know how foolishly *connected* they remain. In which order should I do this to cause them maximum anguish?"

There was so much to unpack there that I didn't know where to start. "Foolishly connected." It was a good thing I wasn't expecting love or even an emotional connection that went both ways from Lord Ego along with the sharing of blood, or that might have been a real blow for me. I shook my head to clear it.

Remember, you fool, you don't want *love or connection from him. But how to answer this question? Specifically, how do you answer it to skew the results toward defeating this calculating bastard?*

"That is…a good question. Hmm. They love each other pretty equally. I don't know that waking up to find out the other is dead would hurt more one way or the other. To have one actually *watch* the other being given the tokhmarenc—that would hurt *most*, I think."

It wasn't much, but it was the best I could do. Having them both awake at the same time drastically improved our chances. I hoped Lord Ego's thirst for revenge was strong enough to encourage him to make less-than-practical decisions.

"Of course, being made to watch the other be put down would be the most wounding." I could see Kurgan coolly considering the optimum emotional anguish, and it sickened me. Even more sickening was still feeling lust for him throbbing inside me like a second heart.

"But they are each formidable and canny enemies, Lord," Norvyn interjected. "It does not make sense to bring them both into the state of play when you can easily deal with them one at a time. Or, Lord, dispatch them both as they currently are, and let us move on."

How I hated the vile little toad. That was the worst suggestion he could make, but obviously the most sensible one. Happily, one didn't need to worry overly much about am'r making sensible choices. Kurgan frowned so disapprovingly at Norvyn that I felt a wash of nerves, despite it not being directed at me. Toady-boy, under the full force of it, took a step back and held up both hands in supplication.

"This is not about *easy*," Kurgan growled. "Do you think me a craven little *trus* such as yourself? You clearly understand nothing of the need for vengeance, nor of the value of seeing defeat in an enemy's eyes before you take his life away. It is...incalculable, a treasure beyond any other.

"And you have no instinct for the *art* of inflicting suffering, one of the things that makes existence worth waking up every night. If you wish to serve me long, you will quickly gain an appreciation of these matters."

"Yes, of course, my Lord!" Norvyn almost tripped over his words, nodding eagerly. I wondered if Kurgan had captivated him as strongly as he had done me. If so…well, I wasn't planning on having any sympathy for Toady-boy, but it would be *some* explanation for his behavior. I wasn't entirely certain I wouldn't slide back down into being Kurgan's Toady-girl at any moment, and if that happened, I wasn't certain I could *ever* emerge from it.

"I have been awaiting this perfect moment for longer than you can fathom, *mal'chik*, and I will not have your fretfulness ruin my long-deserved victory.

"However, I do not want any troublesomeness from either of our *friends* as I deal with each of them. It was demonstrated by Popper how easily Bagamil can be incapacitated by ancient methods that I myself helped originate. The old ways are so often the best, eh? It is no big deal to put him out of action while I give Wladislaus his deserved tokhmarenc. That will be a satisfying warmup to a final dance I've been waiting to join since the wheel was a new idea."

Dismay coursed through me as I remembered Bagamil hogtied tightly to prevent healing of his broken limbs. *Not again.* I somehow had to prevent that.

"Can't you just make Bagamil give his word not to interfere in your duel with Sandu or something? His word is very important to him." But when I saw the look that moved across Kurgan's face, I knew it was a lost cause.

"Myshka, you have read too many stories of the olden days. One's word was once very important among the kee, that is true, but we am'r are more practical creatures. I would not trust Vohuni-sura to keep that word for a moment longer than is useful. In fact, I *do* trust him to break his word the instant it suits his need. As would I. As would Wladislaus.

"Norvyn here would like to get it over with quick-quick. And, I admit, the thought of putting those helpless bastards through the woodchipper is...not unpleasing." Kurgan stopped to enjoy imagining it for a moment. Norvyn grinned hopefully. I tried not to pass out. *Think faster!*

"Oh, of course," I said, trying to sound comfortably sanguine about shredding my beloveds. "But I know that would leave you profoundly unsatisfied for, like, forever. You said yourself you need things to be hands-on. Can't you tie him up so he can't get free?"

"While most bondage would not slow down an am'r, myshka, there is a specific arrangement that will do for even the Aojysht-of-aojyshtaish," he said with a disagreeable grin.

Lord Ego began giving orders to Norvyn and bustling around the room. He looked pleased and entirely comfortable with the situation, which boded poorly for my beloveds and me.

It was understood that with my inferior am'r-nafsh lack of strength, I would only get in the way. I backed into a corner and up against books that normally I could never stand facing *away* from, uninterested in relishing every title and gently caressing their spines. I watched as the huge desk and piles of tomes surrounding it were shoved into a far corner, making a large central space. I realized this library was probably the largest room in the house, the rest being claustrophobically tiny rooms. Indeed, from the odd angles and differing ceiling heights, this room had obviously been expanded more than once, perhaps as the collection of works outgrew the available space.

I was improbably noticing architectural details in this tense moment because Kurgan had directed Norvyn to get some rope, and Toady-boy had returned quicky and eagerly with a long, all-too-sturdy-looking length of it. They'd thrown it up over an exposed beam in the tallest-ceilinged section, and it dangled ominously. Norvyn was tying another length of the rope to a rusty old metal ball that might have had some agricultural usage in its past life, but it had obviously been used as nothing more than a door-stop for possibly longer than I'd been alive. Even he had lugged it in with some difficulty, so I most likely couldn't even lift it.

I didn't have the slightest idea what was going on, but I didn't like it.

"Have you done the *corda* before?" Kurgan asked Norvyn, who shook his head, eyes wide. "It is quite obvious once it begins. In the meantime, once he is awakened, we will move without delay. Hold him upright, facing you. You need do nothing except ensure that he does not break free as I prepare him."

"Yes, my Lord."

"Myshka, come over here."

I resented his casual dominance, and part of me wanted to tell him where to shove it. But the part of my brain that was still functioning reminded me I was supposed to be spell-bound by his every word and gesture, as eager to please as Toady-boy. I bit my lip and walked over, hoping my silence would be taken as submission.

"Your vhoon is what will awaken our sleepers. Norvyn, a blade for my myshka."

If Kurgan was unaware of Sa'mah, I wasn't going to bring her to his attention. We hadn't needed to bother with my boots in the, erm, incident on the cold hillside, so why would he guess I was armed? Even if my blade *was* only three inches long, she could do him enough damage to distract and imbalance him at the right moment.

No. No. NO. You could not *have dispatched him by yourself while he was fucking you. Don't get it twisted. You've now got him trusting you, and you've broken out of his mind-control. You can angst about the other shit all you like later. For now, work with what you've got, which is probably the best you could have gotten. It doesn't feel like that, but this isn't the time for feelings.*

I kept my mouth shut and let Norvyn glare at me, then provide me with his personal blade: a Bowie knife he produced from an unexpected horizontal sheath on his lower back, reminding me yet again that in the am'r world, underestimating your enemy is the quickest way to the tokhmarenc. Six inches of polished steel with a pretty stag antler-and-brass decorated handle, with "Sheffield England" marked on the blade. She was well-weighted, and I felt a reluctance to return her. The more weapons I had right now, the happier I would be.

"Wake Vohuni-sura with your vhoon. Just enough to bring him to consciousness, no more," Kurgan directed me.

I was saved from pointing out that it was hard to awaken an am'r from the ahstha when said am'r wasn't present. Norvyn had left the room after giving me his knife and now returned with Sandu in an awkward firefighter carry. He dumped him on the floor with decided contempt and went out again. Kurgan stood holding the rope that was dangling so ominously from the crossbeam.

I wanted to ask, "What the fuck is going on?" but Kurgan started giving me instructions. "When Norvyn returns with Vohuni-sura, we will bind him here. Once that is complete, you will wake him, then his frithaputhra. I will heal your cut immediately after. Norvyn is still not so good with his control."

That made me wonder about the fate of the Wee Strumpet. I could still faintly smell her in the room, but only barely. The last I'd seen of her, she'd been slumped unconscious on the floor but most likely still alive. She had, however, seen a lot of suspicious shit, and I doubted she would be let go to tell her stories down at the pub later. I didn't have a good feeling that Kurgan would find it worth his time to hypnotize her. It seemed more likely that one of them would take care of the situation by bloating himself like a tick on her until the problem was resolved.

I looked at Norvyn more closely as he carried Bagamil's wiry body into the room. He did look healthy—too healthy. *Poor girl.*

But I didn't have time to think about anonymous kee anymore. Norvyn was holding my gharpatar up almost like they were slow-dancing, except that simile didn't work when Kurgan was standing there, pulling Bagamil's arms tight behind him and trying them at the wrists. For some reason I couldn't guess, my gharpatar had been stripped to his trousers.

I couldn't see how just tying his wrists behind him was going to incapacitate one of the most powerful am'r to ever walk the Earth, so this was obviously going to get worse. I just didn't see how yet. But Bagamil wasn't going to be put through a woodchipper while unconscious, he was going to be woken up. There were no metal medieval torture devices. I told myself this *had* to be better, but on the other hand, if it made Lord Ego grin like that, it justified the knot of fear that roiled in my belly.

Once the knots were fast, Kurgan looked at me. "Myshka, awaken him now. Not full vhoon-berefteh, just a taste."

Bagamil's head was resting on Norvyn's right shoulder, and that was far too close to Toady-boy's ill-controlled mouth. I glared at the back of his head but stepped forward and used the pretty Sheffield steel to make a shallow slice on my wrist. I moved as fast as I could to get the wound to Bagamil's mouth before the white of shocked dermis could turn red with rising blood. There was a pause, then Bagamil started drinking before consciousness even stirred in him.

How many times had I done this? Wakened my gharpatar with my blood? The first time had been in a burnt-out cave system under the Karakum desert. The second and third and however many other times were in a damp cave system in Tierra del Fuego, and now here in this ramshackle old farmhouse in the even damper back of beyond in England, with unexpected sheep sounds still startling me. It was the oddest nostalgia imaginable, but it was so very am'r.

I could sense, don't ask me how, when Bagamil moved from unconscious gulping to awareness. Was it the vhoon-bond between my gharpatar and me? Sadly, Kurgan and Norvyn caught it too, although in Norvyn's case, it was probably from feeling a change in how Bagamil held himself within Toady-boy's unwelcome embrace.

"Stop!" Lord Ego demanded. I didn't obey fast enough, so he shoved me, and I stumbled backward, overwhelmed.

"Hold him until I say." Kurgan barked the command and tugged on the dangling end of the rope, and Bagamil's arms were pulled up behind him. At first, he straightened, but then a point came where Norvyn quickly stepped back and Bagamil was raised off the floor.

My gharpatar cried aloud, and I understood he would not be getting out of *this* bondage anytime soon. Norvyn busied himself at Bagamil's ankles, then the weight was tied to them, and with a few extra hoists of the rope, that weight impacted his body even further. Even Norvyn looked a bit dismayed by the sound that was made by Bagamil's shoulders dislocating. I would hear that sound in my nightmares forever. Kurgan, however, looked as full of joy and vibrancy as I'd ever seen him, possibly even more than when he was fucking me.

I wasn't sure what of all of that sickened me the most.

My beloved was groaning in agony, shocked fully awake by the pain of the torture he was undergoing. His body twisted slightly as his bones and muscles rearranged themselves to accommodate pressure and gravity, and every movement wrung another agonized sob from him.

Kurgan took on the air of a lecturing professor. "You see, *il tormento della corda* is a most perfect solution for an am'r. A kee would die of this in an hour or so, from the shock of the pain and perhaps a blockage in the arteries in his lungs. But an am'r will not die, and their bodies will heal in this position, so they are quite encumbered until the dislocated shoulder sockets are relocated and healed afresh. Oh, yes, he will eventually slip back into the ahstha, but we shall not take so long, shall we, *father?*" He gave a friendly slap to Bagamil's right buttock, spinning him a little on the rope and producing gasping cries of anguish.

"Now, myshka, waken cousin Wladislaus so I may give our captive audience some entertainment. Norvyn, ensure he is aware from first consciousness that he is to make no sudden movements."

I knelt before my patar and reopened the wrist wound that had mostly closed up. Norvyn was too close behind me, and I could feel the intensity of his interest in my am'r-nafsh blood. The corresponding rush of nausea was the last thing I needed right now, but I made myself focus on getting the blood where it needed to go, which was into my love's mouth. I snuck him as many extra mouthfuls as I could to strengthen his body and his wits for everything that was about to come.

Again, he did that am'r thing where one in a maadak-coma starts suckling blood like a baby before anything like consciousness is reached. Again, I had that sense of knowing when my blood-bonded-one crossed the threshold into awareness.

Sandu got some good pulls from my wrist before he made the cardinal mistake of reaching up to grab my arm. While it was instinctual, it signaled to everyone else that he was properly awake. Everything went a bit wrong at this point.

"Myshka, *stop!*"

When I didn't respond instantly, Norvyn, attempting to ensure my compliance with his patar's command, made the mistake of grabbing my upper arm. Toady-boy found himself facing a snarling Sandu and an enraged me, wielding his own knife against him.

Norvyn had gotten more than a little overstimulated from my vhoon-smell and then the precipitous rush of adrenaline. He bared his teeth and hissed like a cornered weasel. Things almost kicked off right there, but Kurgan imposed himself between us, facing Sandu and me.

"Norvyn, back!" When that was ignored, Lord Ego turned his head slowly, each millimeter of movement demonstrating how unacceptable having to repeat his command was. He hissed, "*Now.*"

That got through Toady-boy's single-minded lust for violence. He blenched and stepped back. Kurgan's head swiveled, almost owl-like, back to us. "Myshka. Come. To. Me."

The crash of conflicting urges nearly broke me. For a moment, I almost gave in to pressing myself to Sandu's side and going out in a blaze of glory with him, but an annoyingly practical voice in my head reminded me that giving in to the pull of Kurgan's voice was the wiser move to make, even if it felt like I was just caving to his hypnotic control. *Pretend, but don't give in to it. It's not the coward's path, not the weakling's path. This is the bravest, hardest choice.*

Those thoughts didn't just stiffen my spine. As I forced myself away from Sandu to Kurgan, it felt like all my muscles had contracted to the point of near-immobility. I hoped my zombie-like movement was put down to my body blindly following the hypnotic command, at least by Lord Ego. I could all-too-easily imagine what *Sandu* was thinking.

When I reached Kurgan's side, he smiled down at me, victorious and prideful. There was not one shred of warmth or affection. It would not have bothered me if I were back in the mesmerized state. I tried to take comfort from knowing I was hiding full physical and mental integrity. "Myshka," he said, his voice full of pseudo-warmth, "let me close that wound for you." He nipped the fleshy part of his palm and then, turning up my wrist, which was mostly closed, so this was clearly performative territorial pissing for Sandu's sake, smeared the few drops of his blood across the cut, causing it to close up before my eyes.

Kurgan turned his smirk to Sandu. "She is *mine* now, little cousin Wladislaus. My stronger vhoon has made her mine entirely, washing your influence from her body and mind."

Sandu didn't even look at me. He met Kurgan's eyes with steady hatred. "*Fută-te dumnezeu.* I could taste that you had desecrated her good vhoon-anghyaa. So. Did you wake me up merely for cocky self-aggrandizement? Because if so, I'll take some more of that maadak now. Better yet, why not grow some balls and give me the pleasure of stopping that braggart mouth for all time?"

Impossibly, Lord Ego's grin grew wider. "Why, cousin, that's the very reason I woke you from your slumber. It's time to determine whose vhoon-anghyaa is the most potent: that of Vohun-ukhra, who rose from the first tokhmarenc, or the offspring of the untested Vohuni-sura, who has yet to fight his way back to the true am'r existence."

"I would hardly call Bagamil 'untested,'" Sandu pointed

out almost agreeably. A fight had been promised him, and that put him in his comfort zone. "He has *existed* for longer years than you, *coz*. I think he may have met a test or two in that time."

"He has not met me, *yunets*. And neither have you."

"Oh, I admit, I have not yet had the pleasure of kicking your ass. But surely your memory is not so deteriorated that you've forgotten that Bagamil fought you all those years ago and that *you were beaten most profoundly?*" Sandu was beaming by the end of this, an Impaler twinkle in his eye. Normally, it disconcerted me to see that well of violence in him. Right now, I hoped it would take him over and turn him into a creature who could destroy our enemy while hardly breaking a sweat.

Kurgan growled, "You were not there. You have heard only his side of the story. And the old fraud has *not* tested himself against me, not since I rose from the tokhmarenc. But it matters little. I will demonstrate the strength of my vhoon-anghyaa to *you*, and I will make sure you survive just long enough to fully despair in your loss, and ensure you appreciate the suffering of your patar at your defeat."

He turned his head to bring attention to poor Bagamil. Sandu had been too quickly smacked over the head with my seemingly obvious betrayal and then challenged to a battle of wits, all while fighting off the lingering effects of the maadak for him to immediately notice the dangling agony of his patar. His spasm of shock brought the nasty smirk back to Kurgan's face. He made an abortive lurch in Bagamil's direction but controlled himself because he knew he wouldn't be allowed to rescue him. He brought his eyes back to

Bagamil, and the affable aggression was gone; there was only a monster looking out now. *"Futu-ți dumnezeii mă-tii!"* he snarled.

"What about my knife?" Norvyn's tone was not as bold as he was probably trying for, but his words pulled everyone's attention to him anyway. And then, sadly, to the Bowie knife still in my hand, which instinctively tightened around her. I didn't want to give her back.

"Myshka, return Norvyn's blade," Kurgan instructed me. I was torn because I had to obey him to keep up the pretense of being under his control, but I really didn't want to trade the current situation of "I have a big knife and Norvyn doesn't" for the alternative.

Inspiration flooded through me, and I smiled at Norvyn. It was not a very nice smile, but I was learning from the bad company I was keeping. I said, "Sure thing!" then threw the knife into a corner of the room. It was in Norvyn's general direction, but it didn't pass close enough for him to catch, even with am'r reflexes. I'd had no practice with throwing knives, so it did not land tip-first in the bit of wood paneling I'd aimed for. The butt thudded against the thin strip of wall between shelves and fell with another thud to the floor. The thuds were the precursors to a silence that reverberated.

After what seemed like a million years, Kurgan said, "Ha! Norvyn, this am'r-nafsh has taken more from my vhoon-anghyaa than you ever have. *She* is my true fritha-puthra, despite my generosity to you with my strong vhoon. Hasten to find your strengths if you wish to keep serving me."

He turned back to me. "You have made your point,

myshka. I like a frithaputhra who can think for herself...*up to a point*. Beware of testing those limits."

I couldn't help but breathe a sigh of relief, and was thankful it would be read as relief that my act of typical am'r social climbing wasn't being punished. "Yes, my Lord," I responded, eyes downcast. He was certain of me now, and I could get away with a little buttering up because he was accustomed to being treated that way.

Sandu had paid little attention to the drama playing out with Norvyn and me. He was mostly staring at Bagamil and then studying Kurgan. Bagamil, for his part, had lifted his head as best he could and was looking very intently at Sandu. I wished they had real psychic communication abilities. They did sometimes finish each other's sentences, like any couple who has been together for ages. Literally ages. I hoped they were coming up with some plan and would then find some way to let *me* know said plan.

Kurgan was not unaware of the urgent looks between my two beloveds. I couldn't wait for one of us to somehow wipe that damn smile off his too-handsome face. Or, if that weren't possible, that I could find some way to die that seriously inconvenienced him, so the last thing I'd see would be Lord Ego *not smiling*.

"I see you appreciate the complexity of your situation, cousin," he drawled to Sandu.

"I do have *some* experience with torture, coz," Sandu replied. He was standing tall now, free of the post-maadak cobwebs and looking ready to step to Lord Ego. "No detail of what you are attempting has gone unnoticed."

"When I finish you, would you prefer it to be quick, or

would you like to say goodbye to your patar in your dying moments? I offer you that choice out of kindness."

"*Suge-mi-ai pula.* I think you do not know the meaning of *kindness.* This is more of the torturer's art, a finishing touch of suffering like an after-dinner mint. But assuming you will be sated by this meal is more assumption than you should make."

"Do you really believe you can best me? *Pozhaluysta,* I am asking this with genuine interest."

"To answer you in all honesty, *da.* I believe my vhoon-anghyaa is as strong as yours, and my skills are at an equal level. You may have lived and fought for many millennia, but I was trained by one who has lived and fought for just as long. I am not worried, *nenorocitule.*"

"Neither you nor your pathetic patar can imagine what increase of power and skills I have gained in these long years."

Sandu shrugged, eloquently conveying his complete lack of impressedness. "So, how about you show me how superior you are to me?"

Before the words finished leaving Sandu's mouth, the energy of the room changed. Up until that moment, they were in some kind of foreplay zone. The fight was inevitable, but there were still steps to go through to get there. Apparently, some people enjoyed those steps enough to draw them out. I had not yet gotten to a place of comfort and self-assurance from which I could enjoy anything before a fight; I just wanted it over. But these were connoisseurs, and I was not sure I'd ever get to their level. Or that I wanted to.

Foreplay was decidedly over now. They both stood

relaxed but expectant. They were holding eye contact. Then they started moving. Not much, just little things: cracking their knuckles, shifting their weight from one leg to another, loosening their shoulders. Even I understood that this was preparation combined with intimidation. They still made eye contact. I had learned how *intimate* a fight could be, but this was next-level stuff.

Kurgan's right arm flashed, and suddenly a black blade was in his hand. It was angular and ugly, with a slightly curved tip sharpened on both sides and a nasty serration on the top edge. The bottom edge was a straight length of razor-sharpness. It had what on a sword you'd call a "cross-guard," the top one jutting forward and the bottom one sticking straight down. Kurgan was holding it still enough that I could see "СМЕРШ-5" marked along the blade. He noted that our attention had been caught by it suddenly coming into play and drawled, "Oh, do you like this? I've had it since the Great Patriotic War. It's such a young knife, my Smersh, but it fits my hand pleasingly."

"How nice for you, *târfă*," Sandu replied evenly. "I notice you took the precaution of disarming me after poisoning me. Are you so nervous about fighting me that you cannot fight me fairly? That's not very *cousinly*."

"Hah! I suppose you feel you had to try, little Wladislaus. But we both know that not one am'r would choose a fair fight when they can put things to their advantage. I am far too ancient to fall for your immature tricks, so do not waste your final words."

"I am more than ready to stop your endless flow of words. Must I call you a coward directly?"

"Call me what you like, you insignificant speck." Kurgan

used the last insult to lunge unexpectedly at Sandu, the Smersh an extension of his arm going straight for Sandu's belly.

Sandu stepped neatly to the side like a dance-step, and he had his hand around Kurgan's wrist, trying to break both it and his hold on the knife. Kurgan spun his body in the same dance, and somehow his other arm was in just the right place to catch the knife as it dropped. Then he spun out of Sandu's grasp.

Kurgan rushed him again, attacking before Sandu could re-center himself. Sandu proved more than ready and got hold of both Kurgan's arms at the wrists, trying again to disarm him. Kurgan, too fast, used the hold against him and pulled Sandu down from the waist as he brought up a knee. His arms almost blurred as he reached up, grabbed his Smersh-wielding-hand, and clubbed between Sandu's shoulder blades with the butt of his knife. His arms raised again, spun his knife pointy-end down, and started to deliver the blow that would sever Sandu's spine.

But Sandu dropped, and just as fast, shot his arms out to Kurgan's ankles and pulled. Lord Ego toppled over backward with an almost comical look of surprise on his face.

I had to remember to breathe, and doing so reminded me I had other things to do besides watch my beloved and Lord Ego eagerly attempting to finish each other. I glanced at Norvyn. He was as engrossed as I.

I started thinking about moving toward Bagamil, who was still hanging in agony, watching his oldest son try to kill his youngest son. I focused on holding my body loose and not looking anywhere but at Sandu and Kurgan, who were rolling on the floor like dueling octopuses, fighting so furiously that they seemed to have more than the usual number of limbs. I tried to let my body slide along as imperceptibly as an am'r, not taking steps but almost gliding where I desperately needed to go.

CHAPTER FOUR

I wasn't an am'r yet; I still moved too unsubtly. Toady-boy picked up on it and appeared in front of me like a bad hallucination.

"You wouldn't be trying to help *him*, would you? Betraying Lord Croglin so fast?"

"I'm just trying to keep out of *their* way!" My point was made when Norvyn and I had to jump away from the fighting am'r whirlwind that spun in our direction. Happily, it moved us closer to my tortured gharpatar.

"My Lord may trust you, but I do not."

"That's fine. I don't trust *you*." Why was I cursed to always be dealing with pissy minions?

"I will not let you free him." He gestured at Bagamil.

"You mean, not over your dead body?" The fury I'd been stifling had become insuppressible. "I'm OK with fixing that."

His face stretched into a leer. "Stupid cunt! I will drain you so dry that you cannot rise from the vistarascha."

I just smiled at him and didn't bother to mention that

his ungentle patar would be very displeased with him for disobeying direct orders. I found myself ready to make the world a better place by the removal of Toady-boy, and so full of adrenaline that fear and reason were no longer factors in my decision-making.

He rushed me; *we* weren't going to waste time with lengthy foreplay.

He was going for my throat. I got my arms up and knocked his away with something like Fosse choreography. He didn't want to dance, so he knocked me over. It was a good policy overall, but it didn't take into account that one of the parts of training I liked best was wrestling, because I was naturally good at it.

As momentum moved him down onto me, I had enough time to realize gravity was my friend now. I grabbed his head as I would a lover's and, rolling in the direction he was already moving, pulled it with all my force onto the floor beside me. It made a really satisfying *thunk* as it made contact. While he was stunned, I pushed him off me to the side and sat up, reaching desperately for Sa'mah, who was waiting eagerly in my boot. I missed her; my hand slid outside my boot. *Fuck.* I reached down again more carefully, but he had risen behind me and grabbed my shoulders, his grip eloquently expressing his anger.

I had an equally eloquent answer. I thrust my left arm forward and brought the elbow back *hard* into the delicate area that was conveniently right beside me.

I have very sharp elbows. Everyone who'd practiced with me in Sandu's training hall knew that. Norvyn learned that now.

The result was not all I'd hoped, however, because he

collapsed *onto* me, making a deep grunting noise, and sadly also knocking my hand away *again* from Sa'mah's sheath in my boot.

Since he was regrettably not out of his mind with pain, he used his weight to force me onto my back again. He wasn't quite as full of am'r grace as he processed the blow to his 'nads, but he still outweighed me, and was a full am'r to my am'r-nafsh. He made sure my arms were no longer above his so I couldn't pull the head-to-floor stunt again, but I was fine with that because I, with some "seeming like she's struggling to free herself" wriggles, curved my body into the right shape for reaching Sa'mah.

Doing that exposed the side of my neck to him, which was like a red flag to a bull, especially when said bull was full of adrenaline and excitement. He was more than ready to end this fight in the most pleasurable way possible, and he went for it.

I let his teeth scratch my skin, moving my head at the last minute to keep him from biting deeply. I knew the smell of blood would completely distract him, so the injury was worth the pain and risk. He almost gently nuzzled the blood on my neck as he prepared for his big *chomp* while I finally—*finally*—slid my fingers correctly into my boot.

As Sa'mah slipped into my fingers, I became calm and in control. My ultimate security blankie. Time slowed, and I could deal with everything without rushing.

Norvyn had pulled his head back again and was coming down toward my neck teeth-first. Now that holding Sa'mah had clarified my universe, I didn't recoil to protect my neck but left it temptingly available. My left hand, holding the blade, slithered smoothly above my head, and I was able to pivot the elbow to get real force into my strike. Norvyn was so engrossed by my am'r-nafsh vhoon that he didn't catch my movements in his peripheral vision until the point of my little obsidian dagger was moving inexorably toward his eye.

Sa'mah seemed to glide syrupy-slow through space and time, but that was just my perception. Norvyn didn't have enough time to react. Sa'mah hit the center of his pupil like it was the bullseye of a target. I'd built up enough force through acceleration for her to sink deep into the eye. I let go of the handle, then used the heel of my hand to slam her the final inch into the brain.

Norvyn sagged lifelessly onto me. He seemed to weigh even more, and I had to work to roll us over and get out from under him. One eye stared blankly at me. The other eye was mostly the butt of Sa'mah's hilt. Around the hilt, clear fluid dripped out like tears. From some long-ago science class, the term "aqueous humor" came back to me. *Ugh. Move on.* I knew I hadn't given Toady-boy his tokhmarenc, but he wasn't going to be healing on his own any time soon, so for now, it was good enough.

A crash to my right sharply reminded me that my patar was in a fight for his life against a more powerful adversary. I looked over to see Sandu bent backward over the desk, his head at an awkward angle against the row of books behind. Kurgan was hunched over him and was hitting him in the face so hard that Sandu's head was getting hit first in front by Kurgan's fists, then recoiling into the books for a disorienting secondary blow. I wondered why Sandu hadn't just pushed him away, then I realized that one of his arms was hanging loosely at a bad angle—broken, obviously. It hadn't time to heal or wasn't able to heal right without help.

It was a suboptimal situation for Sandu, but I had to trust that he could hold his own until I could bring help. Sa'mah was going to be too difficult to extract from Norvyn's brain, so I looked around for the pretty Bowie knife I'd tossed this way centuries ago.

There it was! I scrabbled across the floor to her, and she felt good in my hand. Toady-boy didn't deserve her, and this time, I didn't have to give her back. "Shall I name you Suffragette or Queen Bitch?" I murmured to her as I climbed to my feet and moved to Bagamil. My ability to joke was torn away when I saw his face.

It wasn't that I had forgotten he was dangling in agony, but things had moved pretty fast for a while there, and you can only have so many life-or-death considerations on your mind at one time. Now, this one was front and center, and it was more horrific for having lasted this long.

Bagamil's arms had clearly been torn out of his shoulder sockets, up and behind him at a terrible angle. His body was twisting gently as it hung, but of course, the sensations he was experiencing had nothing *gentle* about them. The weight pulling down on his legs had made the shoulder situation worse. Probably messed up his hips and legs as well.

His eyes met mine, and I winced at the look in them. He was not screaming on the outside, but that did not mean he was in any less torment. My patar's calm acceptance of the pain made me feel shame for taking so long to release him from it.

I cut the string of the weight, freeing his ankles in the

process. I thought it best to cut his feet free before lowering him, but a keening sound escaped from him as my actions caused him to spin. I forced myself to meet his eyes before I moved behind him, promising without words that I would get this done as quickly and thoughtfully as possible.

Kurgan had done a fancy knot to hold Bagamil several feet off the floor. I was torn between taking the time to figure it out, and the Gordian solution; that would be faster, but it would drop him too suddenly. Happily, when I pulled on one end of the rope, the knot came undone easily. Then I was dealing with the problem of what rate of descent was correct for someone with their whole weight being supported by ruined shoulders. Not too fast, not too slow, but "just right" was a wild fucking guess.

He ended up in a broken heap on the floor. Still, I'd seen him look worse. As I lowered myself with him, I could hear his breath rasping. I couldn't tell if it was from damage to his chest and lungs or the effort it took not to scream.

The separate knot around his wrists had tightened enough that it was easiest to use Queen Bitch to carefully slice them free. When I was done, I stupidly waited for him to raise his arms and push himself up from being a pile of limbs. *Oh. Fuck.* Those dislocated shoulders. I was almost certainly going to have to put his shoulders back in the right place before giving him vhoon-vaa. I didn't have the training for this, and the only reason I would have the nerve for it was that *not* having the nerve for it wasn't an option.

"You must do as I tell you." It came out of him in a harsh gasp, no extra breath for niceties.

Thank everything he could talk. I couldn't do this without his knowledge of anatomy and physiology. "Just tell me and I'll do it," I replied, my tone a lie of confidence.

"Make me straight, flat and straight." I rolled him onto his back, ignoring the pain in his breathing, trying gently to nudge his spine straight and his limbs into the right places.

"You start with my right." A moment of measured raspy breathing. "First you lift my arm up, bend the elbow." Pause to breathe. "Sit with your foot—left foot—on my ribcage below my armpit. Other foot against my neck." He rasped some air while I tried to remember to breathe as well, deeply dismayed. "Then. You will straighten arm. You will pull it up *hard* until it clears..." Pause to breathe. "Until it moves freely. You can feel that. Then. You lower arm in correctly. I will tell you when you have done it."

More than ever in my life with am'r, I wanted to run screaming. How the fuck was I supposed to manage this? But I just pulled off my boots, scrunched to the right spot, and tried to gently lift his arm without causing him extra pain, i.e., do the impossible in a quietly competent way. He wheezed. I placed my left foot under his armpit against his ribs. My right, I tried to situate optimally against his neck in such a way that he could still breathe and talk to me.

"Where do I hold on?" I asked, not letting my voice quaver.

"Just above elbow. There. Now, straighten."

Using my other hand, I reached for his wrist and pulled it straight, leaning back to accomplish it. He gasped. I rested his now-straightened arm on my shoulder and got a good grip with both hands right above where the elbow started.

"This will be hard," he told me, and I almost said, "No shit," but instead, I just listened. "There is a thing like cup. You must put ball of shoulder. Back into it. Some muscles. May get caught on edge. Must not let happen."

He paused to breathe. I asked the dreaded question. "What if that happens?"

"Pull out and start again."

So that was something to avoid at all costs.

"Start," he instructed me, so I pulled out his arm. Or I *tried* to pull his arm out from the place it had been dislocated to. His wiry ancient muscles had no plan to cooperate with me. After being actively wrenched out for hours, they had found new places to rest, and they weren't ready to go anywhere again. My gharpatar made a high-pitched sound through his gritted teeth.

I got a better hold of his arm and started again with a better idea of how much strength I'd need. This time it worked better, and I closed my eyes to better visualize what I was doing. Without visual distraction, I could more easily feel the bones in the arm lifting. I tried simultaneously to pull out and center the arm where it ought to go in the shoulder socket.

Bagamil gasped, "OK! Release! *Slowly!*" Despite my foot against his neck blocking some of his air, the pain in his voice was all too obvious, and I had to fight letting it affect me. I discovered I was holding my breath and breathed out and in slowly as I lowered the arm into a spot that seemed to accept it well.

My gharpatar just breathed for a moment. "Yes. It is in."

Triumph washed over me, as good or better than the first time I had killed an enemy. It was immediately quashed by Bagamil saying, "Now the other."

Fuck. I have to do the left arm, too.

He pulled me out of my overwhelmation by saying, "The minute it goes in correctly, there is relief. Also. There is haste."

As if to emphasize this, we heard two bodies crash to the floor behind us and continue thumping each other. Even in the severest pain, *he* had remembered that his frithaputhra was fighting for his life while I was getting lost in my feels. *Get it together.*

Trying for speed, not haste, I slid around him and got my feet placed, then gently bent and lifted his left arm. We both took a breath before I straightened it. That part seemed to go less stressfully than the first time.

"OK." Bagamil took the deepest breath he could, which still didn't sound very healthy. I lifted the arm with all my strength, trying to find the right spot on his shoulder to let it slide in. A cry interrupted me from outside of my immediate focus. I looked up, and Sandu was wrestling with Kurgan, but with only one unbroken arm, so not very well. He also had blood on his neck and lower face, and there was blood smeared all over Kurgan's face and slicking his shirt, so I wasn't able to tell who was doing the bleeding, if they both were, or what.

It was a bad distraction, and what made it worse was that I let up on the pressure on Bagamil's arm and was only brought back to what I should be doing by him giving a thin scream like a boiling kettle.

"*Focus*," he hissed when he could talk again, but I was already doing that, drawing my whole self into the area of his shoulder, raising my arms, and trying to stop them from shaking from the continued effort. I felt the end of the arm bone—humerus, maybe?—lift free again, and I slowly moved it around, looking for the sweet spot. When I found what seemed right, I was terrified to lessen my upward pressure but forced myself to do so, and it smoothly nestled back home. When Bagamil took a deep breath of relief, so did I.

"It is in. Thank you, cinyaa." I could tell he was in less pain, and my gratitude for that buoyed me. At least I knew what to do next; by now, it was something I could do well. Vhoon-vaa. I had never felt so relieved to get to this least sexy style of blood-drinking.

I crossed my legs and moved in close. He still couldn't put his weight on his arms, so I gently lifted his head onto my lap. "Come here, cinyaa." We didn't have any time, but we *had* to make time for this, or else we would be no good to Sandu.

I reached to the side and grabbed Queen Bitch, then ran my finger along her edge. This was going to hurt a bit more than Sa'mah, whose obsidian edge was so sharp you barely noticed her slicing you open. QB was sharp enough, but the steel of the blade could never be quite as keen. That extra iota of pain was not even worth considering, however, because having Bagamil back in action was worth anything.

His eyes met mine. "Where is Sa'mah?"

I was very tired and very rushed, so I answered him plainly. "In Norvyn's brain."

"Ah. Good." We usually bantered during extreme situations to make surviving them more bearable. The fact that neither of us had a witty quip available marked how bad shit was. I looked away long enough to do a serious slice of my wrist, then rushed it to his mouth.

I'd cut myself far deeper than I ever had before. I had already noticed that my healing was far speedier with Kurgan's vhoon-anghyaa in me—and Bagamil was about to find out about *that*. But we could have the recriminations later; right now, I just wanted my am'r-nafsh goodness thrumming down his throat as fast as he could drink it.

And that was just what he was doing, chugging my blood like a fraternity guy at a kegger. I could feel the pull of his drinking in my veins, which was disconcerting when there wasn't sex happening to distract from it. But he had to drink fast and deep and get as healed as he possibly could.

I was surprised at how fast my gharpatar sat up on his own, looking almost his old self, just a little older and more tired. "Thank you, cinyaa, for the good healing." He looked into my eyes as he said it in that very formal way he always had.

"I—" I had so many things to say, and I almost started crying from the wave of emotions.

"Now we fight, Anushka. Yes?"

"Yes. Sorry. *Yes.*"

Kurgan and Bagamil were still grappling on the floor. Kurgan was on top again, or perhaps he'd been on top the whole time. His nose was broken, and his face underneath was thickly coated with blood. He had scratches on his face as well. I couldn't imagine how Sandu had managed to impose those wounds on him with one arm broken, but the Impaler had learned how to work around pain in his time.

Bagamil was on his feet and moving toward them. Maybe he was a little slower than normal, but not that you'd notice. I didn't think the am'r had adrenaline, but they more than made up for it with sheer force of will.

My gharpatar bent down, lifted Kurgan off Sandu, and threw him across the room. Kurgan bounced off the rows of books like he was made of rubber and was back on us in a second, looking like a kid with a new toy.

I rushed to Sandu's side since he was slowed by his broken left arm. I wanted to help him up or offer him vhoon-vaa, but he shook me off. "No time, *draga mea*. Heal later."

I thought him having the full use of his body in this fight was probably worth it, but didn't have time to argue. "Take my knife!" I insisted as he started moving forward to engage Kurgan again. He tossed back, "No, you need it more!" then he and Bagamil were both fighting Kurgan while I fumed from the sidelines.

They had started my training one-on-one, then we had done some training with me trying to keep multiple opponents engaged. We hadn't had time to train me in how to be useful when there were three of us taking on one crazy-strong, crazy-fast am'r who was powered with five thousand years of pent-up resentment.

Bagamil and Kurgan fought like it was a dance they had practiced together for years. Sandu had five hundred or so years under his belt, and had trained for many of them with Bagamil. I felt like an onlooker at a flash mob when music came out of the blue and the bustling people in the train station began a choreographed routine. I stood there with my knife and hated them all for my lack of training. Unless something changed, I could only get in the way right now.

Kurgan, who never let being a gentleman get in his way, was the only other person who was armed, his angular black knife an extension of his arm. Sandu and Bagamil didn't seem to mind it, however, and as I watched from the sidelines, my anger drained as I realized I was watching the fight of a thousand lifetimes.

It went too fast for me to fully appreciate the artistry. Their bodies flowed like they were living Impressionist paintings, and that each attempted strike was done with the most calculatedly harmful intent could almost be forgotten in the beauty of the movement.

For a short while, while Kurgan's knife did not meet flesh, neither did any of my beloveds' hits or kicks meet any unblocked part of Lord Ego's body. If I hadn't known better, I'd have said it was like contact between dancers, planned and counted upon. But I did know better, and while part of me was being blown away by the skills on display, part of me was throbbing with profound anxiety. The two of them *had* to be able to overpower him. It was simple math, right? Even if I couldn't be a useful third, two trained and powerful fighters had to eventually take down a lone combatant. *Right?*

And when they did, I would be holding QB at the ready. I would find a way to help, *dammit.*

They circled. They spun. They kicked. They dodged. They struck. They blocked. They danced death.

And then the pattern changed. With unspoken communication, my patar and gharpatar rushed Lord Ego together, seemingly leaving him no way out.

But he found a way, impossibly slipping between them like a leaf on the breeze, and then that breeze blew him to me. I tried to respond in time, but it was like he was on fast-forward and I was stuck in slow motion. His Smersh knife slashed out at my stomach, and I felt something very bad happen there. Then he was around me, and his knife, almost clean of my blood, was against my neck.

"I have your weakness, you fools. She was almost my weakness as well—such *intoxicating* vhoon—but she has proved stronger than I anticipated. It is too bad I shall have to destroy such a near-masterpiece, but clearly, I can never trust her. Your vhoon-anghyaa corrupts her person with the cunning manipulation you always tried to use on me.

"I was going to pay you back, *father*, by killing your most cherished frithaputhra and tearing the other from your side to serve me. I do not mind adjusting my plans. I will simply kill you all and ensure that none of you ever rise again. And just as you never rose from the vistarascha, your little granddaughter never will, either! You will be broken by my hands and finished with fire. I will burn *you* last of all. It will be enough to satisfy my revenge, just to finally have you off this Earth for good."

I listened to Lord Ego do his monologue with a funny sort of calm. I'd been in this hated place before, used as the Achilles' heel because my beloveds had made the mistake of loving me and not hiding me away, but we'd always found a way to prevail. Some weakness in our enemy became apparent in the last seconds before all was lost, and we took advantage of it. It was how all the stories went, and it was how this story had to go. Anyway, he hadn't bothered to disarm me. I still had QB, and I'd find a way to stick her into him, goddammit.

Then the blade at my throat moved. I saw his arm moving out of the corner of my eye as well and I thought, *So, that's what it's like to have your throat cut. I thought it would hurt more.*

CHAPTER FIVE

I remember Queen Bitch dropping to the floor.

I remember my arms, now free, grabbing at my throat to try to do...something. Stop the flow of blood? Keep my head properly attached to my neck? It wasn't logical, especially since my insides were slithering out of my tummy, along with a lot of blood.

I remember crumpling, still stuck in that damned slow motion.

I was still thinking the thoughts I'd last been thinking about how I would help kill Kurgan. I remember trying to force my brain to catch up with this newest development.

I couldn't think.

And then darkness. *Nothing.*

CHAPTER SIX

I was hungry; that was my first thought. It had been a long time since I'd had anything to eat. A really, really long time. *I need to eat something.*

I opened my eyes, and everything swam into focus. Eventually. I was unusually groggy, and I was having way more trouble than usual pulling my thoughts together. The only clear thought was just how damn hungry I was.

I was in a new place. I couldn't remember where I was supposed to be, but I knew this wasn't the last place I'd been in. *That* didn't make any sense, so I shook it off. I closed my eyes and opened them again, hoping that things would make more sense.

The neon signs around the room gave me one distinct piece of information: I was in Nthanda's London warehouse lair. Sandu was sitting just to my side, looking loving and...something else. And there was Bagamil, with a similarly weird expression. Nthanda was over there, smiling his usual killer smile. There was someone I didn't know beside him.

That someone was kee.

Hunger blinded all my senses except smell and muted all my thoughts except *Now we feed.*

I stumbled up out of the thing I was in, tripping over the high edge and falling on my hands and knees to the hard floor. I didn't stop to swear but scrabbled in a combination of crawling/clambering on all fours toward the kee.

I could smell the hot blood, could already taste it in my mouth.

The kee didn't move, and that was good, or I would have chased it down and torn it apart. It stood against a wall, and I could smell it was nervous, which added a piquancy and made me lurch even more ungainly toward it.

And then I was there, climbing it and the wall behind it, throwing myself against it, burying my mouth in its soft neck. My mouth opened wider than I thought it could, like a snake's, and I sank my teeth through the flesh, freeing the blood.

The blood. *The blood.* It was better than anything I'd ever had before; it blew away every previous best moment of my life. It rushed to greet me like a lover, poured like sweet water down my throat, and tingled with life through my entire body, an outward wave of healing and satiation. This was it, and all I'd ever wanted, and I wanted it to last forever.

Too soon, I was interrupted. Unwelcome hands pulled me away. *No! This blood is mine!* I lashed out. There were too many to fight off as I kept trying to drink, so I tore my mouth away from the source of all delight and snarled my intention to destroy my disturbers.

They danced away from my claws and teeth, but they did not go far enough. Multiple arms pulled me inexorably from the one place I wanted to be, and I growled at them and threatened them—maybe not with words, but the noises were clear enough.

They pinned me down. There were three of them, and even in my frenzy, each was stronger than me. There was nothing I could do but hiss and growl at them. After a while, the frenzy started to dissipate. It took a good long time, and three full am'r sitting on me. As I came down, I started to feel embarrassed about my lack of control. On the other hand, the hunger, somewhat tamped down, was still very real and present. This was all confusing.

"Um." My voice was scratchy and weird, and it almost hurt to talk. I tried again. "Um. Um. I think you can stop sitting on me."

"*Cinyaa!*" and "*Sufleţel!*" my beloveds cried at the same time. They gracefully lifted themselves off me, as did Nthanda, who, as I tried to find my own graceful way up from having just been flat on the floor, gave me a little bow. He looked unusually disheveled. "Anushka, fritha-puthra of Vlad Dracula, I am honored to be here and to welcome you to our number."

He's honored to be...in his own home? Huh? Welcoming me to what?

"Thank you, Nthanda...but I don't understand." My head felt like it was full of cotton candy or something, and I was still so hungry I couldn't think properly.

"*Draga mea*, come here," Sandu said. Everyone's voices were funny, not just my own. They sounded like they had new depths in them, or maybe they echoed differently.

He held open his arms, and I rushed into them, grateful for the comfort. The proximity to him made me realize that I could hear everything so much better. His heartbeat was so loud that I wondered if we could talk over it. The sound of the blood in his veins was like being by the sea. And there were rips in his clothing, blood clotted on them, long scratches quickly healing underneath. His *blood*—my hunger threatened to overcome me again, and I tensed in his arms, not sure what my body was going to do next.

"*Taci, micuțo*, it's alright, it's fine, relax." He held me tightly enough that I knew I couldn't fight my way out of his arms, and I forced myself to relax into it.

Bagamil came over and put his arm around us. This overwhelmed my senses even more, but I practiced breathing in and out. "Cinyaa," he said, his voice very gentle and low, "What Nthanda meant was that he was honored to be here when you awoke from the vistarascha."

I didn't respond.

He tried again. "Noosh, darling frithaputhra, you have had your vistarascha and risen to life as an am'r."

"Oh," I said. I didn't have any feelings, except how hungry I was and how annoying all my senses were being right now.

"Do you understand, *dragă* Noosh?" Sandu looked very concerned.

"I—I." I had to pause and think. "Yeah. I guess so."

Nthanda broke down laughing. We all looked at him. "Greatest. Fuckin'. Evolution. One. Can. Make." He wheezed. " 'N she *guesses so!*"

Sandu looked down at me with a grin starting on his face. Bagamil was trying to bite back his smile, so I gave up and let Nthanda's laughter be contagious to me and thus to us all.

That helped. It helped more than anything, possibly even more than more blood. (But I would have liked more blood, too.)

When we collected ourselves, I looked at them and asked seriously, "OK, I think I've processed the fact that I died—"

"'Died' only as a mortal, *draga mea*—"

"Yes, yes, I get that. And then I was dead down in the vistarascha for a while. Um. *How long?*"

"Ah. A fortnight."

I stopped and practiced my breathing some more. I tried to remember what a fucking fortnight was. "I was dead for *two weeks?*"

"Not dead. Becoming new. Becoming your whole am'r self. And actually, the vistarascha can last for many months. I was in the vistarascha for a month myself."

"He was *very* injured," Bagamil said, as if defending Sandu's ego. "And so were you, cinyaa. You were disemboweled, and your spine was severed."

"We could not have given you enough vhoon-vaa," my gharpatar added anxiously, "to be able to hold off the vistarascha. That was why Vohun-ukhra gave you those killing blows. He thought Sandu would waste his time trying to save you as am'r-nafsh, that it would be enough of a distraction to us both to give him the edge."

"He called me Wladislaus enough," Sandu muttered. "You'd think he'd remember what the name *Vlad Dracula* means."

I was having trouble coping with all this, plus the

continuing hunger. I looked around for somewhere to sit. There was a loveseat that beckoned to me, but I got distracted by the open coffin beside it.

"Was I in...*that?*"

"Yes," Bagamil explained, still gently. "You had to rest somewhere."

"I brought it up," Nthanda said, pleased to let me know. "They wanted the safest, most respectful way to transport you back to London. This is Victorian. Hand-carved ebony. The lining has been reupholstered recently."

"Am'r don't...sleep in coffins."

"Ah, well, they are good for protection against light. And curious glances. As well, the vistarascha is more than just *sleep*. Most in the vistarascha were buried until they rose. We do not often bury our resting ones now, but the coffin, well, it has become...customary. Traditional."

"It's a good *storage solution?*" I asked. My hunger was making me a little cranky.

"That's a good way to put it." Nthanda grinned at me, perfectly aware of my mood.

"*Draga mea*, you were in a sacred state." I turned and listened more respectfully because Sandu didn't often use words like "sacred." That was Bagamil-talk. "You joked about the vistarascha before, talking of butterflies and chrysalises. It was not entirely wrong. Do not mind us showing our love for you and our respect for your trans-formation."

Well, when he put it that way... Shit. I finally went and sat on the loveseat. Sandu followed, pulling his torn clothing into the best order he could. He put an arm around me as he sat. Bagamil came and sat cross-legged at our feet, resting an arm on my leg. He didn't seem to care about his slashed shirt, which hung loosely on his wiry frame. Nthanda lounged on another piece of vintage furniture, legs swung over one arm, watching the family meeting with amusement.

"OK, so, you lovingly put me in a coffin and brought me down to London. *What the hell happened before that?*"

"That's a reasonable question," Nthanda piped up. "I'd like to hear that, too."

"As you *know*," Sandu shot a look at Nthanda, "we need to keep this explanation short for now, but I will try to give an adequate summary.

"*Dragă* Noosh, when we saw the cut to your neck, we knew that to try to come to your aid would be folly. Thus, we focused on Kurgan, which surprised him. He had come to believe that he had the exclusive rights to being dispassionately calculating.

"We managed to get on either side of him, and your gharpatar finally disarmed him of that stupid knife. I managed to knock him down by snapping a knee and keep him there for long enough for Bagamil to pin his arms, and then we drained him of enough blood to seriously discommode him.

"That is the short of it. You did not miss much. Then we attended to you."

"What do you *mean*, I didn't miss much? I missed Bagamil killing his son! It was a big deal!"

Bagamil chimed in, "We didn't say I *killed* him, cinyaa."

"Wha… Why the hell *wouldn't* you have killed him? He's a powerful am'r who has basically existed with the worst of intentions for millennia. He's been sending am'r to assassinate you, and when that didn't work well enough, he lured you to a private place to murder you himself and everyone you love, too!"

"We didn't kill him, my practical one, because we left that for you."

I just sat there and stared at them. Since they flanked me, I took turns staring at one, then the other, and then glaring at Nthanda, who was beaming obscenely.

"Why?" It was the only thing I could say.

"Ah, cinyaa. For many reasons, so many that his death becomes almost poetic. It feels to me fated that he lived long enough to give to *you* his final drops of blood and the ending of his long and wretched life."

What could I say to that? I waited for him to continue. "Most practical first. I know the hunger of the vistarascha. I know that you are barely hanging on through your unsated appetite this moment, which is why I am trying to keep this as brief as possible, while also giving you the information I know you crave just as strongly.

"It is not just a tradition, such as resting in a coffin or other secure burial place, for the quiescent period of the vistarascha, but when we awake to our new lives as am'r, the vhoon-need is profound, as you now truly understand. The death of *at least* one kee is common for the fraheshteshnesh, for we awakening am'r cannot stop ourselves from draining every drop of vhoon from their bodies.

"One reason I tried to put off your transition from the state of am'r-nafsh to am'r was that I knew you were not ready to be responsible for the death of a kee, and most especially not *that* way. And now you know you could not have restrained yourself. It took the three of us to do so, and not without injury."

I looked around at the ripped and tousled clothes on them. I realized they were all wearing the sort of loose cotton outfits you'd see at martial arts practice. They had dressed in anticipation of me going berserk. I shuddered. All the scratches and other damage I'd managed to inflict had healed, but the smell of the blood drying on their clothing made me shudder again for a different reason. I tried to just keep sitting and listening.

Truly, it was fear that held me in place. Fear that Kurgan's blood in my system had made me into a monster like him. Did they know I was so polluted, so *ruined*, that they would always have to be ready for me to attack like a wild animal?

But if so, why was Bagamil telling me he wanted me to drink *more* of Kurgan's blood? *This makes no sense.*

I realized Sandu was now talking, and I tried to overcome hunger and terror both for myself and *of* myself and maybe reach some understanding.

"—and without us needing to say anything, I knew my patar's mind and could not agree more that this was the perfect solution. He says it is poetic, but to me, the poetry is to *do unto Kurgan what he wanted to do unto us*, and what he has done unto too many am'r over the millennia: tortured them, kept them in agony, and finally given them their tokhmarenc at the moment which best suited *him*. The rightness of this *satisfies* me."

It was pure Vlad-darkness in his eyes at this moment, and I shuddered again. If I was corrupted by Kurgan's vile vhoon, it was mixing with the vhoon-anghyaa of Vlad-the-fucking-Impaler. Was I already an accursed thing? Had the last thin string tying me to my humanity now been severed, and I would spend centuries creating new torments for am'r and kee alike, surpassing my progenitors with my new nadirs of depravity?

Nthanda's low voice interrupted my downward spiral of catastrophizing. "My dear Lord Bagamil and Sandu, mate, your frithaputhra's freaking the fuck out. Will you let me speak to her while you go make sure things are in order with our favorite villain?"

"But—" Sandu started hotly.

"*Nu, nu, dracul meu*," Bagamil soothed him. "Perhaps someone not so close to her explaining things is better. Come, let's inspect matters."

Once he had practically dragged Sandu away, Nthanda came and sat by me on the loveseat. For a dizzying moment I wished he hadn't, because the smell of his distinct vhoon-anghyaa and the beat of his heart were confusing and upsetting.

"This has all come as a real shock for you, Noosh." His warm concern cut through my bloodlust and refocused me on dealing with the present.

"Yeah. Yes. I didn't realize at first that I'd, you know, *died*. I've, like, passed out from shock and blood loss, but still come back as am'r-nafsh. I didn't expect to become fully am'r. Not this time, not this way."

"What other way?" he asked, mockingly me gently. "No am'r-nafsh dies of old age in their bed. You were doing exactly what most of us were doing when we left our kee lives—proper knock-down-drag-out. Doing unto others before they did unto you. Better than those who were ambushed and drained dry by some enemy of their patar's before their am'r lives even started.

"But I think your special status—not just as an am'r-nafsh of Vlad the Impaler, with all that implies, but then vhoon-nourished by Bagamil himself, and by other am'r as well—if the rumors are true, by the formidable Neplach and the inscrutable Astryiah herself?—may have left you feeling a bit *invincible*. I was there when they kept you from starting the vistarascha in the Tierra del Fuego kerfuffle. You'd be very excused for thinking you'd never die the kee death, the way they went to work with the vhoon-vaa then.

"You're strong, treasure, but the vistarascha comes for us all, and the tokhmarenc, too…except Bagamil, *apparently*. They've been a bit cagey about all that, and I do hope you'll fill a mate in sometime? Anyways, there you were feeling safe from all that death nonsense, and then that toffee-nosed mingebag goes and slices your Gregory Peck right in half—" At this point, my hand raised to my neck, checking to see if there was a scar, maybe, or that it wasn't still split open. "No, no, luv, there's no defacement of your lovely skin.

"But now, here you are. You've gone through that, and it's behind you. Not that your men didn't scare the hell out of you with how they chose to catch you up on it all. But now you must take some deep breaths and just get on with the next bit. Once you've finished your proper frahesht-eshnesh, it'll all become much easier to get used to."

"And a *proper fraheshteshnesh* is waltzing in to Kurgan—who they've no doubt put in some torture-thing to keep him from trying to kill us again—and draining whatever blood he's got left in him?"

"Pretty much."

I closed my eyes and tried his suggested deep breaths. They didn't help as much as one could wish.

I opened my eyes to find him watching me, interested. "So basically, you're telling me to suck this all up and just get to it."

He laughed delightedly. "That's my treasure!"

"I will do that if you answer one more question. The kee, the one that I drank from." I tried to remember them through the haze of my frenzy. I honestly couldn't remember if they were male or female, *not any details at all*, and that bothered me. "Why bother with that? And where are...*they* now?"

"Right. So you're am'r now. Drinking from another am'r is a pleasure and does have some bennies, but you'll need regular frangkhilaat from kee. Don't ask *me* why; ask your gharpatar that shit.

"You drank from one of mine, a kee lad goes by Mikey. He's used to giving *donations*, and I explained the situation to him, so there wasn't too much surprise when you went a bit like a rabid badger. I got him out right away and came back to help them put you in a time-out. Mikey is fine—you didn't fuck him up half as bad as the rest of us! He's been given a cuppa and probably something stronger, too, and some remuneration. Don't worry about him, treasure. Worry about *you*; you've had a good nip of kee blood, but not enough. Your men think Croglin's blood will fill you up a treat, and Bagamil would know best. So, let's go sort that."

I sighed. Life as an am'r apparently wasn't going to be any less confusing than life as an am'r-nafsh had been, but maybe Nthanda was right about a full belly making it easier to think. The cravings were still painful, and it would be really, really good for that pain not to be wearing on me anymore.

I let Nthanda offer me a hand up, although his nearness and touch reawakened the full-body hunger pangs. He led me to the freight elevator, and down even farther under London we went. I'd only been at the first of the three buttons; now we went down to the second.

It was a "final storage dump" kind of place. Ridiculous how ironically spot-on that was. Battered crates and chests and packages rotted slowly down here, their contents long abandoned. It was a large, echo-y area, but the closely stacked boxes of the forgotten made the space claustrophobic and labyrinthine.

Kurgan, a figure now very much brought down from the vainglorious Lord Ego, was in a position I remembered too clearly having seen Bagamil trapped in it: his limbs were broken and hogtied behind him like a disfigured spider.

Even after every horrifying thing I'd heard of Kurgan doing over the span of too many evil years, even after his repeated attempts on the lives of my beloveds, even after he'd mesmerized me and tried to keep me as his mind-slave, even after he fucking killed me as a *distraction*...still, I did not like seeing anyone in such a condition. As Nthanda led me through the towers of detritus, the confusing welter of emotions resurged to the point where I stopped dead.

"*Haide!*" Sandu beckoned me over. It threw me back to practice sessions, where he called it out more often than "Come!" because he'd forget English words in the heat of the moment. "Let us finish this, *draga mea*." His eyes sparkled with Vladish excitement.

I looked down at Kurgan. His twisted form was resting on a narrow crate, so he had the choice of holding his head up to look around or letting it hang off the side of the crate, which probably made him dizzy if he stayed like that for too long—an extra nasty perk of the torture.

His broken nose had not healed, so he *was* in seriously bad shape. Having not seen a wash since I died—since he killed me—his face still had a few flakes of dried blood, and it crusted the top of his shirt.

I tried shutting off my emotions and viewing him simply as what was needed to make my cravings stop. Where was the best place to drink from? I tried every- where but the neck first, but a hogtie makes the veins of the wrists and inner thighs less accessible—and even with Sandu and Bagamil and Nthanda there, and Kurgan in pretty bad shape, I didn't want to risk setting him free. I had to admit the neck *was* the best option, even though that would put me uncomfortably close to his face.

As if he could feel me thinking all that, Kurgan lifted his head as best he could and met my eyes. I shuddered, waiting to feel his influence washing over me again, but I felt nothing. At least, not a compulsion to do whatever he wanted. The first good thing about becoming fully am'r occurred to me. *I'm my own vampire now.* There were some worrying aspects to that as well, but I needed more time to contemplate them fully.

Bagamil appeared at my side and took my hand in his. He pressed a comfortingly familiar shape into it. "Do this as you prefer, cinyaa, but I regift you with her now, as she may be convenient."

He slowly withdrew his hand and stepped back, smiling at me. I could sense his concern for me, but he was being respectful and leaving me in charge.

I kind of wished he wasn't.

I looked down at Sa'mah and felt the conflict increase. The last time I had seen her was just the very butt-end of her hilt buried in Norvyn's brain.

Honestly, *that* wasn't what caused any inner struggle, because Norvyn was without a doubt one of those people who needed killing to be his best self.

Why was I being squeamish now? I'd worked very actively to dispatch am'r in the past, sometimes so fast and furiously that I couldn't keep track of them. It had taken emotional work to get over it at first. But after you'd actually lost count of how many am'r you'd killed—and it had, very demonstrably, always been "it's them or me" situations—you did just *get over it*. So why was I having trouble now?

Well, this was *new*. The one time I'd drained anyone with the purpose of their never recovering had been deeply traumatizing for me. I was steadfastly ignoring that I'd have been happy to mindlessly do just that about half an hour ago. But I should be angry enough at Lord Ego that ending his days ought to be a delight, or at least a solemn duty. There was something *else* bothering me.

A memory of lying on damp grass in the cool darkness, looking up and seeing Kurgan backlit by the starry night, his hands ripping off my clothing, his mouth and teeth possessively taking my body and my blood.

Oh. *Oh.*

I turned to the lads. Sandu was hovering anxiously. Bagamil was pretending he wasn't. Nthanda was leaning against a huge wooden chest, enjoying the continuing spectacle of our little family drama.

"I...don't know if I can *do* this. Oh, not because I don't want *him* dead! But...but... Look! You all know I *let* him drink from me, and I drank from him. You can smell it on me, taste it in me. *He had control over me.* I...don't want that to happen again. What will more of his blood do to me? Will it make me a narcissistic psychopath like him?"

My patar smiled grimly at me. "He can't control you if he's dead, so you don't have to worry about *that.*"

My gharpatar answered more gently, "The psychoses that come with us from our kee lives, or the potential for such which the intensity of am'r existence brings to the fore? Those are not things that are passed on in the vhoon-anghyaa. V'ukh was obviously not a well young man before he ever had his first vhoon-sip.

"I have had many years to learn that certain people should not be given the chance of becoming am'r. Best if they die a kee death, and sometimes best of all if that death comes straightaway. But I did not know that all those years ago. The world has paid for my ignorance many times over, but I have learned much about both vhoon and people since then. You will not be harmed by draining him dry."

"OK, I might not be *physically* harmed. But..." I ran out of words and gestured my feelings helplessly.

"But what, *dragă* Noosh? I do not understand your reticence."

318

I was suddenly angry. I didn't want to be forced to admit any of this out loud.

"Are you trying to *make* me say it? After you tasted his blood in my veins, are you that angry with me, disgusted by me? Are you *punishing* me?

"I let him enthrall me. I let him drink my blood. I drank his. I offered myself up on a fucking plate to him. I let him use my body and control my mind. I was away from you for like five fucking minutes, and there I was, rolling in the grass with him like a horny teenager, no thought for the danger you were in. I literally fucking slept with the enemy!" By the end I was shouting, and I was aware that I was not angry at *them*, but yelling still seemed like the best way of dealing with things. Or at least the way that was immediately available to me.

They all stared at me. Well, Kurgan did not. His head had sunk down, and his eyes were closed. As I looked at him to avoid looking at *them*, I gazed past his tortured limbs at his face, his skin. He was the grayish color I associated with very unwell am'r. I was honestly surprised as I looked at the dry, rough texture of his skin and the ugly circles under his eyes that he had any blood left in him to be drained.

I found no sympathy in my heart. He was in visible pain, but it barely scratched the surface of the pain he had caused me and my beloveds—and that wasn't even the tip of the iceberg for the suffering he'd caused for millennia. My agonizing connection with him was the only thing keeping me from seeing him as Norvyn, one whom the world was better off without.

Finally, a noise broke my introspection. My gharpatar

gasped as if he'd forgotten to breathe for a while and was just remembering to do so. "Noosh. *Noosh.* It is not something to make much of." He spoke like he was having trouble remembering English. "The thing to make much of was that you *never* were entranced by Mehmet, by any of the am'r, powerful am'r, who tried their powers of persuasion on you. I saw you resist it when no mere am'r-nafsh could be expected to do so. Even Astryiah, a most compelling am'r, only shared vhoon-vayon with you after you had taken our advice and chosen the practical solution."

"The thing that mesmerized you about *me* was my damn *books*," Sandu muttered, but Bagamil pressed on.

"If you are doing this unnecessary self-flagellation, it is *we* who are at fault, cinyaa. Your impressive strength of self should have been praised and applauded at every turn. But I am afraid we both," he glared at Sandu, "felt it was an attribute of our strong vhoon-anghyaa. We were smug as you stood against all odds. But whatever came to you in our vhoon, it merely enhanced the strength in you. I spoke before about the weakness that comes from the kee-side of an am'r. I did not think I needed to speak about the strength, the competence, the invaluable core of stability that choosing the right frithaputhra brings.

"We have told you we meant to make you as strong as mingled vhoon-anghyaa could possibly do. But we have failed you by not saying that Sandu started by finding a strong, capable, rational, well-balanced kee with whom to vhoon-share three times."

"*Fir-ar să fie*, patar, I did not *choose* her based on those things! I fell in love with her!"

"Frithaputhra-mine, how *few* kee women have you fallen in love with over the centuries? What you did was *exactly* choosing her for those reasons. You are just an emotional creature, sometimes, not a logical one. At least not when it comes to love. You are very logical when it comes to war and death, *dracul meu*."

They stopped to exchange intense looks, and as always, seeing their love was distracting to me.

"As much as I hate to break up this moment, are we going to get around to killing the baddie, chaps?" Nthanda grinned at us.

Again, everyone looked at me. "Uh, well, I guess there's more to talk about eventually, but I think I'm ready for this."

I sat down, scrunched over. Now that my distracting feelings had been put aside, my hunger roared painfully back to my primary consciousness. It was a perfect time not to think too much.

Kurgan had possibly passed out. I grabbed his hair and pulled his head up. The new me washed away the part of me that worried and thought too much. I was a predator now. This was my moment to accept it.

By now, I knew the perfect spot to slice, what angle to hold Sa'mah, and how deep was "just right." As I reached out, Kurgan's eyes opened and met mine. Those brown-black almond eyes snapped into focus, seeming to hold every bit as much intensity and power as before.

They did not move me. I carried his vhoon-anghyaa— for the rest of my life, I would—but the changes of the vistarascha had set me free of his brief control over me, and relief poured through me. I saw him see it, understand it—*and it was a blow to him.* His eyes lost their focus. He was still beyond gorgeous, but now he looked depleted as if the long years of his life had fallen upon him all at once.

If I were my patar, I'd have mockingly asked him if he had any last words, but what I'd just seen was last words enough for me—and I didn't give a fuck if he felt unsatisfied. I flicked Sa'mah out, brought her down, and placed my open mouth on the sluggish runnel of blood. At first it trickled out on its own, but all too soon, I had to take long pulls on the cool, dry skin of his neck, trying to reach down to his toes, to take into me every last drop of the vitality to which he'd lost the right.

Finally, Bagamil's gentle fingers pulled me away. Since I was barely getting enough to taste anymore, I did not fight. He pulled me into his arms, and I let him hold me. I realized my hunger was sated. Well, mostly. I could eat, but also, I could wait—oh, for a *long* time, like a day!—until hunger was an issue again.

When I looked up, Sandu had hoisted the body in a fireman's carry, and off we went to the elevator and pressed the third button. *Fucking am'r and their tunneling like ants. Crap, I am an am'r now. Will I suddenly start looking at the shovel and pickax sections of hardware store websites like they're porn?*

As we exited the elevator, we were hit with the stench of old burning, and I knew what we were here for. Kurgan was technically still in the ahstha, and nobody wanted to chance him waking up all vengeful and voracious because some idiot did resurrection shit. Nobody wanted a sequel to Kurgan's miserable life-story.

There was a fire pit in the center of the room. A large

one that hinted at stories I probably didn't want to hear. Kurgan's dried-out husk was tossed into it. Lighter fluid was not needed; am'r bodies were strangely flammable. *Shit. That's me now.*

We all stood around and watched him burn. After everything we'd been through, this quiet time of reflection was needed. We waited until the flames were gone and there was only a human-shaped pile of ashes. Not out of respect, just a deep need for closure.

After some thousands of years, Vohun-ukhra, V'ukh, Kori'kan, Kurgan, Croglin—however many names he'd gone by, but always Lord Ego—was dead. No matter how vile and malicious he had been, the end of that profound a lifespan required a moment of silence.

Then we all trooped back up in the clangy old freight elevator to the main floor that was lit by neon signs. Nthanda called his people. We had a party.

———

"A bit of a bash" was what Nthanda called it, but it wasn't really a party. This was for the purpose of seeing if "house-cleaning" would be easy: if Lilani would show up, with no idea about the changed circumstances. If she did, Nthanda would make an example of her, and we'd all go back down to the fire-pit level. *Ugh.* If she'd gotten the news about Kurgan and fled, then housecleaning would necessarily be more complex.

All of it made me sick. I still couldn't accept the infor-mation I'd passed on to Nthanda, that Lilani had been Kurgan's creature all along. I admired her. I *liked* her. She was an am'r I'd come to feel reasonably safe around with no supervision, back when I was an am'r-nafsh, and that had meant something to me. It meant even more, in a bad way, that I'd been so wrong. But then, Nthanda had looked like someone had stuffed a lemon into his mouth when I told him, so I wasn't the only person experiencing those emotions.

I'd tentatively tried to express my feelings to him when I'd given him the news.

"I'm so sorry, Nthanda. I hate this. I hate having to tell you this." I had said, wringing my hands, not wanting to meet his eyes and see the hurt in them.

But he wouldn't have it. "In long lives like we have, this shit happens, right? You can't always be right about people. Some of them fool you. This one played it real cool, didn't she?"

Damn, he wouldn't even say her name. He stood stiffly, holding all his pain and rage inside him. I wanted to reach out to him, but I knew he wouldn't let me. I tried a little wry humor. "I thought it was Roy, you know."

Nthanda made a sound between choking and coughing like he'd tried to inhale and exhale at the same time. It was as close to a laugh as I'd get from him at the moment.

"Ha! Too fuckin' right! He's a dodgy piece of work is our Roy, but I saved him from a pretty bad place. He might sell everyone else out, but he feels he owes me. Still. I got a few lifetimes before he decides to betray me, and he may evolve into a decent bloke in that time. More likely, I'll get bored of him and give him his fucking tokhmarenc."

It seemed like a really good time to give Nthanda some space.

Vivian was back to looking intensely solemn, and I felt for him, knowing he'd also believed he had a close relationship with Lilani. Feeling more secure in my new am'r status, I went over to him, and after looking into his eyes and moving slowly to let him avoid it if he wanted to, gave him a hug. Am'r are not huggy creatures, but Viv let me offer him my comfort and hugged me back.

"I'm so sorry," I told him when we had broken from the hug but were still standing close.

"It is not your fault or your doing," he responded, his voice as somber as his face.

"It *feels* like it is," I admitted.

"Bollocks. If you had not let Nthanda know immediately, *that* I would have held against you." I assumed that was his idea of being comforting.

Beautiful Nadim, dressed to the glittery nines, joined us. "I've not felt so angry in a long time. We all gave Lilani much trust."

"It feels like too much trust." Vérène spoke from behind me, making me jump. I stepped back to let her into the group. Her anger was very clear on her face and in her movements.

Sikandar joined us as well. "We whom Nthanda have brought together must not let the betrayal of one of our number destroy the unique connection we have. It is rare for am'r to come together like this. We must fight the urge we are all feeling to go be solitary, to lick our wounds alone."

"He's fucking right," Nthanda said from where he'd been talking to Sandu, Bagamil, the stunning Sandhya, the utterly perfect priestess Nahid, and even fucking Roy, who

I *still* would have been happy never to see again. "We're a crew. You're my family. Don't you fucking go slinking off. Yeah, trust is hard for us. Yeah, that bitch fucking broke that trust. Doesn't mean all the other trust is bad, innit? We will sort this out, and none of you lot needs me doing you a lecture on how 'pushing through the hard shit makes us stronger,' so don't make me." He followed up this pep talk, which had to be the most British *and* am'r thing I'd ever heard, with a huge grin. It was a bit forced, but it did the trick. His people smiled back at him.

I thought about how the am'r always claimed to be these solitary creatures of the night, but Sandu had his Romanian crew, Lope had his family in Buenos Aires, and Bagamil was downright worshipped by all of them and got warm welcomes wherever he went. Well, when someone wasn't trying to give him his tokhmarenc. Mehmet had had his "jinn" collective, and the less said about the collections of minions gathered by Julio the Super-Colonizer and Orélie the Self-Anointed, the better. Maybe it had been different in the past, or maybe it was a cultural myth the am'r preferred to believe about themselves—much like the notion that they were more intelligent than the kee, of which I'd never seen much evidence. Whatever. I had a long time in which to figure it out, at any rate.

Lilani never showed. After about an hour, Nthanda announced that those who had not already fed should continue the party elsewhere in the style of their choice.

"There is no point in checking airports or train termi-nals," he said, and a few of his am'r looked disappointed. I wondered if they might not find some frangkhilaat at Heathrow or King's Cross station just to make sure. "She got the news. She's already fled my wrath. Tomorrow, we'll discuss her most likely destinations and start hunting her down. We will have our vengeance, trust."

While I was about as glad as I could be *not* to be present for an evening of watching Lilani get interrogated and then given her tokhmarenc, Nthanda's words still chilled me. *This is what I have become.*

EPILOGUE

Eventually, we were back in our private flat, just the three of us, in each other's arms.

Somehow, we had survived again. Well, except I *hadn't*. Not as my old self.

They wanted to fuck. I needed to talk. *The more things change...*

It took me a long time to work up to my real problem. I started by avoiding it completely. "So...Croglin Grange and all those books. What's going to happen to them?"

"Do you want them, cinyaa?"

"The books? Fuck yeah, I do!"

"The house, too. Kurgan has no heir. Well, he *did*, but you slammed a knife into his brain. Nthanda says none of his people have any desire to move up north. Not yet, at any rate. So how would you like a vacation home?"

"Uh. Really? Are you serious?"

Sandu jumped in. "My frithaputhra lives with me. She already has a vacation home, one in much better shape, I would add."

"She may eventually want some space from us, *dracul meu*. She is fully am'r now. She will eventually want her own household, to take a frithaputhra of her own."

Nobody was ready to contemplate *that* yet. I turned back to the topic I'd been avoiding, just to get away from it. "OK, look, I'm afraid if I ever become truly comfortable, it will mean I've become a...a monster."

They were both quiet for a long while. "Do you think I am a monster, *dragă* Noosh? Is your gharpatar a monster?"

"I—I'm saying this wrong. But right now, for example, Nthanda is all violent vengeance. This isn't a case of 'If I don't kill them, they will kill me first.' I don't have trouble with defending myself. But just hunting down someone who is running from you? That feels different."

I thought about how Sandu, in his Vladian past, had been rumored to take some pretty drastic vengeance himself. I knew some of that had been part of the world's first printed propaganda campaign, and he had a *real* sore spot about it, so I swerved off those conversational train tracks.

I tried again. "I really like Nthanda, but the retaliation thing scares me. That could easily lead to becoming a Mehmet. Kurgan spent his whole fucking life revenging his perceived injustices. I just feel like I can't find the difference between the good guys and the bad guys. I need to find that divergence. What is the difference between me and a monster?"

There was another long pause, long enough to get me worried.

"Cinyaa, I hear your concerns. They are not invalid." He paused again.

"I do not know if you will like my answer. Among the am'r, the main difference is that of *intention*. Let us draw from the 'bad guys' you have personally dealt with. Mehmet would have made everyone join his side or die. What he envisioned for the kee of the world *started* at being controlled by his jinn and would not have stopped there. With Julio Popper, he was a bad guy before he ever was an am'r, so it is not entirely relevant, but do not doubt that if he *had* grown in power by removing me and strengthening his vhoon-anghyaa with mine, he would have resumed his egomaniacal, despotic ways in both the am'r and kee worlds. Orélie was a madman from the earliest reports of his kee existence, so who knows what he would have done? Nothing good is all we can be certain of.

"But the am'r world is a violent one, Noosh. It is our nature. If you prefer to call us monsters, then that is up to you. Nthanda, who is a valuable ally and one who I am proud to call a friend, is in a complicated position. He must continue to prove to the rest of the am'r that he is strong enough to be the head not just south of a certain line anymore, but for all of England. If he does not make an example of an am'r who so foully betrayed him, he would have challengers, not just semi-regularly but *constantly*. His chosen family would have am'r going after them to make him more vulnerable. He must now prove to all that he is still the am'r who fought his way to the top. He was not *voted* leader of the English vampires.

"The kee world has moved in the direction of non-violence, or at least, some parts of it have made that their goal. The am'r world is a different culture. Our long history of solitary distrust kept us from evolving in that direction, that lofty goal. I hope someday we get there. I will work toward that aspiration my whole life. But I will also not deny our intrinsic natures. We drink the blood of the kee to exist. We therefore must be hunters. I, who have fought strongly for the evolution of animal husbandry for the kee, would just as strongly fight against that for the am'r. Think, Noosh! Would you have us keeping kee as domestic animals? No? I thought not.

"Maybe with your help coordinating the collected knowledge of our species, we can come up with a way to create synthetic blood in our future, so that none need frangkhilaat from living kee again. But our species has evolved around it, as has our whole culture. And how would that impact the making of am'r-nafsh and their role, so vital to am'r life and love?

"Your patar and I brought you to the am'r world to help us move forward. If you choose to regard us—and yourself —all as 'monsters,' how will that help you in that effort? If you hate yourself and hate your whole world?

"We are who we are. There are good among us. There are bad among us. How does that make us different from kee society? Why are we monsters—but they are not?"

Well. Shit. When he put it that way... Hitler had been kee, not am'r. Pol Pot. Stalin beat out Kurgan, especially considering he had far fewer years to commit his atrocities.

Sandu had kept his mouth exceptionally shut during all this—probably since his beloved partner had just said she couldn't tell if he was a monster, and he did still have lingering anger issues on that topic. I felt shitty about that, and I couldn't *unsay* it.

I did the only thing I could. I reached out to him,

wrapped him in the tightest hug I could give him—which now might be enough to damage a kee, but I never had to worry about that with his powerful body. I said softly, but both my beloveds had that good am'r hearing, "I am comfortable with my chosen monsters. I love my life with you, and I wouldn't change a thing. How about I demonstrate that right now?"

And we did.

THE END

AUTHOR'S NOTE

Hey there, Dear Reader.

Here we are at the end of Book III, and I don't even know what to say. There was a time when all I wanted in the world was for *Blood Ex Libris* to be published. It took five years, but it happened. And then, next thing you know, *Blood Sine Qua Non* had been published, too.

And now I'm getting *Blood Ad Infinitum* ready to be held in your hot little hands, and I'm still overwhelmed by it all. It never gets less terrifying to send a book out into the world.

As I was doing the first editing pass on this one, I hit a section I remembered writing while sitting out in the backyard on a hot summer day. Looking out the window, snow was thick on the ground, and my little heater under my desk was doing its best to warm my toes, and I realized this book is a *year of my life*. And what with the pandemic, I really mean that. I lived more in this book than in the real world through most of 2020 and all of 2021 so far. Noosh has been more real to me than I am. If you ask me about what I did at the end of the day, I am more likely to tell you what Noosh has gone through. (Don't say, "What *you* put her through"—I don't want her to get pissed off at me!)

That's probably not a healthy state of affairs, but on the other hand, if I had left my basement office and gone out into the world—kicking ass as Noosh does along the way, *of course*—I would have risked infecting myself and others. So I have lived through her, been to that glorious conurbation London, and up to the endlessly gorgeous Cumbria, been all across the Near East and through the steppes to Russia, and back and forth across the span of human history. It is vastly preferable to being in a basement office, even one that has a heater and a drawer full of good snacks.

I can't believe that all three of my novels thus far have been published during this pandemic. It's insane. But as I said in both previous books, at least I am doing *something* useful in giving you, Dear Reader, a place to escape for a while from the difficulties of the real world.

I hope this third book has brought you new characters to identify with and fall in love with and passionately hate. I hope it's made you think and imagine some things that might not have otherwise crossed your mind. I hope you had a *good fucking time* reading it.

One thing that has gotten me out of the house has been all the live video interviews and book readings I've done. Those have been the highlights of my last twelve months. The other thing has been all the amazing fans who have welcomed me into their lives, emailed me, chatted with me online, and cared passionately about Noosh and her journey. When I remember fighting so hard just to get her story out to people, that is still completely amazing to me. So, as always, I write these stories, but now they belong to you—and a finer bunch of fans I could never have hoped for! Please find me on social media and geek out with me!

Raven Belasco, May 2021

ACKNOWLEDGMENTS

And again, I've had just a stunning amount of help writing this. People who have no spare time have been beyond kind in sharing their valuable time and knowledge with me. Any mistakes are one hundred percent mine.

Bagamil would never have been the am'r he is without Mary Settegast's *When Zarathustra Spoke: The Reformation Of Neolithic Culture And Religion* and *In Search of Zarathustra: Across Iran and Central Asia to Find the World's First Prophet* by Paul Kriwaczek. Both authors exemplify incredible scholarship, and I totally got a piggyback from them. And, I would never even have *thought* of Zoroaster if I hadn't read Gore Vidal's *Creation* at a tender age.

Thank you to my publishing team at LMBPN: Lynne, Kelly O., and her beta/JIT team, Grace S., Steve C., and David B. Also, the finest cover artist a writer could hope for: Jude Beers, who with grace and patience handles me digging my fingers waaaay too much into the cover art pie, and Jeff for the fantastic cover typography.

Adam Phippen & Trent Stewart: Thank you for helping me ensure that my descriptions of violence are graphic, not *silly*.

Charles Weir: Thank you so much for being my "man on the ground" in Cumbria when this pandemic kept me from a long-overdue visit. I hope for tea with you and your beautiful family again sometime in the not too far future!

Sir Tanaka Raiko: Asking for your kind assistance on setting dislocated shoulders was not *just* an excuse to hang out with you by phone—really, totally, absolutely not!

Ligia Buzan has been there to keep me from ineptly bungling the beautiful Romanian language since the first book. She is a goddess in every way, and every writer should be lucky enough to have a Ligia!

Cyd Thomlinson saved my bacon (proper British bacon!) by "Brit-picking" my British character's dialogue. Mike Naylor was indispensable with the impenetrable Cumbrian dialect.

Amanda Steward is a "sensitivity reader" *par excellence*, and just generally a most superior human being. I am beyond lucky to have her patient guidance.

Ayize Jama-Everett has been there with sage advice and laughter through this whole "becoming and being a published author" thing. I *literally* cannot thank him enough.

Trent, Bethany, & Christine: Thank you again for sharing a home with a surly writer who can't be interrupted on pain of profound crankiness and who is practically *useless* when in the throes of creation. Your patience is always deeply appreciated.

Finally, thank you to all the fans of this series. Knowing you are out there impatiently waiting for the next book helps keep me going! Thank you for your amazing support.

GLOSSARY OF THE AM'R LANGUAGE

Am'r Word • Definition

adharmhem • one who endangers am'r as a whole, or the act of endangering the am'r as whole

ahstha • coma am'r fall into when deprived of too much blood and/or oxygen

am'r (sing. & pl.) • commonly known as a "vampire" or "strigoi mort"

am'r-nafsh (sing. & pl.) • In Romanian, a "strigoi viu." A living human being who shared blood with an am'r three times but has not yet died.

Aojasc' am'ratv! • "Strength and immortality!"

aojysht (sing), **aojyshtaish** (pl.) • am'r elder

bakheb-vhoonho • giver of blood, used for am'r who give blood to other am'r or kee. This is a term used for the stronger blood going to the weaker, whether am'r or kee

cinyaa • my lover

fraheshteshnesh • first blood meal as a newly awoken am'r

frangkhilaat • to feed/take nutrition from a kee

frithaputhra (sing.), **-ish** (pl.) • "beloved child," title used by an am'r for an am'r / am'r-nafsh made with the former's blood

gharpatar • grandfather, maker of my maker

izchha (sing.), **izchhaish** (pl.) • a "sacrifice," a mortal who is selected to donate blood (with or without sex)

kee (sing. & pl.) • mortal, non-vampire, living human being

maadak • intoxicating drink; poison, gets humans high; effects am'r like strong hallucinogen / tranquilizer and makes them sick

maadakyo • corrupted with maadak, a mortal who has drunk maadak

pat'rkosh • patar-killer

patar • "parent" or "maker"; title used by an am'r or am'r-nafsh for the am'r who made them

tokhmarenc • finishing another vampire, dying the final death

vhoon • blood

vhoon-anghyaa • blood influence, blood-line, the traits that come down from your patar, also the smell of your patar in your blood

vhoon-berefteh • to be bled

vhoon-vaa • am'r-style healing with blood

vhoon-vayon • am'r love making, with other am'r or am'r-nafsh

vistarascha • dying the mortal death, becoming am'r

INDEX OF NON-ENGLISH PHRASES

Phrase • Translation • Language

Ahl nut dyeu it! • I'll not do it! • Cumbrian English

ahreet, mate • all right, buddy • Cumbrian English

amuse-bouche • a bite-sized hors d'œuvre, literally: "it amuses the mouth" • French

bona fide • "in good faith" / authentic, genuine • Latin

bonhommes • Literally "goodmen," Cathar adepts • French

chyortov (чертов) • fucking, frigging, infernal, flipping, doggoned • Russian

Cine dracu sunt eu? • Who the fuck am I? • Romanian

compos mentis • having full control of one's mind; sane • Latin

Cum ar trebui să te cunosc, nenorocitule? • How should I know you, you motherfucker? • Romanian

da • yes • Romanian / Russian

da bineînțeles • yes, of course • Romanian

de fapt • actually • Romanian

draga mea • my darling, my sweetheart • Romanian

dragă Noosh • dear Noosh • Romanian

dracul meu • my dragon/demon • Romanian

e adevarat • it's true • Romanian

Eh, where's thy car? Ah can see nowt! • Eh? Where's your car, then? I don't see anything! • Cumbrian English

ei bine… • well… • Romanian

fir-ar să fie • damn it • Romanian

fiul meu • my son • Romanian

Fută-te dumnezeu! • God fuck you! • Romanian

Futu-ți dumnezeii mă-tii! • Fuck your mother's gods! • Romanian

Haide! • Come! • Romanian

Hei—pur și simplu nu e cinstit! • Hey—it's just not fair! • Romanian

il tormento della corda • "the torment of the rope," also known as strappado • Italian

je dois dire • I must say • French

khorosho (хорошо) • good, well, OK, fine • Russian

mal'chik (мальчик) • boy, lad, houseboy, man-child • Russian

micuțo • little one • Romanian

micuțule • little man • Romanian

modus operandi • a particular way or method of doing something, especially one that is characteristic or well-established • Latin

mon amour • my love • French

Mouais? • Yeah? • French

myshka (мышка) • little mouse, mouseling • Russian

nenorocitule • (you) motherfucker • Romanian

nu • no • Romanian

O, sărăcuțul! Îmi pare rău! • Oh, you poor dear, I'm sorry! • Romanian

Oui, madame! • Yes, ma'am! • French

Parfait(e)s • Literally "Perfect," Cathar adepts • French

pog • peak, hill, mountain • Occitan

polnaya zhopa (полная жопа) • "Full ass," implies "failure in something," used for absolutely hopeless situations • Russian

proigravshiy (проигравший) • loser • Russian

prostie • silly girl • Romanian

sans • without • French

SMERSH (СМЕРШ) • an acronym meaning "death to spies," which was the name of a Soviet counter-intelligence agency • Russian

sotto voce • in a quiet voice, as if not to be overheard • Italian

stiu • I know • Romanian

sufleţel • my soul • Romanian

Suge-mi-ai pula! • Suck my dick! • Romanian

suka (сука) • bitch • Russian

taci • hush • Romanian

târfă • bitch • Romanian

te rog • please • Romanian

tempus fugit • time flies • Latin

There's ney milk so there's nowt else • There's no milk, so there's nothing else • Cumbrian English

Thoo lot frey owert watter reckon thoo can hannle laal lonnins bloody white liners! Thoo shud mon lait a taxi! • You foreigners think you can handle the roads. You should take a taxi! • Cumbrian English

trus (трус) • chicken, poltroon, coward • Russian

Voivode • "War Lord"; medieval title used in Wallachia and Transylvania • Old Slavic

Yon jalopys a spanker, and thoos darn weel dunshed it! Thoo cud a gitten a bus throot gap! • That car's brand new, and you've darn well wrecked it! You could have gotten a bus through there! • Cumbrian English yunets (юнец) • stripling, cub • Russian

CONNECT WITH RAVEN

Website: http://ravenbelas.co/
Facebook: https://www.facebook.com/ravenbelascoauthor/
Instagram: https://www.instagram.com/raven.belasco/
Twitter: https://twitter.com/RavenBelasco
Email her: ravenbelasco@gmail.com

CPSIA information can be obtained
at www.ICGtesting.com
Printed in the USA
BVHW07075220821
614336BV00003B/18

9 781649 718068